"Why do you continue to think this is a big joke?"

"A love potion! I just can't get over it. It's so out of character for you. Unbelievable!"

"Whatever," she said with a sniff of disdain. "The company is closed tomorrow. Come to my lab Monday afternoon and I'll give you the lab results. Then I'm done with you."

Done with me? I don't think so, babe. "Okay. Let's seal the bargain."

She reached out a hand.

She thinks I mean a handshake. Hah! "With a kiss." *For now.*

Her eyes went wide with shock and her mouth dropped open.

Open mouths were good. He moved in swiftly. Putting one hand on the nape of her neck and wrapping the other around her waist, he hauled her up on tiptoe, flush against his body.

She gasped.

He gasped.

That brief moment of her lips against his was like the headiest aphrodisiac. Forget her love potion. Sylvie Fontaine's lips were pure ambrosia.

Romances by Sandra Hill

THE RELUCTANT VIKING
THE OUTLAW VIKING
THE TARNISHED LADY
THE BEWITCHED VIKING
THE BLUE VIKING
THE VIKING'S CAPTIVE (formerly My Fair Viking)
A TALE OF TWO VIKINGS
VIKING IN LOVE
THE VIKING TAKES A KNIGHT
THE NORSE KING'S DAUGHTER
KISS OF PRIDE

THE LAST VIKING
THE LOVE POTION
TRULY, MADLY VIKING
THE VERY VIRILE VIKING
WET AND WILD
HOT AND HEAVY

FRANKLY, MY DEAR
SWEETER SAVAGE LOVE
DESPERADO
LOVE ME TENDER

SANDRA HILL

The LOVE POTION

AVON
An Imprint of HarperCollinsPublishers

This is a work of fiction. Names, characters, places, and incidents are products of the author's imagination or are used fictitiously and are not to be construed as real. Any resemblance to actual events, locales, organizations, or persons, living or dead, is entirely coincidental.

AVON BOOKS
An Imprint of HarperCollins*Publishers*
10 East 53rd Street
New York, New York 10022-5299

Copyright © 1999, 2012 by Sandra Hill
ISBN 978-0-06-201907-3
www.avonromance.com

First Avon Books mass market printing: August 2012

*To my old friend, Rhonda Paul/Zaveckis/Hammett/?,
who was more outrageous than any of my romance
heroines. Where are you today, Rhonda?*

"Love's chemistry thrives best in equal heat."

—JOHN WILMOT, EARL OF ROCHESTER
The Imperfect Enjoyment

The LOVE POTION

Prologue

A born rogue . . .

"You wanna dance?"

"No!" Sylvie looked with horror at a red-faced Lucien LeDeux. He stood before her, cowlick standing at attention, in his shiny Sunday Mass suit.

"No?" he asked, the blush of embarrassment on his dark-skinned face deepening to anger. "Why? Sylvie Fontaine is too good for me?" He made a derisive tsking sound by clicking his tongue against his teeth. "A high-class cat and a Cajun swamp rat? Talk about!"

Oh, it was just like that awful Luc to single her out at her first boy-girl dance at Our Lady of the Bayou School! Painfully shy, she glanced quickly around the crepe-paper-festooned cafeteria to see if any of her classmates, or Sister Colette, was watching as the wickedest boy in the whole parish asked her to dance. "You are too bad for anyone, Luc LeDeux. But not because you're Cajun. Because you are too . . . too . . . bad."

His lips curved into a nasty smirk. "And you are too goody-goody, Sylvie-*chatte*. Here, kitty, here, kitty. Meow." He danced around her in a teasing Acadian shuffle.

"Go away," she urged in a mortified whisper.

He stared at her for a long moment, then turned to walk away. Over his shoulder he tossed a parting shot. "Ah, well, I ain't gonna die of a broken heart. But some-day, Sylvie, you're gonna beg me to dance with you, I guar-an-tee."

"Never!"

"And it's gonna be real close and slooow. And . . . and it will prob'ly be sexy, too. Yep, we'll dance together . . . naked."

She could tell that the latter was a last-minute inspira-tion, not intended to be mean or harassing, but it was so outrageous, even for Luc, that Sylvie gasped for breath. In all likelihood, he'd gotten the idea from those dirty magazines he and the other boys were always snickering over at the far end of the playground. But twelve-year-old boys shouldn't have such indecent thoughts about twelve-year-old girls. At least, Sylvie didn't think they should. She would have to ask her best friend, Blanche, later. Blanche had had the good sense to hide out in the coat room with a forbidden romance novel, instead of coming inside to the dance. Sylvie wished she had been so wise.

"You better go to confession, Luc. Right now. Father Phillipe will give you a penance of fifty Hail Marys, for sure." Fifty seemed like an extremely high number to her. The most she ever got was three.

"I'll just add it to the hundred from last week, then," he said with a shrug and an I-gotcha wink.

Luc was swaggering now toward Mary-Louise Delacroix, who had the distinction of being the only girl in sixth grade with noticeable breasts. Mary-Louise smiled at Luc as if he was a sweet beignet.

"I hate you, Luc," Sylvie called tearfully to his back. His step faltered, and she saw his ears grow pink. "I really do."

Just before he reached Mary-Louise, Luc turned, his black eyes dancing mischievously. And he mouthed a silent message to her. "Naked dancing."

From that day forward, Lucien LeDeux became the plague of Sylvie Fontaine's life.

Chapter One

HOUMA, LOUISIANA, 1999

Forceful seduction, for sure ...

Samson was a stud, no doubt about it.

With his usual raw animal magnetism, he stepped through the low doorway, then reared up, bracing a shoulder against the glass wall. Nostrils flaring and body quivering with tension, he surveyed the far corner where his "harem" huddled together in fear.

Or was it anticipation?

Immediately, his beady eyes honed in on one female ... Delilah. She was nibbling on a tiny red jelly bean. It mattered not that her mousy brown hair stood up in spikes, unlike the renowned beauty of her namesake. Or that she darted her head this way and that, seeking escape ... a clear contradiction to the famed

Biblical siren who supposedly craved sexual attention. At the same time, her timid glance kept returning to Samson. Clearly, she was attracted, despite herself.

Samson was not so shy. His widespread stance and outthrust pelvis sent a message as old as time. *I am male. I am aroused. And I want you.* There would be no escape for Delilah. Not from this glass-walled prison. Not from the scurvy rat who would have his way with her.

But Samson was a cool dude. He didn't force his attentions on any female. He didn't have to. Snagging her gaze, Samson held his prey transfixed . . . the first step in eroding her defenses. Then he waited.

Delilah made a little squealing sound of protest, but couldn't seem to break the eye contact. It was as if she were under some spell. Nervously, she gulped down her jelly bean, followed by two more, a yellow and a green. Gradually her body relaxed, and her eyes dilated with some strong emotion. The only thing missing from her surrender was the white flag.

Samson moved forward slowly, cutting Delilah from the pack. Every movement he made, from narrowed eyes to self-assured body movements, bespoke a fever pitch of sexual arousal. Delilah was becoming equally affected, a shivering mass of excitement, the closer he got.

Acting swiftly, Samson pounced on Delilah, giving her no chance for second thoughts. Without foreplay, he mounted her and was soon thrusting frantically, as if he had not done this a hundred times before. As if they would get no other chance to repeat the ecstasy.

Then, when they were both exhausted with sexual satiety and the door to Delilah's "prison" swung open providing a means of escape, Delilah did the strangest thing. Instead of darting for freedom, she cuddled next to Samson and nuzzled his neck. The victim was staying with her seducer, *by choice*, even after the fever had passed. It was almost as if Delilah loved Samson. Amazing!

Amazing . . . because Samson really was a rat.

Success is sweet . . .

"I did it! I did it!" Dr. Sylvie Fontaine shrieked with exhilaration. "Move over, Viagra. Here comes JBX . . . 'The Jelly Bean Fix.'"

Her best friend, Blanche Broussard, stood with her arms crossed over her chest, shaking her head at what she must consider an overexuberant reaction on Sylvie's part to a mere scientific experiment. *Mere?* There was nothing *mere* about this. It was so much more . . . the breakthrough of the century!

Sylvie had just run the hundredth trial run on her JBX project . . . the hundredth *successful* trial run. Despite her methodical, time-consuming analyses, she was still stunned at the fact staring her in the face . . . through two sets of beady, sex-glazed eyes.

"I have invented an honest-to-God, legitimate love potion," she said in an awe-filled whisper. "In two weeks the human experiments will begin, but there's no doubt as to the outcome."

Unable to contain her elation, Sylvie boogied a little victory dance around her research lab, witnessed only by a bunch of unimpressed rats and the equally unimpressed Blanche.

"Yech!" Blanche had a profound dislike for rodents of any type, even the cute, miniature variety of rats that Sylvie used, which were more like large mice, and she stood tentatively on the far side of the room, away from the animal cages. She brushed a hand with perfectly manicured lavender nails over the front of her long, gauzy dress, as if she might be contaminated, even from that distance.

In her white lab coat, plain linen shirt, and jeans, Sylvie felt frumpy and staid next to Blanche, but after more than thirty years of friendship—thirty-three, if you counted the time they'd spent lying next to each other in high-wheeled, designer carriages while their nannies strolled them to Magnolia Park as babies—she'd long ago given up on competing with Blanche's beauty or flair for style.

"Really, Sylv, you've gotta get a personal life. Watching rats have sex is not . . . well, normal."

"Is that a professional opinion? From 'The Love Astrologer'?" Sylvie asked with a grin. Blanche was a self-trained astrologer, a local radio celebrity whose "love horoscopes" were must-listening every morning across Louisiana—a combination star chart analysis and philosophy for daily living.

"I develop horoscopes for all aspects of life, not just love charts," Blanche corrected her with a little harrumphing sound of consternation. "But you're changing the subject, Sylv." She let out a whoosh of exasperation. "You've been cooped up in this dreary place for too long, hon."

"Do you think this is dreary?" Sylvie was so used to the dim light lab rats preferred that she no longer noticed. "You just don't get it, Blanche. I have invented a love potion . . . *a love potion!*"

"Well, big whoop! A potion to reduce thighs . . . now *that* I could get excited about."

"As if you have to worry about your thighs!" Sylvie made several more notes on her clipboard before casting a sidelong glance of disgust at Blanche's perfect figure. At five-foot-ten, Blanche didn't carry an ounce of excess fat. Sylvie, a good four inches shorter, didn't either, but she had to work at it every single day. Darn it!

"Every woman in the world has to worry about her thighs, honey. Especially after she passes the big Three-Oh. Forget cellulite. *Everything* starts to swell up or slip down then."

"That's precisely why my discovery is so important. It moves the emphasis away from physical appearance."

"With rat aphrodisiacs? Disgusting!"

Blanche just didn't understand.

In this spare room, off the main laboratories of Terrebonne Pharmaceuticals, Inc., a company that dealt almost exclusively with birth control and hormone replacement products, Sylvie had been conducting her experiments for the past year on dozens of rodent couples in their glass-walled cages. It hadn't started out that way. She'd been immersed in her regular work involving progesterone when she noticed an elevation in pheromone levels as different ingredients were manipulated. Out of that had grown her JBX Project, which would be of special interest to any for-profit company, especially after the way Pfizer stock had almost doubled in price following the announcement in mid-'98 of its little blue pill.

Of course, there was a world of difference between Viagra and JBX, but they were both drugs that could enhance a person's love life. The public would love it . . . there was no doubt about that fact in Sylvie's mind.

She'd given her chemical formula to just the male rat, the male and female, just the female, two males, two females, every combination possible. She'd adjusted the proportions, measured heart rates and blood pressure, tested blood samples, studied changes in physical characteristics. Samson and Delilah were the standard against which all the other "guinea pigs" were studied, and they'd proven in more than a hundred encounters that physical and emotional attraction could be directed *on a short-term basis.*

Oh, the idea of inciting or heightening lust had been around since the beginning of time. Everything from amulets to oysters. And, of course, Viagra. But being able to orchestrate the emotions, perhaps even love itself, through chemistry, now that was a big-time breakthrough.

"Isn't this illegal or something, hon? Drugging someone without their permission?"

"Well, in the wrong hands it could be problematic, but that will never happen . . . well, any more than Viagra, or any other substance, is misused. Besides, it will be at least a year before we're ready to go public with this . . . lots of time to iron out those little wrinkles."

"But it sounds sort of like that date rape drug, GHB . . . you know, the one they call 'Easy Lay.' "

"Absolutely not! Gamma-hydroxybutyric acid knocks a person out; my love potion turns them on . . . *emotionally.* Well, physically, too, but the most important part is that the receiving party is attracted temporarily, on an emotional level, lasting anywhere from a few days to several weeks."

"I just don't know, Sylvie."

"Think about it, Blanche . . . How many times have you and I said that the mating game is based too much on youth and physical appearance . . . that men and women often overlook the perfect partner? This potion gives that perfect person an opportunity to be with the mate they want, to have that person get to know the *real* individual. Hopefully, when the potion wears off, the lovin' feelings will remain."

"But the ethics of it all! The manipulation!"

"Hah! How is this any more unethical than following

the advice of that popular book *The Rules*? Or wearing a push-up bra? Or seductive perfume? Health food stores are loaded with bottled love aids. Heck, women have been manipulating men, and vice versa, for centuries, ever since Eve gave Adam the apple."

"I know you've worked hard to conquer your shyness, Sylvie, but I still can't visualize you setting yourself up for the publicity this would engender. *You* would be the spokesperson for this potion when it hits the market, right?"

"No! Never!" She shivered with distaste at the notion of making a spectacle of herself, not having come that far in her shyness therapy. But she did want credit for her work. She came from a family of overachievers, and it was her turn to get some much-overdue credit. Fame and fortune, without being the deer in the headlights, that was what she wanted.

"Your company might feel differently."

She shook her head. "I may be working in Terrebonne facilities, but this is my project. All the project data is stored in my safety-deposit box, and the essentials of my everyday work are kept in that locked briefcase," she said, pointing to the desk, "which I carry home with me every day. I have no interest in being personally associated with this product in the public eye, but I do expect recognition behind the scenes and in the professional scientific community."

"This is all about your boss, isn't it, Sylv?" Blanche walked over to the coffeemaker in the corner, the multi-colored bands of purple in her skirt shimmering in the thin stream of sunlight coming through the single window.

"Partly," Sylvie admitted, taking one of the cups her friend handed to her. Before she continued, she took a sip, savoring as always the pungent scent of the thick, black Creole coffee, with enough caffeine to revive a corpse. In fact, it was one of the secret ingredients in her love potion formula—an idea she'd gotten from the voodoo ritual handbook that had once belonged to her great-grandmother many times removed, Marie Baptiste, the demented antebellum mistress of a sugar plantation out on Bayou Noir. "I mean, I didn't start this experiment with Charles in mind, but once I saw the implications, I knew that I would volunteer to be one of the dozen female guinea pigs when the human experiments began, and Charles would be one of the dozen male targets. It took a little convincing, but eventually he agreed . . . for the sake of the company. We're starting in two weeks."

"Charles Henderson is a middle-aged dweeb . . . an executive stick-in-the-mud. Bo-o-o-ring, with a capital B," Blanche asserted. "You can do ten times better than him. Besides, you're approaching this whole seduction business wrong. You zap a man with a love potion and it takes all the mystery out of romance. What's wrong with the old-fashioned way of falling in love?"

"Ah, but that's why I've been thinking that I would be better off with a man like Charles."

"Honey, you've been dating the wrong men if you think that. I wonder if you realize what you're doing here."

"I know exactly what I'm doing. No more handsome men with overinflated egos. No more BMW-driving, bottled-water-drinking, exercise-addicted, vitamin-conscious, suntanned hunks of testosterone in Gucci loafers. No more boring nights of deep discussions on the lofty subjects of golf handicaps or 401K portfolios or mega-amp woofers. It's time for a 180-degree turn in my life. All I want now is a quiet, scholarly type, like Charles . . . or a reasonable facsimile. A companion. A husband. A man to make a home with me and give me children. Lots of them." She sighed with frustration, knowing she was failing miserably in explaining her motives, especially since tears of concern were welling in Blanche's eyes.

"Where's the sizzle in that picture, my friend?" Blanche asked.

"I don't need sizzle." Sylvie raised her chin defensively.

"Sylvie Marie Fontaine!" Blanche declared, setting down her coffee and planting her hands on her hips. "Everyone needs sizzle. Are you sure there's Creole blood flowing through your veins? Every Creole woman has passion in her soul."

Oh, there was Creole blood in her veins, all right. Some families prided themselves on having ancestors who'd come over on the Mayflower. Sylvie's family took great pride in being one of the original white Creole families of French or Spanish descent who settled in the Louisiana colony centuries ago.

Sylvie laughed at the notion of anyone questioning her Creole bloodlines. Meanwhile, Blanche swiped at her tears with a tissue, careful not to mar her makeup. "Do you really believe my mother or my grandmother have experienced a lustful day in their lives?" Sylvie asked. "Or Aunt Margo or Aunt Madeline? Even my cousin, Valerie?" She made an exaggerated shiver of distaste. Valerie was the perfect example of Breaux womanhood, held up to her as a role model from the time Sylvie first demonstrated her profound shyness as a young girl. Shyness and timidity in any form were considered a weakness in the Breaux family.

"Well, in every family there's an aberration," Blanche conceded.

"Aberration about says it all," Sylvie said with a

sigh. In Sylvie's matriarchal family, there were no men. Mostly, they just gave up and died under all that feminine domination. In her family, the women didn't divorce their men; they buried them. The Breaux women were known throughout Louisiana as the Ice Breaux, in recognition of their cold ruthlessness in pursuing their goals. Her mother, Inez Breaux-Fontaine, was a state legislator with aspirations of being elected to the U.S. Congress. Her grandmother, Dixie Breaux, was a hard-as-nails oil lobbyist. Her aunts, Margo and Madeline Breaux, had stopped at nothing in setting up their mail-order-tea dynasty. Valerie Breaux, daughter of her deceased Uncle Henri, made no apologies for her roughshod, fast-track career path from jury consultant to Court TV anchor.

The look of compassion in Blanche's eyes said without words that she understood perfectly how many of Sylvie's present actions were based, deep down, on lifelong insecurities stemming from her family. With a shrug of resignation, Blanche asked, "So, when are you going to do the deed?"

"Soon. Two weeks . . . a month, at most. We're still synchronizing schedules for all the test candidates." Sylvie pointed to a petri dish filled with dozens of jelly beans.

"Jelly beans?" Blanche raised an eyebrow in question.

"Yep. My lab rats like them, and . . . oh, I might as well tell you. Charles has a passion for jelly beans, too."

Blanche snorted with disgust. "It's about the only thing he's ever demonstrated a passion for."

Sylvie shot her a glance of condemnation for that snide remark, even though it was true that Charles hadn't succumbed to any of the normal hints and downright obvious seduction techniques she'd tried the past year.

"Would they work for anyone?" Blanche picked up a handful and let them slip through her fingers. "I mean, if I give them to some guy, would they work for me?"

"Not those. They contain my enzymes. In order for them to work for you, your enzymes . . . in fact, putting your simple saliva, or a drop of blood, even a hair, inside a neutral set of jelly beans, like those over there . . . would work for you. Along with my secret ingredients, of course." She pointed to her briefcase, where a plastic ziplock bag held dozens of the multi-colored candies.

"Be careful, honey," Blanche warned as she picked up her purse and prepared to leave. "Sometimes the worst thing that can happen in life is we get what we wish for."

Sylvie refused to let Blanche's admonition dampen her spirits. Nothing could ruin her good mood today.

Man on a mission . . .

Lucien LeDeux was in a lousy mood.

He was supposed to be on a two-week vacation. The crawfish were fat and sluggish this summer, and he'd much rather be down in the bayou checking his nets than cruising into the sweltering city at rush hour. But duty called in the form of entrapment . . . by his own conniving brother.

"You are in some kind of wild-ass-lousy mood," his brother René griped from the passenger seat of the jeep where he was holding onto the crash bar with white knuckles. The right door had fallen off two months ago, and Luc hadn't bothered to replace it. "I think it's Sylvie Fontaine that has the steam risin' from your ears."

Sometimes René had a death wish.

"I think you've had the hots for her since we were

kids," René went on. "I think your testiness is just a cover-up for deeper feelings. I think you're afraid of—"

"I think you better shut up, René. I only do one good thing a year, and your tab is runnin' out fast."

"Cool your jets, man. I was just pointin' out that you and Sylvie are—"

"Knock off the love-connection talk, René, or I'm outta here."

"*Dieu*, if you don't wanna help, I can get another lawyer."

"I should be so lucky."

"Maybe F. Lee Bailey is available. Or Roy Black. How about that guy with the fringed leather jacket . . . Jerry whatshisname?"

"Hah! You and I both know there isn't another attorney who'd take on your case."

"*Mais oui*, but then I am fortunate to get 'The Swamp Solicitor.'" René smirked at him.

Luc gritted his teeth and refused to rise to that particular bait, but he took great delight in pressing his foot to the accelerator and speeding down the highway, hitting every pothole the parish road crew had missed in the past few years. He got grim satisfaction from the surreptitious sign of the cross René made on his chest.

"I shouldn't have put you in this spot, Luc."

René's sudden contrition surprised Luc. "You had no choice," he admitted. "*C'est ein affair à pus finir.*" It was a much-used Cajun saying, but particularly applicable in this case. "It's a thing that has no end."

René nodded. "Perhaps we can finally put an end to it."

The hopeful note in his brother's voice tore at Luc's heart. It didn't matter if it was a seven-year-old René looking up to a ten-year-old Luc for answers, or a

thirty-year-old René and a thirty-three-year-old Luc.
Their father's misdeeds were never-ending. The scars
never got a chance to heal.

Luc's stereo suddenly kicked on, and René's static-y
voice belted out:

Bayou man is a woman' delight.
Catch fish all the day
And make love all the night.
Don' matter if he rough
Like a scaly red snapper.
Long as he give his baby enough
Good hot Cajun lovin' . . .

Even René's raucous demo tape couldn't raise Luc's
spirits now. His brother was an excellent small-time
commercial fisherman, a fair singer and accordionist
on the side, and a horrible lyricist. But he fancied himself the next Garth Brooks of the Bayou with his combination of country, zydeco, and Cajun music, which he
played on off nights going from one dive to another
across Louisiana.

Swerving his jeep off the highway, Luc ignored the
sounds of a half-dozen horns blasting behind him. His
turn signal hadn't been working for the past year.

He took a quick look at the crowded parking lot of
Terrebonne Pharmaceuticals and muttered, "That figures!" Without hesitation, he pulled his jeep into the "No
Parking" slot reserved for the company president. The
car continued to rumble even after he turned off the ignition, finally coming to a halt with a loud belch from its
rear end.

"Your car needs a tune-up," René advised, unwisely.

"My life needs a tune-up."

"Yep."

Luc glanced over at his brother to see what that terse remark implied.

"You're a pain in the ass. A royal *chew rouge*." René was grinning at him.

"I know." Luc couldn't help grinning back.

"Let's hope Sylvie Fontaine has a taste for pain-in-the-ass, over-the-hill Cajuns."

"Oh, yeah! Ab-so-loot-ly!" Luc shook his head at the futility of this whole mission. "René, my agreeing to come here today isn't about impressing Sylvie. As if I could!"

"It wouldn't hurt you to try. You don't have to nail her, or nothin'. Just be nice."

Pour l'amour de Dieu! Where does René get these ideas? "Nail her? Where did that brain-blip come from anyhow? Me and Bunsen Burner Barbie? Ha, ha, ha." He shivered with exaggerated distaste.

Come to think of it, he always felt kind of shivery when he was around Sylvie . . . nauseous, actually. He couldn't stand the woman. Never could. Without a word—just a toss of her aristocratic head—she always managed to reduce him to the small, ill-clothed, bad boy from the bayous, anxious for a favor from an uptown Creole girl. Not that he ever showed it. Instead, he played down to her expectations.

"I still can't see why I have to be the one to approach her, René. You know her, too. I remember her greeting you at the Crawfish Festival last summer. Seems to me she gave you a big hug of welcome. 'Oooh, René, it was so sweet of your band to come play for us.'" The last he mimicked in a high falsetto voice. Then he added in a grumble, "All I got was her usual frown."

René laughed. "Sylvie likes you, deep down."

"It must be real deep."

"Here," René said, offering him the rearview mirror,

which he picked up off the floor. "Your hair looks like a
bayou hurricane just swept through."

Luc raked his fingers through his windblown hair,
then gave up. Was he seriously buying into René's
warped idea of impressing Sylvie?

"I still say you should have worn a suit."

"A suit! What, you don't like the way I'm dressed
now?" He looked down at his jeans and the black T-shirt
emblazoned with the logo "Proud to be a Coonass." He
lifted his chin defensively. "My clothes are clean."

In truth, his clothes were always clean. Rumpled,
yeah. But always, *always* clean. One time Sylvie had
looked kinda funny at his muddy jeans and sniffed, as if
he smelled. It didn't matter that he was only eight years
old at the time. His clothes were never dirty again, even
when he'd had to wash them in cold bayou stream water
in an enamel basin at night, along with those of his
younger brothers Remy and René, and wear them damp
to school in the morning. A slap or two from his father
would be thrown in there somewhere. By mid-morning
his head would often droop with exhaustion, and Sister
Colette would rap him awake with a ruler to the head,
deriding, "You bad boy, you! You're never going to
amount to anything but a *gougut* . . . a slovenly, stupid
person."

Lordy, he hadn't thought of that in years. No wonder
it rankled like hell that he had to go to Ms. Goody Two-
Shoes for a favor today.

"Well, come on," he urged as he climbed over the
driver's door, which was rusted shut. "Time to put our
pirogue in the water and see if we float or sink."

"Uh, me, I think I'll stay here. Better you should
dazzle Sylvie with your moves in private."

Moves? What moves? Watching his brother squirm
uncomfortably in the seat, avoiding his eyes, Luc real-

ized that he'd been set up good and proper. René had never intended to go in with him. Whatever. He might as well get it over with. Maybe he'd still get in an hour or two of fishing tonight.

"Bonne chance," René called after him as he headed for the front entrance of the pharmaceutical research company, where workers were beginning to stream out, ending their workday.

Yep, it is a thing without end, he decided. *Sa fini pas.*

Chapter Two

Zapped by a jelly bean...

Samson and Delilah were at it again.

And that was truly amazing, Sylvie reminded herself, since the jelly beans Delilah had been indulging in the past week were placebos. It proved once again that the attraction continued even after the potion wore off, just as she'd told Blanche earlier this afternoon.

Sylvie hung her lab coat on a wall hook, then rolled down the sleeves of her long-sleeved shirt and buttoned them at the wrists. The lab technicians had already left for the day, and she had completed her own official duties an hour ago. She would close up soon, once she took a few more notes. She stooped forward, clipboard in hand, to observe more closely the activity in the glass cage.

"Hey, *chère*, you wanna dance?"

Lucien LeDeux, Sylvie thought instantly. She'd recognize that voice anywhere . . . the plague of her life . . . the man most likely to dampen her good mood.

"Slooow dancing?" he added as usual, chuckling.

The Cajun clod! Uh-oh! What if he's looking at my lab rats? What if he suspects what I'm doing here? We can't let news of this project become public yet. God, he'd like nothing better than to spread the word from one end of the bayou to the other, giving his own twisted spin to my project. He'd make me a laughingstock. Sylvie, the hard-up spinster with the horny hamsters, or some such nonsense.

She peered back over her shoulder at the jerk, and could have died. His dark eyes weren't planted on the animals after all. He was staring, wide-eyed and openmouthed, at her behind, where the denim fabric stretched taut due to her bending.

She'd always adhered to that womanly adage, passed down through the ages: Never bend over in front of a man. Especially not one with the instincts of a bad-to-the-bone connoisseur of females like Lucien LeDeux.

"Man, oh, man! You have the sweetest heart-shaped ass this side of Opoulousa, darlin'," he murmured begrudgingly. Then he shook his head, like a shaggy dog, seeming to realize belatedly that compliments, even crude ones, were not his usual M.O. when dealing with Sylvie.

Oooh, it's just like the lech to say the opposite of what he thinks. Heart-shaped? As if! Instantly, she straightened with affront, and banged her head on an open cage door in the second tier. "Damn!" she swore as her clipboard fell to the floor with a clatter and papers scattered everywhere.

Luc hunkered down at the same time she did to help her gather up the mess, and they knocked heads.

"Nice running into you, *jolie fille*," he drawled.

The lazy grin that tugged at his full lips was the last straw. "Go away," she said.

"Am I sensing a little hostility here?"

Sylvie gave him a hard shove in the chest.

Taken by surprise, he fell backwards. But, to her dismay, the idiot grabbed her by the upper arms and took her with him. She landed flat on top of the laughing lout.

In all the years she'd known Luc, he'd never once actually touched her. Odd that she would recall that now. That must be why she was so disconcerted by the light pressure of his fingertips on her arms, when he'd only been trying to break her fall.

She tried not to notice the silky texture of his unruly, overlong black hair . . . or the dancing amusement in his dark, dark, brown eyes . . . or his even, white teeth. Instead, she frowned at his well-worn, form-fitting jeans and at the logo on his T-shirt with its self-deprecating slur on his ethnic origins—Coonass. If she, or anyone else, ever referred to him as such, he'd probably fly into a rage.

Then, the worst thing of all happened. Luc stopped laughing as his attention was caught by the sawdust flying in one of the cages, where Samson and Delilah were still at it. She saw the instant he comprehended what she'd been observing on his arrival.

"Ah, *chère*, if I'd known you were into . . . perversions," he teased, "I could have introduced you to this place on Bourbon Street. They have two-way mirrors and—"

Feeling her face heat, she tried to squirm away, but his arms were locked around her waist.

"A blush, Sylv?" he whispered huskily. "At your age, you can still blush? You give me faith, darlin'. You give me faith."

"I'd like to give you something, you dumb dolt," she snarled, and scrambled to her feet. "What are you doing here anyway?"

"I need a favor, *bébé*." He had the good sense to duck his head sheepishly.

"A favor?" She started to snicker. "Me do a favor for you? What's the occasion? All Pigs Day?"

Sylvie saw Luc's jaw clench and the visible effort he made not to retort with his usual teasing insult. "Now, Sylvie, don't be sayin' no till you hear me out. I know I didn't start out right, teasing you and all. Come," he coaxed, pointing to two tall stools next to a long, stainless-steel table. "Come, sit your sweet self down over there, and let me explain it to you."

Geez, his obnoxiousness is so bad it's almost adorable. Adorable? Yikes! Watch yourself, Sylvie. He'd done it again. Rattled her composure. Made her feel all flustery and insecure, like a twelve-year-old girl at her first school dance. Sylvie took a deep breath for patience. "Let's cut to the chase, LeDeux. I was in a really good mood before you came on the scene. I'd like to end my day the same way."

"Watching rats have sex gets you in a good mood?" he asked, blinking his deliciously dark lashes with seeming innocence.

I never realized how good-looking he was before. No wonder women fall like dominoes for him up and down the bayou. "A zillion Louisiana bimbos must have gone down for the count with that sexy ploy," she blurted out.

"What ploy?" He tilted his head, genuinely puzzled now.

She hesitated, then disclosed, "That come-hither, eyelash-batting trick."

"Come-hither? Me?" He burst out laughing, and Sylvie had to admit he was pretty near irresistible when he

threw his head back and laughed with unaffected abandon.

Finally, he wiped the tears of mirth from his eyes,
and took her arm, leading her with gentle pressure to the
table. "Truce, Sylvie. Okay?"

She refused to sit next to him on one of the high
stools. Instead, she folded her arms over her chest and
waited, tapping her foot impatiently.

He remained standing, too, though he chuckled at
her silly act of defiance. Then he picked up a small
Mason jar filled with a murky liquid that he must have
laid on the table when he came in. Handing it to her, he
said, "Will you test this for me?"

Now, that surprised her. He really had come here for
some legitimate favor. Well, *maybe* legitimate. "What
is it?"

"Water from Bayou Noir, near the old Farraday plantation."

"Bayou Black?" Her forehead creased as she tried to
picture that particular stretch. "Isn't that where your
family land used to be located? Isn't that . . . why does
the water look so cloudy? And what are those particles?"

His lips thinned, and his jaw jutted out angrily.

She opened the jar and sniffed deeply several times.
"Oh, Good Lord, Luc . . . are you expecting to find
petroleum wastes in this water?"

"Possibly."

She narrowed her eyes suspiciously. "From Cypress
Oil?"

The red stain creeping up his neck and filling his
cheeks told all.

"Your father would be livid to know you're going
behind his back."

"This has nothing to do with my father . . . at least,

not directly," he said. "I was contacted by a group of shrimp fishermen who've noticed dramatic changes in their catches the past few years."

Dramatic changes in their catches. That was an understatement. The past few years, various oil companies had been widening many of the bayous into navigation canals and dredging an interconnecting network of drilling and pipeline canals, often without regard for the ecosystem or the public water supplies. Despite the concern of environmentalists, a great number of Louisianans worked for and supported the oil industries' offshore rigs; instead of supporting clean-water activists, these people displayed bumper stickers that read, "Oil Feeds My Family." Their defense of their livelihood was understandable. But there *were* pockets of resistance throughout the state, especially in Terrebonne Parish. Luc was asking her to insert herself in the midst of this battle.

Still, she didn't want to appear entirely unsympathetic. "I thought the DER had gotten serious about pollution control."

He shrugged. "Money talks."

"That's a serious charge, Luc."

"We're talking serious money. Oh, I doubt that any high mucky-mucks are involved, but local water inspectors keep coming up with perfect reports on Cypress Oil. Bad business, that. It just isn't believable."

"And these fishermen came to you?" she inquired skeptically. "The Swamp Solicitor?" She saw him bristle at that appellation. Heck, she would have thought he relished the nickname. "Don't get your nose out of joint. I apologize if I was offensive, but you must admit you've gone out of your way to earn a reputation for being a loose legal cannon on some occasions."

"Some apology!" He was leaning against the wall, his long legs crossed at the ankles, gazing at her with amusement.

She exhaled with disgust. Talking with Luc LeDeux was like talking to flypaper—always had been; you never knew what was going to stick. "If a nutball, born-to-lose legal case comes up in Louisiana, you're sure to be handling it . . . in your own slightly underhanded, not-quite-legal, not-quite-illegal manner."

"Hey, why don't you say what you really think, Sylv?" His eyes continually swept Sylvie's body as he talked.

"Why me?" she asked.

"I need someone totally disassociated from the oil companies or the government. Someone whose opinion can be trusted."

"And you trust me?"

He hesitated, then nodded. "I think you'd castrate me with a spoon if I blew in your ear, but on a nonpersonal level, yeah, I suspect you're honest to the bone."

She refused to succumb to that faint praise, even though it did strike an unexpected spark of pleasure in her. "Bottom line, buster. You're nuts if you think I'm going to get involved in a dispute with the government, Cypress Oil, a bunch of Cajun fishermen, and your"— she shuddered—"father." She stooped down, her behind deliberately pointing in the opposite direction from Luc, and began to pick up her papers.

When she stood, he was still standing there. Obviously, the jerk couldn't take a hint. She turned her back on him, and began to tuck the papers into folders inside her open briefcase.

"Hey, these are great," Luc commented idly.

She decided to ignore him, even though he was probably observing her lab rats. *I refuse to let him ruin my wonderful day. I refuse to let him ruin my wonderful day. I refuse—*

"Are they Jelly Bellies?"

—to let him ruin . . . What? . . . What did he say? Eek! Chills erupted over Sylvie's skin. "Wh-what?" she squeaked out, spinning on her heel.

Oh, my God!

Luc was tossing jelly beans up into the air, one at a time, like peanuts, and catching them in his mouth. She looked quickly at the petri dish at the other end of the table. It was only half full.

Oh, my God!

The bayou bad boy had just scarfed down a double dose of her love potion jelly beans.

"Sylv?" Luc asked with concern. "Your face is turning purple. You having a fit, or something?"

Her scream was probably heard all the way to Lake Pontchartrain.

Luc hit the side of his head with the heel of his hand— one, two, three times—to clear the ringing.

"You ate my jelly beans," she said accusingly. "Without even asking."

"Well, ex-cuuuuse my poor manners. I'm just a clumsy ol' swamp rat. We don't have no hoity-toity Emily Post down on the bayou to teach us lowdown Cajuns proper etiquette."

"You fool! You idiot! You crude, rude, stupid oaf!"

"Boy, talk about overreacting! It's not as if I stole your car . . . or your virginity."

"Aaarrgh!" She was yanking at her own hair.

Sylvie Fontaine always had been a high-strung holier-than-thou paragon, Luc knew, just like the other cold-blooded Ice Breaux broads in her family. Maybe all those years of suppressing emotions had caused her to

snap. Weren't there rumors that some of her ancestors
had dabbled in voodoo? She sure was acting crazy.
"Don't get your knickers in a twist, darlin'," he said with
as much compassion as he could muster. "I'll pay you for
the lousy candy . . . wh-what?"

Sylvie was approaching him with clawed hands.

He backed up slightly, hitting a utility sink. Hey, compassion only went so far. Sylvie was beginning to look
like Bette Davis in *Whatever Happened to Baby Jane?*
Right down to the bulging eyeballs. Even her hair, which
had been tucked into a neat, single braid down her back,
was coming undone. With strength he never would have
suspected she had, Sylvie shoved him around and forward so that he bent over the sink.

"Throw up," she ordered.

"I beg your pardon?" He slanted her a sideways
glance of incredulity. "They were only jelly beans, for
chrissake."

To his utter amazement, she tried to stick her fingers
in his mouth. "Vomit, you jerk. Vomit."

He would have laughed if he weren't gagging. Her
nimble fingers were practically tickling his tonsils. He
bit down hard enough for her to pull out.

"Ouch!" she yelped. "Oh, God, you have to vomit."
Now she was slapping him on the back, hard.

He grabbed her by the shoulders and shook her till
she started to settle down. "Have you lost your freakin'
mind? Are you crazy?"

"I'm not crazy, but I will be if you don't vomit." She
took several deep breaths. When she was no longer
trembling, she eyed him speculatively. "I don't suppose
you'd let me ease a rubber tube down your throat and
pump your stomach."

"Only if you're straddling my lap, naked as a French

Quarter hooker, doin' the hula. Even then, I'd have to think about it."

"Oh, this is no time for your crude jokes. Get serious. You've been tormenting me for years, but you have no idea what you've done now."

"Why don't you tell me?" A sudden thought occurred to him. He seemed to remember seeing tiny jelly beans in some of the rat cages. Could they have arsenic, or something, in them? His stomach churned ominously. "Those jelly beans . . . they weren't poisoned, were they?"

"Of course not, but . . ."

"But?" he prodded.

"But they had a love potion in them," she divulged with a sigh of resignation. "Can you see now why you have to vomit?"

"A love potion?" he hooted. "Oh, darlin', if you wanted to get laid, why didn't you say so?"

She closed her eyes for several seconds, as if counting to ten. When she opened them, her blue eyes still glittered with anger, but her words came out calmly, as if he were a half-witted child. "Listen, and listen good, because I'm only going to explain it once. I have invented a real love potion. JBX—the Jelly Bean Fix—is a little side venture of mine and Terrebonne Pharmaceuticals. I've run experiments on my lab rats for over a year, and believe me, the potion works."

"A love potion? Ha, ha, ha. You been sniffin' some voodoo-hoodoo incense or somethin'? I got news for you, honey. There ain't no such thing as a love potion."

"How about Viagra? If someone had told you a few years ago that there was a little blue pill that could perform such . . . well, magic, you probably would have pooh-poohed that, too," she said, lifting her chin with affront.

"Pooh-pooh? What's a pooh-pooh? I do not pooh-pooh." Then he thought about her other words. "You've been giving your rats Viagra? Isn't that kind of weird? And illegal? Maybe I should call the animal-rights people."

"No, I have not been . . . oh, this is an impossible conversation. Listen. You swallowed a love potion, you big baboon. Get that through your thick head. We have to do something about it, *now!*"

He looked over to the cages where some of the rats were humping away, while others were nuzzling each other like little lovebirds . . . or love rats. Still others were nibbling on miniature versions of the jelly beans he'd just eaten.

He didn't believe for one minute that there was any such thing as a real love potion . . . no matter what she said about Viagra. But there wasn't a chance in hell that he wasn't going to pounce on this opportunity. "So, when do I go into lust mode? Will I be makin' love to you on the floor, like those rats? And no one will be able to blame me 'cause I'll be out of control from your potion, right? And you'll lose all your inhibitions and jump my bones like a hobo on a hot dog, right?"

"The potion isn't about lust . . . well, not totally. It's a *love* potion. Please, Luc, try to vomit, or go to the hospital and have your stomach pumped, if you won't let me do it."

"You're serious, aren't you?"

"If you only knew." She sighed and rubbed the fingertips of one hand over her creased forehead.

"I thought Terrebonne Pharmaceuticals made birth control and hormone replacement pills."

"They do. This is a . . . um, special experiment. But we haven't started the human trials yet."

"Special? Human?" His head cocked in puzzlement as he watched her face redden again, and she avoided his eyes. "Aha! You're going to be one of the experimentees, aren't you? Whooee! Sylvie Fontaine taking a love potion! And, man, you wouldn't want news of this to get out any too soon, right?" A rush of exhilaration ran through his veins, just like when he had a good hand in *bourré* and knew he was going to win the game. Sylvie Fontaine didn't know it, but she was going to help him and the shrimp fishermen. Or else . . .

The possibilities were endless . . . and surprisingly tantalizing.

"Project heads often volunteer to be their own 'guinea pigs.' And it will be a long time before this product is ready for market. That's the only reason Terrebonne Pharmaceuticals wouldn't want a premature announcement of our tests." Her eyelashes fluttered as she spoke.

She was a rotten liar. He kind of liked that about her. "I don't understand why *you* would be working on a love potion. And by the way, are you the only one I'm going to be lusting . . . oops, I mean loving? I'm not gonna be in rut for every woman I meet, am I? That could be really time-consuming, and I have a date with some crawfish down on the bayou."

Her shoulders slumped, and he almost regretted his vulgar taunting. Almost.

"Luc, why do you talk to me like that? You've been doing it for years and years. What have I ever done to you?"

"'Cause you're so uppity-uppity, always looking down your nose at me." *And you react so quickly to the least little jab.*

"I am not. I do not."

"*Mais oui*, you do. Not that I care."

She raised her brows in disbelief. "In answer to your

question, no, you won't be attracted to just any woman. Only me."

"Well, isn't that convenient?"

"The jelly beans you ate had my enzymes in them." She put up a halting hand when he was about to make another smart remark. "If I'd put your enzymes in a neutral set of specially prepared jelly beans and I ate them, then the process would be reversed."

"Enzymes?"

She shrugged. "Enzymes can be obtained in lots of ways, or simply by taking a tiny drop of saliva."

"Yech! I ate your spit?"

"Luc, that's the least of your problems."

Her words were beginning to sink in, which raised more questions. He narrowed his eyes at her. "Who are the males who are gonna be sucking up love potions with you in this little human test run?"

She jutted out her chin stubbornly.

"I have a right to know, dontcha think?"

She refused to budge.

He tried to think. Houma and the bayou region were a vast network of gossip grapevines. A guy couldn't piss in his own toilet without the entire parish counting the drops. Luc figured Terrebonne Pharmaceuticals wouldn't be bringing in outsiders for this experiment. It would probably be men within the company, in order to preserve secrecy. And he didn't care what Sylvie said, secrecy would be important. He couldn't think of anyone . . . except . . . no, that was impossible. "Your boss," he guessed.

Sylvie's cheeks immediately turned bright red.

He clapped his knee with glee at the absurdity of the situation. "Don't try to deny it, *chère*. I can see the truth on your face."

"Oh, all right. Charles Henderson will be one of the participants," she confessed hesitantly. "But don't you tell anyone."

Like anyone would believe me! Once he snapped his gaping mouth shut, he burst out laughing. He couldn't help himself. "You're giving a love potion to a gay man? Talk about!"

"Gay? Gay?" she shrieked, and his ears started ringing again. "He's not gay."

"Honey, Chuckie boy is one-hundred-percent lah-di-dah. I guar-an-tee."

"How do you know? Are you gay? Oh, this has got to be the worst thing you've ever said to me. The worst."

"*I'm* not gay," he said with affront. "But I have gay clients." Well, he'd had one gay client two years ago . . . a female impersonator at a gay nightclub in Lafayette, The Blue Lily.

"It's not true," she whispered weakly.

"It's true, Sylv. It's true."

Tears filled her eyes . . . eyes that were really rather pretty, a luminous shade of blue, like the sky seen through a bayou mist on a summer day. *Whoa!* He caught himself up short. It was one thing to be a sucker for a woman's tears, but now he was beginning to notice nice things about Sylvie.

Could her jelly bean potion really be working?

Nah!

He felt kind of low unloading such bad news on Sylvie, though. Was she in love or something with a gay man? "Does it matter so much, Sylvie?" he asked with as much sensitivity as he could summon. He was still having trouble holding back a smile at the whole ludicrous situation.

"Drop dead!" she said with a sniffle.

So much for sensitivity. He walked over to the table and picked up his jar of water. "When can you do the tests? I need an answer ASAP."

"I'm not doing your tests."

"Oh, yes, you are, Sylv." Setting the jar back down, he picked up the dish of remaining jelly beans, scooped them up, and stuffed them in his jeans pocket. Patting the bulge with satisfaction, he said, "Evidence."

"Don't you mean blackmail?"

"Whatever."

"I'll do it on one condition. You have to go out of town for at least a week. You can't be anywhere in my vicinity."

"A week?" he sputtered.

"You did suck up a double dose of those jelly beans," she said defensively. "So, yeah. At least one week. I'll put off the human trial runs until your ingestion runs its course."

Ingestion? Now, it's an ingestion? Hell! "Oh, all right." He didn't have any pressing cases on deck, and he was on vacation; he'd been planning a trip deep into the bayou. He wasn't sure he wanted to stay away for even a week, though. Well, she didn't need to know that. As a parting shot, he added, "I hope I don't get hungry tonight . . . for jelly beans." He patted his pocket again.

"You wouldn't!"

Maybe he would, Luc decided. Then again, maybe he wouldn't. But one thing was sure. If he was getting into the blackmail business, he wanted something more than a lab test for his efforts. And he knew just what it was gonna be.

Slooow dancing.

Chapter Three

He was the sexiest gate crasher to hit the bayou . . .

"I've never seen so many men with no behinds in all my life," Sylvie observed the next evening.

"You've got a point there," Blanche agreed. "Most of them are politicians, and everyone knows they have unleavened buns. Comes from all that hot air, I think. Yep, their inner tubes are leaking."

Sylvie and Blanche were sitting on lounge chairs beside the pool behind the Breaux family plantation house. The estate was renowned for its spectacular garden of native and imported irises of a thousand different species, which were in full bloom now.

Tonight Inez Breaux-Fontaine was holding a cocktail party for a few of her closest friends . . . about two hundred people. Some of the men and women wore bathing suits and were enjoying a swim, but most had

come for the political and social networking. Sylvie
and Blanche, in sundresses and sandals, were people-
watching as they sucked down watermelon margaritas
like salt addicts, and listened to Paul Trebel's band
playing soft jazz over by the archway of live oak trees.

Sylvie licked the crust on her stemmed glass and
continued her observations. "God really must be a man,
don't you think? Either that or He has a warped sense of
humor. Why else would a woman's behind blossom into
Rubenesque proportions after a certain age, while a
man's behind just disappears?"

"C'est la vie," Blanche slurred with margarita-
inspired wisdom. "What kind of buns does Charles
have?"

"How would I know?" Sylvie was still in a state of
shock over Lucien LeDeux eating the jelly beans intended for her boss. She hadn't lost faith in her potion,
but she wasn't about to try her experiment on Charles or
anyone else till she was sure Luc wasn't lurking about.
He'd promised to stay away for a week, but she wasn't
taking any chances. And no way did she believe his contention that Charles was gay. No way. Blanche grinned
at her, as if reading her thoughts.

"It's not funny," Sylvie said.

"Oh, yes, it is, Sylv. You and 'The Bad Boy of the
Bayous.' Ay-yi-yi!" She fanned herself dramatically.
"Seriously, hon, isn't this the greatest test you could
give your potion . . . two archenemies? You should
take advantage of the situation. I hear those Cajuns are
fab-u-lous lovers."

Sylvie arched a brow with skepticism.

Blanche finished off her second margarita and nodded her head as if agreeing with herself. "Best of all,
their buns stay hard longer . . . not to mention *other*
body parts." Blanche rolled her eyes meaningfully.

Sylvie couldn't help laughing. "You should say that on your talk show. You'd have women flocking to Louisiana like homing pigeons, searching for a hot Cajun. The tourist commission would declare you a state treasure . . . just like that John Berendt guy promoted Savannah with his book *Midnight in the Garden of Good and Evil.*"

"It's the truth, honey. Didn't you ever hear the story about the beginning of the oil boom in Texas?"

Sylvie groaned. There was nothing Blanche liked better than to tell a story . . . her own embellished version.

"All these Cajun men crossed the border to work on the oil rigs, and the Texas women went full-tilt-boogie wild for them," Blanche said. "Pretty soon all the Texas men were wondering what those swaggering Cajun men had that they didn't . . . what made them so *virile.*" She jiggled her eyebrows at Sylvie on that last word. "Well, the wily Cajuns told them that it was the fat in those ol' crawfish they ate all the time. And sure enough, those dumb Texans commenced scarfing up mudbug fat. Some people say that's what started the popularity of crawfish." The whole time she talked, Blanche gave her story the drawn-out, Southern Creole accent that endeared her to thousands of radio fans.

Sylvie reached over and squeezed Blanche's hand. Thank God for this good friend who could make her smile, even when her world might conceivably be about to self-destruct. All because of Lucien LeJerk.

"Sylvie Marie, you know Mr. Sommese, don't you?" her mother said, having come up behind them unexpectedly. The cool stare Inez leveled her way said clearly that Sylvie was failing in her responsibilities as a dutiful daughter to mix with the crowd. Sylvie had always failed in her mother's eyes, in one way or another.

As usual, Inez Breaux-Fontaine was decked out in

understated elegance, from her Cartier diamond-stud earrings to simple pleated slacks of cream linen topped by a tailored, rose silk blouse. *A lady never makes herself conspicuous, Sylvie Marie.* Inez's face was tight-skinned perfection that would do a forty-year-old woman proud, let alone one of fifty-five, thanks to a lifelong regimen of Erno Lazlo facial products and a few nips and tucks. *Have you been out in the sun again, Sylvie Marie? Tsk-tsk. A real lady does not freckle.* Not a single hair on Inez's trademark chic black bob would dare be out of place or, God forbid, turn gray. *When are you going to find a hair style that suits you, Sylvie Marie? Do you like being so plain?*

Sylvie and Blanche both stood, though they were a little wobbly on their feet, which drew another icy glare from Inez. Sylvie was bound to hear more about this indiscretion later. *A lady never overindulges, Sylvie Marie.*

"Hi, Matt," Sylvie and Blanche both said at the same time.

Matt Sommese was a *Times-Picayune* reporter they'd met on innumerable occasions over the years. After exchanging a few pleasantries, Inez drifted off to perform her hostess duties. Inez had drifting down to an art form, while Sylvie still suffered inside from chronic shyness, a condition she fought to hide and overcome. Blanche excused herself to go to the ladies' room.

After some small talk, Matt asked, "So, Sylvie, when you gonna let me examine that voodoo journal of your great-grandmother's?"

"It belonged to my great-grandmother many times removed," she corrected. "And the answer is the same as it was last time you asked. Never. It's a private family possession."

Matt was working on an in-depth series of stories

about voodoo and its continuing existence in Louisiana. In fact, there had been two suspicious ritual-type deaths during the past year that locals attributed to powerful gris-gris. Matt probably hoped to get a Pulitzer Prize, the way his fellow journalists at the New Orleans paper had gotten one for a 1997 series on the failing bayou ecosystem. Well, he wasn't going to get it with her family secrets . . . especially since she already had reservations about having used some of the information from the voodoo journal for her formula . . . especially since there was an unwritten family agreement that the journal's contents were to be kept secret.

"It's a piece of Louisiana history, Sylvie, and you know it. Don't you have any community spirit?"

Sylvie was spared making an answer when Blanche returned, grinning from ear to ear. Sylvie made a mental note to cut off her friend's supply of margaritas. But then Blanche jabbed her in the arm with an elbow and whispered, "Here comes boot-scootin' trouble."

She peered toward the house through eyelashes that felt intensely heavy. Then she gasped.

Lucien LeDeux.

Uh-oh!

Chugging down the last of her margarita, she tried to remember if she'd had two or three . . . whatever, it wasn't enough.

The brute had promised to stay away for a week. One day had passed, and already he'd broken his word.

As to Blanche's reference to "boot-scootin' trouble," well, trouble didn't begin to describe the long, tall Cajun in jeans, white T-shirt, navy-blue blazer, and scruffy boots, headed in her direction with fire in his eyes.

With hysterical irrelevance, Sylvie wondered how much crawfish fat he'd ingested over the years.

"Sommese, Blanche," Luc said, greeting the other two with a nod, then adding bluntly, "Get lost."

Matt and Blanche glanced at each other, then back to the spectacle about to unfold before them. "Hah!" they both muttered, not budging an inch.

Directing his attention to Sylvie, Luc pulled her off to the side and got right to the point, barely able to keep his voice down to an outraged undertone. "What the hell have you done to me? That love potion you invented is driving me up the wall."

"Shhh." She put a hand of caution on his arm. Even though they were several feet away from Matt and Blanche, she worried that they might be overheard. "What are you doing here? You promised to stay away."

He shrugged her hand off angrily. "I went deep into the bayou, just like I promised, and the only thing I could think about was you."

"Did Luc say that Sylvie has invented a love potion?" she heard Matt ask Blanche. "I wonder if she got her ideas from that voodoo journal?"

Oh, Lord! The man must have a reporter's sixth sense, or else he could read lips.

Luc noticed and deliberately turned his back on them. He whispered raspily, "I can't sleep. I can't eat. I can't even fish. All I do is daydream about a woman I loathe."

Loathe? Sylvie cringed.

"*Dieu*, you have me picturing you in some hokey Acadian house on stilts, along a stream, with a white picket fence and a horde of grimy-faced kids with blue eyes and heart-shaped asses. But that's not all. I—"

"I am *not* flattered by that heart-shaped business, you know."

"I picture you in my boat, in a thong bikini. Red. Made of some lacy material. And you know what the best thing is about lace, don't you, *chère?* All the holes."

Sylvie inhaled sharply. "I have never worn a thong bikini in my life. In fact, I don't even own a bikini."

"Worst of all, I picture you in my bed . . . oh, Lord, do I picture you in my bed! Hot damn, I didn't even know they could do that with licorice whips."

Licorice whips?

"Then there were those black fishnet stockings. Man, I about had a heart attack."

Oh, my God! Sylvie thought her face would burst aflame. Even if she weren't chronically shy, that last remark would be embarrassing. Lucien LeDeux made a habit of not only crossing the line between good taste and crudity, but pole-vaulting over it with great glee . . . at least, he did when around her. "You are making this all up," she accused him huffily, and punched him in the chest.

"Am not," he asserted, making a cross over his heart with a forefinger. "Really, can a man die of a perpetual hard-on? And mushy emotions are banging against the walls of my brain like ping-pong balls, and each of them has your picture on it, sweet cakes." He took a glass of Scotch off the tray of a passing waiter and belted it down in one long swallow, then let out a whoosh of exasperation.

Forget about Luc dying of . . . that thing he'd said; Sylvie was the one who felt like dying . . . of mortification. It wasn't that Luc was speaking loudly. Far from it. His words came out in more of a low growl.

"Give me an antidote. Right now," Luc demanded.

"There is no antidote."

He appeared taken aback by that news. "Well, then, you'd better be prepared to spend the next week or so on your back, sweetheart."

He couldn't mean what she thought he meant.

"And another thing . . . did you start on the pollution

tests I asked you to do? Shrimp are dying as I speak. Am I going through this torture for nothing?"

"Shhh," Sylvie warned once again. Matt had taken out a small notebook and was engaged in some serious scribbling, the whole time inclining his head toward Blanche, who was babbling away. "I did some of the preliminary tests, you jerk," she gritted out. "And the results were just as you expected. Worse, even. Wait till you see the components in that sample. You may be able to make a direct connection with Cypress Oil. I'll mail them to you in the morning."

"Mail? Mail?" he sputtered.

"Hold the bloody presses!" Matt came up and hooted at Luc, as if suddenly enlightened. "I just made the connection between you and Sylvie . . . a lawyer and a chemist. Don't tell me you're representing that bunch of ragtag fishermen that are trying to fight Cypress Oil? 'The Swamp Solicitor' and the shrimpies? Man, you guys must have a death wish. And isn't your father involved with Cypress?"

Luc blinked at Matt. Horror soon replaced the expression of fury on his face as he realized how much he'd risked by coming to a public place to confront Sylvie. Of course, it was all guesswork on the newshound's part thus far. Still, Luc would have to be more careful. "You're way off base, Sommese," he lied. "And if you print one word, I'm gonna sue the pants off you. Then I'm gonna cut you up into gator bait, starting with that flapping tongue of yours. Don't think I've forgotten the last hatchet job you did on me."

"You mean, the one about the dingbat Vermilion Parish farmer who sued the electric company? The guy whose ducks stopped laying eggs when the power went dead for a day, cutting off the Cajun music piped into their pens?"

Luc put his hands on his hips and glared belligerently at the foolhardy reporter. "I won, didn't I?"

"That's because the judge was a Cajun. And you kept playing 'Jolé Blon' in the courtroom to illustrate your case. The judge couldn't stop tapping his feet. The atmosphere in the jury box was like a regular *fais do-do* . . . a Saturday night dance down on the bayou."

Luc told Matt to do something anatomically impossible to himself.

Out of her peripheral vision, Sylvie saw her Aunts Margo and Madeline approaching. The fire in Luc's eyes was nothing compared to the bonfire in theirs. The legal-eagle gate-crasher, now chugging down another Scotch, had represented a client five years earlier who'd prevented them from expanding their herbal tea company onto a neighboring trailer park property. He'd claimed he was preserving local culture. Apparently, there were some antique trailers there . . . pieces of rusted-out Cajun Americana, much like the vanishing steel highway diners of the past.

Luc had lost the case, but managed in the process to give the trailer park so much publicity that its market value increased dramatically, beyond her aunts' willingness to pay. Now, every time they looked out their office windows, they were forced to view a neon-sign-blinking tourist attraction.

But her advancing aunts were only a small part of the soap opera that was becoming her life.

Behind her aunts, Sylvie saw two late arrivals. Valcour LeDeux—an older, alcohol-dissipated, though still handsome, version of Luc in an expensive, tailor-made suit—strolled forward with a bourbon in one hand and his nymphet common-law wife in the other.

Luc's body went completely tense the minute he noticed his father.

Rumor claimed that the man had physically abused his sons when they were children, and Sylvie could recall Luc with black eyes or a limp. At the time, she'd assumed he'd been brawling with boys his own age. Now she wondered. It would seem that Luc's father had a lot to answer for.

Despite his unsavory reputation, Valcour LeDeux had money and power, thanks to his dumb-luck interest in Cypress Oil, and for that reason alone, he was her mother's guest. Probably, he'd donated a pigload of cash to her last campaign.

She and Luc stared with horror at the two aunts . . . at the lech and the bimbo . . . then at each other. Without a word, Luc grabbed her hand, spun on his heel, and fled the scene, pushing her in front of him toward the old carriage house, which had been converted to a four-car garage, then beyond that to a massive magnolia arbor, which was fortunately empty.

Thawing the ice (princess) . . .

Luc closed his eyes and breathed in and out, deeply, to settle his raging temper. The scent of magnolias was cloyingly sweet in the close confines of the bower.

How could he have taken the chance of speaking in a public setting about the lab tests? He should have known better. Secrecy was critical at this stage. He and Sylvie shouldn't even be seen together. He'd never had trouble protecting his clients' needs in the past. His only excuse was that he seemed to be under the influence of some madness.

A love potion?

No, that's impossible. Maybe the stress of hating my father for so many years, and finally having an oppor-

tunity to retaliate, has made me snap. Maybe I've been alone too long. Maybe Tante Lulu is right when she predicts a big thing is going to happen to me this year. I only hope the big thing isn't jeopardized by misdirected lust. It's burning out the circuits in my brain.

When he opened his eyes, he saw that Sylvie had moved to the other side of the arbor, putting some distance between them. Smart woman!

Well, not so smart. Look at the mess she's made with her stupid experiments. Look at the mess she's made of me.

Twilight came abruptly, as it always did in the bayou region, like a celestial light switch, hazing the already shady arbor. Against the backdrop of huge blossoms in vivid shades of coral and pearlescent white, Sylvie resembled a paper doll inserted in an impressionistic painting. Unreal and hauntingly beautiful.

Sylvie? Beautiful? He really was going mad.

She wore a long gauzy dress of variegated shades of indigo blue—much like those in the fine fabrics Cajun women still hand-dyed and weaved. With its rounded neck that barely exposed her collarbone, its loose, waistless construction, and ankle-brushing length, it could have passed for an old-fashioned gown of another era, except that the back dipped low, low, low, exposing the delicious curve of her lower back.

He knew this because he'd followed her a short time ago as they'd escaped the prying eyes and ears at the party. He knew because his heart had dropped about two feet when he got his first gander at all that creamy, made-to-be-caressed skin.

No doubt about it, Sylvie Fontaine was pretty. Not that he'd ever been attracted to her in that way. At least not before. Or not consciously. No, he preferred wild redheads. Or wild blondes. And taller. He liked a woman

who would fit better against his six-foot frame. And he
sure as hell didn't favor her haughty, touch-me-not attitude.

He didn't like her one bit. That was why his sudden
obsession with her was so confusing and intolerable.

Sylvie had been a thorn in his side for years . . . a
visible reminder of all his shortcomings. For that reason, he jabbed at her whenever they met. Oh, she'd
pretended to be timid when they were younger, but she
was Ice Breaux to the bone, even then.

"How come you never got married again, Sylv?" he
surprised himself by asking. He surprised himself even
more by closing the distance between them and leaning
against a trellis post mere inches away from her.

Her eyes shot up. Wide blue eyes framed by thick,
silky black lashes. It was probably just mascara. As
Tante Lulu always said, "Put beauty on a stick and it
look fine, but the stick, she is still a stick." Usually,
Tante Lulu was making that remark to his half-sister
Charmaine, a former Miss Louisiana who owned a
beauty spa over in Thibodaux. Charmaine claimed
she could make any woman beautiful.

"Why?" Sylvie snapped, regaining her composure
and recalling him to his question about marriage. "How
did you know I was married? It was fifteen years ago."

"Everyone knew you were married, *chère*. Houma is
a small town, after all." And the speculation over why
one of the Ice Breaux would marry a lowly street gui-
tarist had provided meat for juicy gossip. He'd personally given her a mental salute at the time, but later
learned that the marriage had lasted only six months.
Mama Breaux-Fontaine had come riding to the rescue
with a posse of lawyers. Actually, he hadn't given her
all that much thought back then. He'd been in a youth
correctional home for a year, till his eighteenth birth-

day, and had just been offered an opportunity to turn his life around by attending LSU.

Sylvie's cheeks flushed with embarrassment, but she lifted her chin.

"What's the ex doing now? Is he a famous musician or something?"

She flashed him a sheepish grin. "He's a stockbroker."

He grinned back. Dangerous territory, that . . . sharing a grin with Sylvie Fontaine. Soon he'd be wanting to share other things. Hell, he already wanted *that*. "You didn't answer my question. Why haven't you married again?"

"Frankly, my personal life is none of your business." At least she wasn't exposing him to any more of her deadly grins.

"You made it my business, darlin', when you gave me your potion." He reached over and plucked a white blossom, tucking it behind one of her ears. The flower softened her features, giving her an almost wanton look.

At first, Sylvie was too stunned to react to his touching her. But not for long. "Don't touch me," she said, and put a good three feet between them.

"Why?" Lord, he'd forgotten how much fun it was to tease Sylvie. He never remembered having this urge to touch her, as he did now. No, it was more than an urge, it was a compulsion. He brazenly closed the distance between them.

"Why? Because I don't like you," she said.

"I don't like you either. So?"

She put the back of one hand to her forehead, then sliced him a withering glare.

Except he wasn't withering. Not anywhere.

"Go away, Luc."

"Come with me."

"Are you crazy?"

"Yeah. But no kidding, sugar, you should come with me down to the bayou."

"I wouldn't be caught dead with you down on the bayou, or anywhere else."

He chuckled. "I meant that I want you to check out some of these contaminated streams, in person. What did you think I meant?" He batted his eyelashes at her with presumed innocence.

Her face grew redder at having misinterpreted his words. "I'm not getting any more involved in your she-nanigans than I already am. Matt Sommese is already sniffing around as it is."

That threw a dash of cold water on his "shenanigans." Raking the fingers of one hand through his hair, he exhaled with disgust. "Do you think he overheard any-thing I said? Dammit, I can't even recall if I revealed anything important."

She shook her head. "You really didn't say much. No, I'm sure you didn't give anything away in that regard. I'm more worried that Matt might find out about my love potion. He *was* talking to Blanche, and she had had a little too much to drink."

He grinned.

"Why do you continue to think this is a big joke?" she demanded.

"A love potion! I just can't get over it. It's so out of character for you. Now, if Blanche had done it, I would just shrug it off. But you? Unbelievable!"

"Whatever," she said with a sniff of disdain. "The company is closed tomorrow. Come to my lab Monday afternoon, and I'll give you the lab results. Then I'm done with you."

Done with me? I don't think so, babe. "Okay. Let's seal the bargain."

She reached out a hand.

She thinks I mean a handshake. Hah! "With a kiss."
For now.

Her eyes went wide with shock, and her mouth
dropped open.

Open mouths were good. He moved in swiftly. Putting one hand on the nape of her neck and wrapping the
other around her waist, he hauled her up on tiptoe,
flush against his body.

She gasped.

He gasped.

His lips feathered over hers lightly, shaping, coaxing
hers into pliancy.

"Salt," he murmured against her open mouth. "And
watermelon."

"Margaritas," she whispered back.

That brief movement of her lips against his was like
the headiest aphrodisiac. Forget her love potion. Sylvie
Fontaine's lips were pure ambrosia.

Then he stopped thinking. With a hunger that had
been building for the past twenty-four hours, Luc used
his mouth and tongue and teeth to alternately punish her
for the hell she was putting him through, and thank
her for the hell she was putting him through. Who knew
a kiss could be so powerful?

In the midst of the one unending kiss, Sylvie made
little mewling sounds that caused him to press her lower
body against his raging erection. Which then caused
him to make little mewling sounds. He was about a hundred and ten on the arousal scale, with a hundred being
blastoff.

"Sylvie," he rasped out, breaking their kiss with a
groan. He put his hands on her upper arms and set her
away from him. "Sylvie, let's go somewhere. To my
place. Or yours."

She blinked at him, as dazed as he was by the

explosive chemistry that had ignited between them
with just one kiss.

Chemistry? That's right. He'd forgotten. He was
under the influence of a chemical concoction. But what
was Sylvie's excuse? Her glazed eyes and parted, kiss-
swollen lips could only be attributed to . . . what? He
had no chance to figure out the answer because Sylvie's
expression was morphing quickly from "Kiss me" to
"Kiss off."

"The only place you and I are going is our separate
ways," she stormed, grabbing for the magnolia in her
hair and tossing it to the ground.

She was right. He had to get out of there . . . before he
made a complete fool of himself. But he was pleased to
have learned a few things about Sylvie Fontaine tonight.
Like where the chinks were in her armor. No way did
she have ice in her veins.

Not that he was planning to stick around for the deep
thaw.

He wouldn't mind a little ice sculpting, though.

"I'll see you Monday afternoon, then," he said, decid-
ing to give her a break. He headed out of the arbor, and
had just reached the end of the carriage house when he
noticed that the band had changed its program to swing
music, allowing the partygoers to dance up on the patio.

He turned back to Sylvie, whose shoulders were
propped against the arbor like a rag doll. Yep, the heat
was definitely on, and the ice was about to flow.

"You wanna dance, *chère*?"

"In your dreams!"

He winked at her. "Guar-an-teed!"

Chapter Four

And then the jelly beans hit the fan . . .

Sylvie had thought her life was hell. Little did she know there were degrees of hell, like Dante's Inferno, and she'd only entered the first level.

When she awoke late the next morning—suffering from the aftereffects of the previous night's numerous margaritas—Sylvie shuffled out to the front stoop of her town house in a Dilbert nightshirt and a pair of fuzzy bunny slippers. With an open-mouthed yawn, she reached down to pick up the Sunday edition of the *Times-Picayune*.

And went stiff as a show dog on point.

She wasn't sure if it was the pouring rain that caught her attention or the strange flash of light. Peering upward from her bent-over position—luckily, her rear end was facing the open doorway and not the street—Sylvie saw

a photographer raise his camera and then another brief
flash of light. Then she noticed Matt Sommese, leaning
against her car.

"Nice negligee, Sylvie. Victoria's Not-So-Secret?"
Matt inquired with a smirk. His photographer sidekick,
who continued to click away, snickered in agreement.
"Can I assume the love potion hasn't kicked in yet?"

Swiftly, Sylvie spun on her heel and was back in her
hall, closing the door, even as Matt called out, "Come
on, Sylvie, gimme an interview. I just wanna know a
little more about your . . . ha, ha, ha . . . love potion. And
those lab tests. Is LeDeux in there with you? He hasn't
been answering his phone for the past eight hours."

Oh, no! Blanche had confessed last night that she
might have blabbed a little too much to the reporter,
under the influence of those stupid watermelon margaritas. Sylvie had been hoping Blanche's concerns were
unwarranted. Now she knew better.

She opened her door a crack, with the chain attached.
"No, Luc isn't here. I can't imagine what would make
you think he would be. There is no love potion. It was
just one of Blanche's sick jokes. Now, go away. I wouldn't
give you an interview if you were Dan Rather."

With that, she slammed the door.

An hour later, Dan Rather called.

Then Larry King, Sally Jessie Raphael, Sylvie's
mother, her aunts, a dozen newspaper and magazine reporters, Blanche, an enraged woman who claimed to be
a voodoo priestess, a lawyer for Cypress Oil, even Valcour LeDeux, and most ominous of all, her boss, Charles
Henderson.

Sylvie didn't talk to any of these people. She just let
them spout off into her muted answering machine
while she chugged down cup after cup of thick Creole
coffee, and stared blankly at the front-page articles in

the *Times-Picayune*. Somehow, Matt had managed to piece together two stories based on what he'd pumped from Blanche at last night's party; the rest he'd filled in with conjecture.

One article carried the headline "Is the Swamp Solicitor Fishin' for Oil?" It was accompanied by a photo of Luc coming out of the Houma courthouse last year—following a triumphant win, she presumed from the wide grin on his handsome face. His hair was tousled, but he wore a suit with a loosened tie and opened top shirt button. Pure Cajun rogue lawyer.

The other article carried the headline "Chemist Discovers Love Potion; Terrebonne to Give Pfizer a Run for Its Money." It was accompanied by Sylvie's eleven-year-old college yearbook photo in which she resembled a dark-haired Martha Stewart . . . after swallowing a lemon. Pure Creole nerd wallflower.

Neither article was heavy on fact. Luc's was mostly filled with rumors that had been floating around for months about Louisiana's lower-triangle shrimp fishermen banding together to fight Cypress Oil. And there was lots of rehashing of Luc's legendary bad-ass attitude; his maverick career, or non-career; teenage stints in reformatories; and his father's rise to wealth from poor shrimp fisherman to major shareholder in Cypress Oil, thanks to the controversial sale of oil-rich lands that had been passed down in his family for generations. Tossed into the mix was a reminder of the problems affecting the entire bayou ecosystem.

Sylvie's article was more brutal. Matt had managed to dredge up her education and work history, her failed marriage, her mother's political record, her aunts' business dealings, her cousin Valerie's recent smash hit on Court TV, the unsavory appellation given to the women of her family, "Ice Breaux," even the fact that Sylvie had been a client of a famous shyness therapist for years. The only news was that Sylvie had invented a love potion based on some chemical formula inserted into jelly beans and that it might have something to do with an old voodoo recipe passed down in her family. There was also some rehashing of the international hoopla when Viagra had first come on the market. Matt speculated—but luckily had no proof—that Lucien Le-Deux, the bayou bad boy, had taken the love potion by mistake. That last *had* to have come from Blanche.

Unfortunately, it happened to be a slow news day.

Unfortunately, Matt's love potion article was just quirky enough to be picked up by the wire services and the Internet, where it was catching the attention of the national media.

Unfortunately, Sylvie Fontaine was fast becoming the laughingstock of the world. The headlines said it all: "Love Potion Gone Awry." "The Chemist and the Rogue." "Forget Oysters, Try Jelly Beans."

With a headache the size of Big Mamou, Sylvie finally picked up the phone and called Charles. He wasn't at home, nor at the office. Just on a hunch, she tried her lab at Terrebonne Pharmaceuticals. He answered on the first ring.

"Where in God's name have you been, Sylvie?"

"I overslept."

"Overslept?" he sputtered. "Do you have any idea what you've done?"

I'm beginning to get a clue. "I never intended any of this to become public, Charles," she started to say, but then realized there was a lot more that needed to be explained first. "Why don't I come down there and fill you in on the whole picture?"

"No! There are some reporters outside." He put his hand over the phone and spoke softly to someone else.

"Who's there with you?" She didn't like the idea of people being in her lab, possibly touching things that might upset her experiments.

"Frank Daley."

She groaned. *The chairman of the board? Oh, Lord!*

"On second thought, maybe you should come down, after all," Charles said. "Slip in the back door. I'll have a security guard let you in."

Some rats have only two legs . . .

Within a half hour, Sylvie entered her lab.

"What could you have been thinking, Sylvie?" Charles asked without preamble. He was alone and riffling through her files, which recorded the daily rat activities. The formula files were still in her briefcase in the trunk of her car, where she'd left it after work on Friday. "Timing is everything in a venture of this magnitude. You know better than anyone that the research is far from complete on JBX."

Sylvie didn't at all like the lecturing tone in Charles's voice, but she bit back an angry retort and explained as briefly as possible what had happened.

Charles stood, drumming a pen on the desktop as he contemplated her words. Instead of his usual conservative business suit, he wore khaki slacks and a white oxford shirt. To her absolute amazement, she noticed a plastic pocket protector in the shirt pocket. She didn't realize people actually used those things. Luc and Blanche would have had a good laugh over that nerdy accessory.

"It never occurred to me that you would have a loose tongue," he added. "It never occurred to me that you'd do something to reflect badly on the company's good reputation."

"Now, wait a minute. It's not my fault that snoopy reporter pieced together a story from eavesdropping and . . . whatever."

"And you blew it over a man like Lucien LeDeux?" he sneered. "The Swamp Solicitor?"

Sylvie was really starting to dislike Charles's attitude. "I am not involved *personally* with Lucien Le-Deux, not that it's any of your business." She raised her chin haughtily.

"Oh, it's my business, all right. We could be talking lawsuits here."

Her face heated, but she held her ground. "No one but Luc ate the potion . . . no human, that is." She motioned with her head toward the cages, where Samson and Delilah were indulging in their favorite pursuit, along with a half dozen of the other rodent couples.

"Can't you stop them from doing that?" Charles inquired with a sniff of distaste.

"How would you suggest I do that?"

"Put them in separate cages."

But that would be so cruel. "I'll take care of it." She walked over and opened the window blind, letting in a stream of sunlight. Now that the rain had let up, the sky was bright and cloud-free. "The rats will settle down now. They don't like the light," she explained.

Further, she decided to protect at least one of her pet couples—Samson and Delilah—from Charles's or the company's neglect or inadvertent abuse. She saw an empty Happy Meal carton that must have been left by a cleaning person. She poked several holes in it with a ballpoint pen, then gently placed the squealing lovers into their new nest of crumpled wax paper, which still smelled of cheeseburger. The two rats immediately latched onto a half-eaten french fry. Rat heaven.

"What . . . are . . . you . . . doing?"   Charles   demanded. Sylvie really, really disliked the underlying condescension in his voice.

"I'm taking Samson and Delilah home with me . . . for a few days."

"Why?"

"Because I want to." *Now that was a mature answer. Why didn't I add a "nyah, nyah, nyah"? It must be my exposure to Luc that's causing my personality to split.*

Charles snorted with disgust, then asked, "Speaking of lawsuits, did you use generic jelly beans, or the name-brand ones?"

"Huh?"

"Surely you see the possibilities of a lawsuit there, too," he pointed out snidely.

"No, I didn't use name-brand jelly beans." She inhaled and exhaled deeply with exasperation. "Look, there's no real harm done here. Tell the reporters it was just a joke, that there is no love potion. I'm sure I can get Luc to go along with that." *Well, reasonably sure.*

"It's gone too far for that. Uh . . . actually . . . we . . . I mean, the board . . . are contemplating a rush trial on humans."

"What? You made this decision without consulting me?" Sylvie was overwhelmed with fury. "And did you bump me from the trials, too? Are you by any chance taking over *my* project?"

Charles's eyes looked everywhere but at her. Even more telling was his refusal to answer her questions. "In the meantime, we could schedule a press conference giving preliminary results on JBX," he said. He shifted from foot to foot and rubbed a forefinger nervously over his upper lip.

The fine hairs stood out on her neck. "No! Absolutely not! I will not jeopardize the success of this venture because of a silly newspaper leak. Surely, we can do damage control."

"Frank and I were talking about it, and of course we won't know for sure till we examine your formula, but . . ."

"But?" Her eyes narrowed suspiciously.

"Well, you see, the company earnings have been down this past quarter, and we were thinking that, if it really is a viable love potion, and it's already been proven with lab rats, well, what's the point of waiting till . . ." His words trailed off at her gasp of outrage, and his face flamed slowly into a beet-red color.

"The FDA would never give approval without human testing."

"We could market it as an herb, rather than a drug, and bypass the FDA."

"Here's a flash, Charles. You are not turning this love potion into a commercial product, *until* it is proven safe and effective under at least six months to a year of human testing," she asserted. "I may not be entirely certain of all my legal rights, but I do know I have the authority to stop *that* insanity."

"It's not up to you. Any work done on this property belongs to the company," he asserted.

"Not if you don't have the formula. Besides, you're forgetting one not-so-minor point. I own an equal share in this formula."

Charles's face turned pale and greenish.

Thank God she'd had the foresight to seek legal advice last year when she'd first stumbled on this promising venture. She'd offered to resign from Terrebonne Pharmaceuticals and set up her own private lab. And she could have done it, too, thanks to a substantial trust fund left her by generations of independent Breaux women. But Charles had talked her into staying . . . the incentive being an equal interest in the project results.

"Now, Sylvie, don't go off half-cocked. I'm sure we can straighten out the situation. We need a cooling-off period, though."

She snorted her assessment of that wheedling suggestion, picked up the closed Happy Meal box by its cardboard handle, then slung her handbag over her shoulder, about to leave. "Remember, Charles, we have signed legal documents. But you're right, we need each other." She'd completed too much research on company property to veer off on her own now.

In a more placating tone, he said, "Go home and think about it, Sylvie. Take a few days off till this settles down. The board is meeting tomorrow night. Why don't we talk again on Wednesday? Maybe we can work something out that will be mutually beneficial."

Mutually beneficial? He and this company didn't care diddly how this news could ruin her personal life and professional career, so long as they could make a profit. She stared at him, really seeing him for the first time. *What a fool I've been!* "Do you mind if I ask a personal question, Charles?"

"No. Anything," he offered magnanimously.

"Are you gay?"

She saw the surprise in his eyes, but only for a second. "Yes," he said.

Yes? Just like that, he says yes. Then something else occurred to her. "You're gay, and you were going to participate in my experiment. Why? Did you have your own agenda in mind . . . like maybe proving that homosexuality isn't genetic?"

"Hell, no," he said, face flushed. "I intended to tell you before we began experimentation. You need to provide all types of statistical samples, Sylvie. In fact, I was going to suggest *all* kinds of additional combinations. Man-woman. Man-man. Woman-woman. Gays. Straights. Different ages. Maybe even different ethnic or race groups. Without all those, there would have been too many questions left unanswered. You were severely limiting the trials."

He was on track about the necessary adjustment in trial samples, but still Sylvie's mind kept going back to the one fact she had overlooked. *Gay? Charles was gay.*

Much as she hated to admit it, Luc had been right.

She could only wonder if Luc had been right about anything else.

An unexpected wake-up call . . .

Luc awakened Monday morning in his Houma apartment with a head the size of the Goodyear Blimp, a tongue with enough moss to fill one of those bonsai terrariums, and a lower body part that felt as if it could double as a pogo stick.

That latter called to mind the fact that even a bender hadn't been able to wipe out the effects of Sylvie's love potion, or whatever the hell it was.

"Wake up, sonny boy. Time, she is a wastin'."

He cracked one eye open, just a tiny bit, and saw a blond Chia Pet standing next to his bed.

Both eyes opened wide at that discovery.

Oh . . . my . . . God!

Correction. It was his great-aunt, Tante Lulu, with a blond Chia Pet on her head. She was wearing purple spandex biker's shorts, K-Mart sneakers with little white anklet socks sporting pink pom-poms, and a T-shirt with a logo that proclaimed, "Ask Me To Yodel," all topped by what looked like a helmet of tight blond curls.

"Hi, sugar," Tante Lulu cooed.

Uh-oh! Tante Lulu is not prone to cooing. What's wrong with this picture?

Although her greeting was warm, her eyes said he was in big trouble. And Luc knew why. It had been a long time since he'd drunk to excess, and his aunt would be thinking that his hell-raising days were starting all over again. The way Luc was feeling, there was little chance of a repeat of this dumb performance anytime soon. Tante Lulu's lips thinned into a little moue of disgust as she continued to contemplate him.

Luc allowed himself the brief luxury of remembering another pair of lips and a killer kiss.

Sylvie.

Aaarrgh! The woman was driving him nuts. Somehow, she'd managed to imbed herself in his brain . . . like an erotic splinter. But he couldn't think about that now, not in front of Tante Lulu. His wily great-aunt, a noted bayou *traiteur*, or folk healer, would probably be able to read his mind.

"René says you won the booger contest."

"Huh?"

"He says you drank ten Dixie beers at The Swamp Shack—"

"René always did talk too much."

"—then you started dancin' with that waitress, Marie Dubois, and the two of you fools won the booger contest."

Comprehension dawned. "That's boogie, Tante Lulu. Not booger."

"Whatever," she said, waving a hand airily. "Did you hear the new song René wrote? 'How Can I Love You When You Keep Rattlin' My Chain?' " She rolled her eyes meaningfully. "I bought a new car."

What that last had to do with dancing or René's

songwriting talents, he had no idea. "I figured maybe you were taking up biking," he teased, giving her spandex pants a little snap. His aunt was skinny as a rail and had no curves at all. She'd lost her behind around 1973, if she'd ever had one. What would possess her to don such an outfit?

His aunt swatted his hand away. "Nope. These pants match my new car."

"A purple car?"

"Yep. A 1965 Chevy Impala."

"Tante Lulu! What would you want with a big gas-guzzler like that? Betcha a dollar you can't even see over the steering wheel."

"You lose. I can see just fine, with two cushions."

He sat up in the rumpled bed, making sure the sheet covered him below the waist, though he was pretty sure he was wearing boxer shorts.

"What happened to your hair?" he asked grumpily. He wouldn't even bother to ask how she'd gotten into his second-floor apartment. She'd probably conned a second key from René or Remy.

She flicked the ends of her Chia Pet. "Charmaine gave me a perm. Spiffy, huh? She tossed it in for nothin' after I bought her car."

So, that was the story of the car. Luc's half sister Charmaine was a former Miss Louisiana who operated a beauty salon over in Thibodaux called "Kuts & Kurls." Her mission in life was to turn the entire state of Louisiana into big-haired bimbos—at least, the female half. He'd have a good talk with Charmaine later today, once his head stopped growing. It felt the size of a medicine ball right now.

"What? You don't like my 'do?" Tante Lulu asked the question with belligerence, but Luc caught the underlying tone of hurt and insecurity in her voice.

The last thing Luc wanted to do was hurt his aunt. "Oh, yeah, I like it just great. It will probably last a really long time."

Tante Lulu frowned, not sure if he was being sarcastic.

"I don't know much about perms, but I bet it would take a long time for those curls to . . . um, relax." He was on a roll now. Next, he'd be discussing mousse. God!

Apparently that was the right thing to say because Tante Lulu beamed at him. "Charmaine says that Demi Moore is gonna get a 'do just like this one. Imagine that. Me and Demi Moore havin' the same 'do."

I'm imagining, all right. "It's just a little . . . well, blond." He knew immediately that he'd said the wrong thing. He would have bitten his tongue, except it was taking over his mouth with fuzziness.

"So what's wrong with blond?" She braced both hands on her almost nonexistent hips.

"Tante Lulu," he said with patience, "most seventy-five-year-old women don't have *bright* blond hair."

"I am *not* seventy-five," Tante Lulu lied indignantly. "I'm only sixty-five."

In your dreams, Auntie, he thought. But what he said was, "Oh, I forgot."

Actually, Luc couldn't care less what Tante Lulu did with her hair. He loved the old bat to pieces, would do anything in the world for her. She'd been there for him through all the agonizing years of his youth. How many times had she hidden and protected him when his father had come looking for him, belt strap in hand? How many times had she taken blows for him?

Besides, when it came to hair, all Luc could picture in his sluggish brain was silky black hair, highlighted by a white magnolia behind one ear.

But he refused to succumb to that ongoing fantasy.

Yawning widely, he glanced over at the bedside clock and saw that it was noon. "Shouldn't you be at Bingo Heaven? You always go to Bingo Heaven after Mass on Sunday." Tante Lulu was a bingo fanatic. And a lottery fanatic. And a racetrack fanatic. In fact, for her last birthday—her seventy-fifth, no matter what she said—he'd taken her to Pelican Track to bet on the ponies. She'd had such a good time, you would have thought he'd taken her to Buckingham Palace.

"Sunday? This ain't Sunday. You've lost a day, sonny boy. It's Monday."

"Monday? It can't be! I have an appointment in two hours." He jumped up, which caused his head to throb like a fifty-pound jackhammer. Making some swift mental calculations on how long it would take him to shower, shave, and get on over to Terrebonne Pharmaceuticals, he rubbed his bristly face and realized that he must not have shaved in days.

How had he lost a day? He'd been at Swampy's—The Swamp Shack—where René's band had been playing last night—no, it was the night before that . . . Saturday, after he'd left the party. The party where he'd seen Sylvie in that Frederick's of the Bayou backless sundress.

Aaarrgh! There I go again . . . thinking about Sylvie.

Well, she did look hot in that sundress.

Good Lord! Where did I ever get the idea that Sylvie Fontaine is hot? Hell, she's Ice Breaux to the frigid bone, guar-an-teed.

"Stop those dirty thoughts, Lucien LeDeux," Tante Lulu chastised. She was picking up dirty clothes off the floor and placing them in a hamper. Then, she opened a large armoire and started to lay out clean, neatly pressed slacks, shirts, socks and underwear, still in their laundry packets. "Go take a shower. I'll make you a good Cajun breakfast . . . *boudin* sausage, scrambled eggs with shrimp, fried okra, pan bread, *beignets*, and coffee."

After a quick visit to the bathroom, he shrugged on a pair of sweat pants and followed her into the kitchen, where she was unloading a bag of groceries she'd brought with her. Leaning on the open refrigerator door, he contemplated the nothingness inside the refrigerator and said, "You don't have to cook that stuff for me." Besides, he was sure to lose every mouthful if he put anything other than coffee in his stomach.

"I want to," she said with a shrug, "although you should be havin' a wife to do for you." It was her continual gripe. *Find a good woman, Luc. That's what you need.* "What you need is to find a good woman, Luc."

"Women today are liberated, Auntie. They bring home the bacon, they don't fry it up no more. In fact, they probably buy turkey bacon—less cholesterol—and make the husband do the cooking."

"Humph! Not a good old-fashioned Cajun girl."

He just grinned at her. "How come you're here on a Monday morning?" he asked, idly scratching his chest.

"Two reasons," she said, and continued to unload her grocery bag. She'd brought enough foodstuffs to last him a week.

"Well?" he prodded finally.

"I brought you some more embroidered pillow cases for your hope chest. And a new Cajun blanket I just finished weaving. Oh, and another St. Jude statuette. You can put this one in the bedroom," she offered meaningfully. St. Jude was the patron saint of hopeless cases. Needless to say, his aunt thought he was pretty nigh hopeless. He had enough St. Jude statues in his apartment to open a gallery, except they were mostly plastic.

He groaned. "Tante Lulu, men don't have hope chests.

And I have enough handmade, embroidered linens to
open a department store. Sheets, pillow cases, blankets,
bedspreads, dish towels, napkins, doilies." Tante Lulu
meant well, but she was making him the laughingstock
of the bayou with this hope chest nonsense. When he
walked down the street, he often heard his friends hooting with laughter as they told hope chest jokes.

"How many Cajuns does it take to fill a hope chest?"

"Just one. Luc LeDeux."

Needless to say, the jokes weren't even funny.

No one made St. Jude jokes, though. Cajuns were a
superstitious lot, and there was no fooling with the
saints.

The problem was, he couldn't hurt Tante Lulu's feelings by refusing the gifts. In truth, he was beginning to
think he gave meaning to the last days of Tante Lulu's
life: find the boy a wife.

"You can't never have enough linens . . . especially
when you first get married." Tante Lulu must have been
talking while his mind had wandered. She had already
gotten the coffee perking, and the thick pungent smell
of chicory filled his small kitchen. Now she was cracking eggs into a bowl . . . *four* of them. Lordy, Lordy!
Four eggs!

But the overabundant breakfast she was preparing
wasn't his biggest concern. "Tante Lulu," he cried, putting his face in his hands, "I am not getting married.
How many times do I have to tell you?"

"You will someday," she insisted. "I'm just making
sure you're ready when the thunderbolt hits." To Tante
Lulu, the thunderbolt was her version of falling head
over heels in love. "By the way, have you ever made it
with her?"

"Made it? Tante Lulu, I'm surprised at you!" Luc
exclaimed with shock. He couldn't believe his great-

aunt was asking him if he'd *made it* with some woman. The bleach must have seeped into her brain. "Made it with *whom?*" he finally sputtered out.

"Sylvie Fontaine. *Mon Dieu*, she looks like Martha Stewart on a bad-hair day in that picture."

"Picture? What picture?"

"Maybe you could get her over to Charmaine for a makeover."

"A makeover? Where do you get these ideas? Sylvie Fontaine is fine just the way she is."

"She is?" His aunt smiled, though Luc had no idea why.

Then, finally, she gave him some answers by holding up the front pages of several newspapers that she'd apparently brought with her. Newspapers that appeared to contain his name and Sylvie's. It was probably both the Sunday and Monday morning newspapers, he judged, by their bulk. This must be Tante Lulu's second reason for the unexpected visit. He blinked several times, but all he could make out in the headlines, from across the room, were the words "Swamp Solicitor," "Oil" and "Love Potion."

"You didn't tell me you were a celebrity," she said. She was adding shrimp and heavy cream and herbs to the whipped eggs, while another frying pan was sizzling with thick Cajun sausages.

Luc hadn't even known he had two frying pans. He had Domino's Pizza on his speed dial, and practically his own parking space at The Ragin' Cajun Red Hots stand.

"A regular F. Lee LeDeux, you becomin', huh? And since when you go sniffin' round Creole girls? Ain't there 'nough Cajun girls for you?"

With a groan, he pressed his forehead against the wall, especially as his aunt's earlier question sank in.

"Sylvie? You're asking if I ever nailed . . . I mean, *made it* with Sylvie Fontaine?" He started to laugh, but stopped when even that slight movement caused tiny explosions of pain inside his head. "Never."

"And guess what?" she said. He could hear the excitement in her voice. "You're gonna be on TV at twelve-thirty . . . the midday news. Hurry up and turn on the set. Maybe you could call in or somethin'."

I'm gonna kill Sylvie. I swear I am.

"I wonder where I might be able to buy some of those jelly beans," Tante Lulu commented. "Do you have an in with Sylvie Fontaine?"

"An 'in'?" he choked out. "Hardly."

He gaped at Tante Lulu for a long moment, wondering why she thought she needed a love potion. But then he'd been surprised that Sylvie would want such a thing, too. Women! Go figure. He'd like to see the guy who'd rely on such a harebrained idea for a chick magnet. Nope, real men sucked in their guts, slapped on the ol' aftershave and a tight pair of jeans. If they were really dumb, fancy boots and a cowboy hat, too. Sometimes it worked, sometimes it didn't. Those were the breaks.

Tante Lulu flipped over the eggs, and winked at him.

Oh. She must have been kidding.

Whew! That's a relief.

He pressed the fingertips of one hand to his forehead, which was aching rhythmically to some inner drumbeat. This was more than a hangover.

God, my life is going down the drain. But then he stiffened with determination. *If I'm going down the tubes, you're coming with me Ms. Ice Breaux Chemist.*

Sylvie didn't stand a chance.

Chapter Five

Father Dearest sure beats Mommy Dearest . . .

Luc never got a chance to kick Sylvie's butt. Her butt had somehow disappeared from the face of the earth . . . well, at least from Houma, Louisiana.

After Tante Lulu left, he showered and put on clean clothes for his afternoon appointment at Sylvie's company to pick up the lab results. Even though he had a long-playing tape on his answering machine, the damn thing had wound itself out during his drinking binge. He must have been really dead to the world. The red light bleeped now that dozens of voice mail messages had been recorded.

Having read the papers from Sunday and Monday, he wasn't surprised to have messages from his frantic brother René, as well as newspaper and TV reporters. René probably thought this publicity was a deliberate ploy on his part . . . his usual outrageous M.O. Truth be told, his reputation far exceeded his boring life. Luc decided he would find a way to make that misconception work for the benefit of the fishermen. Sort of like that old adage: If someone throws lemons your way, make lemonade.

The plight of the shrimpers was a serious one, especially since shrimp represented the most important fishing catch in the Gulf region. Shrimp were dying by the truckloads in Louisiana, or their numbers dwindling off, and someone was to blame. Part of it was due to overfishing by commercial enterprises and sport fishermen, but mostly it was due to habitat destruction.

A person didn't have to be a tree-hugger to care about what was happening, and Luc felt guilty knowing his loose tongue, or association with that dingbat Sylvie, might have mucked up their case. He had a lot of damage control to put together today.

While René's calls had been expected, the other calls were a bit of a shock. Most hurtful were the anonymous calls from plain folks who said Luc's meddling threatened their livelihoods.

Then there was Sylvie's grandmother, Dixie Breaux, a lobbyist for a conglomerate of Southern oil companies, who asked him to stop by her office. Her voice was businesslike, the underlying tone was uptown pissed.

Joe VanZandt, a lawyer for Cypress Oil, threatened, "LeDeux, I'm gonna put your ass in a legal sling if you don't stop screwing with matters that're none of your business." He knew Joe from way back. Joe was a prick, not worth worrying about.

The Department of Environmental Resources was another matter. The DER would naturally be perturbed by any insinuation that they weren't doing their job. Frank Early, the regional director, demanded, "LeDeux, it's nine A.M. Monday morning. Be in this office by noon with all the lab work and files you have on Cypress Oil."

Luc looked at his watch. It was already one o'clock. Not that he'd kowtow to any pencil pusher anyhow.

The last call before the machine tape ran out was the clincher. His father.

Luc went stiff. His father never called him. Never. Even when they ran into each other in public, they barely exchanged more than a few civil words. The company must be really worried if they'd convinced his father to approach his estranged son.

"Lucien, this is Valcour LeDeux." God, the man didn't even have the sense to know how offensive it was to refer to himself that way. Not Dad. Or Papa. Even father.

With a snort of disgust, Luc threw a sofa pillow at the answering machine.

"For once in your life, take my advice, boy. Don't get involved in this bullshit with René and his loser pals. It's an unwinnable battle. You know it. I know it. Everyone knows it."

Boy? Luc could barely understand his father's slurred voice. He must have been drunk when he called. As usual.

Which caused Luc to be assailed by a wave of self-loathing at his own drunken lapse. *Like father, like son. No! I am not like my father. I'm not!*

But then he thought of his father's youngest son, ten-year-old Tee-John, and had to admit that he very well might be.

Letting out a whoosh of exasperation, his father continued with boozy recklessness, "If this is about revenge, forget it. You can't hurt me. No one can. Your mother was the only one, but the bitch went and died on me."

With a howl of outrage, Luc picked up the machine

and threw it against the wall. Still, the hated voice droned on with self-pity and recriminations. If he were in the same room with his father, and if he were twenty-five years younger, now would be the time when the belt would come off and the beatings begin. *"You're a bad boy, Lucien. Bad, bad, bad. Someone's gotta beat the badness out of you. Bad seed, that's what you are. Devil's spawn. Bad, bad bad."*

Luc stormed out of his apartment, slamming the door after him.

It never ends. Never.

She was smarter than he'd given her credit for . . .

Things weren't any better when Luc arrived at Terrebonne Pharmaceuticals. The first clue was the half-dozen police cars in the lot. Thanks to a Cajun police officer he knew from high school, Luc finally got through to the lab, which had been cordoned off. He discovered that there had been a break-in the night before. Drawers had been pulled out, file cabinets were overturned, bottles smashed, papers scattered everywhere. A detective he'd represented once in a messy divorce suit told him off the record that all of Sylvie's files and some of her experimental rats had been taken, though Luc noticed that a few of the rodent couples were humping away in the corner, despite the turmoil surrounding them.

But there wasn't a sign of Sylvie. Apparently she hadn't been seen since yesterday.

"Where's Sylvie?" he asked her boss, Charles Henderson, who was standing in the open doorway of his office, talking with a police officer.

The officer left and Henderson gave him a disdainful once-over, apparently because he hadn't shaved in two days. Some hidden part of him wondered if his clothes were dirty or wrinkled, as they had been when he was a little boy, but, no, he'd donned clean jeans and a cotton shirt, fresh from the laundry packets. Maybe Henderson looked down on him just because he was who he was. Yep, that was probably it.

"I have no idea where Sylvie is," Henderson replied. "I thought maybe you would know, LeDeux."

Me? Why does everyone think I have some relationship with Sylvie? "She was supposed to meet me here this afternoon."

"Why?"

"None of your freakin' business, that's why." He inhaled deeply to control his temper. "Where's Sylvie?"

"I don't know. I told her when I saw her yesterday not to come in today, but—"

"You fired her?"

"No, I didn't fire her."

"Suspended?"

"Look, I don't have to explain myself to you. But if you must know, I advised her to stay away for a few days till the board met."

"What does the board have to do with her coming to work or not?"

"Are you her lawyer or something?"

"Something."

"The board needs to discuss all the ramifications of Sylvie's . . . I mean, our . . . uh, product."

Luc's eyes went wide with sudden understanding. "You intend to market her love potion? Now? Before the human testing?"

"Well, that hasn't been decided yet."

"And Sylvie agreed to this?"

"Well, not exactly. But it's not up to her. Any work done on Terrebonne Pharmaceuticals property belongs to the company," Henderson proclaimed. His eyes shifted craftily with those last words.

"Is that, so?" Luc swung on his heel, about to leave and hunt Sylvie down elsewhere. Apparently, Sylvie needed a good lawyer. Not that he was about to volunteer.

"If you find Sylvie, tell her she'd better deliver those formula files to me right away. We need to put them under lock and key. And she'd better bring those two lab rats back, too."

"So, let me get this straight," Luc said, peering back over his shoulder. "Neither you, nor the perps, got your hands on the precious formula?"

Stains of red bloomed on Henderson's cheeks, but he clamped his thin lips together.

Luc smiled. Maybe Sylvie wasn't as dumb as he'd thought.

On second thought, Luc concluded a half hour later, Sylvie Fontaine was the dumbest broad this side of the Mississippi.

Her home was a god-awful mess. Drawers pulled out and emptied, their contents tossed here and there. Paintings ripped off the walls. Oriental carpets flipped up. Chair and sofa cushions lifted off and slitted, their stuffing pulled out.

Dumb, dumb, dumb! How could she have left her front door unlocked? Well, maybe it had been unlocked by the vandals once they'd entered. But that didn't excuse her other dumb mistakes. How could a single woman live in a town house with first-floor French doors? All that glass was an open invitation to a burglar, as evidenced by the broken panes he'd seen first thing on entering her home. Hadn't she ever heard of an alarm system? Or a guard dog?

Good thing she wasn't home, or the person who'd broken into her home might have done more than ransack the place. Obviously the burglars were out for something other than loot, or they would have taken the television, or VCR. Hell, there were enough silver doodads and fine antiques scattered about the place to fill a small museum. That upended porcelain umbrella stand in the hallway, for instance. It looked like one of those Chinese thingamajigs, *So-sue-me* or some such name, that they sold in the French Quarter antique shops for a gazillion dollars.

What could the perps have been searching for?

Sylvie's love potion? he speculated to himself with a groan of incredulity.

It seemed too ludicrous to be true, but hadn't Henderson hinted that even his conservative business enterprise was entertaining the possibility of marketing the love potion? Well, not so ludicrous when you considered the huge profits Pfizer had made with Viagra.

But who would be anxious enough to break into a lab and a woman's apartment for the formula? Industrial espionage agents? Reporters out for a scoop? Family members seeking to prevent a scandal? The FDA?

Something caught his attention then. A slight motion near the still-open front door. When he got there, though, all he saw rushing down the street was the back of a woman, clothed all in black, from turbanned head to ankle-length gown. Looking down, he saw something usually witnessed these days only in the deepest bayous . . . a gris-gris, of all things. The small gris-gris or *conjo* bag was attached to a voodoo curse doll, which wore a white lab coat and looked like a dark-haired Martha Stewart.

It was one thing for Lucien LeDeux to be after Sylvie Fontaine's butt. The press, her family, business spies, and every government agency in the Washington Beltway might pose a threat. But voodoo hoodoos were a whole other territory.

Yep, Sylvie Fontaine was in big, big trouble.

Her Prince Charming had to be a jerk . . .

The first thing Sylvie noticed when she arrived home Monday afternoon was the open doorway to her town house.

The second thing she noticed was the mess. Someone had broken into her home and savaged it. She leaned down and picked up a closed umbrella on the hall floor.

Stepping quietly into the living room, she set her Happy Meal container on the floor, then noticed a third thing . . . Lucien LeDeux.

She'd been gone since yesterday evening after giving up on responding to the numerous phone calls that kept coming in on her answering machine. Blanche had offered her the use of her parents' summer home near Avery Island. After four straight hours of sightseeing at the famous bird sanctuary, hearing every birdsong imaginable, Sylvie had decided it was time to hightail it home and face her own music.

Little did she know she'd be confronted by her own personal vulture first thing. Luc stood on the other side of the room with his back to her, casually listening to the messages on her answering machine. The nerve of the dolt!

"Ms. Fontaine, this is Fred Daltry at the Food and Drug Administration. Please give me a call immediately. We need to talk about this . . . ahem, uh, love potion you've invented. Are you aware of FDA regulations regarding substances which are sold as medicinal products? Now, if this is just a vitamin supplement, or herb . . . well, really, I can't explain over the phone. We need to talk. My number is . . ."

"Aaarrgh!" Sylvie shrieked, and went after Luc with the upraised umbrella. "How dare you break into my home? How dare you listen to my private messages? How dare you smirk?"

Luc ducked just in time, and the umbrella came down with a whack on her great-grandmother's Queen Anne side table, knocking the phone and answering machine to the floor.

Aunt Madeline was spouting off now. "Don't forget now, dear. You mustn't make any deals for your love potion. The formula could be very valuable. In fact, Margo and I might be able to help you out . . . for a fee, of course. We might even be able to market it through our herbal tea company. First things first, though. You need a good lawyer, sweetheart. May I suggest . . ."

Talk about vultures!

"Hey, babe. This is your lucky day. I just happen to be a lawyer," Luc pointed out in response to her aunt's suggestion. He was still smirking.

"Aaarrgh!" she said again, this time more softly. Tears filled her eyes as she surveyed the damage to her home. "How could you do this, Luc? I told you there was no antidote to the love potion."

"You think I did this? For a lousy antidote?" Luc stiffened, no longer smirking. "God, you must consider me lower than pond scum."

She counted to ten to stop herself from saying something really vulgar. "Who else, then?"

"Well, how about your boyfriend and his cohorts at Terrebonne Pharmaceuticals? How about some over-zealous competitor who wants to get in on the love potion market? How about your scandal-shy, nutcake family? How about the FDA, EPA, the FBI, the CIA? And by the way, where are my lab results?"

"The FBI? The CIA? Give me a break!"

He ignored her interruption. "Not to mention"—he held up the gris-gris doll—"some voodoo fanatic."

Her eyes bugged out at the voodoo doll.

People who lived in the South might not believe in voodoo, but they would never be so foolish as to disbelieve. Uh-uh! Superstitions ran deep below the Mason-Dixon line, and Sylvie felt a shiver of trepidation run through her.

"This is your fault, Luc. If you hadn't opened your big mouth at my mother's party, none of this would have happened."

"My fault? My fault? If you hadn't been poking around with human nature, inventing a jelly-bean aphrodisiac, none of this would've happened. And if your friend Blanche hadn't blabbed to a newspaper reporter, we wouldn't be in this fix," he declared icily, moving to the French doors, where he examined the broken glass on the floor, being careful not to handle anything that might have fingerprints. "And, by the way, it works just fine, in case you were wondering."

"What works just fine?" She was having trouble following his rambling train of thought. Was he talking about the doors, or who was at fault, or . . . *oh, my God!*

"I've been drinking nonstop since Friday night, and I don't even like to drink all that much anymore. Despite being snockered, I still kept . . . *keep* thinking about you." Sheepishly, and with way too much candor, he explained, "I've had a hard-on for you the past forty-eight hours straight."

She looked down, without thinking, at the flat denim area near his crotch.

"Believe me, it'll be salutin' any minute now. And its national anthem ain't no 'Star-Spangled Banner.' It's 'Star-Spangled *Red*-Hot, *White*-Heat, *Blue*-Flame' Sylvie. Put that on your Bunsen burner, babe, and think about it."

"You are the crudest man I have ever met."

"Yeah. Maybe that's what you need in your life, *chère*. Maybe you've had too many la-dee-dah, polite namby-pambies in your life. Men who say, 'Can I?' and 'May I?' when what they should've said was, 'Park your ass on my lap, sweet buns, and let the good times roll.' "

"I hate you."

"Likewise."

They were practically nose to nose now, gritting out their insults to each other, when a loud cracking noise erupted just above their heads. Another pane of glass shattered, followed by a whizzing noise, then a thud against the far wall.

Startled, they turned as one to see a bullet hole the size of a quarter in the cream-colored plaster wall.

"Duck!" Luc shouted, and shoved her to the floor, just before another bullet winged its way through the French doors.

Sylvie was too stunned to scream or cry, even though one of her palms was grinding against a sliver of glass . . . even though Luc was lying on top of her with his full weight.

"Oh, I forgot," she said in a panic. "Samson and

Delilah. I left them by the front door." Sylvie shoved him off her and proceeded to turn and make a snake-like path back through the living room.

He grabbed her by the back collar of her blouse, halting her progress. "Are you nuts? You can't go back there . . . not yet. And who in blazes are Samson and Delilah?"

"Rats."

"Rats?" he repeated incredulously.

"Yes, I brought Samson and Delilah, my two main lab rats, with me yesterday when I left the company."

"Holy shit!" he muttered. The woman was risking her life for rats.

She stared at him, wide-eyed with unspoken supplication.

Oh, hell! He was the one doing a snake dance then, making his way on his belly to the foyer, then back again carrying a Happy Meal carton that made tiny squealing noises. He handed it to Sylvie, who checked to see if the occupants were okay. The two little rodents squeaked with delight, but he wasn't sure if it was because they were happy to see Sylvie, or happy to be able to hump in peace once again.

Sylvie was making cooing noises at the animals as they shook the wax paper in their usual erotic frenzy. They were real sex machines, these two were . . . a regular X-rated Mickey and Minnie.

"You are really weird, Sylv. No kidding."

The most important thing, though, was that there were no more shots. He pushed the Happy Meal carton to the wall and motioned for her to follow him, crawling on his belly to the far side of the room. Finally, they made it to the dining room, still lying low on their bellies, and gazed at each other in amazement.

It was the craziest situation Luc had ever been in . . .

and there had been a few humdingers. He propped his
elbows on the floor and braced his chin in his hands,
staring at the witch who'd conjured up this unbelievable
plot.

"Why is someone shooting at us?" Sylvie, also
propped on her hands, was wearing black pleated trou-
sers and a white silk blouse. The top few buttons of the
wispy shirt must have come undone when he'd thrown
her to the floor at the first gunshot, or when he'd pulled
on her collar. Not that he noticed her exposed skin. Or
cared. Or even looked.

Hah!

"Not *us*, necessarily. It could be me. Maybe someone followed me here," he suggested.

She tilted her head in puzzlement, causing the blouse
to gape wider.

I'm not looking. I'm not looking. "They would have
no reason to shoot at you, Sylv. They'd never get the
formula, then. Me, on the other hand," he said, with a
shrug. "They're banking on the fact that the fishermen
might give up without an advocate. They'd probably
never find another lawyer dumb enough to represent
them."

She thought for a moment, worrying her bottom lip
with her small, even, white upper teeth. She had really
nice teeth . . . thanks to a good orthodontist, no doubt.
And really, really nice lips. Not that he noticed. Or
cared. Or—

"Luc?" Sylvie prodded.

"Huh?" She must have been talking to him while his
mind was on . . . other things.

"I said, how about the gris-gris doll? That was surely
a threat to me."

"Yeah, but voodoo practitioners are more likely to
use poison. Or kidnap you and employ slow torture with

a knife during one of their rituals. Or drop you in a snake pit."

"You're making that up."

Despite her accusation, he saw a flicker of fear in her wide blue eyes. She had really nice eyes. This was the second time he'd noticed how pretty her eyes were. *Stop it*, he chastised himself. *Stop noticing nice things. Hate Sylvie like you always do. Hate, not like. Or love. Definitely not love.* He answered her, then, with the definitive male response: "Am not."

"God, you are so juvenile!"

"Some women like a man with a sense of humor."

"Aaarrgh!"

"You say that a lot. Is it a speech impediment?"

"Do you have a death wish?" She tried to swat him on the shoulder, but he rolled away onto his back.

It was fun baiting Sylvie. It always had been. But this was no time for fun and games. "Look, it's been swell, but I better get out of here while I still can. If the Cypress Oil people don't get me, you will." He rose to his feet and walked into the living room and over to the French doors. Carefully, he checked the front yard and street. Empty. Amazing that none of the neighbors had heard the gunshots. Well, it was a Monday afternoon . . . a workday for most folks.

"Shouldn't we call the police?" Sylvie asked, rising, too.

"I sup-pose," he said slowly, rubbing his chin in contemplation.

"What? Why do you hesitate?"

"Well, I hate to draw the Houma police into this till we know for sure what we're dealing with."

"You're saying they're corrupt, too?"

He shook his head decisively. "No, but there would be publicity if we call them to investigate. It's hard to keep a lid on it, especially when we've garnered as much press as we have so far, with so little effort. Putting ourselves in the limelight even more will make it all the harder to find out who's behind this crap. Besides that, it will be awfully hard to continue my investigation or your experiments under a spotlight."

Sylvie's shoulders slumped with disappointment. "So we do nothing?"

Luc was a little concerned about the way both of them were using "we," but he could address that later. "No, we have to do something. Make a record of this incident, if nothing else. I have a fishing pal who's a P.I., a former police detective from Dallas. We need some expert advice."

Sylvie brightened visibly.

Luc wasn't feeling so bright, though. Too many things were happening too fast. Still, he reached for the phone.

"What's your friend's name?" Sylvie asked enthusiastically as he punched in the digits.

The P.I.'s number was ringing, and Luc looked up at her, a slow grin tugging at his lips. "Claudia Casale."

This P.I. was no dick . . .

Claudia Casale was a six-foot-tall blonde with the sharply honed physique of a female bodybuilder. None of her assets were hidden by her crisp white T-shirt, proclaiming "Extreme Exercise," or her tight designer jeans. Sylvie couldn't help wondering what type of fishing she and Luc engaged in. She'd bet it was strenuous stuff. Extreme to the max. And, for sure, Ms. P.I. wasn't the type who would need a man to bait her hook.

Claudia had already dusted for prints; there were none. She searched for but found no physical evidence that would identify a suspect. She took photographs of the crime scene, regardless, and made a call to a locksmith and window glazier to come and secure the broken French door. She checked the bullet holes and gathered bullet casings, preserving them in little plastic zip bags. A small but efficient tap had been discovered in Sylvie's phone, and photographic devices planted near her front and back doors.

The gris-gris held some interest for Claudia, which was surprising since Sylvie had expected a detective to dismiss the importance of voodoo. Claudia planned to show it to an ancient swamp woman who still dabbled openly in the voodoo arts. Everyone knew a gris-gris held a powerful curse that could only be removed by a certified exorcism of the spirits. Sylvie only hoped she wouldn't be required to burn black candles every night, or carry around a bat's eye, or make an animal sacrifice or some such thing. Perhaps the purchase of some magic charm would do the trick.

Geez, she couldn't believe she was even contemplating such nonsense.

"Motives," Claudia said, plopping down on the sofa next to Luc. Sylvie, sitting on a nearby upholstered chair feeding bits of bread to Samson and Delilah, noticed how Luc's arm immediately went up over the top of the sofa—sort of, but not quite, embracing the woman. "Without evidence, the only way we can narrow down the suspects you've already mentioned is to examine their motives," Claudia went on. "I can look for witnesses, though I doubt there will be any, and I'll check police computer files for a similar M.O., but motive is our strongest working element right now."

"We've already told you everything we know," Sylvie reminded her. "Can you figure out anything from that?"

Claudia's big brown eyes gave her a thorough sweep from head to toe. It wasn't really an insulting examination . . . almost clinical . . . like it was part of her job. "Possibly," she concluded, then glanced at the Happy Meal container, where the paper was rattling noisily. It was clear to everyone what was going on . . . *again.* With a grin, Claudia asked, "Did you really invent a love potion?"

Sylvie shrugged.

"And Luc swallowed it by accident?"

Sylvie shrugged again.

Claudia's eyes shifted to Luc and lingered in a questioning fashion. "Are you feeling as . . . uh, feisty as ol' Samson is?"

It was his turn to shrug. And blush.

"Wow!" Claudia threw back her head and laughed. "You two are a piece of work."

What? What does she mean by "you two"? Is her investigative mind seeing something neither of us do? Hey, I'm an investigator of sorts, too. I don't see a thing. Definitely not.

"Can you help us?" Luc grumbled.

"Well, I agree with you, Luc, the break-in was probably done to find her chemical formulas. The gunshot was to frighten Sylvie, not to kill her."

"That's a relief," Sylvie said sarcastically.

Claudia just raised an eyebrow and continued. "I can't rule out the possibility that you weren't followed here, Luc, and that the gunshot wasn't intended for you . . . as a threat, mind you. The person firing into this unit was using a sophisticated weapon. If he, or she, had wanted, they probably could have hit either of you."

She and Luc both nodded.

"With regard to you, Sylvie, the suspects thus far, as

I see it, are industrial espionage agents, who often move in quickly when they hear of promising new products; parties at Terrebonne Pharmaceuticals, who want to ensure they hold all rights to a potential financial windfall; your aunts, who'd like a piece of the action; voodoo fanatics, upset over your possible use of their dark secrets; and the media, snooping for a hot story. How does that list sound to you?"

"It seems unbelievable, but I guess I would have to include all of them, even though I refuse to believe that my aunts or anyone at Terrebonne would harm me."

"Honey, anything is possible when money is involved." The P.I. then directed her attention to Luc. "You are a different matter, my friend. Hell, you've pissed off half the state at one time or another. It could be Cypress Oil. Your father. Some corrupt EPA or law enforcement official. Just about anyone. Even an old lover." That last she offered with a grin.

Luc fake-jabbed her on the upper arm with a fist and laughed. "Darlin', 'old' would be the operative word here. I've seen so little action lately that there's rust on my zipper."

Sylvie doubted that very much. And so did Claudia. Sylvie could tell by her raised eyebrows and husky chuckle. It was more likely Luc had a speed control on his zipper. Both women made a deliberate effort not to look down.

"This is my private number," Claudia said then, giving them a Houma cell phone number. "Memorize it, and call me if you get into any further trouble. In the meantime, I would suggest that both of you go into hiding for at least a few days till I do some preliminary investigative work. No need to provide a target till we know what we're dealing with here."

Just before Claudia left, she looked directly at Luc

and said, "Call me." There was no doubt in Sylvie's
mind that she had plans for his zipper.

Not that Sylvie cared.

Much.

She offered an irresistible bribe . . .

"Where are you going?" Sylvie asked a short time later
as Luc gathered his jacket and looped it by one finger
over his shoulder. He was preparing to leave.

"I don't know. A few days in hiding, as Claudia suggested, seem in order for me to regroup. Somewhere beyond the range of these deranged lowlifes." He started to
walk toward the front door.

Sylvie hesitated for a moment before calling after
him. "Take me with you."

Little alarm bells went off all over Luc's body at the
suggestion. "No way! Uh-uh!" He turned to glare at
her, hoping she would see just how impossible her suggestion was.

"You'd leave me here, unprotected? You really are
pond scum."

"Hire a bodyguard. I can recommend a few, and I'll
wait till one gets here. Better yet, why don't I drop you
off at your mother's? She'd probably hire you a truckload of Rambos."

"I am not staying at my mother's," she said with a
vehemence that was telling.

Hey, he could understand that. It would take a gre-
nade to make him stay with Inez Breaux-Fontaine, too.

Then she tossed in the zinger. "Would you stay with
your father?"

Guilt . . . she's gonna blindside me with guilt. "You
are not coming with me," he asserted firmly. "It's too

dangerous where I'm going." *Not that I know exactly where I'm going, but I'm pretty sure it will be dangerous.* "So, take your pick. The police or your mother's."

"I could do some more lab tests for you," she offered as a bribe. "In addition to the data I have in my briefcase, I could even show you some different ways to test that you might not have even considered."

He was tempted. Almost. But the prospect of spending days . . . maybe even a week . . . with Sylvie Fontaine looking down her nose at every little thing he did . . . He shivered with distaste. "I could make you do the tests anyhow," he said.

She raised her chin defiantly. "You don't know me at all, Lucien LeDeux. I don't do anything under pressure . . . not anymore."

Huh? What the hell does that mean? Don't ask. It's a lure. The guilt trip again. Don't freakin' ask. "Whatever. I'm outta here."

"There's one other thing I could do if you'd take me with you." She combed the fingers of a shaking hand through her mussed-up hair, making the strands even more tangled. Her bottom lip trembled. Bright red blotches of mortification mottled her cheeks. His heart stopped, then thundered wildly against his chest. She looked unexplainably brave . . . and adorable.

Adorable? Luc should have run like hell then. The alarm bells in his head had dropped about three feet and had set off the love potion, big-time. He felt as if a time bomb were ticking between his legs and in his heart. Still, he stood his ground, put both hands on his hips, and cocked his head in question.

"Honey, there isn't anything you could offer that would make me change my mind. Save your breath."

"Slow dancing."

"No."

"Real slow . . . with you."

"No."

"In the nude."

"On the other hand . . ."

Chapter Six

He promised to be her Cajun knight . . .

Luc wanted to kick himself a short time later, even before they arrived back at his apartment.

It was a risky business, sticking around town, where gun-wielding, voodoo-practicing criminal elements abounded, with guess-who targeted in their crosshairs. His immediate concern was establishing a safe haven from which to operate. But first he needed to pick up his cell phone before leaving town. And, yes, a pistol, too.

Because of the laughable nature of the alleged love potion, Luc found it easy to forget that there was nothing to laugh about here. Not when his libido was stuck in overdrive . . . not when fanatics were making gris-gris dolls . . . not when weapons were being fired. In the midst of all that, what could he have been thinking to have agreed to bring Sylvie with him? It was too damn dangerous, physically and emotionally.

Sylvie thought it was the "slow dancing in the nude" offer that had convinced him in the end, but she was wrong. True, the invitation held some appeal. Okay, a lot of appeal, considering that it had been a twenty-year fantasy of his . . . the highlight of many an unconscious erotic dream. But it was the look of fear and vulnerability in her blue eyes, not nude dancing, that had snared him. As she'd stood in the midst of shattered glass in her plundered home, chin lifted with bravery, some powerful and frightening emotion had grabbed hold of his heart and shot all his common sense to hell.

It was too much to hope that it might be indigestion from his big breakfast. He couldn't help wondering if the blasted love potion had affected his reasoning. He hoped so, unbelievably, because otherwise he would have to face an even more untenable conclusion . . . that he harbored feelings for Sylvie Fontaine . . . and had for a long time. *Feelings!*

Mon Dieu, he was becoming a freakin' Knight in Shining Armor. Next people would be calling him The Cajun Knight, as well as The Swamp Solicitor, for chrissake! Talk about!

"Why are you frowning?" Sylvie asked.

He glanced to the right as his jeep idled at a red light on Verret Street near the courthouse. With her precious briefcase on the floor near her feet, Sylvie was holding onto the overhead crash bar with one hand and the equally precious Happy Meal box with the other. Her ebony hair looked as if she'd stuck her finger in a light socket, partly due to the tussle on the floor back at her town house and partly due to the wind produced while riding in his open vehicle. Her face was flushed from fear and warm sun rays. Her silk blouse was plastered against some rather enticing curves.

Not that he paid any particular attention to these irrelevant details.

"I'm frowning because I'm driving around with two rats. I'm frowning because someone is trying to kill me, or you, or both of us. I'm frowning because we should be the hell out of Houma by now, instead of hanging around like clay pigeons. I'm frowning because you conned me into taking you into hiding with me. I'm frowning because . . ." He saw that she was about to protest the "con" remark, but he went on quickly before she could speak. "Most of all, I'm frowning because you make me want impossible things."

Now, what made me disclose that? For sure, my emotional circuits have gone haywire.

Her mouth opened, then shut, then opened again as she stared at him incredulously. "Things?" she finally squeaked out. "You want things from *me?*"

"Yep," he said. When he saw the panic on her now-beet-red face, he winked. Let her think he was just teasing, as usual. He *was* just teasing. Really.

Oh, God! First feelings, now I want things from her! Damn, I should have gone fishing today.

But, man, I would really, really like to kiss her. For a long time.

And other things. Oh, yeah, definitely other things, including . . .

A driver behind him honked to alert him to the light change, and Luc moved forward in the late afternoon traffic.

This whole situation was crazy. So many strange and deadly serious events had occurred in the past three days, ever since he'd entered Sylvie's lab. He needed answers to some important questions to figure out who the perps were, but he couldn't do any investigating while under fire. Claudia Casale was tops in her field, and he trusted her to do the preliminary investigative work for him. But, holy hell, it was going to be hard enough to cover his own ass, let alone Sylvie's little heart-shaped butt.

What made him think he could do a better job of protecting her than Sylvie's mother? Without giving it another thought, he swung the wheel of the Jeep and proceeded to make a sharp turn in the highway and over the bayou, much to the fury of the drivers behind him. The operator of a battered pickup truck that fishtailed around him flipped him the bird. As the vehicle— better known as a Louisiana Cadillac—rattled on down the highway, Luc noticed its bumper sticker. "Keep honking . . . I'm reloading."

Luc continued to drive, now in a different direction.

"No!" Sylvie exclaimed with alarm. "You are not taking me to my mother's."

He gave her a sideways glance of surprise. "How do you know that's where I'm headed?"

"I can read your face," she said, "and your face says, 'How do I dump Sylvie and ride off into the sunset?' Well, think again, cowboy. I'm going with you. We're in this together."

"Oh, yeah?" *That was real bright, LeDeux.* He surreptitiously peeked her way to see if she shared in his low opinion of his conversational skills. Then he did a quick double take.

Sylvie still held onto the crash bar and her mouse hotel with white-knuckled intensity, but her hands were shaking, and her overwide eyes glistened with tears that she blinked to hold back. The woman was clearly in shock. Plus, she'd probably never ridden in a Jeep with no door before. Lots of firsts in her life today, for sure.

Without hesitation, he swerved the Jeep off the highway, to the tune of blaring car horns, and into the parking lot of a twenty-four-hour, drive-through daiquiri stand. Cutting the motor, which, of course, continued to run till it came to a sputtering halt, he pried Sylvie's hands off the crash bar and Happy Meal box, setting the latter on the floor next to her briefcase. Then he dragged her across the gear shift and onto his lap. Not an easy task in the close confines of the Jeep's cramped interior.

"Someone's trying to kill us, Luc," she said, weeping freely now.

No kidding.

"I've never been so scared in all my life. I feel like such a fool, crying like this. I never cry. My mother taught me to never be weak . . . never weep or whine . . . hold in emotion. Oh, God, I am such a weakling."

Someone should have wrung the neck of Inez Breaux-Fontaine a long time ago. Lord, the woman really is made of ice, like everyone says. It would seem Luc and Sylvie were both scarred by a parent.

He hugged Sylvie tightly, tucking her face into the crook of his neck and running a comforting palm up and down over her quivering back, the whole time crooning soothing words of assurance. "Hush, *chère*, you can stay with me if you want. Guess you're just like all the other women . . . sticking to ol' Luc like suckers on a gater's tail. Just kidding, just kidding. Ah, don' be cryin', babe. I won't let anyone hurt you. You'll see. I'm gonna be your Cajun Knight."

Here comes the bride. What bride? . . .

Luc drove into a parking space in front of his building on Lafayette Street a short time later, and Sylvie breathed a deep sigh of relief. She had to admit that she was touched by Luc's comforting words and arms when she had broken down so ignominiously a short while back. But riding in his open-air Jeep had quickly jolted her back to the reality of whom she was dealing with here, especially when his brother René was singing the most outrageous song on a demo tape in Luc's tape player, "I Gave Her Tongue, She Gave Me Teeth."

Some Cajun Knight Luc was turning out to be. Whoever heard of a brave protector riding in a broken-down jalopy, cursing a blue streak under his breath? She was pretty sure she was the object of some of those curses since she'd virtually latched onto him like Krazy Glue.

Still, her heart warmed in the strangest way at the idea that he would even suggest such an outrageous concept . . . *her very own Cajun Knight.* Okay, she admitted to herself, reluctantly, she liked the sound of it. And she sure as Louisiana rain qualified as a damsel in distress.

Even now, she cringed at the thought that she had offered to slow-dance in the nude in exchange for his protection. Having battled so many years to overcome her chronic shyness, she had probably set herself back a decade with that definitely-not-shy proposition. She didn't want to even think about the fact that her palms sweated and her head pounded with anxiety now—clear sighs of regression to her old shrinking-violet self. She wiped her free hand on her slacks in a nervous, repetitive motion.

Luc noticed, and slanted her a questioning look as he left the jeep. She got out, too, and handed him her briefcase. Clutching the Happy Meal box in one hand, she inhaled and exhaled several times . . . to settle her nerves.

Taking Sylvie by the other hand, he laced his fingers with hers and led her toward the door of the pale yellow brick, shotgun-style building that housed his office

and private residence. His calloused palm pressed
against hers . . . not what you'd expect from a seden-
tary lawyer . . . but not surprising for Luc. What *was*
surprising was how good that rough skin felt next to
hers. Sexy and comforting at the same time.

Did Claudia Casale get to feel that rough skin abrad-
ing her flesh? Did he offer to be her Cajun Knight,
too? No, Sylvie immediately rejected that notion with a
little smile. The more-than-fit private investigator was
more likely to offer to be Luc's protector. Sylvie would
like to see what that independent woman's reaction
would be if the rude, crude bad boy of the bayou ever
tried to comment on the shape of *her* behind.

Hah! She'd probably like it, Sylvie's contrary mind
quickly opined.

Sylvie stole a glance through lowered lashes at said
bad boy. He wore neatly pressed jeans and a soft cotton
denim, collarless shirt, the sleeves buttoned at the wrists.
Although he hadn't shaved, he smelled faintly of some
piney soap. His thick hair was mussed a bit, and his
black eyes stared straight ahead with solemnity, checking for danger.

Sylvie had been critical of Luc for many things over
the years, but she'd never been able to deny his hand-
someness. He was ten kinds of sexy . . . and then some.
Truly, with his dark good looks and his roguish personality, the man was way, way too appealing to certain
types of women—*like Claudia Casale, no doubt*. It was
oddly disconcerting to discover at this inopportune moment that she was one of those women, too.

*Why do I care about his relationship with other
women?*

Other women? Was she going crazy? What was it
with this "other women" business? She didn't have a
relationship with him.

While her mind had been wandering, the keyless jeep, which had been shut off, was idling away noisily behind them . . . a crude, belching reminder of the image Luc liked to portray in their mutual hometown of Houma, which was situated at the heart of winding bayous and moss-draped oak trees. Houma was a sophisticated city, despite its earthy Cajun influence and its distance from decadent New Orleans, sixty miles northeast, and from the state capital, Baton Rouge, ninety miles northwest. For the first time, she wondered if perhaps Luc deliberately tried to mask his true self with his outrageous outward appearance. Could she have been wrong about Luc all these years? She'd always thought *he* had an attitude problem, but maybe . . . just maybe . . . *she* had a perception problem. Had she been viewing Luc all these years through prejudiced eyes?

No, she was just softening under all the stress today. He was the same rude, crude bad boy of the bayous as he'd always been. She wasn't going to be tricked into changing her opinion at this late date, Cajun Knight or not.

"Nice place," she commented, regarding the building in front of them. And she meant it. The structure was old . . . probably pre-Civil War . . . and had the charm and character of many of the South's vintage structures. Not quite the choice she would have expected of Luc. A rusted-out trailer would have been more in line with his rusted-out Jeep. As the old joke went . . . tornadoes and Southerners going through a divorce have a lot in common . . . including the fact that someone's going to lose a trailer.

Geez, there I go again. Basing my opinions on outmoded stereotypes. Why do I find it so difficult to give him the benefit of the doubt? What do I have to lose by granting him a few admirable traits?

Luc turned to her, and she noticed the surprise, then pleasure, on his face at her praise. "I call her The Buff Bimbo."

"Huh?"

"You know how lots of old mansions and plantation houses are given feminine names, like The Grande Dame or The Pink Lady? Well, behold." He waved a hand proudly in a *ta-da* fashion toward the two-story, pale-yellow edifice before them. "The Buff Bimbo." He grinned at her then, but she could tell that he loved the place.

Why that should endear him to her, she could not say. But somehow she liked the fact that a maverick like him would appreciate the timeless beauty of faded bricks, picturesque ironwork, and time-rippled glass. It was almost as if he had to give the building a coarse appellation to hide his affection, which might be construed as sentimental. God forbid that The Swamp Solicitor might have a mushy spot or two.

"Do you own the building?" she asked.

He nodded. "Some construction crews were about to raze the site and put in an annex to that modern office complex next door," he explained. "It used to belong to a sugar broker before The War, and I paid an overinflated price to save her." He shrugged, not bothering to mention which war he was referring to. Everyone in the South knew which war was "The War."

Then Sylvie thought about his other words. "So, you rescue buildings, as well as damsels, huh?"

He blushed. He actually blushed. And Sylvie once again felt that odd tugging in the region of her heart. And a sense of guilt that she might have misjudged him these many years.

His street-front law office was on the first floor with a "Closed for Vacation" placard in the many-paned, leaded glass window. A low, black wrought-iron fence in the form of twining acanthus leaves encircled the small yard in front. He lived in an apartment on the second floor.

"Well, at least your office seems to be intact. No sign of forced entry," she remarked as they entered the door to the left and then the corridor, off of which was another door to his office and up ahead a staircase leading to the second-floor apartment.

Luc nodded in agreement. "Perps wouldn't dare break in through the window, fronting on a busy street as it is. It's patrolled heavily by police. Not that burglars don't try to break in on occasion, coming through the back entrance," he noted, pointing to pry marks on the heavy oak double door to the right, with the brass nameplate "Lucien LeDeux, Attorney at Law." "But this door has enough dead-bolt locks to secure the federal mint. Doesn't stop the everyday criminal from tryin', though. They seem to think we lawyers have a bundle of cash stashed in our desks. Too much Court TV and gold-chained Johnny Cochrans are ruining our image."

Luc steered her with a hand on her elbow up the narrow stairway with its wonderfully carved cypress wainscoting and handrail. The upper walls were papered in a reproduction antique stripe of beige and burgundy offset with green acanthus leaves. Here and there were framed etchings of famous bayou settings. Astonishingly tasteful.

But Sylvie had something else on her mind. She hesitated at the top of the steps and turned to Luc. "I want to apologize for my behavior earlier. You should not have been subjected to my embarrassing . . ."

"Sylvie Fontaine, don't you dare apologize for behaving like a normal human being. You're upset and scared, with good cause. Hell, I'm sure-God scared, too."

She blinked at him with disbelief. "You don't act scared."

"*Dieu*, why do you think I was holding on to you so tightly back in the Jeep?" He winked at her then, causing her heart to skip a beat.

Even though she recognized that he was just being kind, she stood on tiptoe and gave him a quick kiss on the cheek. "Thank you," she whispered.

"Oh, darlin', you should not do things like that to me." He was shaking his head at her.

"Why?"

"Because you shouldn't rub the lamp if you don't want the Genie to come out. Because it tempts me to kiss you back, *chère*, and not on the cheek either. Because, if you knew the impure thoughts I've been having about you, you'd put a Mississippi mile between us, not a kiss."

She still clutched her Happy Meal carton in one hand, and her other hand was still twined with his, but Luc leaned down, ever so slowly, and pressed his lips against hers. They were a perfect fit.

Sylvie closed her eyes, the lids of which suddenly felt heavy. It was amazing that, in the midst of all the danger, they stood in a hallway smelling of old wood and a century of beeswax polish, kissing. And it felt so very right.

He moved his lips back and forth across hers—a restrained, non-threatening whisper of a kiss. And yet it was all the more powerful because of its restraint and, for a certainty, it threatened everything that Sylvie had ever been or ever dreamed. He moaned deep in his throat, and that was her undoing.

She pulled back abruptly. Breathing heavily, she struggled to find some explanation for this strange chemistry whirling about them, connecting them in a most compelling way. She could see by the stunned expression on Luc's face that he was equally touched.

"You have no idea how good your chances are with me right now," he whispered huskily.

"Is it the love potion?" she asked.

He thought a moment. Then a quicksilver grin tugged at his lips. "Mus' be."

Sylvie was oddly disappointed at that response. But why, she couldn't imagine. Did she want him to be attracted to her, on her own merits . . . as she obviously was to him, since she couldn't blame the influence of a love potion?

Another thought occurred to Sylvie then. This forced confinement with Luc would be the perfect opportunity for her to study the effects of the love potion formula. Her first human trial run, in a way. Well, finally, there was some good news in this crazy scenario.

Another moan broke the charged silence, but this time it didn't come from Luc, who had been staring at her hotly. Luc exchanged a startled look with her; then they both turned toward his closed apartment door, where yet another moan emanated, followed by a loud bang, as if someone was kicking against wood.

"Sonofabitch!" Luc muttered as he dropped her hand and rushed to his door, key in hand. But the key was unnecessary, since the door was unlocked . . . presumably not the way he'd left it earlier that day. In retrospect, she would guess that some of those pry marks on the office door downstairs were new.

When they entered Luc's apartment, both came to a screeching halt.

Sylvie gasped.

"I'll kill him. Whoever did this . . . I swear, I'll kill him."

His apartment was in even worse condition than her

town house had been. She could see that it would be a
lovely apartment, under normal circumstances. Sparsely
furnished with vintage Louisiana cottage pieces that
highlighted the random-plank Cypress flooring and fine
natural-grain woodwork. But now, the furniture was
upended, drawers pulled out and their contents tossed
to the floor, dozens of dry-cleaners' packets containing
shirts, underwear, socks, and pants tossed here and
there. Did the man dry-clean *everything?*

And most unusual, there were numerous crocheted,
embroidered, and hand-woven bed linens, tablecloths,
napkins, towels, and other household items. Some of
them were made of the yellowish-brown cotton the Cajuns grew and wove themselves, which they called *coton
jaune*, once referred to as slave cotton. Still other items
came from the complex Acadian method of weaving
called *boutonne*, with the intersecting checks and woof
threads raised and tufted to make the intersections stand
out. The most elegant Cajun bedspreads were made this
way with borders of handmade, hand-tied lace . . . like
the one on the floor over there. But all these exquisite
handicrafts were tossed aside now, some of them bru-
tishly slashed or ripped apart.

Sylvie had no time to ponder all this. She set down
her box, and Luc dropped her briefcase, already opening a closet door in his bedroom where a straight-back
chair had been propped under the doorknob and from
which muffled groaning issued forth.

"Oh, no!" Luc exclaimed as he opened the door and
pulled out a short woman with curly blonde hair whose
hands and feet had been duct-taped together, with a
piece of tape slapped over her mouth. "Tante Lulu! What
are you doing here? I thought you left when I did. What
happened? Are you hurt?"

Within moments, the diminutive old lady was free.

Instead of falling into his arms hysterically the way most women would, especially one of her advanced age, his aunt slapped away Luc's concerned hands, which were fluttering about her body, checking for injury. "No, I'm not hurt, but someone's gonna be," she raged angrily. "I came back here after you left to get the knitting needles I forgot, and those hoodlums jumped me."

"Did you get a look at them?"

"No, but I know it was that Valcour who was at the bottom of these shenanigans."

"How do you know?"

"'Cause one of the men referred to me as 'the ol' bitch.' That's what your father called me all the time."

"Maybe I should take you to the emergency room, just to make sure you're not hurt."

"I tol' you I'm okay." She narrowed her eyes at him. "It took you long enough to come back here, though. I coulda starved to death in that closet while you been off doing God knows what. Oooh, lookee there at that Happy Meal box. You been to McDonald's. And did you think of me? I'm just a sixty-five-year-old lady who needs her energy. Whatchou doin' eatin' that junk food anyways when I make you good Cajun food anytime you ask?"

Luc cast Sylvie a hopeless look. The silent message inferred there was no interrupting Tante Lulu once she got started.

"And, Lordy, my behind is so numb from sittin' so long in that closet that I can't hardly feel it at all. Why . . ." Her words trailed off as she seemed to recall her manners in the presence of a stranger. She addressed Sylvie. "Hello."

Her eyes darted between Sylvie and Luc; then she smiled . . . a ludicrous expression with the lower half of her face reddened by the duct tape. She made a quick sign of the cross, then inquired, "Could this be the one, Luc? Finally?"

"No!" he said. "Definitely not."

"The one what?" Sylvie asked.

"Don't ask," Luc advised.

"The one and only." Tante Lulu beamed. "Think thunderbolts."

Luc groaned.

Sylvie's mouth dropped open. "Me? No, no, you've got the wrong person. I'm Sylvie Fontaine, a . . . uh, friend of Luc's." She stepped forward, hand extended.

To Luc, Tante Lulu said, "*Jolie fille*. Pretty lady. She really should see Charmaine about that hair, though. A good oil treatment will tame it down. But you done good, boy."

To Sylvie, she said, "Pleased to meet you. I'm Luc's great aunt, Louise Rivard, his mama's aunt, but you can call me Tante Lulu." The woman, who couldn't be more than five feet tall, glanced upward as she spoke. Then the old woman shook Sylvie's hand vigorously. "Welcome to the family."

The family? What does she mean?

Luc rolled his eyes heavenward. Then he reached into the secret back panel of an open armoire, took out a pistol, and checked for ammunition.

"Well, if it isn't Wild Bill LeDeux," Sylvie said mockingly to hide her concern over the need for a weapon.

"Hey, babe. If I'm Wild Bill, you're damn sure gonna be my Annie Oakley," he countered with a grin. Then he turned serious. "We've got to get out of here," he told them both. "Tante Lulu, you can tell us what happened on the way."

"On the way where?" She was rubbing her sore wrists.

"Bayou Noir."

"Bayou Noir! I can't go there. I have a baby to deliver

in Chacahoula . . . could be this evenin'." She turned to
Sylvie and informed her, "I'm a *traiteur*, sweetie. A folk
healer. Have been for nigh on fifty years. Lots of women
still likes me to act the midwife for them. Maybe some-
day I'll catch one of your *bébés*, yes?"

Sylvie's face heated up at that suggestion, while Luc
just chuckled. The clod.

"You got any French fries in that box?" Tante Lulu's
question contradicted her earlier implication that she
wouldn't eat junk food.

"No," Luc stated dryly. "Just rats."

"Rats?" his aunt shrieked, jumping backwards and
almost falling over. Having a second thought, though,
she peered forward as Luc picked up the Happy Meal
container and showed his aunt the contents.

"There is a sick side to you, boy," Tante Lulu commented with a shake of her head. "Reminds me of the
time you collected toads when you was a little one. Had
thirty-seven of them slimy buggers, as I recall . . . till
your daddy found out." Her eyes went dark then at some
remembrance. Sylvie suspected it had something to do
with a beating Luc's father might have administered for
that misdeed. "Used up all my wart remedies on you
that time. Seems to me you even had a wart on your—"

"They're not *my* rats," Luc informed her with a
laugh. "They're Sylvie's pet lab rats."

"What are they doing in that box . . . why are they
making all that noise?"

There was a brief silence as Luc looked at Sylvie to
answer, and she looked at him to answer.

He gave in. "Boinking."

"Boinking? What's boinki . . . oh, I get it." Tante
Lulu sliced Luc a condemning glare. "You gettin' a foul
mouth on you. Don' be thinkin' you too old for a taste
of my homemade lye soap."

Tante Lulu seemed to think of something else then
and cocked her head to the side . . . a head covered with
the most outrageous blond curls, almost as outrageous
as the purple spandex biking outfit she wore. His aunt
glanced up at Sylvie, then over to the lab rats, and back
up at her again. "*Sylvie Fontaine*. Are you the chemist
with the love potion?"

"Yes," Sylvie said, face heating with embarrassment.
"I'm a chemist."

"Your newspaper pictures don't do you justice, dear."

"Well, thank you." Sylvie's face grew even hotter. Ac-
cepting compliments had been one of the hardest things
for her to learn in shyness therapy. Compliments called
attention to a person, whereas the timid person would
much rather be invisible.

"Is it working?" Tante Lulu asked out of the clear
blue sky.

Sylvie knew instinctively what *it* she referred to. The
love potion, of course.

Luc answered for her. "Hell, yes, it's working."

"Lu-u-uc," Sylvie chided. "You can't tell your aunt
things like that."

But Tante Lulu looked as if her nephew had just
handed her a pot of gold. She made another sign of the
cross. "Praise God. My prayers are answered."

"Not *that* kind of working, Tante Lulu," Luc inter-
vened quickly, raking the fingers of his right hand
through his hair. The left hand still held the pistol. "The
other kind."

"What other kind?" Tante Lulu's eyes slitted at him,
then went wide with understanding. "Don't you be givin'
me that lust-not-love business. Who said anything about
that hop-skip-and-go-naked kind of love? I never said
anything about oinking."

"Not oinking. Boinking," Luc corrected.

"Whatever!" His aunt threw her hands up in an exasperated manner. "I'm not so old I don't remember the difference. You been given a love potion, boy, not a lust potion. Ain't that right, sweetie?" The last was for Sylvie.

"Well, that's technically right," Sylvie sputtered, her face flaming with discomfort. What a conversation to be having with this elderly woman!

"See, Luc, I was right," Tante Lulu said. "Lordy, there are so many things to do."

"Like what?" Luke inquired suspiciously.

"Feathering the bride, for one." She tsked at Luc as if he should already know that.

"What's feathering the bride?" Sylvie asked.

"Oh, my God!" Luc muttered, crossing his eyes with frustration that she would encourage his aunt.

Amazingly, he looked kind of cute when he crossed his eyes.

"That's when all the Cajun women in the community give a prize chicken to the new bride. That way she has her own money, independent from her husband. She gets to keep all the egg money from her flock for herself."

"Bride feathering—what a nice tradition!" Sylvie remarked.

Luc's response was a snort of disgust.

"But who's the bride?" Sylvie frowned with confusion.

Tante Lulu looked directly at her with a wide smile. Luc looked directly at her with pure disgust for posing the question.

"*Me?* You can't mean me," she protested to Tante Lulu. "I'm not a bride-to-be, and I most definitely do not have any place for chickens at my town house."

But Tante Lulu ignored her objections as if she'd never spoken. "Yep, I best get home and finish up my crocheting for you, Luc. I still have the bridal quilt to complete before the wedding."

"What wedding?" she and Luc asked as one, their voices equally filled with shock.

"Dum, dum, dee, dum," Tante Lulu hummed in response as she strolled in front of them into the living room.

Then the old lady screamed.

Chapter Seven

*S*ome women can drive a man batty...

Criminal elements wouldn't prompt a peep from Tante Lulu, but damage to her precious handiworks caused her to scream her head off. So, it was not surprising that two hours later, Luc, Sylvie, and Tante Lulu were still in his Houma apartment.

Danger be damned, his great-aunt was determined that they could not leave till she'd picked up and examined each and every one of her—rather *his*—damaged towels and pot holders and sundry other linens. And Luc understood her dismay. After all, she'd probably spent a thousand hours laboring to produce those priceless items for him.

Claudia Casale had come and gone, once again, after being summoned to assess this new threat. Her opinions had been much the same as those she'd given at Sylvie's place, except that the damage here was most assuredly related to Luc's work for the shrimpers, and not Sylvie's love potion.

He felt comfortable placing the investigative work in Claudia's hands since she was a true professional. He and Claudia had worked together on numerous cases in the past, but they'd never been involved personally, though he couldn't say why, exactly. She was a beautiful woman.

He'd be a fool not to have noticed the jealous gleam of speculation in Sylvie's eyes when seeing them together, and he'd played up her misconception for all it was worth. Hey, he got his fun anywhere he could these days . . . rusted zipper and all that. It was amusing, really, to see Sylvie react to him with another woman . . . not that she had any right to be jealous of him. Still . . .

Most normal people would have hightailed it out of Houma with the threats and actual physical assaults that had been directed against them. But, to his amazement, he had agreed to wait till Tante Lulu could assess and straighten out the damage to his apartment. "Besides, those crim'nals ain't dumb enough to come back again so soon," Tante Lulu had contended.

Luc wasn't so sure about that.

"And if they do, you can shoot 'em smack dab between their eyeballs."

This was a cold-blooded side to Tante Lulu he'd never seen before. He could be mistaken, but he suspected his aunt was enjoying all the excitement.

He sat in the kitchen sipping his third cup of thick chicory coffee as he alternately raked his fingers through his hair, shook his head with dismay, and wondered if a tension headache could actually make a man's brain explode.

In the next room Tante Lulu was chitchatting with Sylvie—*chitchatting, for God's sake!*—about herbal remedies, Cajun and Creole lifestyles, and *him*.

Through the open doorway, he heard Sylvie ask his aunt, "Will you be able to repair these linens?"

"Some of them. But I got plenty of others at my house and in Luc's cabin. Don't you be worrying none."

"I wasn't worried," Sylvie interjected quickly. "It's just that they're so beautiful."

He didn't need to look to see that Tante Lulu was beaming. Thank God, Sylvie wasn't looking down her aristocratic nose at his eccentric aunt, who did make herself a mark for ridicule in a lot of ways. He had to give Sylvie credit for seeing beyond the outrageous exterior.

"Tell me again why Luc needs all these household linens," Sylvie urged.

Propping his elbows on the table, Luc put his face in his hands and groaned.

"For his hope chest, of course."

"His hope chest?" There was no laughter in Sylvie's voice. Just incredulity.

"*Mais* yeah. Certainly."

"A hope chest for a man? Really? And Luc *wanted* a hope chest?"

He spread his fingers, which still braced his face, and peered at Sylvie to see her reaction.

She was looking pointedly at him, eyebrows raised in question.

He rolled his eyes.

"Hah! When it comes to what's good for that boy, he don' know haf'."

Luc rolled his eyes some more.

"Tell me, honey, did you give the same jelly beans to Luc as that male rat there?" Tante Lulu was peering inside the Happy Meal box, where the rodent couple had made love an impressive number of times.

"Well, not exactly the same," Sylvie said hesitantly.

"But they have the same effect on rats as humans, right?"

"They should," Sylvie admitted.

Oh, God! he thought.

Sure enough, his aunt whooped with glee. "Thank you, St. Jude."

St. Jude? She thinks St. Jude is responsible for this love potion nonsense.

"Maybe it wasn't really an accident that Luc ate your jelly beans," Tante Lulu confided to Sylvie.

"Huh?" Sylvie didn't have a clue when it came to the meandering way his aunt's brain wended its path through a conversation.

"Dontchya have a hope chest, honey?" Tante Lulu asked Sylvie. Good, the subject was moving away from him and love potions.

"Well, no."

"*Cou!* Not to worry. We got plenty of time to get you started on one. And on the flocking, too."

Luc bit his bottom lip to stop a burst of laughter. He couldn't wait till Sylvie found out what flocking was.

"What's flocking?" Sylvie inquired casually.

"Same as feathering," he told her.

"I'm assumin' the wedding won't be right away," Tante Lulu continued. A pregnant pause followed. Then: "There ain't no reason for a rush wedding, is there?"

Luc's head shot up. "Tante Lulu!" he rebuked. "There isn't going to be a wedding. And don't you dare start crocheting doilies for Sylvie's hope chest."

"Oh, my God!" was Sylvie's response to this ludicrous discussion. Sylvie was not yet used to the way Tante Lulu's mind worked or to his aunt's obsession with finding him a bride. Her next words were proof that she was searching for some way to steer the discussion away from herself and his aunt's misconception about their marriage plans. "Why are there so many St. Jude statues and night-lights and candle holders here, and . . . was that a St. Jude toothbrush I saw in the bathroom?"

Luc would have been embarrassed if he weren't three light years beyond embarrassment.

"You know who St. Jude is, donthcha?" Tante Lulu asked Sylvie.

"The patron saint of hopeless cases?" Sylvie offered tentatively.

"Yep," Tante Lulu responded. Then she and Sylvie both turned to look at him.

"Enough said," Sylvie stated with a soft laugh.

"This one," Tante Lulu remarked, jerking her head toward him, "he is in bad need of a good woman. Has been for a looong time."

Sylvie made a gurgling sound deep in her throat . . . speechless at the prospect that she might be called upon to be the "good woman." He would have laughed if he didn't feel like crying.

Okay, the foolishness ends now. Time to be a man and take control of this madness. He stood abruptly and walked into the living room, insisting, "We've wasted enough time. We've got to get out of here."

"Uh-oh!" Tante Lulu exclaimed. She was peeking around the drapes of his front window, staring down at the street. Clucking her tongue in a tsking sound, she added, "Bad business, this!"

"What now?" he asked, stomping over.

Two thugs were ransacking his jeep, searching for God knows what. Pollution reports? Chemical formulas? Jelly beans? Happy Meal rats?

"We'd better take my car," Tante Lulu suggested quickly, nudging Luc away from the window. "Hurry up, boy. Why you dawdling here when danger is standing right outside your window?"

Me dawdling? Me? Luc gaped at his aunt for a moment before springing into action.

Is this how The Fugitive felt when on the lam?

No, he immediately answered himself. *This is how Thelma and Louise felt before going off the cliff.*

She drove like she lived. Full speed ahead . . .

A short time later, they were barreling down Highway 90 in a twenty-year-old purple Chevy Impala. Tante Lulu was driving, her head barely topping the level of the steering wheel, even as she sat on two cushions. Beside her sat the Happy Meal rats, who were rustling their wax paper in some activity. He and Sylvie were in the backseat, hanging on for their lives . . . pistol and briefcase in their respective hands.

Horns were honking and brakes squealing as his aunt switched lanes with abandon, never using a turn signal. Houma was called the Venice of America with good reason. It had numerous bayous and bridges fanning out like the spokes of a bicycle wheel. He could swear his aunt hit every one of them.

The getaway car—*God, didn't that conjure up some images!*—left downtown Houma on 90 West, then cut a right onto LA 311, over Little Bayou Black, past the State Sugarcane Experimental Station and Southdown Plantation. The latter's green and pink colors blended into a putrid blur as his aunt tried her best to break the speed of sound.

Eventually they crossed Big Bayou Black bridge and were on 90 West again, following the Old Spanish Trail, which hugged the bayous and cut through the swamps. This was probably the oldest route from Texas to New Orleans. In fact, cowboys used to drive cattle across these very streams, the men latching onto swimming horses' tails. Right now, Luc would much prefer riding a horse's ass—rather, tail—than his aunt's insane driving.

Luc had been involved in some dumb things in his life. This was the worst.

If the hair-raising ride down the narrow bayou roads wasn't bad enough, Tante Lulu was tossing out love counsel to him, like a regular Dr. Ruth with bullets of advice:

"Treat her nice, Luc. Women like men with couth. Best you pull out all your couth. No scratching or crude swear words or nothin'. And you, young lady, best you treat my Luc proper, too."

Sylvie giggled nervously.

He snorted, nervously.

"I don' believe in long engagements for men like you. Yes, I said men like you; don' you be givin' me those dirty looks. You been havin' impure thoughts since you a little boy. And I don' want no hanky-panky 'tween you two afore the wedding, love potion or no love potion. Well, maybe a little hanky-panky. Do you have any of those condos with you?"

A gurgling sound came from Sylvie's throat. She was no longer amused by his aunt now that she was the subject of the love advice. He thought she was mumbling something that sounded like, "Engagement? Hanky-panky? *Me?*"

"It's condoms, not condos," he corrected his aunt with a belated gasp of shock.

She ignored him, continuing her tirade. "I'll start workin' on the wedding quilt once I catch that Dubois baby."

"Don't you dare start any wedding quilt for me," Sylvie snapped. Then she was immediately apologetic. "I mean, I'm sure you make lovely quilts, but it's just that—"

It was as if she hadn't even spoken. Tante Lulu was still fixated on him. "Did you say a proper thank-you prayer to St. Jude for sending you a good woman to love you? Maybe you better make a novena. St. Jude had to work extra hard on you."

Luc gave up arguing with his aunt. Sylvie looked as if she'd been hit with a Mack truck, or Tante Lulu's Impala, which was as big as a Mack truck.

Luckily, the car came to a screeching halt in front of The Swamp Shack. Every bird within a mile took flight in the dust she raised.

Tante Lulu's parting words to him were "How many *bébés* you plannin' to have? Lordy, I ain't even started knittin' baby afghans yet. I been too busy tryin' to get you married off."

Sylvie was stunned speechless.

For a brief moment, he closed his eyes and said a silent prayer. *Dear St. Jude, you are needed here . . . big-time.*

He thought he heard a voice in his head answer, with a lazy Cajun drawl, "Let the good times roll."

Some saints had a warped sense of humor.

Love Bug, Love Potion, all the same thing . . .

It was early evening, and Luc was carrying a tray from the back entrance of The Swamp Shack . . . better known as Swampy's. The tray was loaded down with two pottery bowls of steaming crawfish gumbo, a platter of warm cornbread oozing butter, frosted glasses of iced tea, a stack of beignets covered with powdered sugar, and hot coffee.

His brother Remy, a rancher in Northern Louisiana, would be coming just before dawn with a hydroplane normally used to transport feed to far ranges. Now it would be used to take him and Sylvie to a cabin Luc owned on a remote bayou.

With René at his side now, he walked carefully along the planks of the wharf where his brother had found a temporary hiding place for them that belonged to a friend of his—an ancient houseboat no longer capable of movement over the bayou's intricate waterways. There were a couple dozen other vessels docked there, as well . . . everything from fancy motorboats to air boats to primitive pirogues to "go devils," gas-powered boats that could travel through extremely shallow water. Most of them belonged to customers of Swampy's, the no-fuss restaurant-bar serving hearty Louisiana foods during the day and loud Cajun honky-tonk music at night. Most of the time René lived on a bayou closer to the salt waters of the Gulf, on a commercial shrimp boat that he owned in partnership with two other Cajun fishermen, but he did stay here on the houseboat occasionally when performing gigs at area nightclubs, fire halls, or wedding receptions.

Luc was fairly certain that the half-wits chasing after them were unaware of this houseboat. They were safe . . . for now, at least.

"This is all my fault, Luc. I never should have involved you in the shrimpers' fight. Maybe we should give up before someone gets hurt," René said. Even more ominous than his words was the fact that René was tucking a small pistol into the back waistband of his jeans, which was then covered by a denim jacket. Just as Luc's weapon was hidden by the suede vest he'd grabbed when fleeing his apartment.

"If I thought y'all would give up without me, I might consider tossing in the towel," Luc said. "It's a losing battle fighting these oil behemoths anyhow, as you well know."

"Hey, haven't you ever heard of David and Goliath? That's who we are . . . a bunch of Davids." René grinned at Luc, trying to make light of a situation that was getting darker by the moment.

"Dammit, René, I know you and your lamebrain friends. You'll ditch the idea of legal representation and try to fight Cypress Oil with your own half-ass methods. When the almighty dollar's involved, human beings are disposable roadblocks to the bottom line. Believe me, slingshots don't count for crap with these people." He looked pointedly at the back of René's jeans when referring to slingshots.

"Yeah, but if there are enough slingshots, and if the Davids have extra ammunition, as in The Swamp Solicitor"—René shrugged—"well, who can predict what will happen, eh, big bro?"

Luc chuckled and shook his head. Sometimes it was hard for him to remember that his brother was thirty years old and not the gap-toothed urchin tagging after him in the bayous. In truth, Luc had been playing the big brother to René and Remy for so long, he wouldn't know how to stop now. And René knew it.

They stepped onto the houseboat and René held the screen door open for him, then unlocked the door, before Luc eased himself inside, sideways, with the wide tray. He set the food down on the table of a corner vee-shaped booth in the galley area.

"I'm thinking about leaving Sylvie here with you," Luc said in a low voice, not wanting to awaken the woman, who was napping on a narrow cot attached to the far wall of the large, one-room residence. The events of the past few days had taken their physical toll on her, and she'd barely protested an hour ago when he'd left her to go over to the restaurant and talk with René and his fishing comrades.

"No way!" His brother shook his head vehemently. "I'm going to be on the run the next few weeks as things get hot and heavy. I can't have my movements hampered by a chick. Not that Sylvie's a chick . . . I mean, she's attractive enough, and I may fancy myself a David, but let's face it, she sure as hell isn't any hot-to-trot Bathsheba. Too strait-laced, if you ask me."

They both looked toward Sylvie, who was sleeping soundly, her Happy Meal container at her side. For once, there was no rustling inside the box. Mickey and Minnie must be all screwed out.

If René's assessment of Sylvie was intended to be a criticism of her allure, Luc had to disagree. Her right arm was thrown over her head in abandon, causing her breasts to be uplifted and clearly outlined under her silk blouse. Her legs in their black slacks were parted. It was an uninhibited, inviting position that Sylvie would normally never take when awake, at least not in anyone's presence. Certainly not his.

Worst of all—*or best of all, from my perspective*— her left hand lay loosely over her flat stomach, low down. Was it an unconscious caress?

Like a rush of erotic adrenaline, Luc felt that imagined caress through every inch of his own body. And his overactive imagination zoomed into sensual overload.

Did Sylvie ever touch herself in the absence of a lover?

Had she ever touched herself in the presence of a lover?

His brother was wrong. Sylvie Fontaine could be a Bathsheba any old day. Looking at her, Luc felt his heart soften and another part of his body harden. Correction. Harden *even more*.

"Holy shit!" René remarked in an undertone. Then he softly sang the words to that old Queen song "Another One Bites the Dust."

Luc came back to the present with a jolt. "What? What's wrong?"

"You!" René hooted. "You've fallen for Sylvie Fontaine. *Mon Dieu!* I never thought I'd see the day that you'd tumble for the L-word."

"You're crazy," Luc protested.

"You should see your face when you look at her, Luc. I wish I had a camera. You're a freakin' Cajun Hallmark moment."

"Go away. I'm not in lo . . . lo . . . love with anyone, least of all Sylvie Fontaine. That's ridiculous." *Lord, I'm pathetic. I can barely think the L-word, let alone say it out loud.*

René shook his head in disagreement. "No one is bullet-proof, big brother. Geez, maybe love potions really do work. Oh, man, Tante Lulu must be in seventh heaven."

"I am not amused, René."

"Yep, it mus' be love," his brother continued. "I think I'll write a song about it. 'The Cajun Love Bug.' *Dieu*, I jus' can't believe it. My big brother in love!"

Luc sighed deeply. In his opinion, his brother and his aunt were both wrong. Oh, he'd already suspected earlier that he was developing *feelings* for Sylvie, but he'd marked them down to the effects of her souped-up jelly beans. *No way am I falling in lo . . . lo . . .*

But he was beginning to fear that his heart had a mind of its own. And that scared the hell out of him.

So, he handled the situation the way most men do. He decided not to think about it. Shoving René out the door with a promise to come over later to the tavern where his band, The Cajun Swamp Rats, would be playing, Luc turned the key, locking himself in, and proceeded to the other side of the room. He stood over the cot and said softly, "Sylvie. Time to wake up."

Nothing.

"Come on, darlin'. I've been slavin' over the stove all day. Come eat."

Nothing.

Okay, now what? he asked himself. I could shout. Or I could take other measures.

He thought about opting for "other measures." Those might include easing himself into that small cot with Sylvie and checking out the possibilities of just how far a love potion could go.

Sanity ruled, though. "Hey, babe," he hollered, "move your butt or you're gonna have company in that bed."

Sylvie jackknifed into a sitting position and glared at him through sleepy eyes, blinking with confusion. "You don't have to yell."

"Yes, I do, *chère*. Yes, I do."

She was going to make a graph of his WHAT? . . .

"Do you have an erection?"

Luc's mouth dropped open, then snapped shut so quickly he almost bit his tongue. His hand went reflexively to his crotch to make sure he was decent.

He wasn't, but Sylvie couldn't see that, hidden as his lower body was by the table. They were sitting at the small galley booth, having just finished their meal, when Sylvie made her out-of-the-blue inquiry.

With a flaming face, she put aside the rats, which she'd been feeding leftover gumbo. Then she pulled out a small black-and-white-speckled notebook and a ballpoint pen she'd found on the counter. Unbelievably, she was preparing to take notes.

I have landed in a god-awful Saturday Night Live skit. Pulling himself together, he replied as calmly as he could, "Now? Or ever?"

"Now, of course." She was looking everywhere but at him as she spoke.

"Sylvie, I've had half a hard-on for you ever since I swallowed your damn jelly beans. A five on a scale of ten."

"Oh."

"Wanna see it?" he teased.

"No!"

Luc hadn't realized that a face could get so red just from embarrassment. He kind of liked this shy side of Sylvie, though her question was far from shy.

"Are your nipples sensitive?" she asked.

"They are *now*."

"Do you have sexual fantasies?"

"Do I ever!"

"More than usual?"

He grinned. "Ab-so-lute-ly."

"Is your heart rate accelerated at certain times?"

He nodded. "At certain times."

"Do you ever—"

"Hey, Sylv, do you have any particular reason for asking about the state of my body parts?"

She'd been scribbling like crazy in her notebook, but now she put her pen down. "Well, yes," she said enthusiastically. "I was thinking that, since we're going to be together the next few days anyhow, and since you already swallowed the love potion, and since we don't have any human trial data on the formula yet . . . well, it's a perfect setup for studying your reactions." She stared at him hopefully, waiting for a response.

"A guinea pig? You want me to be your human guinea pig?"

"Yes! I could check hourly on your pulse and temperature and . . . and arousals, not to mention a dozen other variables. I can already envision the separate time/data graphs I could plot. Really, this will be even better than a lab setting for the human trials."

He was gaping at her as if she'd lost her mind. "You're going to do a hard-on graph of me?"

"Well, that could be one of the graphs. But I certainly wouldn't describe it so crudely."

"I'll bet you wouldn't, babe." He shook his head in wonder that she actually thought he'd participate in such a bizarre experiment. "That's all I need . . . to be known as The Swamp Solicitor *and* The Happy Penis."

"This is serious business, Luc. I'm a chemist. We could be making scientific history here."

He had to laugh at that. "My cock a scientific wonder? I . . . don't . . . think . . . so."

"Where are you going?" she said in a panicky voice. He was sliding along the Naugahyde bench, preparing to stand.

"Out. I need a beer."

"Wait. I'll come with you."

He shook his head. "No. You stay here. Lock the door after me. Remy will be here about five A.M. with the copter."

"But—"

"I need some time alone, Sylvie." He was already walking toward the door, tucking the gun into his back waistband.

"But—"

Speaking over his shoulder, he snapped, "Unless you plan on doing something about these erections you've caused with your love potion, and with all your damn questions about them, I suggest you put a mile between your sweet self and my erections."

Silence.

Curiosity got the best of him, and he peeked back over his shoulder. Her pen was flying over the notebook.

He didn't need to ask what she was writing. "Diary of a Penis," no doubt. *Mon Dieu!*

She would show him! . . .

It was midnight, and Luc still hadn't come back to the houseboat.

Sylvie was bored. And worried. And just a little bit angry.

Where was he?

What if he'd dumped her here? No, her instincts told her that Luc wouldn't do that. Certainly not without first providing for her protection. Like calling her mother for bodyguard service. Oooh, she would kill Luc if he'd done that to her.

But what if something had happened to him? He'd said not to worry . . . that they were safe here, at least for a short time. His youngest brother Remy, a pilot for a North Louisiana ranch conglomerate and a Desert Storm Air Force veteran, would be coming to take them to some hideout in a far-off bayou, accessible only by air or a long, long trip in a pirogue. But maybe the bad guys

had pounced on him anyhow. Maybe he was even . . .
Oh, my God! . . . dead.

Sylvie shot to her feet, her notebook and pen falling
to the floor. She made quick work of unlocking the door,
in a hurry to find Luc, to rescue him, or . . . or . . . She
wasn't sure what. She just knew she had to find Luc.

Her eyes darted about thé room, searching for a
weapon—*just in case*. Not a gun, or switchblade knife,
or even a baseball bat in sight. Just a battered fiddle
that had seen better days. Well, it would have to do. She
grabbed the old instrument by its neck and was out the
door, making sure to lock up after herself. After all,
her briefcase was still inside—albeit hidden inside a
fishing tackle storage closet—and the lab rats, too.

That was when the band started up again.

Sylvie had been hearing René's band, The Cajun
Swamp Rats, playing off and on all night. They did
loud renditions of both traditional and modern Cajun
music, from the slow, evocative melodies passed through
generations of French Acadians, to the more upbeat,
lively, sometimes raucous, modern versions, including zydeco.

As the band launched enthusiastically into the well-
known "Big Mamou," a song about one of Louisiana's
largest lakes, and she made her way determinedly toward the tavern, other thoughts entered her mind. Anyone listening to Cajun music soon ended up smiling.
These Cajuns were such a fun-loving people, and they
enjoyed a good laugh, even when the laugh was on
them. That jerk Luc probably wasn't hurt at all. He was
probably in the tavern having fun—drinking, dancing,
flirting with some barroom floozy.

Forget about killing Luc, she was going to whack off
his favorite body part. With a fiddle.

Sylvie stormed right up to the tavern and past the

big galoot at the door, who was a cross between a professional wrestler and Godzilla. He gave the fiddle in her hand a cursory glance, then shrugged, muttering something about crazy musicians.

Stepping into the dim interior of the tavern, she felt a blast of heat from the numerous bodies inside, even though the place wasn't filled to capacity. Then she recoiled from the explosion of rowdy music that seemed too loud for the small space. The band had finished "Big Mamou" and swung without interruption into the equally upbeat "Louisiana Man." Luc's brother René, the lead singer, had a fair voice, but more important, a foot-stomping, grinning, rebel-yelling demeanor that told his audience he was there to have a low-down good time, just as they were.

Then she saw Luc.

The fiddle dropped from her fingers to the floor with a clunk. "You two-timing, womanizing SOB," she muttered under her breath, though why she would think the louse owed her any fidelity, she couldn't say. Her eyes blurred with sudden tears of hurt and blinding jealousy.

Jealousy? Jealousy? No way! Uh-uh! Oh, God, jealousy.

The Louse was leaning back against the bar, braced by his two elbows. One booted foot was propped casually by the heel on the foot rail. A long-necked bottle of beer dangled from the loose fingers of one hand.

Standing in front of Luc was a gorgeous brunette with big hair. Her small hips were stuffed into a pair of skintight jeans and her breasts were pushed all the way up to the North Pole. And Luc was smiling at her. In fact, The Louse threw his head back and laughed out loud at something she said.

Sylvie had never been witty. She'd never had a talent for flirting, as this bimbo obviously did. She didn't have small hips. Let's face it, shyness therapy or no shyness therapy, she was a failure in male-female seduction games.

Seduction? Damn! First, jealousy. Now I'm thinking about seduction. With Luc, for God's sake!

Just then, Luc looked her way, over his girlfriend's shoulder, and he smiled. The Louse dared to smile at her . . . in the same roguish, sexy way he did at all women.

And she melted under that smile . . . the way all women did.

It was untenable. It was humiliating. It was the last straw.

Luc was approaching her now, his smile replaced by a glare as he no doubt recalled that he'd ordered her not to leave the houseboat till he returned. *Hah!* Without thinking, she reached down for the fiddle and threw it at him. He ducked just in time, and the fiddle barely missed the well-endowed bosom of the bimbo following close behind him, swaying in her high-heeled, white snakeskin boots. Both of them wore stunned expressions on their faces. Hell, Sylvie was pretty well stunned herself by her bizarre behavior.

With a sob, she whirled and made a run for the exit. Luc caught up with her before she reached the bouncer at the door.

"Sylvie? What's wrong?" Luc asked, his viselike fingers on her forearm holding her in place.

"You!" she railed, struggling to get free. "You're the problem. I'm locked in that damn houseboat, worrying about you—"

"You were worried about me?" The slow grin that spread across Luc's lips was the absolute last straw, *on top of the previous last straw, that is.* Sylvie made a fist with her free hand and swung hard, but all she connected with was Luc's other hand, which laced with hers and pulled her closer.

"You were worried about me?" he repeated in a husky, too-sexy murmur.

Sylvie smelled the tangy scent of Luc's aftershave. He must have shaved somewhere this evening. For Barroom Barbie?

"Yes, I was worried about you, you louse! You've been gone so long that I thought you might have been hurt, or . . . or killed. And what do I find? You drinking and flirting with some barroom floozy."

Luc's jaw dropped open in surprise.

"Hey!" the barroom floozy said. She was standing right behind Luc, ready to resume whatever had been going on between the two of them. "I'm no floozy."

"Hah! If it looks like a floozy, and jiggles like a floozy, and hangs out in dives like a floozy, then it must be a floozy," Sylvie said. Even she was shocked at the snideness of her remark. She had certainly lost her shyness now.

But the woman just cocked a hip and grinned at Luc, as if they shared some joke.

Luc pulled Sylvie even closer then, and tucked her flush against his side with an arm looped over her shoulder. Then he turned so they faced the floozy, who, Sylvie had to admit, was a very attractive woman of about twenty-five or so. *Darn it!* The big-toothed, pure-white smile the floozy flashed Sylvie's way further infuriated her. She was pretty sure the low, growling sound came from her throat, and not the band, which was now doing a cat-purring rendition of "Tiger in the House."

"I'd like you to meet someone, Sylvie *chère*," Luc began.

Sylvie wished she could sink into the floor. Luc was actually going to introduce her to his girlfriend, and if the twinkle in his dancing eyes was any indication, he must suspect that Sylvie was jealous. Oh, it was so embarrassing!

"This is Sylvie Fontaine, the chemist friend I was telling you about," Luc told his bimbo, who nodded vigorously in understanding. Her well-lacquered hair didn't move a bit.

"And you, sweet thing," he said, chucking Sylvie under the chin. "I want you to meet Charmaine."

Charmaine. That figures. A perfect bimbo name. Oh, God, when did I turn so mean and condescending and—

"My sister."

Chapter Eight

Cajun men dance like they make love. Slow! . . .

Leaning against the bar, Sylvie decided that she needed a drink. Something to wipe away her humiliating rush to The Swamp Shack to save Luc's worthless hide, followed by her humiliating misconception about Luc and what she'd thought was a barroom floozy, not to mention her humiliating jealousy—her second bout that day with the green-eyed monster.

I was jealous. Jealous! Maybe this is one of those Stockholm Syndrome kind of things where a victim falls in love with her captor. Aaarrgh! I wasn't captured by Luc. And I'm certainly not in love with him, God forbid!

She was sandwiched now, like a hot dog on a bun, between Luc and said "floozy," his sister, Charmaine, at the crowded bar.

Yep, that's me. The world's biggest weenie.

Sylvie recalled now that Charmaine Devereaux, illegitimate child of Luc's father and a Baton Rouge stripper, had been Miss Louisiana a few years back. That less-than-proper family background had provided much fodder for the gossipmongers back then. She also vaguely remembered that Charmaine operated a posh beauty salon over in Thibodaux. That would account for the Texas-style hair. Sylvie suspected, on the other hand, that her own hair lay limp and lackluster after all she'd been through that day.

"I'll have a pink zinfandel," Sylvie told the bartender, a huge giant of a man with a bald head and a thick mustache. A gold hoop ring sparkled in one ear, giving the impression of a scruffy pirate.

"Say what?" Blackbeard was obviously harried by a sudden rush of dance-heated customers and not in the mood for fancy drink requests.

Not that hers had been fancy. *Geez!* "A pink zinfandel. That's wine," she explained.

"Lady, I know what zinfandel is," the bartender grumbled in a weary drawl. "We got red wine and white wine, *chère*. You want pink, how 'bout you order a glass of each and dump 'em together?"

Sylvie's upper lip curled. "I am in a bad mood, mister, and I am not amused by your attitude. Remember one thing," she snarled. " 'He needed killin' ' is a legal defense for murder in Louisiana."

"You a lawyer, too?" the bartender asked with a laugh, nodding toward Luc.

"No, I'm not a lawyer, you dunce. I'm a chemist."

"Ah, well . . . me, I feel much better, then. You gonna kill me with some chem-i-cal, 'stead of bullets?" The whole time he was expeditiously filling orders for

other customers . . . mostly beers without glasses for
the no-frills crowd.

Luc snickered and chugged down the last of his beer.

Charmaine ignored both the bartender's snippy remark to Sylvie and her equally snippy retort, as well as
Luc's snicker.

"Can I have a glass of ice water, Gator?" Charmaine
batted her false eyelashes at the burly man, who was
suddenly not in such a bad temper. In fact, Gator smiled
at Charmaine, flashing a gap-toothed, David Letterman-
style smile, and said, "Anytime, sweet cakes."

That irritated Sylvie, for some reason. "I'll just have
one of those," she decided, pointing to the tray of oyster shooters that a waitress was preparing behind the
counter.

Oyster shooters were a Louisiana specialty featuring
a single raw oyster in a shot glass covered with enough
Cajun lightning, or Tabasco, to peel the skin off the
tongue. They were tossed back and down the throat in
one smooth motion, followed immediately by a chaser
of straight, one-hundred-proof bourbon.

I can handle that.

I think.

"Uh . . . I don' think so, Sylvie," Luc cautioned.

Sylvie lifted her chin defiantly.

"Trust me, this is not a good idea."

"Maybe I'll have two."

Luc shook his head hopelessly at her. "Have you
ever had an oyster shooter?"

"Of course," she said. Well, she'd watched other people toss them back like peanuts, and they'd seemed to
enjoy them. And she did eat raw oysters on occasion.
And she did like her food on the spicy side. And, although she preferred a cool zinfandel, bourbon had to be

good if so many people drank it, right? "I can handle it," she concluded with only slightly faltering confidence.

Luc held three fingers up to the bartender, and Blackbeard placed a set of oyster shooters in front of each of them.

"Not me," Charmaine said with a laugh, waving a hand with gold-speckled, blood-red fingernails of an ungodly length. Gator slid Charmaine's set of shooters over in front of Sylvie.

Then everyone turned to watch Sylvie. It appeared she had no choice. She put the first shot glass to her mouth and knocked it back cleanly. Without any chewing, the oyster slid down her throat and landed in her stomach with a thud. The voyage was smooth, but the passage was red-hot. Sylvie thought her mouth and throat and stomach lining were going to burst aflame. Not giving herself a chance for second thoughts, she tossed back the bourbon chaser, hoping to extinguish the flame, but what it did, instead, was fuel the fire. Certain that her eyeballs were steaming, Sylvie exhaled repetitively with short, rapid puffing sounds, much like a mother in labor.

Luc was laughing uproariously, while Gator just stood watching her with arms folded over his chest and an expression on his face that translated into; "Lady, I've seen dumb twits before, but you take the cake."

Charmaine passed her glass of ice water over and advised, "Here, try this, honey," immediately followed by, "The first thing you gotta learn in bayou country, sweetie, is never let a Cajun man goad you into *nothin'* . . . if you know what I mean. Just take my second husband, Justin. He could charm a woman up one side and down the other till she didn't know her engine from her caboose. When he left, he took everything,

including the gumbo pot. I made sure my third husband
wasn't a Cajun, but Lester left, too, and good riddance;
that man was booooring. By the way, Sylvie, who does
your hair? I'd love to give you a little more pouf."

*Pouf? Pouf? At a time like this, she's thinking about
hair, of all things. Geez! My hair doesn't need pouf. It
already feels as if it's standing on end.*

As Sylvie chugged down the ice water and motioned
for another, Luc patted her on the back. "Next time,
maybe you'll listen to me, *chère.*"

That was the wrong thing to say. "Could you possibly be more smug?" Sylvie commented. Then she
sighed woefully because his smugness was forcing her
to do just the opposite of what he recommended.

Sylvie prepared to toss back another oyster shooter,
followed by the bourbon chaser.

"Oh, swell!" Luc muttered.

This time she only hyperventilated a little. Luc
followed suit with his own oyster shooter, and didn't
show any reaction at all other than an appreciative
"Whoo-ee!" accompanied by a single pound of his
closed fist on the bar and a fierce shake of his head.

"Let's dance, *chère*," he suggested, abruptly straight-
ening himself from his leaning position at the bar.

At first, Sylvie thought she'd heard him wrong. After all, there was a loud buzzing noise in her head, and
her earlobes felt numb. But, no, she hadn't been mistaken. Luc turned her with a hand on her elbow, about
to guide her toward the minuscule dance floor. She
wanted to protest, but her tongue was in rigor mortis.
The minute she stepped away from the bar, her knees
gave way. Luc chuckled and held her up with an arm
wrapped around her waist.

"You are pickled, babe," he murmured against her
ear.

Sylvie felt the soft flutter of his breath all the way to her toes and a dozen not-to-be-mentioned-in-public places in between. She wasn't drunk, though . . . just a little off balance. Was that why Luc was having this odd effect on her? "I'm just a little woozy. It'll pass in a moment."

"Well, Ms. Woozy, can I have this dance?"

"I don't want to dance," she declared, digging in her heels. "And I'm tired of you bringing up that dancing business with me all the time. I'm not twelve years old anymore. I'm not so easily shocked."

He appeared taken aback at her vehement response. Then he winked at her. God, she hated it when he winked at her. Well, truth be told, she liked his winks, and that was why she hated them.

"*Mais oui*, but I'm not talking about that *other* kind of dancing now . . . the kind *you* so graciously offered to me earlier today, I might note. A little Cajun two-step, that's all. Regular dancing."

"Hah! There's nothing regular about you."

Luc grinned at her, as if she'd given him a compliment. "Was that a compliment, *chère*?"

Looking around, she was startled to find herself in the center of the postage-stamp-sized dance floor. Luc must have steered her there while they'd been talking. She ignored his question and brought up one of her own. "Shouldn't we worry about being in such a public place? Aren't we making ourselves easy targets here?"

He shrugged with unconcern. "The bouncers at the front and back doors have been alerted to watch for any strangers. This is an out-of-the-way tavern, frequented mostly by local people who know each other, especially on a weekday. There's no real danger . . . yet." Still encouraging her to dance with him, he held his hands out to her, as if she would willingly step into his embrace.

She shook her head stubbornly and ignored the dancers who occasionally brushed against them in the brisk Cajun two-step . . . a dance that wasn't quite fast and wasn't quite slow.

The band was playing an upbeat version of that Joel Sonnier song, "Knock, Knock, Knock," about a bayou rogue who's in the doghouse with his wife once again. Every time the band came to the refrain, René—who wielded a mean accordion, alternating with an over-the-shoulder washboard to give a zydeco touch—yelled out the foot-stomping lyric "Knock, knock, knock," and the house joined in raucously.

Meanwhile, Luc's arms were still open wide, his fingers beckoning, his hips swaying slowly to the beat.

She forced her eyes upward.

Luc winked at her knowingly. "Don't you want to ask any questions about my . . . uh, body parts? Did you bring your notebook with you?"

"No, I didn't bring my notebook." She hesitated. "*Although* . . . if there's some reaction you're experiencing, of course I want to hear about it."

He laughed out loud at that. "I'd rather show you." Now he was circling her, snapping his fingers in rhythm, waiting for the most opportune moment to pounce on her, no doubt.

Sylvie was getting dizzy trying to watch Luc, who couldn't seem to stand still. "Oh, all right," she agreed churlishly. "Let's dance and get it over with." She stepped into his arms, putting one stiffened left arm on his right shoulder, holding him at arm's length, with her right hand in his left one, forcing it out and away from her body.

Now, that wasn't as bad as she'd imagined. With no essential parts touching, her body swayed to the beat along with Luc's. The band moved seamlessly into its next song . . . a plaintive, twangy rendition of "Jolé Blon."

Luc laughed softly. "I can't dance like this, Sylvie. I can hardly feel your rhythm from way over there."

"My rhythm? What do you mean? Oh . . . no . . . what are you doing?"

Luc placed one hand on each of her hips and yanked her flush against his body. Then he forced her arms up and around his neck, meanwhile lacing his hands behind her waist.

She didn't need to ask about his bodily reactions now.

To say they were acutely conscious of each other was the understatement of the millennium.

Both of them stopped, standing stock-still in the midst of the dancers. The most incredible aura seemed to surround them. Being in Luc's arms felt so nice. More than nice. A sensual, compelling mix of emotions filled her . . . a mix that soothed and ignited her body all at one time.

Luc cocked his head to the side in puzzlement. Clearly, he was experiencing the same rush of physical sensations and alarming emotions as she. Bemused, he began to dance again, forcing her to follow.

Sylvie liked to dance, and she was no slouch on the dance floor. She didn't call attention to herself, but she had her own subtle moves. She noticed Luc's lips twitch into a little smile at one of those moves. It was just a sinuous roll of the shoulders, but she could tell that he liked it . . . a lot.

Luc, on the other hand, was a *gooood* dancer. A man at ease with his body, he oozed uninhibitedness. Most women, on the other hand, were self-conscious about their bodies and danced accordingly, afraid of making a fool of themselves. Not that Luc did any outrageous dance moves. He danced the way he probably made love . . . slow and sexy. And he watched her the whole time with a maddening arrogance. Lazily assessing. Waiting.

Eventually, her eyes dropped before his steady gaze. *Lordy, Lordy! What is wrong with me? Speculating about Luc as a lover? It must be the bourbon. It had better be the bourbon!*

She should ask him how he was feeling. She was a chemist. He was a guinea pig, so to speak. It was unprofessional of her not to regard this situation in a clinical way.

Before she could switch into her chemist mode, though, Luc spoke. "I want you so much, Sylvie. Do you know that? You're making me crazy."

Her heart skipped a beat, then hammered against her chest walls. Every woman alive wanted to be wanted, and Sylvie was no exception. It didn't matter if Luc's desire stemmed from a chemical potion; the words still struck a chord in her. There were a million things she should have said, but what slipped out, instead, was the God's-honest truth. "I want you, too." She gasped at what her loose tongue had revealed. "I didn't mean that. It just came out of nowhere. Forget I even said it. Really, I don't know what I was thinking."

"Shhh. Don't try to explain, Sylvie," he said in a grainy voice, pressing a silencing forefinger against her lips. "Some things shouldn't be examined too closely."

She reeled under the influence of the potent alcohol.

Or was she reeling under the influence of the potent Cajun?

Their slow dance had slowed down to a mere swaying from side to side. His smoldering eyes held hers with an intensity of wanting . . . and fear. Yes, that was fear she saw in his dark eyes. And she knew just how he felt. She was scared to death, too.

"It's just the love potion," she assured him.

"Maybe." He licked his lips. The way he was staring at *her* lips, as if he wanted to kiss her, was enough to melt Sylvie's bones . . . if they weren't already butter soft. And the way the crotch of his jeans brushed against her as they danced was already melting some significant portions of her anatomy.

"How do you explain your wanting me?" His one hand was still planted against the small of her back, but the palm of the other was distractedly stroking—*Be still, my heart!*—up and down her back, from shoulder to waist.

"The bourbon," she answered quickly, but she really wasn't sure about that. Still, she sought for logic in what was becoming an increasingly illogical situation. "Luc, don't try to make this more than what it is. It's chemistry, pure and simple . . . whether it comes from a love potion formula or alcohol. You've never been attracted to me in all the years we've been acquainted."

"Sylvie, Sylvie, Sylvie." He shook his head hopelessly at her. "I've had a thing for you since we were kids . . . just like my brother René pointed out so annoyingly earlier today." She could tell that he immediately regretted his admission.

"A *thing*? Oh, Luc, you are so full of it." She had to laugh. "Apparently I remember better than you do just how attracted you were to me then. I distinctly recall the time you said I was the Southern belle who was never going to be tolled."

He grinned at her. "I said that? When?"

"I don't know . . . when we were ten years old or so, I guess."

"Oh, now I remember. That was the time you sniffed

at me, like you always did, as if I stunk like day-old roadkill."

She blinked at him in confusion. Then comprehension dawned. "You, fool! I had an allergy in those days. I was always sniffling."

They stared at each other then. Could they both have been so wrong?

"Is that why you've been tormenting me all these years?" she demanded. "Because I sniffed, for heaven's sake?"

"No . . . well, not totally," he said, ducking his head sheepishly. "The incident that's stuck in my mind is the time you refused to dance with me."

"Now, that I do recall," Sylvie conceded. "We were sixth-graders at Our Lady of the Bayou School, and it was our first boy-girl dance."

"Yep." He nodded. "Do you have any idea, Sylv, how much nerve it takes for a twelve-year-old boy to ask a girl to dance? And to be refused? *Mon Dieu!* Talk about humiliation!"

"Oh, Luc, I was sooo shy, then." *Still am, in many ways . . . though you'd never know it tonight.* "Having the best-looking, wildest boy in class ask me to dance . . . calling attention to me . . . well, I was the one humiliated. But it had more to do with *my* shortcomings than yours." That had been the first time he'd ever brought up the nude-dancing business, but she wouldn't mention that now.

"Really?" He grinned at that disclosure, then homed in on one part of what she'd said. "You thought I was good-looking?"

She punched him playfully in the shoulder and he pretended to be hurt, even as they swayed to the music. Without being coerced, or even asked, she returned her

hand to the back of his neck. Then they smiled at each
other. Just a smile. But it connected them in a way that
constricted Sylvie's heart and made her yearn for something just beyond her reach.

Luc looked a little misty-eyed, too.

If Sylvie didn't know better, she would swear she
was the one under the influence of a love potion, not
Luc.

The band ended its song, and René stepped up to the
microphone. "We've got to take a break soon, folks."

There was a communal groan. The dancers were all
having too much fun.

"But, first," René shouted, trying to keep the crowd's
attention, "I notice that my brother Luc is out there. I
just happened to write a new song today, and this one's
dedicated to you, big brother . . . and the *sweet thang*
standing next to you."

"Uh-oh," Luc murmured.

"Uh-oh," Sylvie said at the same time.

"This one's gonna be slow and sexy, everyone . . .
like my brother."

"I am going to cut out his tongue," Luc muttered
under his breath.

René chuckled into the microphone. "So grab your
favorite gal," he told all the men, "and enjoooy. The
name of this song is . . ."

Luc hadn't released her yet; so, they were already in
dance position.

". . . 'Cajun Knight.'"

"Oh, my God!" Sylvie exclaimed. "Did you put him
up to this?"

"Hell, no!" Luc glowered up at his brother, who
waved at him and grinned. "Forget the tongue. I swear,
I'm gonna kill him."

"Don't be so hard on your brother. It's kind of cute that he would write a song about you," she said, smiling.

Once there was a Cajun knight
who yearned for a Creole flower . . .

"Creole flower? *Creole?* Is . . . is he referring to me?" Sylvie sputtered.

"Still think he's cute?" Luc asked with a lifted eyebrow.

The knight of old . . .
had a mighty big *lance.*
The fair lady,
a tempting *moat.*

The crowd laughed uproariously at the suggestive lyrics while René did a flourishing trill on his accordion that involved spinning on his feet in a 360-degree turn, then waggling his eyebrows at a frowning Luc and red-faced Sylvie.

The crowd joined with much enthusiasm in singing the refrain:

Cajun knight and Creole flower.
Cajun knight and Creole flower.

Sylvie gasped. "You told me earlier today that you would be my Cajun Knight. Did you say something to René?"

"Would I be crazy enough to divulge *that* to my brother? I guess I'm just not all that original."

It was original to me, Sylvie thought.

Through hard times and many a year
the knight did travel the bayou,
his poor *lance* rusting away.
But always in his heart of hearts
were dreams of Delta *honey*.

Hooting with laughter, the crowd joined in again on the refrain:

Cajun knight and Creole flower.
Cajun knight and Creole flower.

"He's awful, isn't he?" Luc commented.

"Yes . . . no . . . I mean, his lyrics leave something to be desired, but his theme is kind of touching."

"Touching? You are definitely under the influence of alcohol if you think references to my rusted *lance* are touching. And you can't be naive enough to think the honey he mentions comes from a bee hive."

The Creole flower was withering on the vine,
her *moat* nigh dried up.
Still, she pined for her Cajun love.
But the *little warrior* just could not *come*.
She was a lady, he was a rogue,
never the twain should meet.
Cajun knight and Creole flower.
Cajun knight and Creole flower.

"Moat? Moat?" Sylvie sputtered. "Is he referring to what I think he's referring?"

"He is." Then Luc seemed to remember another part of the lyrics. "And my *warrior* is definitely not little."

"Withering on the vine? Who says I'm withering on the vine? Oooh! You don't need to kill him, Luc. I'll do it for you."

Luc had to pull her back from going up on the stage after René. The crowd clapped in encouragement.

"Let's get out of here before he moves on to other body parts with his cockeyed metaphors," Luc suggested, pressing his lips against her ear.

The crowd was singing the refrain so loud the floor was vibrating. Or was that the rippling effect of Luc's breath against the inner whorls of her ear, reverberating all the way to her toes?

Panic overcame her suddenly at the prospect of leaving the crowded bar, where she was somewhat protected from her own overactive hormones. "I thought you wanted to dance with me," she complained over her shoulder as Luc steered her off the dance floor and toward the exit with a hand pressed to the small of her back. "It's what you've mentioned every time we've met up in the past twenty years."

He stopped abruptly and pulled her around to face him. "More than anything in the world, I want to dance with you," Luc told her in a low, husky voice. His head swooped low to nip her bottom lip, which was no doubt hanging open. The little biting kiss was over before it began . . . too little time for her to savor how infuriatingly delicious it had felt.

But, wait, Luc was still talking to her in that sexy half-whisper. "You'd better believe I want to dance with you, darlin'," he was continuing, "especially dancing the way you promised this morning."

Oh, Lord!

"But right now, I want much more from you than dancing, *chère*. Much, much more."

He chuckled at the dazed expression on her face,

and made a great show of using a forefinger to tip her chin up to shut her gaping mouth.

"Babe, I've been suffering like a tomcat in heat with what your chemistry has done to my libido," he informed her. "It's time to make some of my own chemistry."

Chapter Nine

*O**ne thing led to another, and whoo-boy!* . . .

Outside the doors of Swampy's, Luc inhaled and
exhaled for strength. He hadn't wanted to alarm Sylvie
when he'd suggested they leave the tavern, but her love
potion was having a powerful effect on him.

Not only had his erection become a living entity, but
explosive currents of escalating excitement were ricochetting through his body like short circuits on a hot
wire. Given the chance, he could probably outdo that
rat Samson. For a certainty, he had a craving to nibble
something . . . or someone.

And, for a certainty, his arousal was affecting his
thinking. *Was I crazy . . . making such suggestive remarks to Sylvie?* Luc wondered, cringing at the mem-

ory of the words he'd whispered a few moments ago: "Much, much more."

As they stood on the porch, he released her fingers.

"Let's walk," he told Sylvie, keeping a good two feet from her. No way could he link hands with her now . . . not in his condition. No way could he return to the close confines of the houseboat with her and not jump her bones like a raving lunatic.

She gazed at him questioningly through eyes that were big and blue and sexy as hell. When she blinked . . . once, twice, three times . . . he felt blood rush to his heart. Or was it to another organ? Hard to tell. Luc was so aroused he felt disoriented. Without thinking, he groaned.

"Luc?" Sylvie inquired with concern, putting a hand on his arm. "Is something wrong? Your teeth are clenched."

He shrugged off her hand, which felt hot on his fevered flesh . . . even through the sleeve of his shirt. Words failed him.

"Are you suffering from the effects of that one oyster shooter, like I am . . . though of course I had two . . . but then two for me is probably comparable to six for you, right? Or was that three . . . or four . . . for me?" She was blathering aimlessly. Clueless . . . the woman was clueless as to her effect on him. "I have to admit, Luc, I feel really, really strange."

"*Strange* doesn't begin to express how I feel, babe." He emphasized his words with a short, strained laugh. "And if you're feeling the same way I am, fasten your seat belt, because we're both in a hell of a lot of trouble."

"Hmmm," she said. "Would you wait here a minute? I want to go get my notebook and pen."

"No!"

"No?" She was gazing at him as if he'd flipped his lid . . . which he had, of course. "There are a million questions I want to ask you, and I need to start taking notes or else I'll . . ." Her words trailed off as her eyes drifted over his body, did a double take back to his crotch, then widened.

It was probably the first time any woman had ever reacted with saucer-wide eyes to his "virility," even when he'd gone full monty with them for the first time. Oh, he had more going for him in that department than the average guy, in his not-so-humble opinion . . . but he couldn't remember one single time that a woman had gone wide-eyed on him.

But wait, his own personal testosterone booster was chatting away blithely. ". . . and if we're going to be away for more than two days, I really must insist on getting a supply of graph paper. A laptop would be great, too, but I can make do with a half-dozen more notebooks. The most important thing is that I absolutely need a thermometer, a blood pressure gauge, and a tape measure."

"A tape measure?" he choked out.

Her only answer was a deep, deep blush.

"Unbelievable," he commented, and stomped off ahead of her, down the steps of the tavern porch, and over toward a path that ran beside the meandering bayou.

"There you go . . . overreacting again," she called after him.

I'd like to show you overreaction, chère. *And maybe I will . . . if I'm as dumb as I seem to be . . . and as reckless . . . and as turned on. Aaarrqh!* As he walked briskly away from her, the neon glow of the tavern was soon left behind, but there was a full moon, which illuminated his way with pools of light. He sensed Sylvie's presence just behind him as she half-skipped to keep up with his much longer strides. Fortunately, she'd opted for silence, having no doubt realized how foolishly she was pushing him.

Finally, he stopped just around a bend, leaned back against the ample trunk of a live oak tree whose vast limbs were draped with Spanish moss, and closed his eyes. Inhaling and exhaling repeatedly, he tried to calm his nerves. When that didn't work, he lifted his head, raised his eyelids, and slowly scanned his surroundings, hoping that the bayou setting would seep into his soul and give him respite . . . as it had so many times as a child when he'd fled his turbulent home, or as an adult when people and life in general seemed to demand too much of him.

Luc loved the bayou. Many people got their spiritual energy from church. Well, the bayou was a church of sorts to him. In fact, it even resembled a church in places where the live oak trees on both sides of a stream formed an archlike canopy . . . not unlike a cathedral. In the ethereal, mysterious gloom, there was an air of spirituality and sanctity.

A warm breeze wafted, causing the *barbe espagnol*, or "Spanish Beard," to undulate. The breeze carried the rank metallic smell of the slow-moving water and fish, mixed with the pleasant scents of verbena, honeysuckle, and pine. Nearby, some egrets and herons floated by on their way home to nests where they would roost for the night. In the distance, he heard a series of alligator bulls roar . . . a sure sign that rain was on the way.

Many people didn't realize that there was a nocturnal food chain in the bayou, as important as the daytime one. Some of the night-feeders were catfish, salamanders, frogs, and snakes. It didn't take a biologist to witness the big water snakes feeding on small Blue Gills, which fed on Mayflower nymphs, which relished good mosquito larvae, which sucked up the infinitesimal one-celled protozoa. Nature in all its glory!

More calm now, Luc looked over at Sylvie, who stood a good five feet away. She was clearly wary of him in his present dangerous mood. *Smart lady.* "I hate what you've done to me," he said abruptly. "I mean, I love it, but I hate it, too."

Her head jerked up, as if he'd struck her. "Huh?"

"Sylvie, I'm out of control here. Everything you do is turning me on."

"Really? Everything?"

Is that a look of pleasure on her face, or alarm? Probably both.

"Yeah, everything," he answered with disgust. "The way you breathe . . ."

She held her breath.

"The way your blouse shifts over your breasts when you move, and I can see your nipples harden . . ."

She glanced downward, gasped, and folded her arms over her chest.

"The way your heart-shaped butt swings from side to side when you walk . . ."

She would probably spend the rest of her life trying to walk in a prissy, tight-assed way. No more shaking her bootie, for sure.

"The way you look at me with a frown on your face and sweet invitation in your eyes . . ."

She used the fingertips of one hand to smooth the frown from her forehead, and she shut her eyelids, refusing to make further eye contact.

"The way you tossed back those oyster shooters. The way you go all blushing shy one minute, and hot, hot, hot the next. The way you moaned when I kissed you. The way you—"

"Enough!" She put up a halting hand to stop his discourse. "Luc, I feel bad about the love potion . . . and that's all this is . . . a chemical reaction. It wasn't entirely my fault, though. Nobody asked you to eat my jelly beans."

"Are you trying to say you're sorry? If so, it's the most defensive apology I've ever heard. You've heard of faint praise, haven't you? Well, I'd say that was a faint apology." His lips turned up in a slight smile.

She shot him a glare. "What I'm trying to say is that I understand the awkward position you're in."

"Awkward? Are you nuts?" This conversation was going nowhere fast. "Listen, it's not so much the effects of the love potion that I hate. Hell, I like being turned on as much as the next guy. I might have even taken the jelly beans willingly if you'd informed me of what they were. I'm game for most anything."

She lifted an eyebrow in question. "So what's the problem?"

"The problem is the lack of control. I loathe this feeling of being unable to put the reins on my lust or my love . . . if you can call it that. You really need to rethink the ethics of this love-potion business, Sylv. It's not fair to manipulate a person who doesn't want to be attracted."

She tapped her chin pensively with a forefinger, as if considering his words. "You have a point, except that the love potion was never intended to be given blindly to an unsuspecting partner . . . even though people throughout time have been trying to come up with the perfect aphrodisiac, with no qualms whatsoever. No one criticizes perfume manufacturers, or lingerie designers, or the makers of tight jeans." She looked pointedly at his jeans.

He had to smile at that. *So, Sylvie noticed the fit of my jeans, huh?*

"I see my love potion as a prescription, given by a medical doctor under careful supervision. Heck, we at

Terrebonne haven't even gotten to the point of discussing the exact market. Married couples who've fallen out of love, maybe. Research studies on male-female chemistry. I wouldn't want JBX to be thrown into the marketplace with any fewer restrictions than, say, Viagra. But, yeah, it could be used as a tool to seduce an otherwise uninterested partner. As I was explaining to Blanche just a few days ago, there are a lot of lonely people in this world who think their perfect mates have to have certain physical characteristics. They don't give themselves a chance to see beyond the exterior. Maybe JBX could help." She shrugged in the end, not having all the answers.

He nodded. "You know what bothers me the most about your love potion and how I'm feeling? It's that you've turned me into my father."

She stiffened. Even she apparently knew of his father's reputation. "That's not true, Luc."

"Yes, it is. My father has always been an oversexed tomcat who would screw any woman willing to spread her legs. The younger the better. He even did it when my mother was alive. Look at all the illegitimate kids he's had. There's ten-year-old Tee-John; Amelie, an executive with Cypress Oil; Charmaine, whom you've met; and LaVerne, a homemaker down in Morgan City. And those are only the ones I know about." He clucked his tongue with disgust. "My father was a walking penis. He was led by his cock his entire life. Maybe I'm the same."

"Oh, Luc, don't say that. You and I have never gotten along particularly well, but I've never put you in the same class as your father. Nobody does. You're wild and outrageous and downright crude at times, but you're also kindhearted and giving and committed and ethical when it comes to the generally offbeat, poor clients that you represent. People in Houma know that it's you who raised your younger brothers, not your father. And one has only to look at you and your aunt to know how much you cherish her. Don't you dare put yourself down like this, Lucien LeDeux. Don't you dare." Sylvie stopped her long-winded response with a loud exhale, then put a palm to her mouth with embarrassment at the vehemence of her defense of him.

Sylvie's constant ping-ponging back and forth, in and out of shyness, intrigued him. His heart tightened then with the most incredible emotion, and warmth flooded through him. "Is that how you really feel about me, Sylv?"

She nodded. Her innate honesty was more appealing than she could possibly imagine.

"Even before this love-potion crap?"

She nodded again. "At least you don't have any illegitimate kids running around, right?"

He felt a roil of nauseousness in the pit of his stomach. All he could manage was a shake of his head.

"See? Give yourself some credit, Luc."

He knew he was lost then. Holding out a hand to her, he said in a voice huskly with need, "Come here, *chère*."

Without hesitation, Sylvie stepped forward and into his arms. He turned so that her back was to the tree, and he faced her.

She put a hand to his face tenderly.

He lurched at her mere touch.

Wrapping both arms around his waist, she tugged him forward so that his body pressed against hers, and she nuzzled her face bashfully into his neck. Instinctively, his arms wrapped around her, pulling her even closer.

Oh, God, it felt so good. Just standing there with Sylvie in his arms. It was more than a sexual experience. All his senses were involved, and most important of all, his heart, which thundered against his chest walls as if to mark the fervor of his long-withheld emotions.

Luc was afraid to move or speak for fear the wonderful mood would shatter. Feeling as if a precious jewel was within his reach, if only he did nothing wrong, he wanted to hold this moment with Sylvie forever.

But he always did things wrong, Luc reminded himself. Hadn't his father told him so, over and over? Hadn't classmates, teachers, and community members given him the appellation "bad boy of the bayou"?

Really, my imagination is going off in some strange directions.

Putting a hand on each side of Sylvie's face, he held her back slightly. Then he smiled at her. He intended it to be a smile of thanks. She was the first person in many a year who'd shown such confidence in him . . . maybe the only one since his mother . . . and he wanted her to know that he appreciated her kindness.

"Don't smile," she said.

He tilted his head to the side. "Why?"

"Your smiles make me . . ."

When she refused to go on—*that blasted shyness again*—he prodded, "My smiles make you what?"

"Breathless," she confessed.

He groaned. Then it was Luc who could barely breathe.

No longer fighting his longing, he decided then and there that he would kiss her. Not just a kiss, though. Luc loved kissing . . . long, short, slow, fast, deep . . . yeah, especially deep . . . and gentle, and devouring; it didn't matter which. And he was a damn good kisser, as a result. He knew he was. Yeah, he'd like to give Sylvie one unending kiss to show her his feelings. He wanted her to become one with his body, through the kiss. *Now, there's a thought.* Then she would know, as well as he, how it felt to be under a love spell. Payback was gonna be hell.

At least, that was why he had this overwhelming desire to kiss Sylvie, he told himself.

"I'm powerless to resist you," he informed her in a voice gravelly with desire.

"I don't want you to resist," she answered candidly. "Not anymore." He could swear her voice was gravelly with desire, too.

Almost as if he stood outside his own body, Luc watched his head descending, inch by inch. Sylvie stared at him with wide eyes and parted lips. In fact, in the end, she leaned forward to meet him partway. A giant leap from shyness.

He tried to be gentle at first, to control the incessant drumbeat of arousal thrumming through his body. With just the barest of skin contact, he settled his lips against hers. Then he allowed himself the intense pleasure of moving his mouth this way and that till they fitted perfectly.

She sighed against his open mouth.

He sighed back.

Gently, gently, gently, he increased the pressure, moving over her lips with an almost reverent caress. That exercise lasted about a millisecond, but red stars exploded behind his eyelids. He drew back slightly and panted for breath.

"Sylvie," he whispered hoarsely. That was all he said, but apparently it was enough because Sylvie whispered back, "Luc." There was such a poignant tremor in her voice that Luc feared tears might be welling in his eyes in reaction.

But this was too much of a stroke of good fortune to waste. He didn't want to give her a chance for second thoughts. Any second thoughts he might have considered had already drowned in the quicksand of his raging excitement. So his mouth came down hard now, demanding a response from her.

Not to worry. Her lips went immediately pliant, opening for him. It was a gesture of utter surrender that reached down into his soul and tugged at that part of himself he'd always kept apart from everyone. Oddly, her ardor did not surprise him. Had he known on some instinctive level all these years that they would be so well suited as lovers?

When he pushed his tongue slowly into her mouth, relishing the sweet drag of each fraction of an inch's progress, she drew on him in welcome. *Thank you, God!*

Sylvie was a good kisser, too, he realized then. Was it from experience, or just that they were so perfectly matched? For some reason, he hoped it was the latter.

Luc's mind went blank, and he lost control then. As his tongue began a rhythm of thrust-withdraw-thrust-withdraw, his hands roamed everywhere. He couldn't seem to get enough of her . . . stroking her back, kneading her buttocks, palming a breast, combing his fingers through her silk-fine hair. And Sylvie appeared to feel the same, moaning into his mouth, around his tongue, her hands touching him wherever she could reach.

There were some other places he would like her to touch, as well . . . places that were unreachable at the moment because there wasn't an inch of space between them . . . but not yet. No, that particular pleasure he could postpone till his rocket was less likely to launch. Besides, there were a whole lot of places he wanted to touch her, too. A whole lot!

He tore his mouth from hers and gave himself only the briefest moment of satisfaction at seeing her sex-hazy eyes and kiss-swollen lips. Bending his knees, he hunkered down a bit so he could take between his teeth the nipple of one breast, clearly delineated through her silk blouse.

She whimpered.

That was all the signal he needed. Luc opened his mouth onto her breast and suckled deeply—an unrelenting, rhythmic pull on that erotic zone. Then, with barely a break, he gave equal attention to the other breast.

Sylvie, whose legs had apparently turned to rubber, was holding on to two low-hanging branches with arms stretched out and over her head. A continuous keening came from between her gritted teeth. Her neck was arched back with the intensity of her arousal.

Forget about love potions and aphrodisiacs. In Luc's opinion, there was nothing more enticing than the sight of Sylvie aroused.

Luc couldn't help himself then. He put a knee between her legs and nudged her thighs wide, allowing her to feel his erection against that most sensitive part of her.

Her eyes shot open.

Please, God, don't let her panic now. He put a palm on each of her buttocks and lifted Sylvie till her toes barely touched the ground. They were perfectly aligned now.

Arranging her legs around his hips, he began to pound himself against her. Slowly, at first, then faster and faster. The whole time, he held her eyes, wanting to see the moment she began to come.

When her legs tensed, he stopped.

"No," she cried out. "Don't stop."

He smiled and rubbed himself against her from side to side.

"Aaaaaaarrrrrgh!" she ground out.

He spread her legs wider and resumed his thrusts.

She began to scream.

He caught her scream with his mouth.

Sylvie's hips were rolling frantically now, and undulating against him with a feverish pitch.

She became wild.

He became wilder.

Finally, he could feel Sylvie spasming against him, and he lost it himself, pounding, pounding, pounding away against her till they were both moaning into each other's mouths and his knees gave way, taking them both to the ground, where he continued to thrust against her, even when he'd reached his mind-blowing orgasm, even when she had come at least three equally mind-blowing times.

Short minutes later, as they lay in each other's arms, Sylvie practically purred as she rested her face against his chest, one leg thrown over both of his. He felt supremely satisfied, and unsatisfied at the same time. When she kissed his chest, ever so gently, he kissed the top of her hair.

This was the worst thing that had ever happened to him.

It was the best thing that had ever happened to him.

Busted! . . .

"Sonofabitch!"

The single expletive came from the mouth of a long, tall man in dusty boots and a sinful length of faded jeans, denim shirt, and battered cowboy hat. He was staring down at them from a height of about six feet two inches, shining an industrial-sized flashlight in their faces.

"Get that freakin' light off of me," Luc snarled.

" 'Scuse my language, ma'am," the cowboy drawled, tipping his hat in Sylvie's direction. "And Luc's, as well." To Luc, he just shook his head hopelessly and made a tsk-ing sound of dismay as he turned the flashlight to some spot over their heads.

Meanwhile, Sylvie and Luc were still lying on the ground, wonderfully/horribly sated . . . she would decide which later when her sanity returned . . . which it was, by humiliating leaps and bounds. *How could I? How could I?*

Luc mumbled some obscenity about getting his rocks off like a teenager as he scrambled to his feet, then extended a hand to help her up, too. Apparently, he was having the same regrets about their reckless almost-lovemaking.

The cowboy leaned against the tree casually, legs crossed at the ankles, while he waited for them to adjust themselves. "Everyone and his brother, from one end of Looz-i-ana to the other, is searching for you. And not to say 'Howdy,' that's for sure," the cowboy told Luc, who was dusting off the back side of his jeans. "And here you are, engagin' in a little early mornin' delight. Are you crazy?"

"Do I look like I'm crazy?" Luc snapped back.

The cowboy must have decided to check, because he was back to playing with the flashlight. This time he made a slow sweep of the light from the tops of their heads, down to their toes, then abruptly back to their midsections, where two wet circles on her blouse and a bigger, wetter circle at Luc's crotch were highlighted.

A lazy grin spread across the lips of the cowboy, whose face was mostly in shadow. "Yep. One-hundred-proof crazy."

Luc reached out and shoved the flashlight to the right

so it was no longer shining on them. Grudgingly, he introduced them. "This is Sylvie Fontaine, the chemist I told you about."

"The hell you say!" the cowboy remarked, still grinning. Then, he added a belated "Ma'am."

"Sylvie, this is my little brother, Remy. He's the pilot we've been waiting for."

"Pleased to meet ya, ma'am," Remy said, taking her hand in a firm shake. The whole time he was trying to get a better look at her while she was ducking her head with embarrassment. "So, you're the one who gave Luc the love potion, huh?"

"I didn't *give* him the jelly beans. He *took* them." Even Sylvie was startled by her quick change of mood from turned-on to turned-off.

"Ma'am, by the looks of my brother, those sweet thangs," he said with an exaggerated drawl, "sure put some kick in his giddiup." He waggled his eyebrows toward Luc's ignominious stain.

"My giddiup didn't need any kick, I'll have you know," Luc contended, snagging Sylvie by the hand and beginning to backtrack down the wide path toward the houseboat. His brother walked on his other side.

"Can I try some?" Remy asked Sylvie. He was leaning his face forward so he could see around Luc. "I'd be much obliged if you'd give me a sample, ma'am."

"Oh, no! Not you, too." Luc threw his hands up in the air despairingly. "First, Tante Lulu. Now you. Who next? Charmaine and René?"

"Tante Lulu wants a love potion?" Remy asked incredulously.

"Yeah," Luc said with disgust. "I think she was just kidding, but who knows!"

"Well, I wouldn't mind trying some, too," Remy persisted.

"I am not giving you any love potion jelly beans," she insisted, then had a second thought. "Unless, of course, you want to participate in the lab trials at Terrebonne Pharmaceuticals."

"Uh . . . I don't think so, ma'am. I prefer my love potions in private."

"Like you've ever taken a love potion before," Luc grumbled.

"I'm game for anything. I took Viagra on a bet, didn't I?"

"You did?" Sylvie and Luc asked, their mouths dropping open with surprise.

"Sure. Best six-hour hard-on I ever had. Not sure I'd ever try it again, though." He tipped his hat at Sylvie again and winked. Then: "Oh, geez, ma'am, I am so sorry. My tongue just has a mind of its own today."

"Since when do you need any extra jingle in your spurs?" Luc inquired.

"There's no such thing as too much jingle, if you get my drift," Remy replied.

"How did you know that I took the love potion?"

Remy raised his eyebrows mockingly. "Everyone knows, Luc. Everyone. Besides, your lady looks like she's been rode hard and put up wet. No offense meant, ma'am; that's a compliment. But you, Luc, you look like you been layin' pipe back here in the bayou . . . and you sprung a leak. Love potion would be my guess."

Sylvie put a hand to her hair. Yep, it was wild. She was afraid to touch her lips for fear of what she would find.

"Remy! *Rode hard and put up wet?* I'm surprised at you," Luc said, reversing the etiquette tables on his brother. "A gentleman always treats a lady with respect. Isn't that what you always say?"

"Could we change the subject, please?" Sylvie begged.

"Hey, I came out in the middle of the night to fly you to the end of nowhere, risking life and limb," Remy was telling Luc, "and this is all the appreciation I get? Criticism, criticism, criticism."

"I have two words for you, Remy. And they're not 'Thank you.'"

"Likewise, bro . . . though it seems to me that you were about to do just that when I arrived on the scene . . . just in time, I might add." Remy glanced toward Sylvie then and groaned, no doubt suspecting he'd used some more bad language.

"Don't you dare apologize, or call me ma'am, one more time," she ordered Remy. Then she turned to Luc. "You, on the other hand, could apologize till the ducks return to Lake Ponchartrain and it wouldn't be enough. And, frankly, a ma'am or two would be a welcome change."

"Yes, ma . . . I mean, Sylvie," Remy said with a grin.

"Yes, *chère*," Luc said with a grin.

"Aaarrgh!" Sylvie said, and she wasn't grinning.

"Enough of this foolishness!" Luc said then. "Do you have the plane ready?"

Remy nodded. "The hydroplane is anchored in the water next to the houseboat."

"You're early," Luc commented.

"I decided to get you out of Dodge quick as I could. All hell's breaking loose back in Houma. Is there anyone you haven't pissed off today?" The cowboy seemed to call himself to task. "'Scuse my language, ma'am. I've been hanging around cattlemen and oil riggers too much lately, I reckon. And my bro."

"That's okay," she said, trying to see his face. Even in profile, Remy was motion-picture gorgeous. Not just classically handsome, he was beautiful. With a perfectly square chin, a straight nose, finely sculpted lips, and what appeared to be mile-long, black eye lashes. "I'm getting used to your brother's foul mouth. Are you sure you're brothers? You're so polite, and he's so . . . not polite."

"I taught him everything he knows," Luc told her in a deliberately loud undertone meant to be overheard.

Remy made a snorting sound of disbelief. "Emily Post, he never was, ma'am," he informed Sylvie. "Luc might have taught me how to tie my shoelaces, and how to sneak a *Playboy* magazine out of Boudreaux's General Store, and how to undo a bra snap in two seconds flat, and . . . and other good things. But *I* was the one who taught him proper etiquette. Yessirree, ma'am."

Luc made a rude harrumphing noise.

"Why do you call me ma'am?"

"He calls all the ladies ma'am," Luc piped in before his brother could answer. "It's a surefire way of getting them to shuck their drawers, I suspect."

Remy and Sylvie both gasped at that crudity.

"What does Luc call you?" Remy asked.

"Babe," Luc said with a grin.

"*Chère,*" she said with a frown.

"Same thing," Luc countered with an even wider grin.

"I'm beginning to think you're both crazy." Remy kept glancing from one to the other of them with puzzlement.

They'd arrived back at the tavern area, with its bright lighting. She noticed the hydroplane sitting in the bayou stream next to the houseboat.

Luc went up ahead to get a few items, including her lab rats, from the houseboat. She turned to say something to Remy at the same time he turned around fully, and she got her first real look at him. She barely stifled the gulp that sprang to her lips.

Oh, she remembered the gap-toothed Remy who had followed his bigger brothers, René and Luc, around Houma as children. Now she remembered something she had heard about Remy as an adult. He'd been a pilot in Desert Storm, where his helicopter had been shot down, causing him massive burns.

Remy was still a beautiful man, depending on the angle at which one viewed him. He was angel-gorgeous on his right side, including intact lips and nose and both eyes, but the left side of his face was scarred and puckered with pink burn tissue.

To Sylvie's embarrassment, she saw that Remy was taking in her survey with a lifted brow and faint smile. He didn't turn away as some men might, but then he was probably accustomed to the scrutiny. Instead, he froze in place and waited for her to register the full extent of what he no doubt considered his grotesqueness.

Neither one of them wanted to break eye contact. Remy seemed to want her to shy away in revulsion. She refused to do so.

Remy was the one to snap the silence, and his words shocked her. "Don't hurt my brother."

"Wh-what?"

"Luc is a good man. He's been a father to me and René. Lots of people depend on him . . . too much, sometimes. I would take it kindly, ma'am, if you wouldn't break his heart."

At first, Sylvie was too stunned to react. "Oh, I can't believe you said that. What makes you think I have the power, or the inclination, to hurt your brother?"

"Just take care, that's all, ma'am."

"Take care of what?" Luc asked, coming up behind them on the dock in front of the plane.

"Nothing," Remy said, casting her a speaking glance of warning. Then he noticed the Happy Meal box in

Luc's hand. It was obvious that something live was inside since the waxed paper was rustling up a storm. "What is *that?*"

"Fucking rats," Luc replied dryly.

Sylvie put her face in her hands, but still she heard Remy exclaim, "Luc! Now you've gone too far with your cursing in front of a lady."

Sylvie peeked through her fingers and saw Luc open the Happy Meal box in front of Remy's astounded face. She could just guess what he was witnessing with Samson and Delilah.

"I told you," Luc said. "*Fuck*-ing rats."

Chapter Ten

This is so not a good idea! . . .

"I want to go home," she said a short time later.

Luc, Remy, and René all looked at her, sighed with exasperation, and exclaimed with a communal "Jeesh!"

René stood next to her on the dock. Luc and Remy were in front of them doing something manly with ropes that would presumably allow the plane to lift off soon.

René had come out of the tavern a moment ago. Even though the tavern was still open, the band had quit for the night. Grinning at her unabashedly, he'd inquired, "How'd ya like my song, *chère*? I'm thinking 'bout sending it to Beau-Soleil to record." Luc had threatened to break his too-pretty nose then, especially when René informed an amused Remy about his "Cajun Knight" lyrics.

God must have been in a really good mood when he created these three gorgeous men, she thought irrelevantly now, just after making her pronouncement. But perhaps not so irrelevantly since the appeal of one of them was the reason for her current panic.

"I want to go home," she repeated.

"Uh-oh," René said.

"Oh, damn," Luc said.

"I smell trouble," Remy said.

"Really, I just want to go home. I don't want to be any trouble, though. I can call a cab . . . or call my mother to send her driver." She practically choked on that last offer.

"Do the words 'spoiled brat' mean anything to you?" Luc asked. "Or 'over my dead body'?"

Raising her chin in silent defiance, she felt like a whiny child insisting on some impossible whim, but she had had enough of this "adventure" with Luc. She hated the way mysterious people or events were steering her life, and her lack of control with Luc had been the last straw. Who knows what she would do if she were in his company much longer?

Actually, she knew exactly what would happen, and that was the problem.

"You can't go home, Sylv. Not for a couple of days, at least," Luc told her with exaggerated patience.

"Yes, I can. I appreciate your letting me tag along so far, Luc, but I'm not cut out for this *Die Hard/Lethal Weapon* stuff."

"And you think I am?" He raised his eyebrows indignantly. "You think I envision myself as some Bruce Willis/Mel Gibson fool?"

He was better than those two, in her opinion, but he didn't need to know that. "I'll hire a bodyguard, like you suggested," she said. "Maybe your *friend* Claudia can give me a recommendation."

"My *friend* Claudia isn't going to give you diddly-squat, unless I tell her to."

Oooh, he was making her so mad. First, he didn't want to take her with him. Now, he wouldn't let her go. "Listen up, Luc, this is the end of my trip with you. That's final."

"Uh, I don't think so, ma'am," Remy interjected, raising a hand like a little boy in a classroom. "There are a few things that have happened in the past ten hours or so that you two are not aware of. My boss needed me to deliver some parts to an oil rigger who lives in Houma. It would have appeared odd if I'd refused. The point is, I picked up some news. I had planned to fill you in during the plane ride."

He had everyone's attention now.

"There's a warrant for Sylvie's arrest, for one thing."

"What?" Sylvie couldn't for the life of her imagine any reason for her arrest. She'd never even gotten a speeding ticket, or a high school suspension. Besides, she was the one who'd been vandalized.

"Terrebonne Pharmaceuticals," he explained, "claims you stole some of their property."

She put her face in her hands. "I can't believe Charles would do this to me. A warrant!" She shivered with apprehension as she comprehended that the spotlight would be on her for sure when she returned to town. A cold clamminess came over her skin . . . the precursor to one of her shyness anxiety attacks, she feared.

"Actually, you might look good in prison stripes, Sylv," Luc quipped. She knew he was just teasing her, to lighten her fears.

"Hey, I could come sing 'Jailhouse Rock' for you in the slammer," René added, also seeming to empathize with her devastated condition. "The Cajun version, of course." •

"If it's anything like your 'Cajun Knight,' I'll pass," she said in an embarrassingly wobbly voice.

"You didn't like my new song?" René cast wounded eyes her way. The boy, who was really only a few years younger than Sylvie, was way too good-looking for his own good. Those eyes probably worked on lots of women, but not her.

Still, she laughed, despite her dark mood.

"Hey, this is nothing to laugh about, guys," Remy said. "At first, I thought the warrant was issued because of the formula . . . which may still be the case . . . but now I'm kinda thinking the property they want back is . . ." He looked pointedly at the Happy Meal box in her hand.

"Samson and Delilah?" she practically shrieked, and hugged the box to her chest. "They belong to me, bought and paid for with my own money."

"Samson and Delilah?" René asked.

"Don't ask!" she and Remy shouted as one.

"Fu—" Luc began, hesitated, grinned, then started again. "Full-fledged, furry sex machines. In other words, Sylvie's lab rats."

"Rats? You have real live rats in that tiny box?"

Sylvie nodded. "They're miniature lab rats."

"And cute as hell," Remy observed.

Luc frowned at his brother. "They are *not* cute."

"What's all that noise they're making?" René wanted to know.

Luc and Remy exchanged a look with each other and waggled their eyebrows at René. "Guess."

Wanting to change the subject back to the important issue at hand, Sylvie said, "Well, a warrant is all the more reason for me to go back home and resolve this misunderstanding. My lawyer will handle Terrebonne

Pharmaceuticals, believe me. Thank God I've got legal documentation for everything."

"Did I mention that your mother held a press conference this evening at the state capitol in which she suggested you might have mental problems?" Remy went on. "She insinuated that a short stay in a restful resort might be called for."

"Short, as in till after the next election?" René offered.

"Exactly," Luc agreed.

Sylvie was horrified that her mother would do such a thing to her, and publicly, too. Anything to protect her reputation and political career from being tarnished by a less-than-perfect daughter.

Luc laced his fingers with hers and squeezed, apparently sensing her hurt. "Is that all?" he asked his brother.

"Well, other than Sylvie's front stoop being loaded down with gris-gris dolls and other voodoo paraphernalia, that's it for Sylvie," Remy said. "Now, you, on the other hand, big brother, have got even more trouble."

"How's that possible?"

"Dad called me, and he's practically frothing at the mouth."

Luc shrugged. "Let me guess. I'm the biggest disappointment of his life. Always have been. Always will be. Must be my bad blood, from Mom's side of the family, of course. Should have beaten the crap out of me when I was a kid . . . as if he didn't try on numerous occasions."

"That's about it," Remy admitted. The sadness of his face, and René's, as well, told the whole story. Sylvie would bet that Remy and René hadn't suffered nearly as much as Luc at their father's hand because Luc—the big brother—had taken the blows for them.

It was Sylvie who squeezed Luc's hand then. He gave

her a questioning glance that was both surprised and oddly touched. He immediately masked his vulnerable expression with a scowl, but she had seen enough. More and more, Sylvie was discovering that Luc was not the man he pretended to be.

"Anyhow," Remy went on, "Dad says that Cypress Oil is flying in their top lawyers, anticipating a court battle. He warned that you might lose your law license over this thing, if you're not careful."

"Did you bring that scientific equipment I asked for?" Luc asked him, undaunted.

"Yep," Remy replied.

"What scientific equipment?" she asked.

"The stuff you and I are going to use in the next few days to test the tributary waters."

She gave him a chagrined look.

"We need something to while away the time," he explained.

"And you couldn't have informed me of that? Or asked my advice about what equipment I need?"

"You probably would have given me another lecture." He shrugged. "Sometimes it's better to just do it than ask for permission."

"Luc! For shame! That's the same advice you gave me when I wanted to kiss Evangeline Arnaud in the fourth grade," René pointed out.

They all had to smile at that.

"Hey, it's a multi-purpose bit of advice," Luc said.

"Back to the problem at hand," Remy reminded them. "From what Dad said, or didn't say, I have to tell you that you are going to be hit from every angle on this water-pollution issue. The DER, the EPA, Louisianans who depend on the oil industry for their paychecks, hired thugs. Are you sure you want to get involved?"

"I'm already involved," Luc said.

René looked at his older brother as if he walked on water. So did Remy.

"Oh, and I forgot. Tee-John is missing and Dad thinks you're to blame," Remy added. Although he threw the news out flippantly, she could tell he was concerned.

"Tee-John! What happened? How's long's he been missing?" Luc asked with alarm.

"Since early this morning . . . almost twenty-four hours."

"Why did he run away?" René asked.

"I swear, if Dad's been beating that kid—" Luc's fists were clenched and his voice icy with anger.

"Maybe he just hightailed it to Tante Lulu's. We all did that when we were kids and the old man was in one of his rages." René was speaking, but Remy nodded as well.

Then Remy shook his head. "She hasn't seen or heard from him."

Luc frowned, obviously worried. "I'd better stick around and see if I can find him."

"No, René and I will handle it," Remy said. "You've got enough on your plate as it is."

"Why is Dad blaming me for the kid's disappearance?"

Remy shrugged. "You started running away about the same age. Maybe he figures you've been giving the kid tips. Either that, or the kid isn't even missing, and this is just a piling on of charges to get you in trouble with the police."

"God, when it rains, it pours around you, Luc," René observed.

"Who's Tee-John?" Sylvie finally asked.

"Our half brother," Remy explained. "He's only ten years old and lives with my father and Jolie Guillot, his . . . uh, mistress. Don't you be worryin' none, ma'am. Tee-John is a tough little critter."

Sylvie thought she heard Luc mutter, "As a LeDeux, he'd have to be."

Luc pulled Sylvie aside then. "You can't go back home till we're sure it's safe . . . both from the greedy bloodsuckers at Terrebonne Pharmaceuticals, and from your bloodsucking mother. Oh, and the voodoo fruit-cakes, too."

After hearing all that Remy had related about the dangers to Luc, she'd almost forgotten the warrant for her arrest, and the ludicrous notion that her mother might have her exiled to some remote resort. Both ideas were so preposterous they didn't merit serious consideration, except that a niggling fear wormed itself into her subconscious. Desperate people did desperate things.

Sylvie didn't even bother to protest his characterization of her mother. "I don't know, Luc. I have a bad feeling about the two of us going off like this."

He lifted her chin with a forefinger and forced her to make eye contact. "This is about us almost making love, isn't it?"

She blushed till the roots of her hair felt hot, then lied, "No."

"Liar."

"I'm afraid," she confessed.

"Of the bad guys?"

"Not at the moment." *Not while I'm with you.*

"Of being arrested?"

"Well, yes, but it would be more embarrassing than anything. I couldn't bear to think of making a spectacle of myself."

"Your mother?"

"I'm not afraid of my mother, but she does have the ability to mortify me with that kind of public exposure."

"So what, then? What are you afraid of?"

She lowered her head and refused to answer or look at him directly.

"Sylvie?" He tilted his head in puzzlement, then gasped with shock. "Of me?"

Her head shot up. "No, you fool. Of me."

He smiled then . . . a slow, lazy spreading of lips over bright white teeth. The jerk!

"See?" she cried. "This is not a good idea. You think it's funny, and I think it's bone-chilling serious."

"Ah, Sylv, come on. You and I are adults. We can handle a day or two in the swamps alone. We have self-control."

"Right," she said, but what she thought was, *Yeah, right!*

Minutes later, while Luc was helping Remy load a few last-minute items in the plane, René gave her a warning. "Hurt my brother Luc and you'll be sorry."

"Me?" she demurred, a palm to her chest. "Why does everyone think I have the power to hurt Luc? Your aunt and Remy gave me a similar warning. Luc couldn't care less what I say or do to him."

"You can't possibly be that blind," was René's only reply.

Within five minutes, they were boarding the hydroplane. That was when Remy gave them one last bit of information he'd somehow forgotten to impart.

"Did you know that Tante Lulu got a citation from the zoning officer in Houma today?"

"Why?" Luc drawled out, as if he wasn't sure he really wanted to know the answer.

"Seems she was delivering some chickens to Sylvie's town house. Seems she made a makeshift chicken coop on her patio. Seems the neighbors started to complain about all the clucking." Remy glanced over at Sylvie and grinned.

She and Luc both groaned and put their faces in their hands.

"Do you have any idea what Tante Lulu means by 'flocking the bride'?" Remy asked with seeming innocence. "And, by the way, who's the bride?"

Then Remy laughed. And René did, too. Hilariously. But she and Luc just groaned again.

Hey, baby! You wanna go camping? (Wink, wink!) . . .

The dark predawn skies lightened slowly to an ashy blue, then suddenly burst open over the bayou like a firecracker into clear blue skies, swirling white clouds, and a full orange sun. A perfect moment for the small Piper hydroplane to set down in the stream in front of Luc's cabin.

Even this early, heat shimmered in the air and mist rose from the slow-moving water. A crimson-headed turkey buzzard wheeled over the trees before swooping down to the water, undaunted by their intrusion into its domain.

As the crow flies, their destination was less than two hundred miles from Houma. By plane, it had taken only thirty-five minutes to get there. But because of the endlessly meandering streams and tributaries, many of them so new that they were unnamed, it would have taken a day or more to reach the site by boat. Fortunately for them, there were a lot of bayous in Louisiana that were not yet civilized or known to men, especially since every time the Mississippi changed its course or flooded over, new bayous were created and old ones swallowed up.

There was no dock; so, Luc and Remy jumped into the shallow water, shoes and all, and made quick work of securing the light plane with ropes to an ancient stump on the sloping bank. It appeared as if Sylvie would have to go into the thigh-deep water as well, if she wanted to traverse the ten feet from floating plane to dry ground.

But no, Luc was holding out his arms to her. "Come on, Sylv. I'll carry you."

"Hah!" No way was she going to put herself in his arms again . . . not willingly . . . not even for such an innocent reason.

Remy waggled his eyebrows at them as he splashed by, already starting to empty the plane of the many canvas bags of supplies he'd brought, some ordered by Luc and some filled by Tante Lulu.

She eased herself onto the ledge of the open door, Happy Meal box securely held to her chest, and eyed the murky water with distaste. It was stained the color of dark tea from the tannin of tree bark and fallen leaves. Out of her side vision, she saw a mama alligator cruise by with a baby gator on its back.

Luc laughed, apparently reading her thoughts, and scooped her easily into his arms.

A small squeak of alarm came from her mouth as she quickly wrapped one arm around his neck, the other still clutching the Happy Meal box. "I'm too heavy for you," she protested weakly.

He chuckled and pretended to sway beneath her weight. But then he turned and headed toward shore, one arm under her legs, the other circling her shoulders. Sylvie didn't even want to think about how good he felt and how secure she felt.

"Don't you be worryin' none, darlin'. You're the perfect size for me." He grinned. "To carry, that is."

"I am *not* perfect," she said, without thinking. Her eyes were fixed on the water, where she could swear she saw a black snake slither by, or was it just a long weed?

"Don't tell me you're one of those women who thinks thin is in, Sylv. Tsk, tsk, tsk. You know what really pisses me off? When a skinny female says, 'I forgot to eat today.' I mean, I've forgotten to mail a letter, or put the toilet seat down. But you gotta be some kind of a dumb twit to forget to eat, right?"

She had to smile at Luc's sweet effort to distract her from the water. In fact, they were already on dry ground, and still he held her in his arms.

"Well?" he said, grinning down at her.

"Well what?"

"Don't I deserve a reward for being your Cajun Knight?"

She shook her head at his foolishness. At the same time, her heart tugged at the vulnerable look in his eyes. Surely, the crude, rude lout didn't care what she thought of him.

"Brave knights rescue fair damsels without thought of recompense. It's known as chivalry," she informed him with mock seriousness.

"Dumb knights," he concluded, setting her on her feet. But then he surprised her by giving her a quick kiss on the lips. "Cajun knights are different from other knights. We believe in giving a little lagniappe with our chivalry."

"You are impossible," she said. "Since when are kisses an act of chivalry?"

"New rules," he declared, and turned away from her to go back into the water and help his brother unload.

"Well, those rules had better not include anything else," she called to his back.

At first, she didn't think he'd heard her, but then she

heard him remark to Remy, "Some women don't know when to pull up the drawbridge."

"Yeah," Remy agreed, hefting a huge duffle-style bag over his shoulder, "a lot of moats are in danger when we Knights of the Bayou start updating the rules." Remy and Luc both glanced at her on the shore, where she stood with one hand braced on a hip, and then they both winked at her.

They were right. A lot of "moats" were in danger when these two rogues were in the vicinity. And the funny thing was, the more she was around Remy, the less she noticed his disfigured face. Even more funny, and alarming, was the fact that the more she was around Luc, the less she noticed his boorishness. Dangerous business, that. Surely, a clear and present danger to . . . well, moats.

Sylvie turned to take in her new surroundings. A raised Cajun-style cabin of ancient vintage stood about twenty feet back from the water's edge. It had been built on stilts to withstand the many floods that assaulted it over the years. That meant the main living quarters were on the second floor, and a roofed veranda and storage rooms were on ground level.

Despite its age and weathered, unpainted logs, it was a lovely, well-kept structure. Wide steps led up the center to a porch where a swing and two sturdy, hand-built rocking chairs could be seen. The windows were shuttered, but there were two large ones in front and another smaller one above where a loft must be located, indicating that the interior would be light and airy. A wide hammock was strung between two tupelo-gum trees on one side of the dwelling . . . a homey indication that this was not just a fishing camp but a place of rest and relaxation for its owner.

Most surprising was the pink and white explosion of wild roses that climbed riotously up the house supports and practically covered two sides of the house. Sylvie had to smile at that whimsical touch—probably added a century ago by one of Luc's feminine ancestors. Then she smiled even wider when she noted another feminine touch . . . this one more recent. Between a gas-powered generator and a huge cistern on the far side of the house was positioned a five-foot-tall plastic statue of St. Jude. Even in this remote hideaway, Tante Lulu wasn't taking any chances.

On the flight here, Luc had informed her that almost no one knew about this secret hideaway, which had been passed down through five generations of his mother's family. It had originally been built by Rivard trappers from another time, before the Civil War era. At one point it had even been a safe house for slaves escaping to the North. Sadly, it had been abandoned for more than five decades before Luc took possession of it ten years ago. He doubted his father remembered its existence.

With a sigh of exhaustion, Sylvie grabbed one of the canvas sacks and began to lug it up the steps to the cabin, being careful not to drop her cardboard mouse house. All she needed was two horny rats on the loose in the bayou. She'd never be able to recapture Samson and Delilah.

"The key is above the doorjamb," Luc yelled, then hastily added, "Check for snakes before you stick your hands anywhere inside the cabin."

Sylvie shivered with distaste as she opened the front door, but then snakes were a fact of life in South Louisiana. She didn't like the slimy things, but she didn't fear them either. A quick examination showed she was safe . . . for now.

She set the Happy Meal box down, dropped the bag, and proceeded to open all the windows and shutters to air out the musty interior. She gasped with surprise when she got her first good look at the large room. It was a rustic cabin . . . ancient in age . . . but it was lovely.

There were straw mats on the wide-planked floors, but precious handwoven Cajun carpets of brilliant blues and pure whites were rolled up in tobacco leaves to preserve them from mildew and moths. On the wooden walls, mosquito netting protected glass-framed prints and primitive tapestries from flyspecks.

The cabin contained only one room, but it was large . . . at least thirty by thirty. A cozy living room with comfortable, albeit well-worn, chairs and ottomans, along with reading lamps, dominated one side. Opposite was an alcove with a built-in bed. In the back was a kitchen with vintage, but probably useable, appliances and a big cypress kitchen table and chairs. Upstairs was a sleeping loft, which had probably been used by the children of the family at one time when the cabin had been an actual residence.

A sudden humming noise jarred Sylvie from her musings, and she realized that the open refrigerator had suddenly turned on. The overhead fan began to whir, also. Luc must have started the outside generator.

"So what do you think, babe?" Luc asked. He and Remy had just come in, each carrying three of the canvas bags. "It's not what you're used to back at your mother's plantation, but it should suit you for slumming a day or two."

There he went again, bringing up the differences in their backgrounds . . . as if it mattered a hill of beans to her. She raised her chin defiantly and said, "This cabin is lovely. And the location is special. I can see why you cherish the place so."

"Cherish? Who said anything about cherish? It's just an old fishing cabin," Luc answered defensively. He wasn't fooling her, he loved the cabin, but for some reason he wanted to keep the fact hidden from her. He had acted the same way regarding his apartment back in Houma.

"Yeah, he cherishes the place, all right," Remy offered, plunking a heavy bag of what must be canned goods on the kitchen counter. Then he winked at Sylvie as if they shared some secret about Luc.

Luc and Remy made another trip for more bags.

"I brought a satellite phone for you, Luc," Remy was telling his brother. "Don't use it unless there's an emergency. My phone will probably be tapped, as well as those of everyone else you know. But I'll call you from a safe phone as soon as I get news."

Luc nodded.

"What's with all this stuff?" Sylvie asked then. There were about a dozen bags of various sizes around the room.

"Tante Lulu wanted to make sure you two were comfortable here," Remy explained ruefully. "I think she may have overdone it a bit."

Luc made a snorting sound of disgust, especially when he untied one of the bags and pulled out an exquisite comforter made of soft quilted patches of colorful cloth, immediately followed by embroidered sheets and a homespun tablecloth. "Hell! What does she think we're doing here, setting up housekeeping?" He immediately realized the truth of his statement, glanced sheepishly at Remy and Sylvie, and then blushed.

Sylvie loved him for that blush.

No, no, no she didn't really *love* him. She just loved the fact that the rogue could blush. It wasn't *love-love*.

Oh, God! I am falling apart here. She put a hand to her forehead and moaned.

"Sylv, you're dead on your feet," Luc observed. "Help me make up the bed with those fresh linens and you can lie down. I'll put the supplies away."

She would have liked to argue, but it was the truth. She was suddenly so exhausted she could barely stand on her feet. The events of the past several days were catching up with her finally, and she feared she might not even be able to make it as far as the alcove.

Thunder ripped through the sky, followed almost immediately by a wild torrent of rain. It would undoubtedly be one of those quick summer storms well known in Southern Louisiana, come and gone in the blink of an eye. If Sylvie wasn't tired before, she was now, with the sound of rain pounding on the rooftop in a metronome rhythm conducive to sleep.

Luc showed her to a small bathroom, where she washed her face and hands and arms, brushed her teeth, and donned an old T-shirt and jogging shorts of his. A short time later, she was tucked in between crisp sheets and was drifting off to sleep.

Before she fell asleep, though, she heard Remy advise Luc, "You're in over your head, brother."

"With Dad and his oil cohorts?"

"No, with Sylvie. This one could break your heart, Luc."

There was a long silence.

Finally, Luc said in a low voice she could hardly hear, "Yeah."

What Sylvie would have liked to say, if she weren't

so sleepy, was that maybe hers was going to be the heart broken. Or worse yet, maybe they would break each other's hearts.

Love potions weren't all they were cracked up to be.

Chapter Eleven

Gonna have good fun down on the bayou . . .

Five hours had passed, and Sylvie was still fast asleep.

The rain had stopped hours ago, and steam escaped from the ground in moist billows under the sun's unrelenting rays. The scent of the roses that climbed over the outside of the house was almost overpowering since their recent dousing.

Luc had put all the supplies away, including a pigload of stuff Tante Lulu had sent along from his hope chest. Not just the bed linens, comforter, and tablecloth, but monogrammed towels, a sofa throw rug, pot holders, a macrame toaster cover, and a St. Jude toilet-paper dispenser.

To his surprise—*he never would have thought of it himself*—Tante Lulu had bought a small critter carrier made of clear plastic with a spinning treadmill, saw-dust, and mice food for Samson and Delilah. They were humping away right now in their new home in a dark corner by the fireplace.

Even worse, Tante Lulu had enclosed a brand-new package of boxer shorts—white with red hearts, for God's sake. *Talk about obvious!* And a flame-red Frederick's-of-Hollywood-style nightie, which she had probably purchased in Wal-Mart. It was called "The Naughty Nightie." *Gawd!*

What could his aunt possibly be thinking?

He was afraid he knew.

Remy had seen those items before he'd left, and had had to practically drag his open jaw off the floor. Luc had heard him laughing all the way outside to his plane, and then until take off. He was probably still laughing when he landed on the ranch near Natchitoches.

His aunt had also sent enough grocery supplies to feed a small army. He was standing next to the alcove bed now, trying to decide whether to awaken Sylvie for lunch, or just to let her sleep.

"Sylvie," he said softly.

She had been sleeping on her stomach, her arms wrapped around the pillow, like a lover. At the sound of his voice, she rolled over onto her back, threw her arms over her head, made a sexy snuffling sound, and contin-ued to sleep.

Luc would have liked to think that the internal lurch he felt then was in his groin area and due to the love po-tion, which seemed to affect him in waves, like a time-release pill. He ran a fleeting hand over himself, and sure enough the evidence was there—half-hard and ready for the wake-up call. But, no, it wasn't that region of his anatomy that he was worried about. He suspected that it was his heart at risk here, and not just from a stupid jelly bean. There was some serious emotional stuff going on inside him. But he refused to think about that now.

He shifted from foot to foot, contemplating whether to make another effort to wake Sylvie with a louder voice, or whether to slide into the bed with her and rouse her another way. *Rouse* being the key word. No, no, no, he wasn't *really* considering the latter.

Sylvie was wearing an old gray Tulane T-shirt of his, and it had become twisted around her upper body, molding to her breasts and abdomen. The cotton sheet, likewise, was tangled around her hips and legs.

Beads of perspiration stood out on her forehead and upper lip. She must be roasting in this noontime high humidity, but obviously exhaustion took precedence over discomfort for her today, at least subconsciously. He should let her sleep till she was completely rested.

Still, Luc lingered. He couldn't keep himself from staring at Sylvie as she slept. Her black hair provided a sharp and appealing contrast to the clear creaminess of her complexion, especially with the slumberous blush that gave a hint of color to her cheeks. Her lashes were full and thick, black as coal, like his own. Her nose was straight, with a slight upturn in the middle. He denied himself the pleasure of looking at her lips, which he knew from memory were full and naturally rose-colored . . . and kissable. Oh, yes, very kissable. He still couldn't believe how responsive she'd been when they'd almost made love last night. Responsive, hell! She'd been hot. Best not to think about that. Instead, he moved his gaze to her chin, which was strong and stubborn, like Sylvie.

In truth, Sylvie's appearance was pleasing enough, but she wasn't beautiful. Not really. So why was he so attracted to her?

Because she's Sylvie.

With that disconcerting admission, Luc eased himself down to sit on the edge of the bed. He knew exactly when this "thing" for Sylvie had begun. They'd been elementary school students together at Our Lady of the Bayou School, and Luc had been suffering horribly from feelings of self-loathing, prompted and perpetuated by his father's constant criticism.

Sylvie had always seemed out of his reach, even then, and perhaps he'd felt that, if he could gain the affection of a girl like Sylvie, then maybe he wasn't as worthless as everyone told him he was. Truth be told, he'd done things he was ashamed of since then . . . a sort of living down to people's expectations. And of course, there was that one reprehensible act ten years ago . . . no, he wouldn't dwell on that now. But one thing had to be admitted . . . in many ways, he was unworthy of a good woman.

Of course, Sylvie had never reciprocated his clumsy attempts at friendship. He knew now that she must have been chronically shy, and that his attentions had probably aggravated her fears, but back then all he'd wanted was a kind word from the girl on whom he'd had a crush. Of course, later he'd wanted other things—things that would shock a shy girl like Sylvie—but from the beginning Sylvie had been to his childish mind all that he was not . . . good and respectable and loved.

Was he falling in love with Sylvie? Or had he always been a little bit in love with the girl?

And if so, was it the fault of the love potion? Or some chemistry that had been between them for ages, just waiting to react?

God! My brain has entered an altered state. How could I even think such unthinkable things?

Enough of this stuff! He and Sylvie had no future. Once the love potion wore off, along with his perpetual hard-on, his life would be back to normal. He didn't want or need this kind of aggravation.

Maybe he should go out and catch some fish to keep his mind off the . . . aggravation. Just then, Sylvie moaned in her sleep. Her lips parted, her back arched, and her legs spread slightly. Man, oh, man, that must be some dream!

He stood carefully, not wanting to awaken her in the midst of . . . well, whatever she was doing. The last thing he wanted was to embarrass her. Well, not quite the last thing. He began to tiptoe toward the front door.

Just then, though, Sylvie did an unforgivable thing. She moaned again, ever so softly, and through her lips came one whisper of a word. "Luc."

Luc stopped dead in his tracks.

And smiled.

Sonofagun! Sylvie Fontaine . . . dreaming about the bad boy of the bayou. I wonder what she's doing. I wonder what I'm doing. Sonofagun! How did that old Hank Williams song "Jambalaya" go? "Sonofagun, we gonna have good fun, down on the bayou . . ."

Good fun?

Yep!

It was one thing to play the noble Cajun Knight when the woman was unwilling to be seduced or vulnerable. But Sylvie was dreaming about him! *Hot damn!* She'd told him back at Swampy's that she wanted him, but he'd figured it was the oyster shooters talking. But maybe it was just the booze making her reveal her secret longings. *Secret longings?* God, he liked the sound of that.

First, she gave him a love potion. Second, she fueled the fire by telling him she wanted him. Third, she dreamed about him.

All bets were off now.

* * *

Bayou mud was in his blood . . .

Sylvie awakened about one P.M., totally refreshed after her long sleep and ready to take back control of her unraveling life. She inhaled deeply, relishing the smell of fresh air after the recent rain and the fragrant scent of roses . . . lots of roses.

First, she checked on Samson and Delilah, who had adjusted surprisingly well to their new home. A pot of canned chicken noodle soup had been left warming on the stove . . . presumably for her. She ate it, standing up, from the pot, with some crackers, discovering she was ravenous. Quick work was also made of two homemade beignets . . . presumably from Tante Lulu's kitchen. Her stomach satisfied for the moment, Sylvie sipped at a cup of black coffee, which might have tasted fine when Luc brewed it many hours ago, but was now bitter and luke-warm. Still, she felt revived, and ready to take on the world. Or at least Luc.

Strolling around the large room, she noted a framed photograph here and there . . . one of the three brothers as teenagers, their arms looped over each other's shoulders, grinning at the camera in a rascally fashion. This was before Remy's accident, and he was almost painfully beautiful to look at. But then, René and Luc were pretty darn gorgeous, too.

Another photograph prompted a giggle from Sylvie. It showed Tante Lulu standing next to a pre-adolescent Luc, coming up only to his chest even then. Based on his cute little three-piece suit, prayer-folded hands, and the rosary around his neck, Sylvie assumed it was a First Communion picture. Hard to imagine Luc ever being so angelic.

Last, there was a picture in an antique frame of a beautiful Cajun woman, about twenty, standing on the prow of a shrimp boat, *Sweet Adèle*, staring off into the watery distance. Sylvie assumed it was Luc's mother, shortly before her death.

One thing she noticed as she walked around the room was that there wasn't a speck of dust or clutter. Even the dishes that Luc must have used for his own breakfast and lunch had been washed and put away. No sign either of all the canvas sacks he and Remy had brought in. The straw matting had been rolled up, the wood floors swept, and the Cajun carpets laid around the room. Even the windows looked as if they might have been washed. A bouquet of fresh-picked pink and white roses held center place on the big cypress kitchen table. Luc had certainly been a busy bee while she'd been sleeping half the day away. What did all this say about the kind of man he was? Had he always been a neat freak? Or had it been pounded into him?

She seemed to remember that the bayou cottage where he and his brothers had lived as young boys had been notoriously filthy . . . rusted cars, hot-water heater, and bathtub in the front yard . . . that kind of thing. Was there something about his deprived childhood that had generated this personality trait? As she recalled, his father hadn't sold his land to the oil companies till Luc was about fourteen. Before that, there was lots of speculation on how Valcour LeDeux, a known alcoholic and brutal father, supported his family . . . or rather, did not support his family.

There were so many things she was learning about Luc that made her wonder who he really was. Like an uncompleted puzzle, the whole picture was not yet clear, but it was slowly taking shape.

Just before she prepared to go outside, Sylvie noticed a sealed cellophane package on a side table. She smiled when she saw what it was: three pairs of white boxer shorts imprinted with glow-in-the-dark red hearts. They had to be a "gift" from his aunt . . . or a prod, more likely.

But Sylvie wasn't smiling when she saw what lay under the boxers. It was a flame-red nightgown that dipped low, low, low in front; its hem would hardly reach the thighs. And it even had a name: "The Naughty Nightie." *Gawd!*

Merciful heavens! What could Tante Lulu be thinking?

She was afraid she knew.

After gathering together her notebook and pen, she found Luc down by the stream, calf-deep in the water, working a net to catch some crawfish. He wore a pair of cutoff jeans, and that was all. Lordy, Lordy, looking as he did, the man could catch a whole lot more than a netful of mudbugs.

Lucien LeDeux was a well-built man. His arms and shoulders and chest, even his legs, showed well-developed muscle definition . . . not the pumped-up muscles of an exercise fanatic, but the healthy muscle tone of an active man. His black hair was a little long on the neck, and Sylvie remembered from the night before how silky it had felt against her hands. His fingers were long and deft and way too interesting as he maneuvered the net.

He was not yet aware of her scrutiny; so, Sylvie watched as he performed his tasks . . . lifting the net; tossing crawfish of a suitable size into a bucket on the bank and the babies back into the stream; rebaiting the traps with what she recognized as cow lips—a favorite Louisiana bait for crawfish—which must have been sent with the supplies; and unfurling the net over the stream once again.

He bit his bottom lip in concentration as he worked . . .

clearly a labor of love. Truly, Luc was a man with bayou mud in his veins . . . a Cajun at heart. It was said that you could take the Cajun out of the bayou, but you couldn't take the bayou out of the Cajun. It was certainly true of Luc . . . a man in his element here in the primitive swamplands. How hard it must be for him to switch personas when he had to enter sophisticated courtrooms for his regular work!

Luc raised his face to the hot sun and stretched with lazy pleasure. Only then did he notice Sylvie watching him.

"Did you have a good sleep?" There was a twinkle in his eye as he asked the question. The man got way too many twinkles in his eye, even for the most innocuous reasons.

She nodded. Faced with the full splendor of his bare chest, she was suddenly at a loss for words.

"Eat?" he asked.

She nodded again. Mercy, the man was a dangerous six-foot bundle of male testosterone.

Splashing noisily through the shallow stream, he walked up to her on the bank. His eyes roved over her, from her bare feet, the toes of which were wriggling in the streamside mud, up her legs, over his shorts and T-shirt, which were too big for her but suddenly felt revealing, to her rumpled hair, resting finally on her lips. Then he smiled . . . with an odd, knowing look on his face.

"What?" she asked.

He lifted an eyebrow in question.

"Why are you looking at me like that?"

"You were dreaming about me."

"Wh-what?" *The nerve of him!*

"You were making sexy sounds and movements while you slept, and then you said my name."

"You're making that up." She refused to ask what sounds and what movements for fear of what he might reveal. But she'd really like to know how long he'd been watching her as she slept, and why.

"No, I'm not." His eyes were smoldering with some heated emotion, and more than a little promise. Of what, she dared not ask.

Her face heated with embarrassment. Oh, this was too much. First, she had to live with the way she'd behaved in Luc's arms the night before. Now, she had to live down what she'd allegedly done in her sleep.

"I love your shyness, Sylv." Luc was bending over the five-gallon bucket, checking on his crawfish, as he spoke in a voice gravelly with appreciation.

"Where did that ridiculous statement come from?" she demanded. Really, the man had a way of disconcerting her. She'd come out here all prepared to tell him how things were going to be between them from now on, and he'd thrown her off guard by mentioning her dreams—which were coming back to her with graphic detail—and her shyness, which he knew had to be a sore spot with her.

"You were blushing so sweetly, like you always do," he explained, standing upright and arching his shoulders back to work out the kinks. "And I realized how much I like that shy side of your personallity."

"As if I care what—" She started to say something about how she couldn't care less what he thought of her shyness, but he put up a halting hand so he could continue.

"I understand . . . at least, I've been told . . . that you hate your shyness . . . that you've even had therapy to deal with it. But I've gotta say, babe, that there's something really appealing about a woman who can be hot in bed and shy over breakfast."

"You . . . you . . . you . . ." she sputtered.

"See?" he said, patting her on the behind as he walked by on his way back to the crab net in the water. "Your face is turning red again. You have the prettiest blush, *chère*."

Outraged, she tossed her notebook and pen to the ground and stomped after him, right into the water. "Number one, my shyness is none of your business. Number two, I am not hot in bed."

"Too bad," he said drolly. "I know you're a hot kisser; so, I just assumed—"

"Assumption is the mother of all screwups." She inhaled deeply to calm herself, and continued. "Number three, my face is red . . . not because I'm blushing, but because I'm furious. You . . . you . . . you . . ."

He just grinned at her . . . which was the last straw. She shoved him in the chest, causing him to lose his footing and fall backwards into the murky water. But in the process, the brute grabbed ahold of her leg, pulling her down with him.

When he came shooting up from the water, he flicked his hair back off his face and laughed. When she came up from the water, there was duckweed in her hair and brackish water in her mouth and she was choking, not laughing. He was still laughing joyously, splashing water at her in a teasing fashion like a little boy.

But Sylvie had gone stone still as she combed her fingers through her hair. She'd just noticed that the top button of Luc's cutoffs had come undone and the denim pants were riding low on his hips, exposing his navel and part of his flat stomach.

Luc's laughter stopped abruptly, and she thought she'd been caught in the act of ogling him. But no, he was staring at her, lips parted, eyes glazed. She looked

down and could have died. She might as well have been
naked for all the coverage the wet fabric provided.

With as much dignity as Sylvie could muster, she
walked stiffly out of the water, up the bank, and pointedly picked up her notebook and pen. "You and I have
to talk," she told Luc then.

He looked at her face, then at the notebook, then back
to her face again. "If you pull out a measuring tape, Sylv,
I swear I'm gonna wrap it around your neck."

We're all just ducks, really. Nibble, nibble . . .

A short time later, Luc was lolling in the hammock, one
arm propped behind his head, the other dangling a
long-necked beer over the side from loose fingers, while
Sylvie acted the dedicated scientist. He was about to
fulfill an agreement he and Sylvie had just negotiated.
The gist of it was that she was going to "interview" him
about his sexuality. *Be still, my heart, and other body
parts.* He didn't know about Sylvie, but personally, he
was planning on having a great time with this interview.

Sylvie sat on a wide tree stump several feet away.
Her long legs were extended forward and crossed at the
ankles while she took notes with so much seriousness
you'd think the future of mankind was at stake . . .
instead of the libidos of mankind. If she knew how
good her bare legs and feet . . . even her cute toes . . .
looked to him, she would run for the hills.

*I wonder how she'd look with pink toenails. Better
yet, I wonder how she'd react if I suggested painting
her toenails for her. Not that I've ever painted anyone's toenails before, but I remember someone doing
that to Susan Sarandon in* Bull Durham. *Was it Kevin*

Costner? Or that whiz-kid pitcher? Whoever! It sure as hell worked for me. Maybe I could . . . yikes, maybe I'd better focus on the subject at hand.

"Tell me again about our contract," he encouraged her, wanting to get his mind off her toes. Who would have guessed his erotic fantasies ran to feet?

"Well, it's not exactly a contract."

Uh-oh. "Hey, I'm a lawyer, remember? An oral agreement is most definitely a contract."

"Oh, all right, a contract, then," she said with exasperation.

He'd been needling her with questions about their agreement for the past fifteen minutes while his brain tried to register the fact that Ms. Cool-as-a-Cucumber Sylvie Fontaine wanted to ask him questions about scx. *Sex,* for God's sake!

He couldn't recall any woman asking him such questions in the past unless she was drunk, or unless he was buried ten inches inside of her . . . well, okay, maybe not quite ten inches. *How about nine?* Yep, if he was going to fantasize, nine was a perfectly good number.

He grinned to himself, especially as the word "delusional" came to mind, and Sylvie glared at him, not understanding why he was grinning.

Should I tell her?

Nah.

"Stop looking at me like that," she said.

"Like what?" He batted his eyelashes innocently. "Oh, you mean like with pleasure . . .'cause you were dreaming about me?"

"I . . . was . . . not . . . dreaming . . . about . . . you," she informed him through gritted teeth.

"Uh-hum," he conceded with a wink.

"Back to our 'contract.' I'll help you with your water pollution tests, even to the extent of appearing in court, if necessary. And in return, you'll cooperate with the JBX experiment."

"I'm not taking any more jelly beans." Another dose of that love potion and he might just reach that magic number nine. Either that, or explode.

"I know that. I meant cooperate, as in answering questions and giving me data related to the effects of the formula you've already taken."

"And you're going to take the pirogue with me tomorrow down to Bayou Noir, where we'll spend the day gathering new samples."

"I already said I would . . . though I don't see why we can't wait till we get back to Houma. Everything doesn't have to be so clandestine."

He frowned at her.

"I gave you my word, Luc. Do you want it in writing?"

"Weeelll . . ." He drew the word out, making sure she knew he didn't trust her totally . . . any more than she trusted him totally.

"Why is the shrimpers' plight so important to you, Luc? Is it just because your brother is involved?"

He shook his head, suddenly serious. "Water pollution should be important to everyone, not just the shrimpers. The threat of sickness, even cancer, is real. But as to my involvement"—he shrugged—"fishing defines the Gulf, Sylv, you know that, especially shrimp fishing. More than that, it's a Cajun way of life. Take that away, and you take away our heritage."

She stared at him steadily, and he could imagine that her brain was working overtime. *Lucien LeDeux. The Swamp Solicitor. Takes on every unwinnable case in creation.* "You sound as if shrimp fishing is being dealt a death blow," she said.

"It is. Maybe not today, but the death blow is sure as

hell on the horizon if something isn't done soon. I wouldn't be surprised if the shrimp of the future come strictly from shrimp farms."

"And that would be so horrible?"

"That would be more than horrible." He hated even talking about what was happening to the fishing industry in Louisiana . . . in fact, to the whole bayou ecosystem. "The shrimpers are already beset with hundreds of government regulations, wetland erosion, foreign competition, fights with the sport fishermen, overdemand, population growth and residential development, farm runoff . . . and God only knows what the effects of global warming will be. The contaminants being released into the shrimp breeding grounds by the oil companies are the last straw."

"But there are so many problems," she argued. "I just don't see how your . . . *our* . . . efforts can make a difference. It's like dog paddling against a tidal wave."

"Don't discount the duck theory, Sylv."

"And that would be?"

"Nibbling away like ducks," he explained with a smile. "I know we can't correct all the problems. There are dozens of environmental and other special-interest groups out there trying to correct some of them. If we attack the oil companies one at a time on their pollution policies, and others hit them on dredging offenses, or political corruption, or whatever, eventually . . . well, eventually we'll have nibbled them away, like ducks."

"Or at least given them a few duck bites," she said with a smile.

"Bingo," he agreed, smiling back at her. And it wasn't just her duck-bite comment that he was smiling about. He couldn't get over the fact that Sylvie had been dreaming about him. And she *had been*, no matter what she said.

"So, you and I and René and the shrimpers involved in this fight are ducks, right?"

"Quack-quack." He hesitated a moment before adding, "There is something else we want from you."

She sat up, alert with suspicion.

"Sometimes we Cajuns are a bit aggressive in fighting the oil companies . . . hell, even our Cajun brothers and sisters aren't all supporting us. Many of them work on the oil rigs, for chrissake. So, I figure we should try a different tactic from the usual cancer scare when we go public with whatever damning information we gather."

"I'm listening," she said warily when he paused to decide just the right way to broach the subject.

"Well, we've discovered some scientific data that shows that petroleum by-products can affect the sperm counts in fish. If it can affect fish virility, maybe it does the same thing with male humans. What better way to get the public behind us than to threaten a man's sexual prowess?"

Sylvie thought a moment. "I'm beginning to see the light. You figured since I'm a scientist who works with testosterone and hormones, I would be the perfect person to help you out."

He felt his ears heat up, but he held his chin high.

"You rat! You told me that you wanted me to work with you because I was the only one you could trust."

"There is that, too, Sylv. Honest."

"I don't know what to believe."

"I've told you why the shrimpers' case is important to me, Sylv. Now you tell me why JBX is so important to you."

She hesitated, at first . . . unwilling to share her secrets. "I know you consider the love-potion experiment a huge joke, and I admit there are some aspects that lend themselves to humor. But this is very serious business to me. If I told you I was working on a new birth-control pill, or a new estrogen-replacement program, you'd be clapping me on the back in encouragement. It really isn't such a far stretch to manipulating testosterone and hormone levels for aphrodisiacal purposes."

He put up one hand in surrender, the other one still held the beer.

"And, okay, I might as well admit it, there's a little bit of vanity involved, too," she added.

His only response was a lift of one eyebrow, and another sip of beer.

"I come from a family of high achievers. Everyone knows my mother, the politician; my aunts, the herbal-tea queens; my cousin Valerie, the Court TV sensation. All the Breaux women are huge successes. By comparison, I'm just a mousy little scientist doing hackwork who will never rise to any great level of success. Maybe my family will lay off me if I can provide just one super-achievement."

"Sylvie! Don't you dare fall into that trap of allowing other people to define you. If you enjoy what you do, and you do the best job you can, then that is success. And dammit, it doesn't matter if that job is laying a roof or climbing Mt. Everest . . . or . . . or playing with a Bunsen burner."

She smiled at his vehemence. "Is that why you take on such outrageous cases, and deliberately give the appearance of being a lazy shyster lawyer?"

"Who says I'm lazy?" he asked with mock affront. "But Sylv, I still can't reconcile your alleged shyness with the publicity this love-potion business is going to generate. Are you prepared to run the gamut of TV talk shows? Are you prepared for the jealousy of your peers? Are you prepared for the potshots Jay Leno and David

Letterman are going to take at you? Are you prepared to open your private life to public scrutiny?"

She looked at him with horror. "Of course not! I *do* want recognition for my work, but I will never allow myself to be the spokesperson for the project. Never!"

"You might not be able to prevent it, Sylv. Be prepared."

"And one more thing, buddy, I'm tired of your innuendoes about my shyness being a scam or nonexistent. Believe me, my shyness was a terrible problem at one time . . . a handicap, really. And it took a long, long time to get this far, overcoming its sometimes debilitating effects; so, lay off the shyness remarks."

"Yes, ma'am," he said, saluting her with the longneck.

"I suspect your constant teasing is a cover-up for something, Luc. I just haven't figured out what it is yet."

Time to change the subject, Luc decided. "I thought you wanted to ask me questions about the love potion, not fish, or your shyness, or my lack of ambition."

"I do, I do. I just got sidetracked a little."

"Let's get started, then, before I fall asleep." Actually, he *was* tired, not having taken advantage of a nap while Sylvie had slept the morning away.

Sylvie poised her notebook on her lap, looking businesslike. "What's your name?"

Oh, God! She's going to bore me to sleep. "Lucien Michael LeDeux."

"Age?"

"Thirty-three."

"Health?"

"Perfect."

"No problems?"

"None."

"Have you ever had a vasectomy?"

He almost choked on his beer. "Hell, no. Have you had your tubes tied?"

She blushed. "These are just routine questions, Luc." She was fidgeting around now, scribbling in the notebook, and he could tell she was avoiding asking him her next question.

He perked up, and waited.

Sylvie didn't disappoint him.

"How old were you when you had your first sexual experience?"

Chapter Twelve

This was the most fun test he'd ever taken . . .

"How old was I when I had my first sexual experience?" he repeated, biting his bottom lip to stifle an outright laugh.

She nodded her head.

"Solitary or in the company of another person?" he asked, still trying to keep a straight face.

"Well, solitary, for starters."

Starters? Damn, she is something. "Five."

"Five what?"

"Five years old. You asked me when I had my first solitary sexual experience, and—"

"Five years old!" Her eyes almost popped out, but then she seemed to recall the fact that this was a professional interview. "Can you recall the circumstances that prompted your . . . uh, arousal?"

"Sesame Street."

"Whaaattt?"

"Yep, the letter B." He nodded his head, as if in re-membrance. "I've had a fondness for the letter B ever since then."

"Luc, could you please be serious?"

"I'm being very serious. Would you like to tell me about *your* sexual experiences?"

"Dream on."

"Dreams. Oh, yes! Of course, I've had *lots* of dreams. I'll tell you about my dreams if you'll tell me about yours."

"Would you stop with the dream business? I was not dreaming about you."

"Whatever you say, *chère.*"

"You look idiotic when you smile at me like that."

"Like what?"

"Slow and sexy."

"Who's the liar now, Sylv? Slow and sexy do not go with idiotic. No way." He shook his head. "So, you think my smiles are slow and sexy, huh?"

"Aaarrgh!"

"Do you have any more questions for me before I take a little afternoon snooze? Some of us didn't sleep all morning," he pointed out.

"All right. When did you have your first sexual rela-tionship . . . one that involved sexual intercourse?"

Well, no beating around the bush with Sylvie. Noth-ing like coming straight to the point. Well, I can be blunt, too. "Twelve."

She closed her eyes as if her questions, or his an-swers, were painful to her.

"Could you elaborate, please? No, don't tell me de-tails. Just an overview."

"An overview?" He grinned. Lord, but she was some

kind of a nutcase. "The cloakroom of Our Lady of the Bayou School, during recess."

Sylvie's mouth went slack-jawed, and he knew she was imagining him as a twelve-year-old kid. That was the same year he'd asked her to dance with him, and she'd refused. She had to be wondering who the girl had been.

"You were certainly precocious," she commented when she was finally able to speak.

He ducked his head sheepishly. "I probably set a record with my world-class, thirty-second screw."

"It was Mary-Louise Delacroix, wasn't it?" Sylvie blurted out. "The slut!" He could tell she immediately regretted her hasty words.

"Syl-vie! It's not nice to call people names. Mary-Louise wasn't really a bad girl. One thing just led to another and bingo-bango. We were just two kids, experimenting . . . and rather clumsily, at that."

"I did not need to know all that," Sylvie muttered under her breath. "Let's fast-forward to the present. We can fill in some of these other details later."

"Whatever you say, babe."

"When was the last time you had sex?"

"Define sex."

She groaned.

He took mercy on her. Besides, her face was so red he feared she might have a stroke. "I had sex *with a woman* six months ago."

"Six months?" She was clearly surprised, no doubt expecting him to live up to his wild reputation. She probably thought he had sex daily, even several times a day. *Hardly.*

"I'm selective," he explained. "And one-night stands don't have the appeal they did at one time."

She nodded, apparently in agreement.

206Sandra Hill

"How often do you come to orgasm during a typical sexual encounter?"

He shot a startled glance her way. Well, she'd certainly blindsided him with that one. When he regained his breath, he chuckled. "Six times."

She peered up at him with skepticism. "Liar."

He winked. Then decided to elaborate. "I never lie, but occasionally I do bend the hell out of the truth."

Her upper lip curled with distaste.

"When did *you* have sex last?" he asked, turning the tables on her.

"This interview isn't about me," she said primly.

"Fair is fair."

She thought a minute, then revealed, "A year ago."

"Unh, unh, unh. Isn't that a wee bit of a fib, sweetheart? I saw birth-control pills in your briefcase yesterday."

She sliced him with a glare. "I take birth-control pills all the time, to regulate menstrual flow. Lots of women do. So, believe me, when I say it's been a year, it has been."

"Well, holy moley, Sylv! The pump should be primed on both of us, then, even without the love potion. Why don't you hop up on this hammock with me, and we'll see what swings?"

She sliced him with a glare which he assumed meant, "No hopping! No hammock! No swinging! *Nada*."

"Back to *my* questions," she said. "How often do you think about sex each day?"

What a question! He exhaled with a whoosh. Hadn't he read an article one time that said men think about sex every fifteen seconds or so? And it hadn't even been in *Playboy*; it had been in *Psychology Today*, or one of those airplane mags. He didn't want to appear too sex-crazed, though, so he said, "Once every five minutes, I suppose." It was probably more than that when he was fishing and less when he was in court, but what the hell.

"And since the love potion?"

"Once a minute."

"Okay, let's get down to the intimate stuff."

"This wasn't intimate already? Maybe I'd better go for a cold swim before we start."

"Stop teasing."

"Who's teasing?"

"Tell me, in general terms, how you've been feeling since you took the jelly beans."

"Like hell."

"Could you be a little more specific?"

"You said 'in general.' How was I supposed to . . . oh, all right. If you keep frowning like that, your face is gonna freeze . . . that's what Tante Lulu always says. Let's see . . . at first, I experienced just a twinge of arousal, thinking about you. It didn't happen when I thought about anyone else. I even tested that theory the first night. I tried thinking about some very sexy ladies I know. Only a mild response. Even thoughts of Pamela Anderson, who isn't really my type, but, let's face it, she has a body that could turn an Apostle to sin . . . well, even she only generated a spark. But *you!* Bonfire city!"

She blushed becomingly and tried to hide it by lowering her head. But he saw, and was pleased.

"JBX is about more than sex. Have you experienced any emotional reaction?"

"Does a frog have warts? Yes, yes, yes. And that's the worst part of this whole jelly-bean mess. I hate it, Sylv. I really do."

She tilted her head in confusion. "Explain."

"If I didn't know better, I'd think I was falling in love with you," he confessed unwisely, "which is ridiculous, of course."

"Of course," she said, but couldn't hold back a wince at his hurtful sentiment.

"Not that I really know what *love*-love is."

"You've never been in love before?" She didn't even try to hide the surprise in her voice.

"Never. In like, yeah. In lust, lots of times. But not really love of the man-woman kind. How about you?"

She astounded him by answering, without protest. "No. I thought I was a few times, but it couldn't have been love if I got over it so fast."

"Not even with your husband?"

"Nope."

"Not even Charles?"

"Most definitely not Charles." Then: "Stop looking so smug."

He couldn't help himself. There was an inexplicable satisfaction in knowing Sylvie had never loved another man, as if she'd been waiting for him. *Aaarrgh!* He chose to blame that brain blip on the love potion. Love was dangerous territory he had no intention of entering. Best to steer clear of that land mine. He hadn't teased Sylvie in a second or so, so he opted for that love sinker. "Hell, Sylv, I can't be having the woman who dreams about me lovin' another man."

"I told you, I was not dr—"

"Yeah, yeah, yeah," he said, waving a hand dismissively. "When do we get to the good part with this interview?"

"The *good* part?"

"Physical stimulus to test sensory results." He waggled his eyebrows at her. "Interpretation: making out."

"You are impossible."

"Yeah," he agreed amiably. "So I guess that means never."

"That would be correct."

"I'd even let you take notes."

"Dream on, buster."

"I intend to," he said, closing his eyes, suddenly bone-weary and in need of a little nap. Yawning, he decided, "We'll have to finish the interview later, babe."

"Okay."

He cracked one eye open to watch her walk toward the house, notebook in hand, heart-shaped ass swaying to and fro in his nylon shorts. "I hope my dreams are as *interesting* as yours were," he called out to her.

Sylvie's bare feet faltered in the dirt, but she didn't turn around.

He drifted off to sleep then, and as the breeze swung him gently in the hammock, Luc did dream. And the star of his dreams was slow-dancing, nude.

It was bound to happen . . .

It was Luc who had taken the love potion, but Sylvie was the one who felt as if she were under the influence.

Earlier, Luc had likened the effects of JBX to a wave . . . not a steady, overpowering arousal, but something that ebbed and flowed. It was different with Sylvie, who didn't even have a love potion to blame. In her case, there was a steady buildup of sexual tension in her body that threatened to explode eventually into the Big Kahuna of all waves of excitement.

She'd better be prepared to surf or swim when it finally hit; otherwise, Luc was going to mow her down. And not with his surfboard, either.

"Sylv, you're not paying attention," Luc chided her. He was sitting next to her at the kitchen table chopping meats and veggies for a potluck jambalaya, while Sylvie was peeling some of the crawfish to throw in his pot.

"I am so paying attention," she lied. "You were telling me another of your crazy Cajun legends . . . this time about crawfish." That was what Sylvie said, but what she was thinking was, *Boy, does he smell good! I wonder if I smell as good to him. After all, we both used the same pine-scented soap in the shower.*

And he looked good, too, even wearing a plain old white T-shirt and jeans, with no shoes or socks. She probably looked like Orphan Annie's big sister in her sink-laundered but wrinkled slacks and silk blouse, also without shoes, and wearing no makeup.

While Luc had taken a nap in the hammock that afternoon, she'd gone inside and taken a shower, then lounged about the cabin, sipping strawberry wine from a Wile E. Coyote tumbler and reading a copy of John Grisham's *The Firm*, which she'd found upstairs in the loft bedroom. Luc had come in an hour later, yawning, with outstretched arms, which caused his denim cut-offs to drop lower on his hips. That image of exposed hipbones, flat abdomen, and half a navel would be imprinted on her memory forever.

He'd gone off to shower, as well. Now, still convinced that she wasn't paying attention, he remarked with a chuckle, "First, you dream about me; now you daydream about me. Hot damn."

"I did not . . . I was not . . . oh, never mind," was her brilliant response.

He chucked her playfully under the chin as they continued to prepare an early dinner. "As I was saying, some people believe that the crawfish is descended from lobsters who followed the French Acadians when they were booted out of Canada and were forced to travel down to Louisiana. The farther they traveled, the tireder and smaller the lobsters became, till they were whittled down to the size of these little mudbugs here."

He cracked one of the critters and stuck the head in his mouth to suck out the rich meat, raw, then made a smacking noise of appreciation with his lips.

As Sylvie watched with fascination the sucking motion of his lips and the mischievous glimmer of his dark eyes, something new and primeval tugged inside her heart. He was a sinfully attractive man.

Luc winked at her.

Sylvie was mortified that he'd seen her reaction to him.

Then he shoved a crawfish in her mouth with the order "Suck." She did, and was pleased to see his mouth part and his eyes darken and dilate as he watched her make quick work of the delicious meat.

"I think you make up half these stories," she said, not wanting to think about his mouth or his eyes.

"Mais oui, chère, but that is the best part of being a Cajun. Back to my legend, which you so rudely interrupted. Those crawfish-nee-lobsters who emigrated from the north liked the Cajuns so much that they emulated them, even down to the way they built their homes with mud chimneys. In some low-lying streams, around water-logged cypress trees, you can still see dozens of those chimneys—a village of crawfish—each chimney telling you there's a crawfish sleeping below, just waiting to be caught."

"You're a great storyteller, Luc."

He grinned at her. "I know."

"Did you hear about the Creole who went to heaven? When he arrived at the Pearly Gates, he asked St. Peter if they had crawfish there. When St. Peter said no, the man told him he might just as well go home."

"Tsk-tsk, Sylv. I've heard that story before, but it was a Cajun, not a Creole. And it was gumbo, not crawfish."

She laughed. "The one thing your people and mine . . .

the Cajuns and the Creoles . . . have in common is good food," she remarked.

"Yep, except that the Cajun dishes are more down-home and basic, while the Creole dishes are uptown-fancy."

"I don't know about that."

"Really? Do you know why red beans and rice is a popular Cajun meal?"

She shook her head slowly, smiling to herself. This pleasant Luc was a new person to Sylvie, and one she was enjoying very much.

"Red beans were traditionally cooked by Cajun women on a Monday, which was, of course, wash day."

"Of course." She smiled outwardly now.

"Shush your sarcastic mouth, babe." He tapped her on the lips with a forefinger. "This allowed the beans to cook for many hours without being tended. Even today, Monday is red beans and rice day in most Cajun households."

"As I said, you're a great storyteller."

"Now it's your turn. Tell me a Creole legend."

"Well, there was supposedly a rich planter living in Southern Louisiana during the 1700's who wanted to provide a spectacular wedding for his daughter. So, he imported thousands of silkworms from China. He fed them powdered gold, which caused them to spin gold thread throughout all the trees in his live-oak alley. Supposedly, this was the origin of the Spanish moss in our trees."

"Sylvie! I never took you for a romantic."

"But I prefer the Houma Indian legend about the Spanish moss. It's said there was once a Houma Indian princess who was killed by an enemy tribe during her wedding ceremony. In despair, her mourning family cut off all her luxuriant hair and spread it on the limbs of the oak tree under which she was buried. A fierce wind came up—probably her spirit—and the strands of hair blew here and there, landing in other tree limbs. Over time, the black hairs turned to gray. And, *voila*, our current Spanish moss—a tribute to those who are ill-fated in love."

"Yep, a one-hundred-proof romantic," Luc declared with noticeable delight.

Eventually, they prepared and ate the meal, which was plain, but sumptuous. Boiled crawfish, dipped in melted butter, as an appetizer. A potluck jambalaya that contained crawfish, Cajun sausage, chunks of Spam, and canned chicken. Luc had surprised her with his talent for making light-as-air beaten biscuits, from scratch. She'd made her great-grandmother's recipe for Creole "dirty rice." On the side, they nibbled at a pokeweed and vinegar salad. All washed down with cold beer. For dessert, they had the last of Tante Lulu's beignets and rich cafe au lait.

As good as the food was, the best part was working side by side with Luc. There was an underlying sexual tension ricochetting between them, but more important, and more alarming, a sense of friendship.

She was growing to like Luc LeDeux, and that was a road that led to inevitable heartbreak. That, combined with the sexual attraction that was growing between them by leaps and bounds, made her feel needy and pathetic. Like a timid teenager with a first crush.

They finished cleaning up the dishes and the kitchen and Luc pulled out a map, which he spread over the table. "I want to show you the route we'll be taking tomorrow," he said, and ran a forefinger along a line indicating a bayou. From the cabin to the spot Luc indicated was roughly twenty miles. Sylvie wasn't in bad physical shape, but she wasn't sure she was up to *that* much paddling.

"I still don't see why we have to travel so far in a pirogue to get water samples when we could wait till next week and do it in comfort by motorboat."

Luc thought for a moment. The only sounds were of BeauSoleil's latest album "Cajunization," which was playing on a portable CD player on the counter, as it had been all through dinner. The music, like Luc, was outrageous, and soulful, and teasing, and fun.

"This is the best way, Sylv. We can maneuver the pirogue into some back bayous that aren't accessible by motorboat. And there's the element of surprise. No one would expect us to show up in Cypress Oil's backyard while they're looking for us. Besides, rushing in there by motorboat would be tantamount to shouting our presence with a foghorn."

She shrugged. "I suppose you're right." But she had something else on her mind now. All this time spent with Luc and she was failing to work on the most important thing in her life—the love potion.

"Why are you looking at me funny?" Luc asked.

"I was just wondering if I could take your pulse now . . . while you're . . . uh, normal. I need to get a base pulse for you, to measure against those times when you're . . . uh, not normal."

He threw his head back and laughed. "Oh, Sylv! What makes you think I'm *normal* now?"

"Give me a break. We're talking about maps and pirogues and oil pollution. In the midst of all that dry stuff, you can't possibly be . . ." She let her words trail off.

"Aroused?" He grinned.

"Yeah," she snapped.

"Exactly what do you consider normal?"

"Oh, forget it," she said. "I'll take your pulse later, when you least expect it . . . maybe when you're sleeping or something."

"Don't you dare sneak up on me when I'm sleeping. I won't be responsible for my actions, then."

Oh, the heck with it! She grabbed for his wrist and began to silently count the pulse beats. He had to be kidding about not being "normal" right now. A minute later, her eyes shot up to connect with Luc's. His heart was racing a mile a minute.

"I told you," he said in a voice gravelly with desire.

She dropped his hand like a hot coal and walked over to the counter on wobbly legs. While BeauSoleil belted out the rollicking swamp rocker "*Tu Vas Voir*," or "Can't You See," she nervously flipped through the half-dozen CDs sitting next to the player. One of them caused her to arch her eyebrows and hold the disk up to Luc for inspection. " 'One Night With You'? Luther Vandross? You?"

Luc laughed. "Nah. That make-out music belongs to René. He brought a girlfriend here one time last year."

On an impulse, or perhaps to be perverse, Sylvie pressed the eject button, took out BeauSoleil, and inserted the make-out king. Immediately, a clear, male voice rang out with the love song "Always and Forever."

"Uh-oh," Luc said.

"What?" She pivoted on her bare feet and watched him slowly and deliberately fold up the maps on the table, straighten the chairs, turn down the lights, then hold his open arms out to her.

She was the one then who said, "Uh-oh."

"C'mon, Sylv. You can't put on that kind of music and not dance." Luther was now crooning "Endless Love."

"Have you lost your mind, Luc? Dancing is not a good idea."

"Yes, I've lost my mind. Dancing most definitely *is* a good idea. And it's time for some paybacks, darlin'."

Her head shot up at that last, and her heart skipped a beat, then went into double-time. "Now? You expect to be paid back *now*?"

"It's as good a time as any."

For the first time, it registered with Sylvie that she was alone—truly alone—with Luc. And the sexual tension that had been sizzling between them kicked up a notch. *Bam!*

"Why?"

He shrugged. "I like to dance, and I love dancing with you."

"You only danced with me once," she pointed out, trying to keep the panic from her voice.

"I know." His face turned suddenly vulnerable as he added, "Didn't you enjoy dancing with me, Sylv?"

"Of course, I did, and you know it, too."

"Yeah, I guess I do," he admitted with a shy grin.

Shy? Shy and Luc LeDeux do not go together.

He beckoned with the fingers of both outstretched hands for her to come closer.

She inched her way slowly, reluctantly, the whole time groaning inwardly. She had given her word to Luc, and she was not a person who went back on her word. *But dancing? In a remote cabin? With Luther Vandross music? And Luc? And, oh, my God, in the nude!* She did a full-body shiver as she stepped into his arms.

"Are you afraid of me, *chère*?" he murmured against her hair.

"Yes." *But not half as afraid as I am of myself.*

"I'm afraid of you, too," he confided, and the whisper of his breath against her exposed ear was excruciatingly sensual.

It was either kismet or total coincidence that Luther then swung into the torchy "One Night With You."

Was that what Luc was hoping for?

Was that what she was hoping for?

Were they both nuts?

They were silent for a while, letting the music seep into their bodies, leading them in the rhythm of the slow dance. Her face rested against his clean-shaven cheek. Her left hand curved around the nape of his neck under his too-long hair. His right arm was wrapped tightly around her waist, aligning her body tantalizingly against his. His left hand held her right pressed up against his heart, which thudded madly.

Not once did Sylvie think of checking his pulse or pulling out her notebook. At some point, without thinking, she had crossed a line. She no longer fought the pull of Luc's seduction. In truth, she was powerless to resist him now.

"I surrender, *chère*." His lips were nuzzling her hair as he spoke in a voice gritty with sex. "I can't fight these feelings for you anymore."

Sylvie went immediately alert . . . or as alert as she could be in her passion-hazy condition. Were their minds really so well attuned? Would their bodies be attuned, too?

No, no, no, she couldn't think that far ahead. They weren't going to make love. They were only dancing.

Only dancing? Hah! Who was she kidding? Slow dancing with Luc *was* like making love.

As if to emphasize that point, Luc released the hand held against his chest. He had one arm still wrapped around her waist, but now used his free hand to roam her back and buttocks, the whole time persuading her with soft, barely coherent words to move even closer, perfecting the fit of their two bodies—breast to chest, groin to groin, and thigh to thigh. Every beat of the slow dance gave her proof of his arousal.

When Sylvie could stand no more of this exercise in torture, she rubbed her breasts against his chest . . . back and forth . . . just once.

A low hissing sound came from between Luc's teeth, and she thought she might have moaned, but it was hard to tell, so overwhelming was the intense pleasure emanating from her nipples, which yearned for more abrasion. She wore the silk blouse and slacks she'd had on when they'd left Houma, but, oh, how she wished she were a more uninhibited woman. She would like nothing more than to feel her bare breasts against Luc's chest . . . to have him kiss her there . . . and place his lips . . . oh, too many wicked thoughts and impossible wishes assailed her. Too much to assimilate, especially when Luc was moving his lips along her jawline, closer and closer to her mouth, which she clamped shut for fear he might hear the sound of her panting.

Sylvie should stop this now. She was way out of her league with a man like Luc LeDeux. If she didn't put a halt to this, he would soon discover just how inexpert she was in love matters . . . how pathetic she was in her need for him.

"Luc, no, wait," she tried to say as he whisked his mouth briefly across hers.

"Shhh, Sylv," he said against her lips. "Let me . . . oh, please, just let me . . ."

Sylvie didn't really want him to stop . . . she had to admit that. Instead of pushing him away, she arched her neck and made a low purring sound deep in her throat.

The anticipation of his kiss was a carnal joy . . . a

goal in itself. But, no, he was kissing her now, and she was wrong. The kiss itself was so much more than the anticipation.

With a sigh, she allowed his coaxing lips to open hers and kiss her with a hunger that would have frightened her with its ferocity, if it didn't match her own.

Amazingly, the whole time this was going on, Luc was leading her in a sensuous slow dance . . . not around the room, but in a small circle . . . enough to still call it dancing and not foreplay. Except, it was that, too.

Luc was a really good dancer, she observed. But even more important, Luc was a really good kisser. *Really* good!

He touched her soul with the gentleness of his clinging kisses, then seared her libido with the rapacious appetite of his wet, open-mouthed kisses. She could not say which she preferred. When he buried himself deep in her mouth, and encouraged her to do the same with him, she felt as one with his arousal. He would not travel this erotic road alone, he was making sure of that.

Dragging his mouth from hers, he stared at her swollen lips through smoldering eyes, then nodded as if satisfied with his work. Before she knew what he was about, he moved to new territory, pulling her blouse from the waistband of her slacks, releasing the buttons in front, while he resumed nibbling kisses along the sensitive curve of her neck.

And the things he whispered to her then . . . wicked, wicked words of what he would like to do to her . . . caused Sylvie's knees to go weak and almost collapse. With a joyous laugh, he caught her and held her upright.

They stopped dancing, and with the expertise of a cat burglar, Luc somehow managed to remove her blouse and bra. The soughing of his breath could be heard above the sound of Luther spinning his magic with

"Your Secret Love." All Luc said was, "Oh, Sylvie." Then his T-shirt was gone as well, and they were dancing again, bare chest to bare chest, and nothing, *nothing*, in Sylvie's life had ever felt this good. He used one hand at the small of her back to guide her in the dance, but the fingers of the other hand were doing delicious things to her breasts . . . skimming, kneading, thrumming.

Sylvie heard a low keening sound, and at first thought it was the background singers on the CD. To her embarrassment, she realized the continuous whimper was coming from her.

Luc was lowering his head to minister to her aching breasts. When he took one breast into his mouth and began to suckle, she dug her nails into his shoulders and cried aloud with one long squeal, "Luuuuuuuucccccc!"

He stopped, and she thought he was going to take mercy on her. But she could see by his beautiful sex-hazed eyes and moist, parted lips that he would not. He was even further gone than she was. With a low masculine growl of pleasure, he attacked the other breast, bringing it to an equal pitch of throbbing need.

Sylvie was mindless with passion, and therefore unaware of Luc making quick work of removing her slacks and panties. It was only when the rasp of his zipper rang loud to her ears that she realized she had come full circle. Luc was going to get from her what he had no doubt always wanted . . . what she had promised . . . nude dancing. He had won, finally.

And she did not care.

Where was the shyness that had always been the bane of Sylvie's life? Why was she not mortified to be naked and exposed to a man's thorough scrutiny? Who was this alien, uninhibited woman who had taken over Sylvie's body?

When he took her in his arms to dance now, she relished the rasp of his chest hairs against her breasts, the whisk of his thigh hairs against her smooth legs, the press of her own hair against his raging erection. It was a dance like none she'd ever experienced before, or ever conceived possible.

It was sinful and soulful.

It was tender and raw.

It was lust and something she refused to name.

It was Luc as she, in her secret self, had always imagined he would be.

When he groaned and whispered her name in a pleading way, Sylvie arched her back and smiled. She was woman, and Luc was man, and, oh, what a wonderful, wonderful combination that was.

Somehow she found herself danced against the table, then pressed backward till she lay flat on her back with her legs dangling over the side. Wasting no time, Luc grabbed her knees, adjusting them so that her bottom was at the edge of the table and her legs flung wide. Holding her eyes, Luc pressed his palm against her and rotated. "So wet," he murmured with appreciation. "Thank you, Sylv."

"For what?" she choked out.

"For wanting me this much." His voice was hoarse with emotion and barely audible. He separated her folds with two fingers, stroked her once, twice, three times, then brought his fingers out and up to show her the moistness.

She turned her face away in embarrassment.

He forced her face back to look at him, then put the two fingertips to his lips and made long, erotic laps with his tongue over the wetness.

Sylvie's eyes went wide with surprise and a little bit of fear. Luc LeDeux was not going to be a genteel lover. He was going to be primitive and crude and rough, as he was in regular life, and he was going to demand the same of her.

But she had no time to dwell on that. Luc had dropped to his knees between her legs and was doing things with his expert tongue that would make a saint cry. She tried to rise up off the table, but he would not allow that. Instead, he plied her with fingertips, and tongue, and teeth till she was thrashing from side to side. While he worked that most sensitive part of her with his firm tongue, he moaned a continuous "Uhmmmmmmmmmm, uhmmmmmmmmmm, uhmmmmmmmmmm. . . ." which caused his tongue to vibrate against her and ripple inside her body up to her aching breasts.

Sylvie couldn't see her toes, but she was fairly certain they were curled. And her hands were clenching the sides of the table with white-knuckled intensity.

Enough! she finally thought. *I can't take much more of this.* Drawing on unknown reserves of strength, she reared up, shimmied her tush toward the middle of the table, and grabbed his hair in both hands, pulling him up toward her. If he wouldn't let her down, then he was coming up.

Without protest, he settled himself atop her on the hard table and kissed her greedily. She tasted herself on Luc's tongue, and should have been repulsed, but was not. This was sex at its rawest best. She'd never experienced it before, but she damn well intended to now.

Luc was out of control, as he'd never been in his entire life. He couldn't believe he was making love with Sylvie Fontaine. Talk about getting lucky!

She was lying on the table, arms and legs outspread, hair wild, eyes luminous with passion, lips swollen and moist from his kisses. And she was staring at him as if he was the sexiest stud to come down the bayou since

Dennis Quaid. A heady aphrodisiac, that. Not that he needed any more aphrodisiacs in his life.

With a low masculine growl, he took her hand and guided it to his erection, which pressed against her pubic hair like a steel rod. "God, I want you so much," he said huskily.

She put her free hand to his face, cupped his cheek gently, then ran the fingertips over his parted lips. "I want you, too," she confessed.

Sweeter words were never spoken.

With the other hand, Sylvie circled him and ran the circle up and down his shaft gently, which caused tiny explosions of red stars to burst behind his eyeballs. Then, without any prompting, she raised her knees so her feet were braced flat on the table, spread her legs wide, and guided him inside her.

He gritted his teeth, his neck reared back, and he groaned loud and long, "Oh . . . my . . . God!"

"Oh, my God!" she echoed. "You . . . you fill me."

That about said it all. "Ah, *chère*, you are so hot . . . and tight . . . and wet."

Her inner folds were welcoming him with little spasms that caused him to grow even more. This was heaven on earth, being inside Sylvie.

Her eyes kept going wider and wider, as if she couldn't believe what was happening down below. He chose to take that as a good sign.

Sylvie's body held him in such a snug sheath that he wasn't sure he would be able to move. But he needed to move with an urge that was primordial and overwhelming. Bracing himself on straightened arms . . . with the greatest, most infinite care, he began to pull himself out, almost all the way . . . an excruciatingly pleasurable exercise, considering the way her muscles dragged on him to stay.

She moaned.

"Am I hurting you?" he asked, stopping and gazing down at her.

She shook her head. "Am I hurting you?"

He laughed joyfully at the naivete of her question. "Yes, but only in the nicest way."

There was no more talking after that as he began the serious business of making love with Sylvie. Lord, that had a good sound to it. *Making love with Sylvie.*

At first, his thrusts were long and deliberately slow. Sylvie caught his rhythm and met him stroke for stroke. Luther Vandross was still belting out his gooey love lyrics, but Luc much preferred the wet sounds of their lovemaking as they slid and smacked against each other. They could not keep this slow pace for long, though, and soon he was pounding against her, hard and fast. Sylvie held tightly to the sides of the table; otherwise, he might ride her right off the surface and onto the floor. At the very least, if they were not careful, there were going to be scrapes on his kneecaps and splinters in Sylvie's butt from the hard table. But who the hell cared now!

Sylvie was moaning almost continuously now, "Oh, oh, oh, oh, oh . . ." When he felt her entire body go stiff, and her hips arch up off the table, he threw his head back, let loose with a guttural, masculine growl of supreme satisfaction, and thrust into her one last time. Sylvie convulsed around him, violently at first as he shot his very essence into her, then with progressively smaller spasms till he felt as if he'd been milked dry.

Luc let his weight come down on top of Sylvie, who looked like a rag doll spread-eagled on the table. A very satisfied doll with a Cheshire cat grin on her face. He kissed her tenderly.

Then, as his eyes drifted shut in utter depletion, he thought he heard someone say, "I love you."

The alarming thing was, he didn't know if the words were spoken by him, or her, or if he'd imagined them.

Chapter Thirteen

Beware of men with "good ideas" . . .

"Hey, Luc, I just got a great idea for promoting JBX. A surefire side effect that will blast this product off the shelves."

Luc, who was still plastered heavily atop her body, murmured into her neck, "Uh-oh. Beware of women with great ideas immediately following sex."

She pounded him lightly on the back with a closed fist.

But whoa! Now that she'd "awakened" the sleeping beast, he was nibbling at the smooth skin of her shoulder, and squirming. The squirming was the worst part, or the best part, depending on one's position, she supposed. For sure, there were some specific erotic zones on her body that were being given a "Howdy" wake-up call.

"Well, what's the great idea for promoting JBX?" Luc

inquired, then began doing the most astonishing things with his tongue in her ear. It involved a fluttering tongue tip, wetness, and blowing.

So distracted was she that, at first, his question didn't penetrate her brain. Oh, that's right, she'd told him she had a great idea for promoting JBX. He'd just sucked her earlobe into his mouth, so her answer came out with a little squeal. "Super sex."

"Well, thanks a bunch, babe. You were pretty spectacular yourself. But you still haven't told me about this great side effect of JBX."

"Super sex," she repeated.

A gurgling sound came from his mouth, which she took for strangled laughter. Then he raised his head enough to look at her through those dancing Cajun eyes of his. "Are you saying I give super sex?"

"Super-duper."

His dancing eyes danced some more, this time with mischief. "What makes you think the love potion is responsible? Maybe I give super sex all the time."

"Do you?"

"Mais oui."

She thought a moment and was slightly disappointed. She tried to tell herself it was because JBX didn't play a part in his performance, but she knew it was more than that. She wanted the sex between them to have been special because she'd been special . . . to him.

"Just kidding, darlin'," he said, taking a tiny nip at her chin. "I've never been this super in all my life. Honest."

Pleasure soared through Sylvie at those words, even though he was probably lying through his teeth.

With an expertise she was coming to expect from Luc, he rolled over onto his back, taking her with him. In fact, his semi-limp member was still imbedded in her. Anyone else would have landed them smack-dab on the floor with such a maneuver. Now *she* was splatted all over the top of *him*.

She had to admit, splatting had its good points.

"Hey, Sylv," he said with sudden, and suspicious, brightness, "you're not the only one with good ideas tonight."

"Oh, my," she said as he sat up abruptly. She wasn't sure if she'd said, "Oh, my," because of what his sitting-up did to her insides, or because he'd had an idea. Probably both.

" 'Oh, my' just about says it all," he choked out. That part of him that was still inside her had sprung to full life with his movement. With Sylvie on her knees now, perched on his lap, he wriggled his behind toward the edge of the table, taking her with him. Then he stood in one fluid move—a testament to his excellent physical condition—causing her to clutch his shoulders tightly and wrap her legs around his waist.

With a smile of self-satisfaction, Luc looked down at her breasts, which were nestled against his chest. Sylvie felt her face go hot with belated embarrassment, and she tried to press her upper body closer to hide her nakedness.

"Don't you dare go shy on me now, Sylv. The things I have in mind for you require more than a little . . . boldness," Luc warned.

"Boldness? Me?"

"In spades," Luc emphasized with a swat on her tush as he walked them toward the screen door at the front of the cabin and out onto the porch. Without any forewarning, he sank down onto one of the low rocking chairs and settled her legs, outrageously, over the arms. "Idea number one," he pronounced.

Then he began to rock.

And rock.

And rock.

Luther was still belting out his songs, which could be heard on the porch. Right now, he was into "Endless Love." Again. Yep, *endless* love just about said it all when it came to Luc LeDeux. He was proving to have an endless amount of stamina in lovemaking. Heck, *she* was proving to have an endless amount of stamina in lovemaking . . . much to her surprise.

The rocking was very slow at first, with Luc setting the pace of her rhythm with guiding hands on her hips and buttocks. Later, when the rocking grew faster and more frenzied, Sylvie didn't need his help in undulating her hips. And Luc was holding onto the top of the back spindles of the chair with white-knuckled tension.

Somehow, they ended up in the shower after that, and although their intention had been to wash away the perspiration and effects of their lovemaking, they naturally ended up creating even more. They ran out of hot water before they ever got around to shampooing their hair. Who knew a loofah and pine soap could be deemed sex toys?

Good thing their next step was to the bed, because they both fell into an exhausted slumber in each other's arms. Of course, she shouldn't have been surprised that she was awakened an hour later by a rascal who had another "idea," this one involving something called "The Perfect Fit."

She got back at him later by showing him that men did, indeed, have G-spots, just like women. Luc had been unable to speak for a good while after that. When he recovered, he spent a really long time exploring her G-spot as well, not to mention a few other letters of the alphabet . . . even the M-spot, which he claimed to have invented. It was pronounced as the "Mmmmmmm" spot.

Personally, Sylvie thought Luc was trying to live up to that fictitious six he'd given her earlier as the number of times he climaxed during a typical sexual encounter. Frankly, she didn't give two hoots why he was trying so hard. She was having the time of her life.

Toward dawn, she came to an important discovery. If she hadn't realized it before, she did now: Sylvie Fontaine had fallen in love with the "bad boy of the bayou."

Instead of being alarmed, as she most certainly should have been, the only thing that Sylvie could think was, *Does that make me the "bad girl of the bayou"?*

He had a surefire cure for shyness . . .

Sylvie awakened soon after dawn the next morning to the scent of roses.

She knew it was daylight, not because she'd opened her eyes yet, but because the sun tended to come up quickly on the bayou, like a light switch, and she could feel the bright rays on her face already.

She also felt the imprint of the hammock on her backside, through a scandalously thin, red nightie. Then, too, she felt the heat of a warm Cajun in Valentine boxers at her side. And, yes, they did glow in the dark, she recalled with a smile.

How they came to be wearing Tante Lulu's gifts, and how Luc had seduced her into trying something "really neat" in the hammock, would bring a blush to her face for eternity. Suffice it to say that she would probably have the diamond pattern of the hammock webbing imbedded in her rump for the rest of her life.

They should probably get up now and prepare for their pirogue trip to Bayou Black, but how did one get out of a hammock gracefully, without breaking a leg? Sylvie cracked open her eyelids, looked to the side, and screamed. "*Aaaccckkk!*"

"Wh-what?" Luc jackknifed to a sitting position, which caused the hammock to sway precariously, then flip them both over and onto the ground.

"Oh, my God!" Sylvie muttered under her breath as she got up on all fours, then struggled to stand and straighten out the nightie, which barely covered her essential body parts. Talk about feeling foolish the day after!

"Sylvie! Are you all right? Is there a snake?" Luc was scrambling to his feet, as well.

She shook her head.

"A gator?"

She shook her head.

"What the hell's wrong with you, then?" Luc asked, brushing off his boxers and giving undue attention to a scrape on his elbow. "I might have bruised some important body parts," he added, waggling his eyebrows at her.

Sylvie motioned with a jerk of her head toward the porch. A young boy, about ten years old, stood leaning against a support post, chomping on an apple. A small pirogue was tied up in the stream next to Luc's larger one.

"Tee-John! What are you doing here?" Luc stomped barefooted over the hard-packed dirt toward the cabin, then stood at the bottom of the steps, hands on hips, and glared at the kid.

It must be Luc's runaway brother, Sylvie realized, the one Remy had mentioned. Even with his rumpled hair and filthy jeans and a New Orleans Saints T-shirt, he resembled a miniature version of Luc.

"Hey, Luc," the boy said casually, as if it were nothing out of the ordinary for him to show up in the middle
of nowhere, uninvited.

"How did you get here?" Luc asked through gritted
teeth.

"I flew my jet. Howdja think I got here?" he answered flippantly as he tossed the apple core in a perfect line toward the cypress tree at the edge of the
stream. It hit dead center.

"You've got a smart tongue on you," Luc snarled.
"You'd better use it damn quick to explain yourself, or
you're gonna find yourself upside down in the stream
gettin' your mouth washed out with bayou slime."

"I came in a pirogue," he offered quickly. "Camped
out yesterday and paddled all by myself. I remembered
the way from that time you brought me las' summer. I
got here a couple of hours ago, but you two were makin' kissy-face in the hammock; so, I jus' went inside
and slept on the bed."

Kissy-face? If only the earth would open up and
swallow her whole! She could only imagine what else
the youngster had witnessed.

"You . . . you came here hours ago and didn't inform
me?" Luc sputtered with outrage.

Not to be put on the defensive, the kid threatened,
"Wait till I tell Tante Lulu you were putting your hand
in a girl's naughty place. Whooee!"

With a gasp at the kid's nerve, Luc sprinted up the
steps and lunged forward. But the little brat was faster.
He swerved to the side and ducked under the porch
rail. The last thing Sylvie saw was his oversized T-shirt
flapping behind him as he dashed into the trees.

Luc noticed Sylvie cowering with humiliation, and
motioned for her to come up to the cabin. She complied
because she had no choice, but her entire body—and

there was a lot of it exposed—blushed with the indignity of her appearance. And Luc noticed, too. *The lout!* Wrapping an arm around her shoulders, he kissed the top of her head, and commented, "You look great in red, *chère*. When we get out of here, I'm gonna take you to New Orleans and buy you a whole closetful of sexy, hooker red nothings."

"Don't you dare," she said, but her heart was warmed at Luc's breezy reference to a future time when they would be together. Entering the cabin, she grabbed her silk blouse off the floor near the table that had been the scene of her downfall last night and slipped it on over the nightie. "Aren't you worried about your brother? Shouldn't you go after him?"

"Hah! The stinker managed to paddle his way here. He'll be back."

Sure enough, the boy was already back, pounding up the porch steps in his pricey athletic shoes. "Now, Luc, I didn't mean nothin'. No need for fightin' with your own flesh and blood." The whole time the rascal was standing outside the screen door, brandishing an oar as a defensive weapon.

Luc laughed at the picture of the filthy imp who was no threat at all to his far superior size. "Put that paddle down before I break it over your behind. And apologize to Ms. Fontaine. Now."

Tee-John dropped the oar and ducked his head. He shuffled his shoes a few times, as if contemplating whether he really wanted to lose his pride and obey his brother's orders. Then he mumbled, "I'm sorry, ma'am."

"Come in here and tell me what happened," Luc said then, in a decidedly gruff voice. "Why did you run away? Dad didn't hit you, did he?"

"Hell, no. I'd hit 'im back if he did," the boy boasted, strolling toward the kitchen area.

"I told you before, Tee-John, to come to me if Dad ever beat up on you. And you came, so . . ." Luc, who was picking up all their pieces of clothing from the floor and stacking them neatly on a chair, apparently still worried about his father's mean temper, despite the boy's words. He spoke to the boy as if only remotely interested, but Sylvie could tell that he was more than interested . . . he was worried, and simmering with anger.

"Nah, I've learned how to hide when he's on the booze," Tee-John boasted, "just like you showed me. Do you have anything to eat for breakfast?"

Luc gave him a look of exasperation as he opened the cupboard door and pulled out a box of Froot Loops. From the fridge, he took a container of reconstituted dry milk. He put them both, along with a bowl and spoon, on the counter where the kid was already straddling a high stool. When the boy reached for them greedily, Luc held them away and glared meaningfully at him.

"Oh, okay, I ran away 'cause Mom wants to send me to a boarding school up north."

"Why?" Luc asked, releasing the food.

"She says I'm outta hand, but I think it's 'cause I interfere with her plans."

"What plans?"

"Mom always has plans. For shoppin', and decoratin' the house, and plottin' to get Dad to marry up with her. You know, plans."

Luc, still wearing only boxers, raked the fingers of one hand through his hair and sat down on another stool. "Running away is no answer."

The boy raked the fingers of one hand through his hair, just like Luc. "You did it all the time. Tante Lulu says so."

Luc muttered something about his aunt having a big mouth. Out loud, he said, "I was in physical danger.

You're not. You could have been hurt, Tee-John, being in the bayou alone."

"I was careful, Luc," the boy said in a shaky voice, "just like you showed me. And I ain't goin' to any fancy-pantsy school for rich boys."

"What's wrong with Our Lady of the Bayou School?"

"Aaaah, Sister Colette is always complainin' 'bout me . . . for the least little things."

"Sister Colette is still there? She was *my* fifth-grade teacher."

"I know," Tee-John said ruefully with a mouthful of food. "She's always sayin' I'm a bad boy, just like my brother Lucien. That's you." He gave Luc a hundred-watt "gotcha" smile.

"I know what my name is, you little brat. That's still no reason to run away and scare everyone to death. How did you know I was here, anyhow?"

"I didn't. I just figured I'd hide out here till Mom and Dad's crazy idea for a boarding school petered out. Oh, there's one other reason I came," Tee-John went on, slurping heaping spoonfuls of cereal as he talked and swiping his wet mouth with the back of a hand. "I have some important papers for you."

Luc raised his eyebrows.

"They're in my backpack over there. I overheard Dad talkin' to that slimy Deke Boudreaux from Cypress Oil. They was sayin' stuff about you and some oil bizness and how if you only knew what was in them papers they was examinin', the shit would really fly." He saw Luc's nostrils flare at his continuing bad language, and added quickly, "I'm sorry, I'm sorry."

Luc went over and picked up a red backpack near the front door. He gingerly removed several candy wrappers, an empty pop can, a styrofoam container of bait worms, a baggie containing fishing hooks, and—of all things!—a pack of Marlboro cigarettes, which caused Luc to narrow his eyes. Tee-John would be hearing more about that last item, Sylvie would bet. Then Luc unfolded some papers. He carefully scanned them, then walked over and handed them to her. "If these are legit, we should have a pretty good case, once we get the water samples today . . . don't you think?"

Sylvie skimmed over the documents quickly, which did in fact appear damning. "Tee-John, your Dad is going to kill you if he finds out these papers are missing," she pointed out.

The boy lifted his chin proudly. "I ain't stupid. I made copies down at Kinko's and put the originals back."

"You did well," Luc said then, patting his brother on the back. Then he walked over to Tee-John's backpack and proceeded to empty the garbage he'd taken from it directly to a trash can. "You shouldn't be eating so much candy," Luc chastised him.

"I'm not the only one eating candy around here. I threw those jelly beans away that fell out of your jeans last night. They were on a hook behind the bathroom door, and the pockets accidentally dumped out when the jeans fell."

"Jelly beans?" she and Luc both exclaimed as one.

"Don't tell me you didn't get rid of those JBX samples you took from my lab," she declared.

Luc's face flushed guiltily. "Well, I intended to get rid of them."

"They were all sticky and had lint on them," Tee-John went on, waving a hand airily, "or I woulda eaten 'em myself."

Sylvie groaned, and Luc just shook his head.

"Well, no harm done," Sylvie concluded. "Where are they now?"

"I threw them outside, and some ducks gobbled them up."

"What?" Sylvie was beginning to think this nightmare was never going to end.

Luc was grinning at her. He murmured in an undertone, low enough that Tee-John couldn't overhear, "Do you think ducks get hard-ons? If so, you may have a bunch of Daffy Ducks trailing after you."

"It's not funny," she said huffily.

"Yes, it is, Sylv."

"So, do you two do oral sex?" the kid asked out of the clear blue sky, which caused Luc to practically fall off his stool and Sylvie to put a hand over her face in mortification.

"John Joseph LeDeux!" Luc choked out. "Where do you get such ideas?"

"The news. All the TV news shows talk about oral sex. President Clinton does it, and I was just wonderin' if . . ." He batted his eyes with fake innocence.

Sylvie figured this would be a good time for her to slither off to the bathroom and wash her hot face. The last thing she heard was Tee-John asking a stunned Luc, "Exactly how do you do oral sex? Huh? Huh?"

The little brat probably knew exactly what oral sex was and was setting his brother up . . . deflecting attention away from himself.

"Coward," Luc called to her back with a short laugh as she slipped inside the tiny bathroom. It had no tub, just a shower stall, commode, and small sink with a mirrored medicine cabinet above it. There was also a long, narrow mirror that hung from the back of the door.

Sylvie turned to glance in that big mirror, did a double take, then sank to the floor by the far wall and started to cry. Why hadn't Luc told her how bad she looked? No wonder Tee-John snickered every time he looked at her!

Her hair was a mass of snarls. Her lips were puffy and red. Her neck and chest had brush-burns on them. What appeared to be a bite mark marred her inner thigh, up real high. She was a poster girl for sex on the hoof . . . a walking advertisement that could very easily read, "Horny Males Apply Here."

She felt an anxiety attack coming on . . . the type that had often debilitated her during her younger years as she'd struggled with shyness. Tears streamed down her face. Her skin was hot to the touch, and yet a clammy chill swept over her. She drew her knees up to her chest and wrapped her arms around herself trying to get warm. No luck. She was shivering uncontrollably. Even her teeth were chattering.

Every time she thought about what she'd done the night before . . . heck, all night long . . . she cringed with embarrassment. And this morning was the worst of all . . . having a ten-year-old boy come upon her when she was behaving with uncharacteristic wantonness. Oh, she wasn't ashamed of having made love with Luc, but she did wince with self-consciousness about her playing such an exhibitionist role. She feared appearing foolish, or pathetic, in her neediness.

There was a light rap on the door. "Sylv? Are you okay in there?"

"I'm fine," she said, but the words came out wobbly.

"Sylv?" He sounded worried now. "I'm coming in. Are you decent?" He chuckled to himself. "No, don't answer that because there's a big part of me hoping that you're not. Decent, that is."

She would have smiled at that, except that her lips were trembling.

"Sylv! My God!" Luc opened the door and shut it decisively behind him, then clicked the lock, obviously not wanting his young brother to see her like this.

Sylvie started to weep anew at the ignominiousness of her position.

"What happened?" he asked, sinking down to the floor beside her, then arranging her so that his back was to the wall and she sat between his legs, her back to his chest. Wrapping his arms around her upper body tightly and his thighs around her legs, he attempted to warm her. The whole time he kept kissing her hair and the side of her face, crooning soft words. "Shhh, it's okay. I'm here. Everything will be all right, babe."

At the same time, he attempted to tease her out of what he must consider craziness. "Hey, *chère*, if you wanted to be alone with me so bad, you didn't have to go hide in the bathroom. I'm easy. With you, anyway. Are you crying because you're happy? Please tell me those are tears of joy. Otherwise, I'll think my lovemaking wasn't all that super after all."

Finally, Sylvie settled down. Her heart rate slowed and her body temperature rose, back to normal. Luc still held her tightly in the protective cocoon of his arms and legs. She didn't tell him she was all right, though, wanting to savor this strange moment of bonding. Strange, because the "bad boy of the bayou" was really rather terrific in a pinch. In different ways, she suspected he'd provided the same kind of solace over the years to his younger brothers and to his aunt . . . maybe even his half sisters, too.

"Did I do this to you?" Luc asked, sounding appalled.

See. Next, I'll be revolting him. "No . . . yes . . . no . . . oh, it's too hard to explain. All through my childhood I got these anxiety attacks when I was put in a situation which my shyness just couldn't handle. You'd think after all those years of therapy, I would be over it by now."

"That was an anxiety attack?"

She nodded. "A mild one."

"That was *mild*?" He thought a moment. "But what happened to make you anxious? What were you too shy to handle?"

"Are you living on the same planet as me, Luc?" she chided. "I engaged in outrageous lovemaking with a man whose expertise is way out of my league. I exposed my naked body, with all its flaws, to inspection in a lit room. I opened myself up for ridicule by donning this skimpy, flame-red nightie. And I was ogled in all my near-nakedness by a ten-year-old boy who asks very graphic questions. How's that list for starters?"

"Are you living on the same planet as me, Sylv?" Luc chided her right back. "Number *one*, if you and I made *outrageous* love to each other—and it was most wonderfully outrageous, in my opinion—then it was because we make a good pair, not because of any particular expertise. Number *two*, it was a privilege to *inspect* your naked body, which is incidentally beautiful; I guess I'll have to inspect it again a time or two or twenty to find those flaws you mentioned. *Three*, as for appearing ridiculous in that red nightie, you must be blind; you look hot, babe, and that's a fact. And even if you did risk ridicule by donning the nightie, and even if I risked ridicule wearing Valentine boxers, what's wrong with laughing at ourselves? *Four*, Tee-John is another matter entirely. I'll take care of him, but you gotta know that his behavior is normal for a kid his age. Don't take it personally."

Sylvie thought about all he had said. It was sweet of him, really, to try to make her feel better. She squeezed his arms, which were still wrapped tightly around her—a gesture of thanks.

He reached behind himself and pulled off a swath of toilet paper, which he used to wipe the tears from her face. She felt rather childish now, letting him comfort her, but at the same time she felt a little bit cherished. It was a nice feeling.

"Sylllvvviiee?" Luc drawled out then.

Uh-oh.

"I have another idea."

Uh-oh.

"You know how they always say if you fall off a horse, the best remedy is to get right back on?"

"Yes," she replied hesitantly.

"And if a person is afraid of water, the best thing is to jump right in?"

"Your point?"

Instead of answering, he put a finger under her chin and lifted, forcing her to look directly ahead toward the mirror, where she noticed, for the first time, the enticing picture they made. Both of them sitting, her cradled between his arms and legs.

"What does that," she asked, pointing to the cozy reflection, "have to do with horses and water?"

He chuckled softly against her hair, and as she watched the mirror, he began to unbutton her blouse, exposing the red nightie underneath. At the same time, ever so slowly, he began to spread his knees wider and wider, forcing her knees to follow suit. "My own version of shyness therapy," he pronounced brightly.

"Since when does a lawyer have psychotherapy skills?" She tried to laugh as she spoke, but her thoughts were distracted by the enticing movement of his fingers and legs.

"We lawyers have lots of skills that would surprise you," he murmured into the curve of her neck, which he'd exposed by drawing her hair back off her face. "Tsk-tsk," he said when he noticed the slight bruise there . . . one that he'd no doubt caused. But he soothed it now with a sensual laving of his tongue, followed by soft kisses.

Somehow, he'd removed her blouse, and was about to tug up the hem of her nightie. She put both hands on his to halt his progress. "No, Luc." She was not going to sit naked on the floor of the bathroom in front of a mirror with Lucien LeDeux watching her.

"Please. I want to show you how beautiful you are."

"I'm not beautiful."

"Yes, you most definitely are." He ran his fingertips over the nylon fabric covering her breasts, and they sprang immediately to life.

She moaned.

He smiled.

The rogue was going to take advantage of her every weakness, and he knew about a whole lot of them after last night. In truth, her nipples and her entire breasts were oversensitized from his earlier attentions. Even the inadvertent whisk of sheer cloth as she shifted slightly constituted an erotic caress.

She pushed his hands away from her chest, but no problem. He just moved on to other forbidden territory.

"There's no time for this," she protested.

"There's always time for this," he countered.

"But your brother—"

"Has gone for a swim."

"A swim? Now?"

"I told him to take a shower or wash in the stream. He stinks, in case you hadn't noticed."

"Luc, I don't want you to see me like this . . . in the

daylight," she told him, peering back at him over her shoulder.

"I'm already seeing you . . . in the daylight. And, sweetheart, I like what I see."

At first, she thought that he referred to having seen her this morning as she scrambled out of the hammock. But then she glanced forward and groaned. He had inched the nightie all the way to her abdomen. She was bare to his view from toes to waist. She scrunched her eyes tight to avoid looking anymore.

"Oh, no, I want you to watch," he ordered, making quick work of whisking the nightie up and over her head while she had her eyes closed. "What's the use of therapy if you're not *fully* involved?"

She raised her eyelids and made eye contact with him in the mirror. "You're not going to give up, are you?"

"Never."

Luc made love to her body then, in ways she'd never imagined possible. He touched her everywhere. Always gentle. Always speaking soft words of praise and encouragement. Most of all, he showed her things about her body that went so far beyond the bounds of shyness, she doubted she would ever blush again. Then again, she might carry a permanent blush forevermore in remembrance.

Most of all, he made generous love, without recompense, to her body. This time, he wanted her to be the sole beneficiary of his healing hands.

How could she not love a man like that?

Chapter Fourteen

Bayou road trips are the best . . .

"Hey, guys, enough dawdling! Time to get this show on the bayou." It was nine o'clock, and Luc was eager to get started.

Sylvie gave him an exasperated look as she finished providing a day's supply of food and water for her rats in their critter cage. He was holding the front door of the cabin open so he could lock it after her.

Sashaying by him—*amazing how a woman so shy could have sashaying down to an art form*—she flipped her hair over her shoulder and remarked, "You weren't worried about dawdling in the bathroom a short time ago."

With a laugh, he pointed out, "*Mais oui*, there is dawdling, and then there is *dawdling*."

"Isn't that just like a man, to see everything through a testosterone filter?"

"Are you saying I think with my . . . uh, joy stick?"

"J-joy stick?" she sputtered, then admitted with a wicked grin, "Well, you do give fairly good joy."

"*Fairly* good?" He attempted to swat her on the behind for her saucy remark as she passed through the doorway, but she danced away at the last minute.

Yep, her shyness is melting away like sweet chocolate on a hot tongue.

Now, there's a picture.

It was good to see Sylvie smiling back at him, though, and being playful. He liked to think he'd had a role in that transformation.

No sooner did she step onto the porch than a flock of ducks came waddling onto the porch, quack-quack-quacking their affection for her. Okay, maybe it wasn't quite a flock, but there were six of them, and they were squawking up a storm and rubbing up against her legs.

Was it possible these were the ducks that had eaten the discarded jelly beans last night? Could the ducks be affected by the love potion, the same as he?

Oh, wow! That brought up pictures to boggle the mind. Could ducks have hard-ons? And how would one check? He wasn't even sure how to tell a male from a female. On the other hand, maybe they were just happy to see her because she'd thrown them some bread crumbs after dinner last night. Yeah, that was probably it.

Tee-John was standing down by the stream, waiting impatiently for what he must consider an adventure—an all-day boat trip. Luc's heart swelled with love for the boy, who was a young, spitting image of all the LeDeux men. His black hair was slicked back off his face, now that he'd bathed. His dark eyes were clear

and intelligent. He wore the same dirty T-shirt and
jeans, but his face and arms shone with a clean, healthy
tan. Yep, he was one good-looking kid. And he was
shooting up like a weed. Pretty soon he would outgrow
his nickname of Tee-John . . . a Cajun prefix for *petit*
or small, as in Small John.

It would be good to have Tee-John along for the trip.
Luc had been worried about Sylvie being able to paddle the whole way. This way, she and Tee-John could
spell each other.

The pirogue was loaded with the supplies they
would need to test the water, a camera and spare rolls
of film, maps, notebooks, binoculars, mosquito repel-
lent, sunscreen, and a styrofoam ice chest loaded with
sandwiches, fresh fruit, and soda pop. They expected
to be gone the entire day, and hoped to return to the
cabin by nightfall.

There was also another essential item Luc had
packed—one that he hoped he wouldn't need today.
The pistol. He'd never risk Sylvie and Tee-John's lives
if he thought there were any chance of danger. Still, it
was best to be prepared.

It was a beautiful day as they paddled silently
through the narrow bayou streams—one of those special Louisiana days when the sun beat down with its
unrelenting heat, but a soft breeze ruffled the leaves
and hanging moss of the swamp trees. Pausing for a
second in his paddling, he let the fingers of one hand
riffle through the cool water, which was pure enough to
drink, even though it was stained the color of dark tea
by a century's worth of tree and bark tannin.

Through its translucent depths he saw an abundance
of catfish, large-mouthed bass, white crappies, known
locally as *sac-a-lait*, and sunfish. Even an occasional
grindle . . . those tough ol' bottom-feeders whose air

bladders enabled them to live in mud and who were often plowed up in fields, alive, weeks after floodwater had receded.

"Wish we had some time to fish," Tee-John called back to him, as if reading his mind. His brother sat in the front of the pirogue, Sylvie in the middle, wearing an old Ragin' Cajun baseball cap she'd found in the cabin, and he brought up the rear. As she viewed all the sights, her ponytail flipped right and left through the back hole in the cap like a, well, pony's tail.

"Yep," Luc answered. "Remember the time we spent a week at the cabin and caught our limits every time we threw out a line?"

Tee-John laughed in remembrance. "We were so sick of eating fish, I about puked. And Tante Lulu said she was startin' to grow whiskers from all the catfish we brought her."

"Do you fish, Sylv?" Luc asked then.

She shook her head. "I never learned. No one ever took me when I was a kid. Can you imagine my mother in her Cartier diamonds and designer clothes down on the bayou ... fishing? I ... don't ... think ... so. I suspect I might like it, though."

"I could teach you," Tee-John offered, much to both Sylvie and Luc's surprise. "Course you'd have to bait your own hook. Ah cain't stand sissy girls." He gave an exaggerated Southern drawl to that last statement.

Everyone went quiet again, and Luc sighed with the sheer pleasure of being in the place he loved most. How he cherished the majesty of this land of his birth ... a virtual Garden of Eden! In fact, there was a saying that God must be a Cajun to have created such a paradise. He agreed.

The bayou, like God, was as old as time, but there was always something new to see or hear or smell.

Every time a fierce hurricane or tornado broke over the
Gulf, the land and water were prone to change places.
With each storm, new bayous were birthed and old
ones swallowed up, as if they'd never existed. In many
places, the swamp wilderness had never been civilized.
It was one reason his mother's family's cabin had re-
mained fairly unknown to his father. As far as Valcour
LeDeux knew, the property no longer existed.

Mostly, it was a silent journey as each of them contemplated his or her own thoughts. The only sounds,
aside from the rhythmic dip of paddles in water, were
the occasional glide of a gator into the stream for an
early morning dip, or a heron swooping down for a tasty
breakfast of crawfish.

Maneuvering the pirogue required expert concentration as they wended their way between the bald cypress
trees that rose smooth-trunked from the streams like
royal queens. Strewn about the grand trees with their
feathery green foliage were their ladies in waiting—the
many knobby "knees" or root protrusions resembling
gnarled stumps that pushed themselves above the water
for air.

Mixed amongst the cypress trees were also the
half-submerged loblollies . . . not as massive in girth
as the cypress but giant in height, sometimes as tall as
eighty feet. The loblolly was a sort of weed in the pine
species . . . an indomitable colonizer that grew wherever its seeds landed, its male pine cones rich in life-
giving pollen. Sort of like Cajun men, Luc thought
with an inward smile.

The ducks followed them, at first, but then soon gave
up their raucous pursuit. They'd come across a particularly succulent patch of what appeared to be green
slime, but was actually duckweed—masses of tiny four-
petaled flowers floating on the surface of the water. A

treat more tempting than Sylvie, he assumed. To a duck, anyhow.

When they turned around one bend, they ran into a huge sheet of water hyacinths covering the entire stream for about thirty feet. With grumbles at the delay, they were forced to bank the pirogue and carry it a short distance beyond the floral mat.

"Damn, I hate this stuff," Luc remarked.

Sylvie nodded her agreement. "How anything so beautiful can be so deadly is beyond me."

The water hyacinths *were* beautiful . . . a floating island of fragile lavender blossoms and bright green leaves, their roots dangling invisibly below. How deceptive! It had all started back in 1884 during the International Cotton Exposition of New Orleans. At the Japanese exhibit, visitors were each given a sample of the flowering aquatic plant native to Latin America. What they didn't realize was the remarkable reproductive abilities it would have, with one single plant producing 65,000 plants in a single season. Throughout Louisiana it had posed a problem ever since: clogging waterways, choking vegetation, cutting off sunlight necessary to aquatic life.

"If I had the time, I'd pull the whole raft of flowers out of the water and build the biggest bonfire this side of hell," Luc proclaimed fiercely.

"And they'd all come back." Sylvie smiled. "Remember the time the Army Corps of Engineers tried to dynamite them out of existence, and they came back in more abundance?"

"A sugar planter near us used a flamethrower last summer, and the year before, a machine gun," Tee-John piped in. "Man, did I learn some good swear words this year when they all came back!"

Luc and Sylvie both shook their heads at the boy's enthusiasm over cursing.

"I think the water hyacinths are a little bit like women," Luc teased as they set the pirogue back in the water. "Pretty and dainty on the outside and man-eaters on the inside, ready to suck the blood out of any male who comes within kissing distance." The whole time he talked, he was watching Sylvie's heart-shaped behind as she bent over in his nylon jogging shorts to pick up her fallen cap.

"How come you're always lookin' at Sylvie's ass?" Tee-John asked with a mischievous grin.

Sylvie's body shot ramrod straight, and she sliced Luc with a glare.

He shrugged. "There are some things a man just can't help."

"Hah!" she said.

"Hah!" Tee-John said at the same time. "I'd rather look at a bug."

Everyone laughed at that.

"And you two are always touchin' each other," Tee-John complained, and made a youthful gesture of disgust by sticking two fingers in his open mouth to denote vomiting.

"We are not," Sylvie protested, but she was lying. Luc had to admit on his own behalf that he couldn't stop himself from laying his hands on her every chance he got, even in the most innocent instances. Fingertips brushing her hair under the cap. Resting a palm on her shoulder when he asked a question. A quick caress of her bare arm when he reached for one of the supplies. And Sylvie had reciprocated likewise, much to his great pleasure.

Sylvie—*smart lady*—decided to change the subject back to their earlier discussion. "Actually, I disagree with your analogy, Luc. If water hyacinths are like women at all, it's because we're the stronger sex," Sylvie argued over her shoulder. They were back in the pirogue and paddling again. "No matter what men do to cut us down, we pop right back up. Hey, water hyacinths aren't called the survival flower for nothing."

"*Touché*," Luc said with a smart salute to her back.

"Yep, I am woman. Call me survivor."

"You know, Sylv, the water hyacinth is also called the pain-in-the-ass flower. So, you could say, 'I am woman. Call me . . . P.I.T.A.'"

"You're impossible," she said huffily.

"Yeah, dontcha just love that about me?"

There was an uncomfortable silence then because he'd inadvertently brought up the dreaded L-word. But the moment passed when Tee-John stood expertly in the boat and used his paddle to push a huge water snake out of their path.

At noon, they stopped for lunch.

To Sylvie, the day seemed magical.

Maybe it was the lunch—an ambrosia of peanut-butter-and-jelly sandwiches, washed down with barely cool soda pop and topped off with crisp apples, which Luc had sliced into bite-size pieces.

Maybe it was the glorious pirogue ride through what had to be God's country . . . a place of such intense colors and smells and beauty that the mind instinctively associated them with some celestial creation.

Maybe it was spending a day with Lucien LeDeux, a man she was coming to love more and more, with each passing moment. And it wasn't anything he said or did, either. It was just being with him . . . looking up to see him staring at her with equal wonder . . . catching him in an easy exchange of smiles with his brother . . . remembering all that had passed between them the night before.

As much as Sylvie cherished this glorious day with Luc, she was frightened, knowing it would soon come to an end. The love potion would wear off, and Luc would no doubt ride off into the sunset, chalking it all up to a pleasant interlude.

But Sylvie wouldn't be able to forget so easily.

"Hey, babe, daydreaming about me *again*?" Luc dropped down to the ground beside her where she was resting on her elbows, legs outstretched, waiting for their trip to resume. He and Tee-John had just finished repacking the boat.

"I was *not* dreaming about you," she reiterated once again.

"Yeah, yeah, yeah." Leaning on one elbow, he grinned down at her.

"Where's Tee-John?"

"Went downstream a piece to fill the empty soda bottles with fresh springwater."

"He's a good kid, Luc."

"Yeah, he is, despite his smart mouth."

"Like someone else I know."

Luc poked her playfully in the ribs.

"He looks just like you, too."

Luc stiffened oddly at that, then relaxed. "Well, we *are* brothers." He said that as if trying to convince her. How strange!

"Wanna make out?" he asked.

"Wh-what?" she choked out. "Is the love potion acting up again? Well, forget it. Your brother will be back any minute."

"Plenty of time," he said, and lowered his head till his lips were a hairsbreadth from hers. "I've missed you, *chère*," he whispered against her mouth.

"How could you miss me when we've been together all day?" she murmured, arching her neck for the little nibbling kisses he was placing in perfect alignment along her jaw. Then, she added, "I've missed you, too."

That was all the encouragement Luc needed. He slanted his lips over hers and moved from side to side, making rough growls of appreciation deep in his throat at each movement. When he had their lips aligned to his satisfaction, he kissed her hungrily.

"Do you know how much I enjoy kissing you?" he asked one time when he came up for air.

She knew, because he was showing her with every tender/tough move of his lips and tongue and teeth.

"If that don't beat all," a young voice said above them. "Sucking tonsils first chance you get. I hope I never grow up if I'm gonna act so dumb-ass stupid around girls."

"Go away," Luc said, even as his lips were still pressed lightly to hers.

"Where?"

"Anywhere!"

"How am I s'posed to learn anything if I don't watch?"

"Watch?" she squeaked out.

"Watch?" Luc bellowed.

There was the sound of shuffling feet. Finally, Luc gave up, giving her a quick, final kiss before coming to a sitting position. He glared at his brother, who continued to stand next to them, shuffling his feet.

"Watch?" Luc repeated.

"Yeah, I was hopin' you would get to the oral sex part so I'd finally see what got the Prez in all that hot water."

"You're the one who's gonna be in hot water if you keep talking like that," Luc warned, getting to his feet.

Tee-John smirked at his brother, proving that he'd been deliberately provoking him. And he added one last salvo. "One of my football buddies, Jake Fortier, says if you hum when you do it, it's even better. In fact, Jake says—"

Tee-John never got to finish because Luc picked him up by the seat of his jeans and tossed him in the bayou, head first. When the kid came gushing up out of the water, tossing his hair back in a wet swath, he grinned at Luc. And Luc grinned at him, shaking his head from side to side.

Sylvie almost said, "Like father, like son," but what she meant was, "Like brother, like brother." Finally, she settled on, "Two peas from the same pod."

They both stood staring at her, hands on hips.

"What's that supposed to mean?" Luc asked, moving away from his brother, who was shaking wet drops of water on him like a waterlogged dog.

"Yeah, are you insultin' us?" Tee-John, who came only chest high to Luc, looked up at his brother for confirmation that it was them against her if insults were going to be thrown.

The two half brothers were adorable, mischief-loving mirror images of each other. "Yep, the Mutt and Jeff of rascals," she decided.

The fool had to go fall in love . . .

They arrived about three o'clock at the small man-made lake near Cypress Oil. Luc and Tee-John followed her directions diligently, and within three hours, dozens of samples of soil and water had been gathered from the various tributaries leading off the holding pond.

Mostly, they worked at a considerable distance—at least a mile—from the plant grounds, which were heavily posted against trespassers. It would be even more damning if the contaminants were concentrated at that distance, especially since these tributaries led to residential areas. Even without performing complicated chemical tests in a lab that would break down the components in the samples, Sylvie knew by sight and smell alone that they had clear evidence against Cypress Oil.

"How could the oil company be so careless?" she asked Luc.

He was pressing the small of his back to get out the kinks after being in a bent-over position for so long. "They've been getting away with it forever, so they probably consider themselves invincible. Hell, in many ways they are. A little money tossed here and there, and evidence disappears, court decisions defy logic, government officials look the other way."

"Then what's the use?"

"If you give up, you might as well lie down and die. There's always hope, sweetheart. When all else fails, there's hope."

"We're Cajuns," Tee-John interjected with pride. "We never give up."

She and Luc exchanged a smile.

Then Luc tousled his brother's hair. "You betcha, bud. Regular Ragin' Cajuns, that's what we are."

Sylvie clucked her tongue at the two of them. "Should we start back now? Surely, we have enough samples."

"Just a few more." Luc shifted uneasily.

The fine hairs stood out on the back of her neck. "What?"

"I'm going up closer. We need samples from the holding pond itself."

"Luc! It's too dangerous for us to go any closer."

"*We* won't be going. *I'll* be going alone."

"No!" she and Tee-John said at the same time.

"Yes. You two stay here. I'll only be gone a short while . . . an hour at most."

"Oh, Luc, I don't like this at all."

"Tee-John, I want you to take care of Sylvie while I'm gone."

The boy's chest puffed out at the responsibility.

"Sylv, come over here and show me which vials and baggies to take and how to label them." When she approached the pirogue, he was already pulling items out and putting them in a backpack. "I'm leaving the boat here with you and Tee-John," he said in an undertone. "No, don't argue with me. I can hide myself better if I travel by foot. If something should happen to me—stop looking like that, *chère*, I'll be careful—you and Tee-John go back to the cabin and call Remy. He'll pick you up and take you to safety."

"No! I won't stay here, and I won't leave without you."

"You must, Sylvie. These samples are too important. Besides, you've got to keep Tee-John safe. He'll run off half-cocked."

She threw herself into Luc's arms then. Hugging him tightly with her face buried in his neck, she cried, "Be careful. Come back."

He hugged her tightly in return . . . so tightly she could barely breathe. Then he kissed her fiercely before setting her at arm's length. "You and I need to talk when I get back."

She nodded.

Why did she keep thinking *if you come back?*

Forty-five minutes later, Sylvie and Tee-John were jolted by the sound of gunfire in the distance. Lifting the binoculars to her eyes, she gasped and grabbed for Tee-John's hand.

In less than a half hour, Luc's limp body was being carried away by two heavily armed security officers. A third officer was stomping on glass vials strewn about the ground.

Was Luc dead or alive?

Then the terrible trouble arrived . . .

"Well, we're finally 'home,'" Sylvie said with a sigh, as the cabin came into sight. She squeezed Tee-John's shoulder.

"We gotta call Remy, right off," Tee-John said.

She nodded as she helped the boy pull the pirogue up and onto the bank. It wouldn't be used again if Remy came soon with the hydroplane.

It was two A.M., and the cabin loomed dark before them. It had taken the three of them five hours, not including lunch, to reach Cypress Oil, but the harrowing trip back, laden with worry about Luc, had taken seven hours with only her and Tee-John at the paddles.

She had to give Tee-John credit. Once he'd realized the seriousness of the situation, he didn't balk or cry, as she'd expected a kid his age to do. Instead, he'd helped her quickly gather up their supplies, turn the pirogue around, and get them on their way before the security officers began to wonder how Luc had gotten there, and whether he had been alone. The boy's sense of direction and memory of the route had been invaluable.

Her sense of relief vanished as she noticed the large, lidded basket sitting on the porch floor. Even more ominous than the fact that someone had been there was the hissing sound coming from the basket.

"Stay back," Tee-John warned. While she held the flashlight, he used a boat paddle to tip over the lid.

Sylvie's heart jumped. "Oh, my God!"

The basket was filled with a dozen writhing, hissing snakes.

"Don't worry. They're just garden snakes," Tee-John informed her, expertly flipping the lid back on and taking the basket to the side yard, where he released the snakes into the woods.

She still had a hand over her chest when he returned. It would take a while for her heartbeat to return to normal.

Tee-John held out a folded piece of paper to her. "This was in the bottom of the basket . . . addressed to you," he explained.

Sylvie unfolded the stiff parchment, which indeed had "Sylvie Fontaine" scribbled on the front in red ink. Or was it blood? *Oh, really, Sylvie! Don't get hysterical now.*

The note read:

> Eye of the newt,
> Heart of the snake.
> Meddle with voodoo,
> A corpse you will make.

"What a bunch of silliness!" she said, making a tsking sound with her tongue for Tee-John's benefit. She couldn't show him how terrified she was.

"You been meddlin' with voodoo?" he asked, obviously impressed with her daring.

"No, it's a misunderstanding," she lied. Tucking the note inside her slacks pocket, she quickly opened the door and flicked on the lights. While she checked on Samson and Delilah, Tee-John said, "I better examine the room for any dangerous objects, like snakes or bombs."

"Bombs?" She was practically hyperventilating.

He shrugged. "Can't be too careful. That's what Luc says all the time."

She took the satellite phone from its hiding place in a loose brick of the fireplace's inner chimney and proceeded to dial Remy's number. Meanwhile, Tee-John began the work of closing down the cabin in anticipation of their departure. While the phone was ringing, she watched Tee-John roll up the carpet, lay down the straw matting, and start to work on the perishable food items in the fridge. It was amazing how like Luc he was . . . a regular neat freak, from the way he stacked all the items to be taken with them in tidy bundles, to the way in which he folded the dish towels and bed linens. It was especially amazing for a kid his age . . . to whom neatness should be anathema.

"Hello," Remy said groggily. He must have been asleep.

"Remy, this is Sylvie Fontaine. You've got to come quick and pick up me and Tee-John," she said all in a rush.

"Tee-John? He's there with you?" Remy's voice sounded worried.

"Yes. I'll explain later. When can you get here?"

"Two hours?"

"That's fine. Hurry."

"Uh . . . you know what I told you about my phone . . ." he began.

Sylvie knew he was referring to the fact it was probably bugged. "Uh-huh."

"Well, can I assume this is an emergency?"

"Absolutely," she said, and her voice cracked.

"Let me talk to Luc." Remy no doubt sensed her desperation.

"Not now," she said firmly.

A heavy silence followed in which Remy digested her words.

Then she couldn't stop herself from panicking. "Oh, please, Remy, just come right away."

Getting out of Dodge, bayou style . . .

Two hours later, they were in the hydroplane flying away from Luc's bayou and a cabin that would hold memories for her forever.

"Luc has been shot," Remy informed them. "When you said he wasn't there, I made a few calls."

"Oh, my God!" she cried.

"If my Dad did this, I'm gonna kill 'im," Tee-John proclaimed angrily.

"Tee-John!" she and Remy both exclaimed with shock.

Then Remy elaborated. "Luc was only hit in the shoulder. He's fine, physically."

"But?" Sylvie prodded, sensing there was more.

Remy took a deep breath, then gave them the bad news. "He's in jail."

"For what?" Sylvie asked indignantly, though she had a suspicion.

"A whole litany of offenses, including trespassing . . ."

That was the one Sylvie would have guessed.

". . . and kidnapping . . ."

"Oh, really! Are they still under *that* misconception? Did you tell them that Tee-John is with us . . . oh, I can see why that might be further incriminating evidence. Well, once we explain, they'll understand."

"Tee-John's not the only one Luc is accused of kidnapping."

"Who else?" She had to think only a second to realize who the other alleged victim might be. "I would *hardly* classify myself as a victim."

Remy slanted her a quick glance, then grinned. "So it's that way with you two, huh?"

She just lifted her chin. "Laugh and you are dead meat, mister."

He laughed anyway. "Tante Lulu will be so pleased."

"Don't you dare say anything to her."

"Say what?" Tee-John wanted to know.

"Nothing," she and Remy said at the same time.

Then Remy continued to list Luc's supposed offenses. "Assault with a firearm. Resisting arrest. Using obscene language to a police officer. Making terroristic threats."

"Is that all?" she questioned sarcastically.

Remy shrugged. "The bottom line is that Luc is in major trouble. There are some big shots pressing him to the wall this time."

Sylvie bit her bottom lip with worry. "Trouble of this seriousness is probably nothing new for Luc, but it's a bone-chilling experience for me, I gotta tell you."

"That's what happens when you're in cahoots with 'the bad boy of the bayou.'" He squeezed her hand to show he was just teasing.

"Well, I'll tell you one thing. Never again will I complain about my life being boring."

Soon, the plane was flying over Houma and preparing to land in a small private bayou docking area. It was hard to believe that she'd been gone less than two days, even harder to believe that it had been less than a week since Luc came into her lab for help, and accidentally swallowed the love-potion jelly beans.

Suddenly, the clouds parted in the dawn sky, showing the place of her birth with all its numerous bayous and bridges. The scene was covered with a dreamlike, impressionist haze. Yes, that was what this whole experience seemed like . . . a dream.

But she feared it was about to become a nightmare.

Chapter Fifteen

Feathering the bride . . . what bride? . . .

Despite her plea to be taken directly to the jail where Luc was being held, Remy took them to Sylvie's apartment. Stubborn-to-the-bone must be a LeDeux family trait.

She was amazed to find waiting there Tante Lulu, Charmaine, Claudia, and René. And it was only seven A.M.

"Luc gave me specific instructions not to allow you to visit him in jail," Remy was telling her in an increasingly louder voice, attempting to be heard over Tante Lulu, who was in the corner alternately scolding and hugging Tee-John at the same time. Boy and great-aunt were a sight to see, about the same height, eyeball to eyeball.

Tante Lulu's helmet of tight curls was dyed red

today . . . *bright* red. She was wearing a black leather jacket and jeans, claiming to have traded in her purple Impala for a Harley. That must be why the white T-shirt visible under the open jacket read, "Rev My Engine." A small emblem on the front of the jacket read, "Biker Babes"; emblazoned on the back in huge red letters was, "Born to Be Wild."

Sylvie had heard of a mid-life crisis before, but late-life crisis? That was a new one. She shook her head to rid it of these extraneous thoughts.

"Why? Why doesn't Luc want me to go see him in jail?" Sylvie asked Remy. She couldn't help feeling a twinge of disappointment that Luc would cut her off this way. She'd thought they were partners in this enterprise. And she'd been hoping they might be partners in another way.

"I'm not sure. I just know he was adamant. 'No Sylvie at the jail!' "

"He probably wants to protect you," René offered, sensing how hurtful those words would be to her. "You know, the Cajun Knight baloney."

Baloney about says it all.

Remy made a snorting sound of disagreement. "All I know is that Claudia is the only one he wants showing up at his cell door."

Claudia? He wants to see Claudia? The green monster of jealousy dug its claws into her heart.

Remy seemed to take particular note then of Claudia, who was sitting on the arm of the wing-back chair where René was seated. She looked as if she'd just come from the gym, wearing one of those black, crisscross spandex midriff tops and silk exercise pants.

"Hey, Clau-di-a," Remy said with a grin.

"Hey, Re-my," Claudia drawled right back at him, also grinning.

The green monster of jealousy evaporated in Sylvie as she took in the serious chemistry ping-ponging between these two. But back to the issue at hand. "I can protect myself," she snarled. "Really, this Cajun Knight business of Luc's goes only so far before it turns sour."

"Did Luc offer to be your Cajun Knight?" Charmaine wanted to know. She was applying nail enamel with careless abandon, while seated in Sylvie's great-grandmother's delicate antique chair made of *pallisandre* or violet ebony. It was a priceless piece signed by none other than the New Orleans furniture maker Seignouret. "That is so cute of him. You should be flattered."

Oh, yeah, I'm flattered. More like furious at his high-handed orders. Keep me away from the jail? Hah!

"Anyhow, shouldn't you be worried about the warrant out for your arrest?" René reminded her. "I would think that a jailhouse is the last place you'd want to be seen."

"I called Peter Finch, my lawyer, from the cell phone in Remy's plane. He'll take copies of the JBX legal documents to the district attorney's office this morning. They'll show my *equal* right to the love-potion formula. There's no basis for criminal action against me." She waved a hand dismissively.

"How about your mother?" Remy asked. "Remember those remarks she made about your mental stability?"

Sylvie bristled at that reminder. "I'm not going to be intimidated by my mother . . . not anymore. If she pushes me too far, she's going to find out that I know more family secrets than she would care to air in public."

Sylvie couldn't believe she was behaving in such a calm manner . . . courageous, really, for one handicapped so often in the past by shyness. She guessed that when the people and things she valued most were jeopardized, fear took second place to outrage.

"Let's have some coffee and make a plan," Tante Lulu suggested, her arm around Tee-John's shoulder.

"Good idea," Claudia agreed. Then, to Sylvie, she added, "I need to update you on some things anyhow."

Seated around the kitchen table, Claudia quickly reviewed all the intelligence she'd been able to gather while they'd been gone. Her data, in combination with the samples they had gathered and the documents Tee-John had pilfered, would go a long way toward putting some high-placed people in legal jeopardy, maybe even prison. Oh, they didn't have the makings of a complete lawsuit at this point, but maybe enough for a pretrial settlement.

"Do you have those documents in a safe place?" Claudia asked Sylvie at one point.

"Yep." Sylvie smiled widely. "Under the newspaper liner in the bottom of Samson and Delilah's cage."

Everyone laughed at that.

"I'll take them with me when I go," Remy said.

While they exchanged information, Tante Lulu took over Sylvie's kitchen, brewing up a better pot of coffee than Sylvie had ever made . . . something about tossing egg shells in with the grounds or some such thing. Where she'd gotten egg shells, Sylvie had no idea, since she didn't recall having any eggs in the house.

But then she heard something ominous, coming from her basement.

"Cock-a-doodle-doo!" the sound came again. "Cluck, cluck, cluck."

"What was *that?*" Sylvie had a sinking feeling even as she raised the question. They were all sitting around her kitchen table while Tante Lulu poured mugs of coffee for them, and diet pop for Tee-John.

Without missing a beat, Tante Lulu answered, "The chickens."

"In my basement?" she squeaked out.

"Yeah, Sylvie, remember me telling you about that the other night?" Remy reminded her. "Flocking the bride?"

"Feathering the bride," Tante Lulu corrected, and went on pouring coffee. Then she pulled a baker's bag off the counter—*did the woman always come prepared with food?*—and laid out on a platter a dozen *les oreilles de cochran*, or "pig's ears"—a Cajun deep-fried pastry sprinkled with sugar. Tee-John downed one of the confections before Sylvie had a chance to register what his aunt had said. "Hope you weren't too fond of that ugly red leather chair down there, hon. I tried to cover everything with those fancy flowered sheets of yours I found in the linen closet, but those birds have a mind of their own. The chair seems to be covered with a *little* bit of chicken poop." She thought a moment. "Okay, a lot."

"But why in the basement?" she persisted, refusing to focus on the leather chair—her dead father's favorite for reading—or the Christian Dior sheets her cousin Valerie had given her last Christmas.

"'Cause your dumb neighbors complained about the noise of chickens squawkin'. Can you imagine? It's not like I was playin' heavy lead music or nothin'."

"Uh, I think you mean heavy metal," René said, rolling his eyes at Sylvie.

"Lead, iron, steel, metal, whatever," Tante Lulu said, waving a free hand in the air. "Don't these people know that the sounds of nature are pleasing? Betcha they'd be complainin' if I dumped a truckload of cow manure on those sorry roses of yours out back, too. Yep, these city folks have lost their connection with the good earth."

"Don't . . . you . . . dare," Sylvie sputtered, ". . . bring cow manure here."

Remy and René were laughing uproariously at her dilemma, while Charmaine and Claudia appeared to be sympathetic. Tee-John just continued to eat.

Sylvie raked the fingers of both hands through her tangled hair. She must look a mess. In fact, she noticed Charmaine eyeing her speculatively, even as she was blowing on her nails to dry the lacquer. No doubt Charmaine would be suggesting a makeover sometime soon. Before Charmaine got a chance, Sylvie wanted to set Tante Lulu straight. "What you don't understand is that I am not a prospective bride."

"Really?" Tante Lulu sank down into a chair with a thud of disappointment. "I was sure that boy would see the light this time."

"Did you have a vision, Tante Lulu?" René asked.

His aunt nodded sadly. "I coulda sworn I saw Luc walking down the aisle with a bride that looked like Sylvie here."

"Well, they was kissin' and touchin' a lot," Tee-John informed the group. He was idly licking the powdered sugar off his fingers as he spoke.

"They were?" everyone else exclaimed with decided glee in their voices. Except Sylvie, of course, whose face felt as red as Tante Lulu's hair.

"Yep," Tee-John said.

Tante Lulu's smile was so wide, it was a wonder her face didn't break.

"And then there was the naughty stuff," Tee-John elaborated. "Whoo-ee!"

Sylvie let her face drop to the table, right on top of her own "pig's ear." She didn't care. Life didn't get any worse than this.

Then her life got worse.

Her mother and Valcour LeDeux arrived.

Sometimes a girl just needs to grow some balls . . .

"Have you lost your mind, Sylvie Marie?" her mother asked, as if she were a child, and not a grown woman. "And what is that ungodly white powder on your face?"

Her mother had walked into the kitchen, uninvited and unannounced, and was regarding each of them in turn with her nose lifted in the air. The Queen Mother stepping down into the servants' quarters couldn't have shown more arrogance. Most of all, her disdain was for Sylvie.

"Hello to you, too, Mother," Sylvie remarked with a snippishness she usually contained around her family. As she scrubbed at her face with a damp dish towel that Tante Lulu handed her, she proceeded to berate her mother. "And I'm just fine, thanks. Yes, I managed to escape, unharmed, from the bullets shot through my front window. The voodoo snakes at the cabin were nonpoisonous, thank you very much. Would you like a cup of coffee? Or a cup of my blood?"

"A lady does not speak with such sarcasm, Sylvie Marie. Restrain yourself."

"Jeesh!" she heard Claudia mutter under her breath. "Talk about a royal poker up the be-hind!"

To which Charmaine added, "Someone ought to tell her that her little girl has grown up."

Oh, to be making such a spectacle of herself! Sylvie felt her palms begin to sweat, and a wave of cold shivers passed over her. Next, she would be hyperventilating.

No, she was a new Sylvie. She was not going to crumble under her mother's condemnation, or from fear of ridicule.

Meanwhile, Valcour LeDeux, wearing a rumpled suit and a dress shirt unbuttoned at the collar, took Tee-John by the nape and pulled him out of his chair. "I ought to whup you good, boy."

"I dint do nothin' wrong," he wailed. At the same time, Tee-John gave Sylvie a look that promised he would disclose none of the secrets he'd learned from her and Luc at the bayou hideaway. Remy had already taken care of hiding the water and soil samples. She had the Cypress Oil papers stored in her own secret place.

"Nothing wrong? I'll show you 'nothing wrong,' Tee-John." His father shook him, hard.

"Uh, I don't think so," Remy said, rising to his feet. "The beatings in this family stopped a long time ago, Dad, and they aren't going to start up now."

René and Sylvie joined him in standing, and they all glared at the man.

"Don't interfere in my bizness," Valcour said icily, still holding a squealing Tee-John by the neck so that he had to stand on tiptoe. "He's caused a lot of trouble to a lot of folks. He deserves to be punished."

"Not with physical abuse," Sylvie declared.

"Stay out of this, missy. You're in enough trouble yourself."

"Don't speak to my daughter that way," Inez Breaux-Fontaine surprised Sylvie by saying. To Sylvie, she said, "Come home with me where we can discuss this . . . uh, matter, in private. With a little creative PR, we can still avoid a scandal, I'm sure."

"I'm not going anywhere till Luc is out of jail," Sylvie said. "And frankly, at this point, scandal be damned."

Her mother sucked in air like a puff fish.

"Way to go, Sylvie," Remy said with obvious surprise.

Inez gave Remy a once-over that included an unkind pause on his damaged face.

Remy stared back at her, unwavering.

Claudia looked as if she'd like to leap over the table and strangle Inez for her rude assessment.

Inez turned her attention back to Sylvie. "Lucien LeDeux has nothing to do with you." She said his name as if it left a bad taste in her mouth.

"I beg to differ."

Her mother went bug-eyed, and everyone in the room turned to stare at Sylvie questioningly.

Sylvie declined to elaborate, which caused Tante Lulu to narrow her eyes as she studied her. Tante Lulu was probably picking out wedding colors in her head, or ordering a few more chickens.

Remy grinned and winked at her. René pumped his fist in the air in celebration of some victory. Claudia and Charmaine exchanged a sappy look that pretty much said, "Ain't love grand?" Valcour LeDeux's face turned practically green; he could probably use a stiff drink.

"Sylvie Marie, we are talking about The Swamp Solicitor," her mother hissed. "A man who takes great delight in being called 'the bad boy of the bayou.'" To her credit, she relayed her message in an undertone, so as not to offend his family.

"So?" Sylvie asked. "What's your point?"

Her mother slitted her eyes in a way that would have intimidated Sylvie into cowering compliance as a child. "Exactly what happened between you and *that man* while you were gallivanting up and down the bayou?"

"I would hardly call running for our lives gallivanting, Mother. And nothing happened between me and Luc that should concern you, except that I got to know him a little better. And it's my opinion that behind his bad-boy image is a different person. He's a good man trying to help his family and a lot of mostly unrepresented people."

"Young lady, I can take care of my own family," Valcour proclaimed in a seething tone. "I don't need any uptown bitc—lady interfering in LeDeux business. And you don't know Lucien as well as you think if you believe he's anything more than bad to the bone."

All of Luc's family inhaled sharply with shock at Valcour's condemnation of his own son, Tante Lulu most of all. The little woman stood to her full five feet and told her nephew-by-marriage, "You are the one who's bad to the bone, Valcour. What Adèle saw in you, I never knew. She mus' be rollin' in her grave now to see you put down your own son."

Valcour's fists clenched and unclenched at his side. Fortunately, he'd let go of Tee-John's nape. The boy stared in fear up at his father, whose face flushed so bright a red Sylvie feared he might have a stroke. "I will not have you, or Lucien, interferin' with Cypress Oil business. He's in jail where he belongs."

"Not for long," Sylvie vowed.

"I don't care if you two are screwin' each other's brains out. I don't care if you stem from some blue-blooded Creole family that thinks its vomit smells better than the rest of us. I don't care what you think of me. You will not do *anything* to affect my holdin's in Cypress Oil. And that's a fact, missy." Valcour was wagging his forefinger at Sylvie the whole time, and spittle clung to the edges of his mouth as he spat out the vicious statements.

Before anyone could protest his horrible words, Valcour spun on his heels and left the house, dragging Tee-John with him.

At first, there was just stunned silence. How a father could have such virulent feelings toward his own son was beyond them all. Sylvie's heart went out to Luc, wondering how he'd survived childhood in the same house with that hateful man.

"Killin' would be too good for that man," Tante Lulu said finally, pretty much summing up all their opinions.

"Will Tee-John be okay?" Sylvie asked.

"Yeah," Remy answered. "Dad won't do anything with so many of us watching his every move. Oh, he'll make the kid miserable, but he'll be safe."

"I'll go over and check up on him later," René promised.

"Back to my . . . *our* problem . . . how we're going to get Luc out of jail," Sylvie began.

"No, Sylvie Marie, it is most definitely not *your* problem," her mother stated. "Let Lucien's family and friends take over from here. Pack a small case and come home with me now. I forbid you to involve yourself further."

Forbid? Sylvie's hackles rose. "I told you before, Mother, I am not leaving till Luc is out of jail. Furthermore, must I remind you, this is my home. I'm not going anywhere."

"Don't you care at all what this could do to my career?" her mother wailed. "Disgrace yourself and you disgrace me, you selfish child."

Sylvie exhaled with a whoosh of frustration. "Of course, I care about your career, Mother. But sometimes it's necessary to take a stand, despite the consequences."

"Personally, I think you need some professional help. Why don't you call your therapist?"

"My therapist?" Sylvie's voice was shrill even to her own ears. She exchanged a glance with Remy, who had told her two days ago that her mother had suggested a mental imbalance. At the time, Sylvie had considered such an idea impossible. Now, she wasn't so sure. "I'm exhausted, Mother. Not crazy. I think it would be best if you and I don't say anything else to each other right now, lest words be said that can't ever be taken back."

Inez stared at her as if she couldn't believe this was her own daughter speaking. "So be it," she said finally, and left in a huff.

The room resounded with an embarrassing silence as everyone avoided looking at Sylvie. How they must pity her! To have such a cold woman for a mother must seem unfathomable to them. Well, no, they had Valcour to deal with in their own family.

The old Sylvie would have slunk off in shame, too mortified to face anyone. The new Sylvie straightened her shoulders, ignored the heat that flamed over her, and said, "Well, what are we going to do about Luc?"

He was the coolest jailbird . . .

"Your bail has been set for $500,000," Lt. Ambrose "Rosie" Mouton informed Luc, who was dealing out new hands of cards for the next set of *bourré*. "Captain just got a call from the court clerk before I came down here."

Luc raised his eyebrows at his longtime friend and former classmate at juvie hall. Rosie had reformed a long time ago, long before Luc had decided to walk the straight and narrow. He'd been lording it over him ever since. "Is that all? Tsk-tsk-tsk. And I'm not even an ax murderer. Talk about!"

Detective Pierre Landry, another cardplayer at the table, laughed. "Hell, LeDeux, you've landed in deep shit this time. Too many important people with their noses out of joint. They're gonna make sure you can't make bail. And when it comes to trial . . . you're gonna fry, man, fry."

Luc shrugged and continued to deal the cards. His shoulder wound bothered him a little bit as he moved his arm, but it was nothing to be concerned about. The bruises on his face and ribs were another thing. He'd like to get hold of those security guards who'd roughed him up before turning him over to the authorities.

His cellmate, Frank Martin, regarded him with awe. "My bail is only $50,000, and I'm in for armed robbery and possession of a controlled substance. You mus' be one dangerous dude."

They were all sitting at a table in the rec room of the local jail, unrestrained. He couldn't be *that* dangerous.

Really, though, Luc wasn't all that concerned about being in jail for a few days. Cypress Oil would have a tail on his butt as soon as he stepped out of the jailhouse door. This way he could have Remy and René and Claudia finish up the groundwork that would seal their case, while Cypress Oil thought its opponent was powerless.

And there was another important reason why he didn't mind being in jail. Sylvie. If he was released, he wouldn't be able to help himself. He would hot-tail it to her house faster than . . . well, faster than a man with two tons of testosterone driving his brain. He would *have* to be with her. He just would. And God help him, he didn't want to do anything more to put her in harm's way.

How had he come to care so much? Was it the love potion? Would it wear off in a few days? Did he want these intense feelings to end?

"You lose, LeDeux," Rosie hooted, tossing his winning hand down on the table. "Where's your mind, man?"

"He's under the influence of a love potion, dontcha

know?" Landry told Rosie with a smirk. "I read about it in the newspaper."

"Really?" Rosie inquired. "Does it work?"

"Is it like that Vi-ag-ra?" Frank asked. "I knew a guy once who had a twenty-four-hour hard-on from taking too much Viagra."

"No shit?" Rosie and Landry exclaimed at the same time, their mouths hanging open with incredulity, and interest, as they stared at Frank.

The dunces!

"Had a heart attack and two strokes, but he died with a smile on his face," Frank hooted, slapping his knee at having played a joke on them.

"Hey, LeDeux, you got a visitor," announced another police officer. "This is becomin' a reg'lar social beehive in here."

He was right. Luc had already seen thus far today: his brothers Remy and René, Tante Lulu, Claudia, and his lawyer, Clovis Dupree. He'd refused to see his father or Sylvie's mother, though why the latter would want to see him, he couldn't imagine.

"This *visitor* put up your bail," the officer informed him as he unlocked the gate to the holding cell.

"*What?*" What jerk had gone behind his back and extricated him? He'd explained the plan fully to his brothers and Claudia. Everyone had agreed with him, or so he'd thought.

"Mus' have deep pockets, this one," Rosie said, following behind him, " 'cause every bail bondsman from Shreveport to New Orleans has been warned away from you. Paid in cash, too."

Luc said nothing as he walked through the cell door into the visiting area. He was gonna kill the person who'd pulled this dumb maneuver. Really, he was gonna . . .

Oh, God!
It was Sylvie Fontaine.

That sound was her heart breaking . . .

Luc is not pleased to see me. Sylvie's heart sank with despair at that recognition.

How could he look so good to her, even with a black eye and bruised lip and prison-regulation uniform, while she apparently held no appeal for him whatsoever? Almost immediately the answer came to her: The love potion must have worn off.

"What the hell are you doing here?" he gritted out; at the same time he yanked her roughly into his arms and hugged her fiercely. With his lips at her ear, he whispered hoarsely, "God, I've missed you so much."

"Uh, you folks gotta sit on opposite sides of that table there," the guard informed them. "No huggin' or nothin' allowed. Prison rules."

They separated, reluctantly, but not before Luc gave her a quick, wonderful kiss on the lips. Joy rushed through Sylvie as she sat down, as instructed, though she was still confused by his angry expression.

"Leave us alone for a few minutes," Luc instructed the guard.

Surprisingly, the guard nodded. "The paperwork's being prepared for your release anyhow."

Luc scowled at him, then at her. "Where did you get $500,000?"

"From . . . from the bank," she stuttered out. You'd think he would be glad she'd obtained his release. Instead, he acted as if she'd performed some criminal act.

Her answer clearly astonished him. When he finally

shut his gaping mouth, he asked, "You have $500,000 in the bank?"

"I have more than that, Luc. A trust fund passed down through generations of Breaux women. Why? Does it matter?"

"Hell, yes, it matters. I have a thousand in savings, if that."

"So what?" She'd come here to secure his release, not take abuse because her bank account was larger than his.

"You should not have posted bond for me without my permission," he berated her.

"What? Are you a flight risk or something?"

"Or something," he growled.

She stood abruptly and slammed her purse on the table between them. "You ungrateful slob. Why don't I go out to the desk and take back my check? You can sit here till the cows come home for all I care." She hated the tearful break in her voice that betrayed how hurt she was.

Luc reached across the table and put a hand on her shoulder, pushing her back gently to her seat. "I'm sorry if I was abrupt, Sylv. I guess I'm a little . . . uh, tense."

"Don't take your bad moods out on me."

"Yes, ma'am." He smiled at her.

"And don't smile at me, either."

"Why? Because my smiles make you breathless?"

"Oh, it's just like you to rub in my own foolish admissions. No, your smiles don't make me breathless . . . not anymore. They make me angry."

"You're pretty when you're angry."

"Ooooh, be forewarned, Luc. I'm about to belt you with my purse, and it's really heavy since I just came from the bank."

"What? You've got another $500,000 in your purse?" he asked with mock horror.

"This conversation is going nowhere fast. I came down here to spring you. Well, you're sprung. I'm out of here."

"Uh . . . just a minute, Sylv. I've been thinking."

She forced herself to smile.

"Why are you smiling?"

"Because you've been thinking."

"That was mean, Sylv. Not like you at all."

"Maybe you don't know me."

He glanced nervously at the large mirror on the wall, which was presumably a two-way glass. "This is the thing, Sylv." He took a deep breath, as if bracing himself. "I don't think you and I should see each other anymore . . . or for a while, anyway. We need to give it a rest . . . and . . . ummm, think things over. Slow down a bit."

Sylvie gasped and put a palm over her heart, which was splintering apart at his words.

"I should have known this would happen. A one-night stand, that's all we shared, right?"

He looked as if he'd like to speak, but held himself back after staring pointedly at the mirror, then at her.

"Well, I don't know what I expected," she went on. "The love potion was bound to wear off eventually. The fact that it did so earlier than I expected is disappointing, but the end result would have been the same. All I represent to the great Lucien LeDeux is a good lay . . . if that."

"Sylvie, you can't really believe that." His body gestures were nervous as he squirmed under the presumed watchful eye of the police.

"Can't I?" She didn't care who overheard their

conversation as she waited for a further explanation
from Luc. When none was forthcoming, she felt she'd
been given her answer.

It took monumental effort on Sylvie's part to rise
with dignity and exit the holding room. Let Luc find a
way home himself. She needed to get out of his presence as soon as possible, before she broke down.

"You don't understand," Luc called after her.

"That's the problem," she answered him sadly, never
bothering to look back. "I *do* understand."

Chapter Sixteen

There was no thunder, but there was a thunder-bolt . . .

Luckily, Sylvie made it home before she broke down.

With shaky fingers, she inserted her key in the front lock. She assumed there was a bodyguard about some-where, though she saw no one. Claudia had assured her that there would be two guards, one in front and one in back, twenty-four hours a day.

The minute the door closed behind her, the tears came. And came and came and came. Slow, silent streams of grief for something so precious that had seemed within her reach. *Such a fool! How pathetic I must seem! He doesn't want to see me again.*

Sylvie had the foresight to lock the door behind her before tossing her purse onto a chair and making her way upstairs, crying the whole time, though in a restrained, gulping fashion. She made quick work of removing her clothing and stepping into her glass-walled shower stall. Only when the water was pulsating hot and steamy did she let loose with all the pain that seemed to have built up inside her.

It was Luc's betrayal, of course, that had prompted this breakdown, but there was more than that. She hadn't realized how much tension she'd built up over the love-potion discovery, the bullets shot into her home, Luc being captured. It was all too much for a normally reticent Sylvie to handle, especially on top of Luc's words this afternoon that he didn't want to see her again. Oh, he'd softened it by saying *for a while*, but she knew he was just trying to let her down easy.

With eyes closed and her face held upward, she basked in the hot pellets of spray that numbed her face and hopefully her heart. She was a strong woman. She would get over this . . . eventually. But, God, it hurt so bad.

"Sylv?"

Sylvie could barely hear the voice over the pounding shower, but before she had a chance to register the danger that someone had entered her house, Luc opened the shower door. He cursed softly under his breath on witnessing her sorry state, and entered the shower, fully clothed.

Luc saw the anguish on Sylvie's face and could have died, knowing he'd caused her pain. Without care for his jeans and T-shirt, or the athletic shoes on his feet, he walked into the watery cascade. He couldn't let another minute go by with Sylvie crying . . . *over him*.

The minute he'd left the holding cell and realized that Sylvie wasn't in the waiting room, he'd panicked. Sure, he'd told her that they shouldn't see each other for a while, but he'd been expecting to have time to explain his reasoning . . . in a private place where hidden eyes and ears couldn't eavesdrop. He had pictured her tapping a foot angrily at the front desk, pissed off at him, calling him bad names, having second thoughts about helping him. But he'd never pictured her *not there*.

When he'd seen that she was gone, and realized that he might have pushed her too far, a sense of utter desperation overcame him. He'd only been involved with Sylvie for a few days. Still, in a flash of insight, he'd realized how miserable his life would be without Sylvie in it. Amazing, but true.

Tante Lulu had always claimed that when the thunderbolt hit, there would be no doubts. Well, he'd been hit with the mother of all zaps to the heart.

The processing of his release had taken only a half hour, but it had seemed like forever. His intuition had told him, and rightly so, that he needed to reach Sylvie immediately and explain himself before it was too late.

Was it already too late?

"Sylvie, let me explain," he said now, not even caring if he looked like a fool standing fully clothed in her shower.

"Go away," she wailed, trying to turn her face and naked body toward the wall.

It didn't matter if it was shyness or resistance on her part. He couldn't allow her to put that kind of distance between them. Small spans soon became canyons, in his experience; best to close that gap now. "Listen to me," he ordered, but Sylvie went wild . . . kicking, biting, crying.

Because she kept struggling, he pressed her up against the wall, his fingers interlaced with hers, and held her hands above her head so they both clasped the showerhead. His already waterlogged body crushed against her nudity, chest to groin, till she was unable to move, trapped between him and the ceramic wall.

"Ah, *chère*, don't cry."

"I'm not crying," she cried.

"Why did you leave without me?" he asked accusingly.

She blinked wetly at him. "Because you told me you didn't want me anymore . . ." Then she added as an afterthought, "You louse."

He inhaled sharply. "I never said that. But I'm a louse, if you say I am."

"Yes, you did, Luc. You louse."

"I suggested we not see each other . . . for a while. There's a difference." He shook his head from side to side, as if she were a thickheaded child. "Can't you tell how much I want you?" he asked, even as his head was descending toward hers. Her lips were full and red and swollen from crying, and he couldn't resist the temptation. He just couldn't.

He saw from her expression the moment she became aware that he was pressing his erection into her lower belly. Instead of being embarrassed, as she usually was, or angry, she looked sad. "You just want sex, Luc. Any willing body would do."

"Oh, *chère*, that's not true." Sylvie thought she was the one with the lack of confidence, but he could match her in the self-doubt department, insecurity for insecurity. All his life, he'd had drummed into him the idea that he was bad. How could someone like Sylvie love him, for himself? He had to prove himself worthy. What if he made love to her? That was something he could do for her. Maybe she would love him for how he made her feel.

Having made that decision—and it wasn't all that difficult, considering his constant half-arousals when around Sylvie—he decided to kiss her senseless. Then he would do all those other things he'd become proficient at over the years. He might not be a good person, but he was a good lover.

Unfortunately, Sylvie had other ideas. "No," she said firmly, and tried to turn her head away.

But his mouth just followed after hers. "Do you need the words, *chère*?"

"No . . . yes . . . oh, God!" He assumed the "oh, God!" was an involuntary admission that she wanted him, too. At least, he hoped that was the case.

His lips were already slanting across hers. "I want you," he whispered huskily against her mouth.

She sighed a wispy surrender, and parted her lips for him.

"I want you," he repeated.

His tongue plunged deep inside her mouth, then withdrew.

When he came up for air, she asked, "Is the love potion kicking in again?" For some reason, she didn't appear happy at that prospect.

"Hell if I know." He was pulling his shirt over his head even as he continued kissing her.

"Is that the reason for this . . . uh, reversal of affection?"

"Huh?" he said against her mouth, which he was devouring with delicious expertise.

"I said, are you feeling the effects of the love potion again?"

"Why? Are you taking notes?"

"Mmm."

He bit her bottom lip lightly in punishment.

"I'm too excited to give you logical answers now, Sylv. All I know is I want you. I want you, I want you, I want you," he groaned out . . . a painfully sweet sexual litany.

His fingers were no longer interlaced with hers, but

still she held onto the showerhead for support. Otherwise, her legs would probably give way with the scandalous things his mouth and hands were doing to her.

But he had an even bigger problem now. He was having a helluva time undoing the wet zipper on his jeans. The damned metal tab just wouldn't move. Where was Houdini when he needed him? With a howl of frustration, he grabbed for a cake of soap and rubbed it over the zipper, up and down. *Voila!* He was free. Well, almost free. He had the same problem with the laces on his sneakers. By the time he rolled out of his jeans, like a banana out of a tight peel, he was feeling more like a . . . well, cucumber. Whatever. He now stood naked before Sylvie.

He looked up to see her smiling. *Smiling?* Hey, at least she wasn't still crying.

Then her eyes traveled down his body and stopped dead-on . . . dead on the *cucumber*, that is. To say she was impressed was probably an understatement. Hell, he was impressed, and he'd been living with that body part for thirty-three years.

Somewhere, somehow, sometime . . . whether from a love potion, lack of use, or a zipper soap-rubbing . . . his organ had taken on a huge, vein-popping, tumescent life of its own.

He shrugged ruefully. "Sometimes you get a blue steeler. And sometimes you don't."

She laughed . . . a soft, ripply sound. "Sort of like an Almond Joy?"

"Exactly."

She was still standing under the streaming water with her hands extended over her head, clutching the showerhead. She began to lower her hands . . . to embrace him or take the ol' bar of LeDeux Joy in hand, he wasn't sure which . . . but he protested immediately, forcing her hands back upward. He wanted to savor this picture of Sylvie standing before him thus.

"Let me," he begged, and took a container of liquid body wash in hand. Squirting the fragrant fluid onto his palms, he began to work it into her neck and arms and underarms.

"I'm mad at you," she said weakly, squirming under his touch.

"I know." He bypassed her breasts and lathered her sides and buttocks, her abdomen and flat belly. Going down on one knee, he concentrated on her thighs and calves, as well, even the arches of her feet, and toes.

"Sex doesn't solve everything, Luc," she protested, but her voice was breathy and uneven as she spoke.

"I know," he agreed once again, standing to refill his palms with the slick soap. He couldn't help chuckling when he added, "But it's a helluva start."

He lathered her breasts over and over with wide, circular kneading motions. Then he used his soapy fingertips on the peaks, over and over and over and over, till she was mewling continuously with pleasure and the need for fulfillment. He let the shower wash the soap off her then, and replaced his fingers with his lips and tongue and teeth, suckling her ravenously.

She was probably crying again, but he didn't care now because it was for sexual need of him. That had to be a good thing.

When he moved his ministrations lower to the dewy curls and hot wetness between her legs, she let herself go limp, the only thing holding her up being her grip on the showerhead. He tipped her face up with a finger under her chin, forcing her glazed eyes to meet with his.

"I love you," he whispered.

He hadn't known he was going to say that, and he was as surprised as Sylvie. But it was the right thing to say and the right time.

"I love you, *chère*. Remember that, always. I don't deserve you. I may never have you. But don't ever doubt that I love you."

"Luc, I—"

Before she had a chance to say anything, he turned off the water and took her in his arms, carrying her to the bedroom. Uncaring of their wet bodies, he laid her on the coverlet, then came down on top of her.

For what was probably only a half hour, but seemed like forever, Luc made slow, endless love to Sylvie. And it was so good, he wept, too.

Whoever said, "Ain't love grand?" didn't know the pain it could bring, in Luc's opinion. Even as he basked in the joy of loving Sylvie, Luc sensed the agony to come.

And so he left.

If all else fails, try voodoo . . .

When Sylvie awakened several hours later, Luc was gone. She wasn't overly alarmed, though, even when she read his terse note on the kitchen counter, next to Samson and Delilah.

> Sylvie:
>   I cleaned the rat cage. Don't call me. I'll call you.
>   <u>Love,</u>
>   Luc

The reference to cleaning the cage had to mean that he'd taken the hidden Cypress Oil documents that

Remy had intended to take earlier, but had forgotten. And as to telephone calls, she assumed all their lines were bugged at this point.

The thing that gave her hope—and perhaps it was a sign of how pathetic she'd become—was that Luc had underlined the word *love*. She was hoping that was his secret message to her, reinforcing what he'd told her earlier, that he loved her.

There was such joy in her, knowing that she loved Luc, and that he loved her in return. Even though she hadn't confessed her feelings to him yet, she was certain he must know.

Throughout the afternoon, she held that joy close to her heart, refusing to let anything pull her down, even when she started a list of all the people she would need to talk to or make appointments with: Charles, Aunt Margo and Aunt Madeline, her lawyer, Claudia, Blanche, Matt Sommese, her mother. She grimaced upon writing that last name on her notepad, but really, she and her mother had some serious issues to resolve . . . ones that had been festering for years.

But first things first. She suspected that Luc, even while he'd been in jail, had already begun the process of discovering who had been shooting at them in her apartment. Between him and Claudia and the police, she was certain the culprits would be caught and her safety ensured. But there was another danger she could work on herself . . . the voodoo curse.

She leafed through the telephone directory, then picked up the phone on the kitchen wall and punched in a series of numbers.

"Hello. Tante Lulu?"

"Yes."

"This is Sylvie Fontaine."

"I know that, dear. Is Luc there?"

"No, he left some time ago."

"Is everything okay?"

"Everything's wonderful . . . with Luc, that is."

"Hallelujah. You'd better say a little prayer to St. Jude, honey."

"I will," Sylvie said with a smile. "But that's not why I called. I have to ask a favor of you. Do you happen to know any . . . uhm, ah . . . well, voodoo people?"

"Why? You wanna get a love charm? Ha, ha, ha. I know some good love charms for you to nail that Luc down good and proper. Alls you gotta do is buy a pure white beeswax candle and under it you place a piece of paper with Luc's name on it. Then you burn that candle down till the name is completely covered with wax so that no one can ever read the name. Oh, and did I tell you the name has to be written in dove's blood?"

"Dove's blood? Where would I get dove's blood?" Sylvie laughed then. "That's not why I need a voodoo practitioner."

"It's not?" Tante Lulu said hesitantly.

"No. I need to have a voodoo curse removed."

"Uh-oh."

A pregnant silence followed.

"Tante Lulu?"

"I'm here, but I don't like messin' with no evil spirits, child. No, I don't."

"I suppose I could go over to the French Quarter in New Orleans. There are a couple of shops that claim to be run by voodoo priestesses."

Tante Lulu made a tsk-ing sound. "Those quacks! They're crooked enough to make ol' Marie Laveau turn over in her grave, I reckon. Let me think on this a minute." After a brief pause, she continued. "Let me ask you a question. Would this be between you and me? Private-like?"

"Absolutely."

Tante Lulu sighed in resignation. "Meet me at Mildred's Gun Shop on Highway 90 tonight at nine."

Oh, Lordy!

"Dress in black."

Oh, my God!

"It would help if you brought one of your chickens. Or two."

Sylvie couldn't help asking, "Why?"

"The ritual sacrifice."

"Oh, my!" was her first thought, inadvertently spoken aloud. The second was, "Luc is going to kill us."

"Guar-an-teed!"

Holy crawfish! What next? . . .

Luc was sitting at the conference table in his Houma law office. Also attending the meeting were his personal attorney; Clovis Dupree; Clovis's two partners; René; three of his shrimp fishermen friends; Claudia; and five Cypress Oil attorneys from Dallas, Baton Rouge, and Washington, D.C., including Joe VanZandt.

There was also Dixie Breaux, Sylvie's grandmother, a longtime federal lobbyist for various oil companies, including Cypress. She was a neatly coifed, white-haired lady who had to be at least seventy years old, despite her tight-skinned, perfectly toned complexion. The navy suit and white pearls she wore had probably cost as much as most people's cars.

They'd been going at it for over two hours, Luc realized as he looked down at his watch. Nine P.M. By now everyone's cards were on the table.

Cypress Oil contended they were pretty much going to whip his ass.

He contended the shrimp fishermen were pretty much going to whip their asses.

Needless to say, they were at a stalemate. Time to pull out his trump card.

"Gentlemen . . . and ladies," he said, nodding to Dixie and Claudia, "unless we come to some settlement within the next half hour, I'm going to have to call a press conference."

"Why? To give a running account of your love-potion activities?" VanZandt sneered. "There are some men who need a boost in that department and some who don't."

All the Cypress people smirked at his not-so-veiled innuendo that Luc needed a boost in sexual energy.

He gritted his teeth and snapped, "Get a life, VanZandt." To the others, he continued. "I think the press would be interested in knowing that there's new research on the effect of oil pollutants, like the ones being discharged into the freshwater supply by Cypress Oil."

"Oh, please, you're going to start that cancer scare again," Dixie said in her ultra-refined voice that implied she was better than the rest of mankind . . . or at least a nobody Cajun lawyer. "People just don't buy it, Mr. LeDeux, or they are willing to take the risks. Oil feeds the local economy here. So, give up that argument."

"Well, actually, I think cancer is serious business, but that's not what I'm alluding to. No, actually, I'm talking about the fact that oil pollutants cause sperm counts to go down in fish." He tapped his pen on the table for dramatic effect, then added, "I wonder if that means oil pollutants affect human male virility as well."

He saw awareness bloom in Dixie's intelligent eyes. She would know immediately what the public would do with this kind of threat. Close down Cypress Oil, that's what.

VanZandt jumped to his feet. "You have no proof of that."

"Don't I?"

The other four Cypress lawyers chimed in as well:

"Do you have chemical data to back up that claim?"

"If the public isn't scared by all the cancer propaganda, what makes you think this sperm-count business will matter one iota?"

"Who's your research company?"

"You're not using Sylvie Fontaine for your researcher, are you? Is that the connection between you two?"

"Wait a minute," Dixie Breaux said. The authority in her voice caused everyone, including Luc, to defer to her. "No one is bringing my granddaughter into this discussion. Mr. LeDeux, if you have research material you'd like to show us, I think it would behoove Cypress Oil to listen."

Thus chastened, the Cypress lackeys all sat down.

"Oh, and did I mention one other thing?" Luc tapped his head with a forefinger as if he were forgetful. "There is the issue of this Cypress Oil document." With that, he passed a dozen copies of the papers Tee-John had pilfered around the table.

There were several subtle gasps as the lawyers began to read.

Just then, the phone in the outer office rang. "Would you excuse me for a moment?" Luc said.

It was perfect timing, really, Luc thought as he closed the conference room door, and picked up the telephone.

"Luc, is your meeting over yet?" Remy asked in a decidedly worried voice.

"Just about."

"And?"

"Nothing settled, but looking good."

"Uh, we have a wee bit of a problem."

"Involving?"

"Sylvie and Tante Lulu."

He inhaled too fast and went into a choking fit. When he regained his composure, he inquired, "Together?"

"Yep."

"What do you want me to do?"

"Can you meet me at Mildred's Gun Shop, ASAP?"

"Mildred's Gun Shop!" he shouted into the phone. "Remy, what's going on?"

"You don't want to know."

"Yes, I do."

"Let's just say this. Do the words voodoo, live chickens, a love potion, and two dingbat females riding a Harley mean anything to you?"

Men! They just don't understand . . .

Luc pulled his jeep in front of Sylvie's house and turned off the ignition. The motor, of course, continued to rumble till it came to a sputtering halt.

He hadn't spoken since he'd hauled her and Tante Lulu out of a voodoo ritual ceremony in the swamp behind Mildred's Gun Shop. Remy, who couldn't stop laughing, had driven their aunt home, and René had been only too glad to take possession of the motorcycle.

Sitting in the passenger seat of the decrepit vehicle, Sylvie attempted to soothe his ruffled temper. "Don't you think you're overreacting a bit?"

"Overreacting? Overreacting?" Both of his hands were clenched on the steering wheel, and his teeth were gritted. "Screaming at you might be overreacting, though I was sorely tempted. Putting you over my knee and paddling that heart-shaped butt of yours might be overreacting, though the thought is appealing. Stopping you from actually drinking that chicken blood during the voodoo ritual might have been overreacting, but it would have served you right." He turned and stared at her. "Babe, you haven't seen overreacting . . . *yet*."

Should she try to explain to Luc? Or was it a losing battle in his present mood?

"Listen, Luc, you and I might snicker over voodoo and pretend that it's all just hocus-pocus, but we both know it can't be dismissed so easily. Strange, unexplainable things happen when voodoo is involved." She took a deep breath and tried to lighten his mood. "Luckily, they'd already finished the ritual to remove the curse before you got there. So, no more worries in that regard."

He stared at her as if she'd flipped her lid. Maybe she had. "How could you?" he asked finally.

"How could I not?" she answered stubbornly. "I needed to have that voodoo curse removed, and that's what I did."

"With dead chickens?"

She shrugged. "Whatever it takes."

"Why did you involve Tante Lulu?"

She ducked her face guiltily at that. "She was the only person I could think of who might know a voodoo person. Besides, you told me not to call you."

"What kind of half-assed logic is that? I'm trying to protect you, Sylvie, and you're making it damn hard. First, you release me from jail when I don't want to be released. Then, you drag my aunt into some harebrained scheme that could endanger you both."

She bristled. "You are the most ungrateful bastard! I've taken care of myself for most of my life, and somehow I've survived, harebrained as you seem to think I am."

"Sylvie, I was in the middle of a meeting with the Cypress Oil lawyers when Remy called me. I do not need any more problems now."

"Oh, really. And who else was at this meeting?"

He was surprised at her question, but detailed all the parties involved. "Why do you want to know?"

She was unable to keep the hurt from her voice. "Why wasn't I there, Luc?"

"Huh?"

"You heard me. You've gone to great lengths to get me to help you with the water and soil samples. I agreed to send the samples to a chemist friend of mine who specializes in oil pollutants. You made me promise to testify in court, if necessary."

"And?"

"And now you exclude me, you jerk."

"Don't you turn this on me, Sylv. Why couldn't you just stay put for a few days and let me handle things?"

"S-stay put?" she sputtered. "You mean, like a good little girl? You mean, like I've behaved all my life? You mean, like other people are more competent to do the job than me? Ooooh, I'd like to give you 'stay put.'"

Luc's eyes went wide at the vehemence of her response. "I just want you to be safe."

She was so angry she was shaking. Jumping out of his Jeep, she stomped up to her house. At the last minute, she turned and told him, "All my life, I've done what's safe. And I've been miserable. I thought you were different, Luc." Her voice broke before she repeated, "I thought you were different."

She had to give Luc credit. He did come after her, pleading, "Sylvie, be reasonable," but she'd already slammed and locked the door in his face.

* * *

Could it possibly be true? . . .

A week went by without Sylvie seeing or hearing from Luc, and her temper had cooled.

She wasn't even upset with him for breaking off communication because she assumed he was either in the process of preparing for a court battle with Cypress Oil, or in the process of negotiating a pre-trial settlement. Besides, she had enough on her plate to worry about without being involved in the shrimpers' fight. And despite her protests to the contrary, it was really rather sweet of Luc to be so protective of her.

The only niggling doubt in her mind regarded the love potion. Had it worn off yet? Did Luc still harbor feelings for her now? Did he want her anymore?

She'd gone in to work at Terrebonne Pharmaceuticals several days this week, although her relations with Charles were strained, to say the least. He'd demanded all her data on JBX, which she'd declined to turn over, for now. Further he'd insisted that she continue working on the love-potion enterprise, which she'd also declined to do. Sylvie needed some time to mull over the new insights she'd gained about her project; so, she'd buried herself in old birth-control and hormone-replacement work, which was always ongoing.

When she pulled up at a red light near the courthouse on her way home, she noticed Tee-John pushing a red bicycle with a flat rear tire along the sidewalk. He wore huge, baggy shorts and an oversized T-shirt, and on his feet, the pricey athletic shoes, the kind that cost several hundred dollars thanks to some celeb sports person's endorsement.

Rolling down her window, she called out, "Hey, Tee-John, need a lift?"

He looked over at her sedan skeptically, then nodded.

They should be able to fit the bike in the trunk and secure the lid with some bungee ropes.

That done, and with Tee-John belted in the passenger seat, she asked, "So what happened?"

"Stupid bike keeps losin' air. Guess I need a new
tire."

"Where were you going?" She turned off on a side
street that would take her to the outskirts of town and
Valcour LeDeux's house.

"I went to Luc's place, but he wasn't there. His secretary said he went to lunch with Claudia."

Sylvie's heart lurched with that ol' blasted jealousy,
but she immediately quelled it. Luc and Claudia had a
business relationship . . . nothing more. She remembered how Claudia and Remy had looked at each other.
She'd never intercepted similar looks between Claudia
and Luc.

"Is everything okay with your dad? I mean, about
your running away?"

"He chased me around the backyard with a switch a
few times, but he couldn't catch me. Mom slapped me
around a bit, though. Says I embarrassed her with her
friends." He shrugged. "I'm grounded for a month."

"Grounded?" Sylvie inquired with a lifted brow.
"You don't look grounded to me."

He grinned at her. "Dad's busy with lawyers all this
week. And my mother went to Dallas, shoppin'. Neither one of 'em really cares."

"Oh, Tee-John, I'm sure that's not true." She was
turning up the winding half-circle drive to the mansion
belonging to Valcour LeDeux. "Your father and mother
love you very much."

"Hah! He's not even my real father," the boy blurted
out, then ducked his head sheepishly.

"Tee-John! What a thing to say!"

"Well, it's true. Every time my dad and mom have a fight, he brings it up. Says my mom's a tramp, and there ain't never gonna be any weddin' till she proves he's my father. And she says he's a two-timin' bastard, and she ain't never agreein' to any DNA tests till he marries up with her."

"Tee-John, you must have misunderstood."

"Nah, I understand lots more than folks think I do. Fer instance, my dad has lots of girlfriends, and I think Mom's been sleepin' with the pool guy."

Sylvie was appalled . . . that parents would fight like that within hearing range of a child, that Tee-John had to live with those kinds of paternity questions, that Valcour and Jolie had such low morals that they slept around the way they did.

"But you look just like . . ." Sylvie started to say, then stopped herself when a most uncomfortable thought occurred to her. Tee-John looked just like the other LeDeux brothers, she had been about to remark.

Could it possibly be?

Oh, God! Please, no.

Even as Sylvie stopped the car and helped Tee-John remove the bike, even as she drove the car away, she couldn't help wondering about one alarming suspicion.

Could Luc be Tee-John's father?

It appeared that he lived down to his expectations . . .

Sylvie had been sitting in the waiting room of Luc's law office for over an hour before he came strolling in, wearing a dark blue business suit, light blue dress shirt, and a Star-Spangled Banner flag tie in shades of red, white, and blue. This was a stranger to Sylvie . . . not the man she'd come to know and love.

But then, maybe she'd never really known him. And maybe the love had been an illusion, too.

His secretary had informed her that he had a civil case on the court docket for two P.M. and that he'd planned to go there right from lunch. It was now three o'clock.

"Sylv!" Luc said on noticing her. "I was going to call you later today."

Hah! Likely story!

There was surprise and pleasure on his face, not the anger she'd seen the last time they'd met. Things must be going well with the oil-pollution case, or he would be upset over her making contact with him.

"Can we talk in private?" she asked, sidestepping his arms, which had been about to pull her into an embrace. The guy had no problem with public shows of affection in front of his staff, apparently. Was it just her, or every woman he treated thus?

In particular, how about Jolie Guillot?

His brows lifted in question at her avoidance of his touch, but he nodded. Tossing some court documents on his secretary's desk with instructions on letters to be written, he then opened his private office door, motioning for her to enter in front of him.

Sylvie should have known better.

No sooner had the door shut behind them than Luc had her pinned to the wall and was kissing her ravenously. So much for the love potion wearing off!

At first, she succumbed to the delicious play of his lips on hers. It had been a week, and she had missed him tremendously, and he was such a good kisser. But she was here for a purpose, she reminded herself. A serious purpose.

Shoving against his chest, hard, Sylvie moved to the other side of the room, putting a desk between them. "I have something to ask you," she said without preamble.

"Will it involve tape measures and body fluids?" He was grinning at her, even as he approached in a slow, predatory manner. Just as he feinted one way, then the other, trying to grab for her, she moved behind his desk. Luc continued to grin, obviously enjoying this stalking game.

Well, she wasn't. And it was time to straighten out a few important matters.

"Is Tee-John your son?" she asked bluntly.

Luc stopped in his tracks, and the grin evaporated from his mouth. "What did you say?"

Sylvie sank down into the desk chair and put her face in her hand for a moment. Once she was calm, she repeated her question. "Is Tee-John your son?"

His silence was damning, and the bleak expression on his face was downright alarming. "I don't know," he admitted softly.

"You don't know?" she practically shrieked. "How could you not know such a thing? Is it even possible?"

"Yes, dammit, it's possible."

Sylvie put both palms to her abdomen. She felt as if she'd been kicked in the gut.

"Eleven years ago, I came home from college during my senior year. I was drinking at a Christmas party, and she was there." He lifted his palms in a weary fashion. "I just don't know."

"Did it ever occur to you to ask?"

"Of course I asked."

"And?"

"Jolie laughed."

"She laughed?" Sylvie repeated. "Couldn't you have had DNA tests done?"

"Not without the mother's permission, and Jolie prefers having my father's purse strings than mine."

"Well, I'd say it's about time you found out for sure. Tee-John has overheard too many things. He's suspicious."

"Oh, God!" The look of horror on Luc's face had to be genuine. "He thinks it's me?"

"No, no, no! He just suspects that Valcour isn't his father."

Luc tilted his head and stared at her. "Then how did you make the connection?"

"Because he looks just like you. Because some of his mannerisms are identical to yours. Because, in retrospect, I realized how green you turned at times when I mentioned Valcour being his father."

He nodded.

"I just don't understand you, Luc. How could you have let that boy stay in the same house with Valcour LeDeux, knowing that he might be yours?"

Luc's chin lifted in defiance. "You can't think any less of me than I have for years. The 'bad boy of the bayou' appellation has been well-earned. Sleeping with my father's common-law wife! Talk about trash! But I've looked out for Tee-John all my life. Don't you insinuate otherwise."

They both stared at each other then, each waiting for the other to say something more.

"I guess that's it then," Luc said, his shoulders dropping with resignation. "I told you over and over, Sylv, that you're uptown and I'm . . . not."

With a sigh, she gathered her purse and was about to leave. "We'll talk about this later, Luc."

"Yeah, right." Luc spoke with his back to her as he stared out the window.

"I need time to think," she said defensively.

"Call me when you have some answers, babe, because I sure as hell am fresh out."

Sylvie closed the door behind her, and felt a door of much more importance closing between them, as well.

Chapter Seventeen

Whoa, daddy! . . .

Luc was sitting at Swampy's bar several days later when his two brothers sidled up to him, one on either side.

"Is it really as bad as all that?" asked René, whose band was taking a break from the second set.

"It's worse," Luc muttered into his beer. Actually, he'd been sipping at the same beer for so long, the bartender, Gator, was giving him a dirty look. Amazing how being on the binge wagon for so long turned serious drinking into such an unappealing experience. He must have grown up somewhere along the way in the past five or ten years without realizing it.

"I thought you'd be happy that the police arrested those two hoodlums who shot at you and Sylvie," Remy remarked, taking a long drink from a frosty glass of draft.

"I am," Luc said, pushing his beer aside, "but I still think Dad was involved somehow. He probably paid them well to say they were hired by some unknown person to scare us off."

His two brothers nodded in agreement.

"I'm not buying their claim that they were from New York, either. Not with those thick Creole accents," Luc went on. "But at least they'll be doing a minimum of three to five in the state pen. And Claudia can call off her guards."

"To tell the truth, I think Dad was scared shitless this time," Remy added. "He's pulled some shady deals in the past, but I don't think he expected his hired guns to actually use . . . well, guns on one of his sons. Maybe he's learned his lesson this time."

They all nodded again.

"So, why the sad-sack face, bro?" René asked, clapping a hand on Luc's shoulder. "You should be happy that everything is falling into place."

"Everything but Sylvie. Luc is in luuuuuv," Remy pointed out in a teasing tone.

"Man, if that's what love's like, I hope I'm never afflicted," Remy commented, motioning for Gator to set another draft in front of him and René. "Are you still under the influence of the love potion, do you think?"

"Damned if I know." Luc took a sip of his tepid beer and grimaced. "All I know is I love her. I want her with a passion. All I can think about is Sylvie."

"Sounds like a love potion to me," was Remy's opinion.

As if Remy knew how a love potion felt!

"Why don't you just call her, Luc?" René suggested.

"Now that the negotiations with Cypress Oil are almost finalized, she's in no real danger. At least not from the oil folks. I can't speak for the love-potion fanatics."

"Yeah," Remy agreed. "If she really loves you, nothing could be that bad."

"She never actually said she loves me," Luc admitted.

Remy waved a hand airily. "No biggie, bro. You should have seen the look on her face when she was defending you to Dad and to her mother."

Luc felt his face brighten with hope that soon deflated. "That was before she learned . . . well, never mind."

"Learned what?" both his brothers demanded.

"There are things about me even you guys don't know."

"What could be so damned bad?" Remy asked.

"Really, Luc, everyone has something he regrets," René said. "I can't imagine anything in your past that couldn't be forgiven."

"Oh, yeah! How about the fact that Tee-John might be my son?" Luc recoiled at the indiscretion of his loose tongue. For more than ten years, Luc had kept this suspicion to himself. Now, in one moment of insanity, he had blurted it all out. He was pathetic.

A deafening silence followed in which Luc felt like crawling into one of the filthy cracks in Swampy's plank floors.

"Uh. Luc, I think you'd better explain." Remy's voice was oddly strangled.

"What can I say? I was a college senior, home on break, suffering from terminal horniness. There was a Christmas party . . . I'd been drinking . . . and Jolie crawled into my bed. So, maybe . . . just maybe . . . Tee-John is mine."

"And Sylvie found out?" Remy guessed.

"Yep. Just call me 'the bad boy of the bayou,' through and through."

Remy inhaled deeply, then let out a whoosh of air. "Well, you'd better make that 'the bad *boys* of the bayou.' 'Cause I was eighteen at the time and living at home. Suffice it to say, I always wondered if Tee-John was *my* son. Like you, there was only one time with the round-heeled Jolie, but I guess that's all it takes."

"Remy!" Luc exclaimed. "Are you saying you've been as guilt-ridden as I've been all these years?"

"Absolutely. I guess it's why we've both kept such a close eye on the kid. I would have moved to Alaska long ago to open my own small aircraft business, but I felt the need to stick close to Houma."

Luc stared at his brother in astonishment. "What a helluva mess! I just can't believe Jolie went after both of us."

"Uh, actually . . ." René raised a hand sheepishly. "I was nineteen, and Jolie came to my shrimp boat one night. You can't imagine how guilty I've been feeling all these years. And I've been keepin' an eagle eye on Tee-John too."

They all glanced at each other, stunned at the enormity of what they'd just discovered.

"What a sorry bunch of sonofabitches we are!" René concluded with a mirthless laugh.

"Man, that Jolie must have been laughin' up her miniskirt all these years," Luc commented. "Pulling all our strings, even Dad's. I'm thinking she's not as dumb as she acts."

"You should tell Sylvie about this, Luc," Remy suggested. "Betcha she'd understand."

He shook his head. "No, don't you see, it's not the possible paternity that upset her. It's that she believes my failure to take responsibility has put Tee-John in physical jeopardy. I'm A-1 reckless scum in her book, guaranteed."

His brothers nodded. Women had a different way of thinking than men, and they knew it.

"Well, one thing's for damn sure. We're going to find out one way or another who the proud papa is. *Now,*" Luc vowed, and everyone agreed.

Whew! . . .

The next day, DNA tests were performed in a hospital lab on Tee-John LeDeux and his three "brothers," not to mention an enraged Valcour LeDeux.

The father was proven to be Valcour, much to Jolie's delight. "Do y'all think I would've risked mah fortune gettin' knocked up by you penniless schmucks?" Jolie remarked to them with a laugh.

"She has a point there," Luc agreed.

"Yep, schmucks 'r us," was Remy's astute observation.

"Do they sell cigars to celebrate non-fatherhood?" René put in.

Valcour just glowered at them all.

Valcour and Jolie were married the following day in a civil ceremony . . . but only after Jolie signed a generous pre-nup, put together by The Swamp Solicitor, no less.

Although some of the burden of guilt was lifted from Luc's, René's, and Remy's shoulders, they were sobered by the secret they'd harbored all these years and the repercussions that could occur when morality wavered. And they'd all confessed to having worried that there was a bit of their father's bad blood in them.

Luc was determined to explain all of this to Sylvie and hope she would understand, but thus far she'd avoided his calls. Not to worry. He had a plan that should redeem himself in her eyes. The world was going to know as well as he did just how great a chemist Sylvie was. She was sure to melt when he made his big announcement.

He hoped.

But just for good measure, Luc pulled out his St. Jude medal and said a little prayer. St. Jude wasn't the patron saint of hopeless cases for nothing.

Under the influence . . . or not . . .

Sylvie had been meeting with Charles for more than an hour, trying to convince him to put a temporary halt on the JBX project.

"Charles, having been with Luc for several days while he was under the influence of the love potion has given me a new perspective on this project. I'm not saying we dump JBX. I'm just saying we need to step back and set some new parameters."

Sylvie had come to some startling conclusions the past few days . . . days during which she'd refused to speak with Luc, days when all she'd done was think. The conclusion was clear: She did not like having a man fall in love with her prompted by a love potion. Whether the love carried over after the effects wore off was beside the point. Love was demeaned when it began because of a chemical formula.

Besides that, Delilah had taken a decided dislike to Samson, and Sylvie thought she understood why. The situation had become so bad that she'd had to buy another critter cage to separate the bickering rats. Could the rat behavior be extrapolated to humans? Would Luc turn on her, the way Delilah had with her lover?

"We don't have the luxury of time," Charles contended. "The cat's out of the bag, so to speak, and other companies will be copying us if we don't act quickly."

"How can they copy us if they don't have our formula?"

"That's another thing. You need to turn over the research data. I've tried . . . and our other chemists have tried . . . to break down those jelly beans you left behind with your enzymes in them, but there are some ingredients we just can't identify."

"I could have told you that," she answered, not liking the fact that they were trying to "steal" her formula behind her back.

But then something Charles had said struck a chord with her.

"You didn't have any jelly beans with my enzymes in them. Those were the ones that Luc took. The ones left sitting on the counter were the neutral set."

"You're wrong. The jelly beans left behind definitely had your enzymes in them." To prove his contention, he motioned toward a microscope that was already set up with a slide on it holding a halved jelly bean.

She peered into the lens, and gasped. He was right.

She frowned with puzzlement. If the jelly beans left behind had her enzymes, then that meant that the jelly beans Luc had ingested . . .

"Oh, my God!" she exclaimed. "That means that Luc never took the love potion after all. There must have been a mix-up in the petri dishes."

"I thought you knew that all along."

"Are you crazy? You thought I went off with Luc, pretending that he took the love potion? Why?"

Charles shrugged. "Good publicity."

"You believed this was all a PR stunt on my part?"

He nodded.

"You are a world-class worm."

There was no love potion. Sylvie reeled as the implications of this news numbed her. If Luc hadn't been under the influence of JBX, then that must mean that he'd been fooling her all along. Sylvie felt as if she'd been sucker-punched in the gut.

Tears burned her eyes while the ramifications kept occurring to her one by one, like dominoes falling in place. It had been a game to Luc all along. The teasing. The seduction. The profession of love. And the whole time, he'd probably been laughing at her.

Grabbing for her briefcase, Sylvie pointed a finger at Charles. "The JBX project halts right now. I'll see you in court if necessary, but *we* are not proceeding till some new ground rules are set."

Charles started to protest, then indicated with a motion of his hand that he acquiesced. "Let's give it a week, then meet together with our lawyers."

"In the meantime, you'll do nothing."

"I'll do nothing," he promised. "But JBX is too promising to discontinue. Agreed?"

She inclined her head in compliance.

Sylvie left the building and the parking lot as soon as she could, still unable to comprehend the full significance of this latest turn of events. She wasn't sure what all the effects would be, but one thing was certain: She was devastated by Luc's deception.

She'd thought the possibility of Luc's fathering Tee-John was bad, but this was worse. The "bad boy of the bayou" had proven just how bad he could be.

She would never, ever forgive him.

* * *

Why do fools fall in love? . . .

That evening, Sylvie sat on the sofa with Blanche waiting for the local newscast to come on. Tante Lulu had called to alert her that there would be a special segment on the settlement between the Southern Louisiana shrimpers and Cypress Oil.

"Honey, you have to put this in perspective," Blanche advised. They'd been discussing the situation between her and Luc. Her friend had already given her candid opinion of Sylvie's red eyes and puffy nose.

"Perspective? The man is a tomcat who screws everything in sight, including his own stepmother, or almost-stepmother. And he lied through his teeth about being wildly attracted to me because of the love potion."

"Okay, I'll concede he deserves a few whaps in some strategic places, but, geez, Sylv, love doesn't come along all that often."

"But *he* doesn't love me. Can't you see? He was just pretending when he said that."

"I was referring to *your* being in love. And don't deny it, Sylv. You love Lucien LeDeux."

Sylvie sighed, unable to repudiate that fact, much as she wished she could.

"Honey, don't throw it away without giving him a chance to explain."

"Explain? Oh, Blanche. What explanation can there possibly be for deliberately pulling the wool over my eyes? I knew I was out of my league with him from the start. I just didn't realize how far."

"And now we take you to the boardroom of Cypress Oil where a press conference is about to take place," the announcer was saying.

She and Blanche sat up.

Seated at a long table in front of a bank of microphones was the president of Cypress Oil, Winston Oliver, who'd flown in from Los Angeles; Joe VanZandt, a Cypress Oil attorney; Deke Boudreaux, a Cypress flunky; several of the shrimp fishermen; and Luc, who looked absolutely gorgeous in a dark suit and white shirt with a floral tie. His hair had been recently trimmed.

"He got a haircut," Sylvie murmured. For some reason, that brought tears welling in her eyes, even though she thought she'd been cried out today.

"You're weeping over a haircut, Sylv? Why?" Blanche was staring at her with alarm.

"Because he's already started to change, that's why. To go on with his life."

Blanche chuckled at her fancifulness.

Sylvie swiped at the tears and forced herself to focus on the TV screen.

VanZandt was giving the press an overview. Sylvie remembered him from grade school. He was an oily slimeball then, and still was. "It's with profound pleasure that Cypress Oil and the Southern Louisiana Shrimpers Association announce a mutually beneficial settlement. A short time ago, the shrimpers called to our attention a pollutant problem that we were unaware of. We were *shocked* to find that a *small amount* of pollutants had accidentally escaped."

"Oh, yeah, they were shocked, all right," Sylvie told Blanche. "Shocked to be caught in the act."

"As you all know, Cypress has an impeccable record for environmental protection. Therefore, we were surprised and gratified to have these issues called to our attention *before* they were cause for concern. We are delighted to announce that the problem has been nipped in the bud."

"God, I'd like to nip something of his in the bud."

Next Luc spoke. "On behalf of the Southern

Louisiana Shrimpers Association, we're proud to announce the establishment of a Bayou Clean Air and Soil Fund, thanks to a five-million-dollar startup *gift* from Cypress Oil."

Sylvie had to smile at his diplomatic choice of words.

"In addition, independent investigators will be given permission to spot-check soil and water samples in and near Cypress property for the next five years, without prior notification."

All of the Cypress people pasted cardboard smiles on their faces as Luc outlined the terms of the agreement. To say they were displeased would be a vast understatement.

"Are you satisfied with this settlement?" one local anchorman asked Luc and the shrimpers.

The shrimpers shrugged, and Luc spoke for them. "Both sides compromised in this arrangement. It's not all that we would have wanted. Five years of inspections is nothing compared to the years of devastation in the bayou ecosystem, but it's a beginning."

"And what did the shrimpers promise in order to gain these concessions?"

Luc answered succinctly, "Silence."

That prompted numerous questions, to which all parties remained mum. There were at least ten more minutes of interrogation, with everyone on the panel getting a turn. Sylvie was so proud of Luc and the way he handled himself. When push came to shove, The Swamp Solicitor was no slouch, that was for sure.

But then Sylvie's attention was caught by a question from Matt Sommese, the *Times-Picayune* reporter. "Hey, Luc, let's change the subject for a minute. I hear rumors that you've been under the influence of a love potion."

Luc sat up straighter.

All the Cypress people exhaled with relief that the attention was now off them.

"Is it true?" Sommese persisted.

"Is what true?" Luc shifted uncomfortably.

"That you accidentally swallowed some love-potion jelly beans."

Luc nodded slowly. "Yep."

"Yep?" Matt and all the reporters stiffened, like hounds sniffing up the scent of fresh game. "Are you saying there's such a thing as a real love potion?"

"Damn straight."

"Oh, no, Luc. Please, just be quiet," Sylvie pleaded to the TV screen.

No such luck.

As if on cue, Luc picked up a handheld microphone and stood, walking to the podium.

"You'd think he was going to give a bloody lecture," she murmured. Which was exactly what he proceeded to do. And it was her lecture he was repeating. The louse!

"Sylvie Fontaine is a chemist at Terrebonne Pharmaceuticals who has invented an honest-to-God love potion called JBX, for you folks out there who don't know about this." She could tell by the ease with which he spoke that this was no impromptu announcement. He had intended to end the press conference in this way from the beginning.

"Oh, my God, Sylv! I thought you were putting a halt on JBX for the time being." Blanche was clearly confused and dismayed.

"I am," Sylvie cried. "Luc is ruining it all."

"Now I see some of you guys smirking," Luc told the reporters, as he leaned casually against the podium, "but really, think about it. If there can be a Viagra, why not a love potion?"

The reporters were nodding.

Sylvie put a palm to her forehead. She felt the birth of a world-class migraine, the kind that felt like razors across the back of the eyeballs.

"And there are lots of legitimate uses for a love potion, not just turning someone on . . . though that's nice, too," the Cajun fool continued, this time accompanied by a waggle of the eyebrows. "Like in marriage counseling. Or with people that have low sex drives, and stuff like that. The world needs to know more about male/female relationships."

Sylvie felt like crying. Why was Luc doing this? To embarrass her? She'd told him over and over that she didn't want to take the spotlight over JBX, that all she'd wanted was peer recognition. She would never live this down. Never.

"Let's cut to the chase, LeDeux," Matt Sommese called out with a laugh. "Did you get turned on by Sylvie's love potion?"

Luc just grinned. The camera cut in close, and the last thing viewers saw before the commercial was that devilish grin, which said it all: *Boy, was I turned on!*

Snickers and guffawing provided the background noise to the fade-out.

"Exactly what did you two do when you were gone?" Blanche wanted to know. "I mean, if you say that there was no love potion, and Luc is swearing that there is, well, something weird is going on. Are you sure he didn't take the love potion?"

"I'm sure. He's just repeating stuff I told him about the love potion."

"But why?"

"I have no idea. To tease me like he's been doing all my life. To put himself in the spotlight as some kind of lover boy. To cash in somehow if JBX ever takes off. To mortify me to death." She threw her arms up in the air.

"He'll probably be filing one of his crazy lawsuits against me and Terrebonne Pharmaceuticals."

"For *not* ingesting the love potion?"

"Oh, stop being so logical, Blanche. For making him think he took a love potion when he didn't."

"Is that illegal?"

"I don't know," Sylvie wailed, pulling at her own hair in frustration. "All I know is I'm gonna kill him. I swear, I'm gonna kill him."

The doorbell rang then, and they both went immediately alert.

"I'll bet that's reporters already," Sylvie whispered. "Maybe we could pretend nobody's home."

"With all the lights on and the TV blaring?" Blanche asked, arching an eyebrow at her. "Let me get it. I can handle these newshounds."

Sylvie went back into the den, where the news program had resumed. Luc was spouting off about something else now, but she was distracted by the sound of Blanche talking to someone with an indiscernible husky, male voice.

Then she heard two sets of shoes approaching and the low murmur of talking.

"Hey, Sylv, guess what? It wasn't a reporter, after all."

Sylvie looked up to see Lucien LeDeux standing in the doorway, wearing the same dark suit and white shirt as she'd seen on TV.

Glancing from him to the TV screen, she realized that the show must have been taped earlier.

"Sylvie," Luc said tentatively.

"Uh, I think I'll go home now," Blanche said. "I have to work on tomorrow's radio show."

The traitor! Before Sylvie had a chance to protest, Blanche was gone.

Sylvie stood, not wanting to be at a disadvantage,

and clenched her hands at her sides. She needed to calm down before she started screaming.

Luc stepped into the doorway of the room. "You haven't been answering my calls, Sylv."

"I needed time to think through some things."

"For a week?"

She nodded.

"And?" If she didn't know better, she would think that was a vulnerable look of hope on his face. Thank goodness, he didn't move any closer . . . just leaned against the doorjamb, ankles crossed, with his hands in his slacks pockets holding his jacket back on his hips. Any closer and she feared she would clamp her hands around his neck and do something outrageous . . . like kiss him.

Kiss him? Where did that thought come from? Kissing is out of the question.

When she still hadn't answered him, he prodded, "And why haven't you called me back?"

"More things keep piling on—"

"Things?"

"Yeah, things that need . . . consideration."

He shook his head in confusion. "Sylv, I found out that Tee-John isn't my son. It's a long story, but the gist of it is that my dad was the father all along." She started to say something, and he held up a hand to stop her. "I know what you're going to say. That my paternity wasn't so much the issue as my lack of responsibility. Well, I can't defend everything I've done, but, geez, Sylv, I was young and I tried my best to protect Tee-John."

She waved a hand dismissively. "That's the least of our problems."

"We have problems?" His voice lacked its usual self-confidence.

"Of course, we have problems."

"Then let's talk them through, Sylv." He walked into the room, and was about to pull her down on the sofa with him, but must have noticed the forbidding expression on her face. Instead, still puzzled, he dropped to the sofa and motioned for her to sit in the chair across from him, which she did, needing something to hold onto. "Sylv, I love you. Please don't close yourself off from me like this. Let me in. Tell me what's wrong. Together . . ." He choked up. "Together we can work things out."

"Oh, don't you ever say that again, Luc LeDeux."

"Say what? I feel like you and I are speaking different languages, Sylv."

"Don't you ever say that you love me again."

"Why the hell not? I love you. I love you. I love you."

He looked so gorgeous and childlike and fierce when he said those words that Sylvie felt herself melting. Still, she braced herself.

"I'm on to you, buster. No more playing games. No more vows of love. No more bull."

He bristled with indignation. "What in God's name are you talking about?"

She pointed toward the TV screen. "Let's talk about that show you put on tonight."

"You watched?" His face brightened. "I did good, didn't I?"

Oh, the gall of the man! "The first part was great. I'm glad you got those concessions from Cypress Oil. René and his buddies must be pleased."

"They are. I can't wait to tell you all the details . . . how my dad almost had a stroke when—"

"It's the other half of the program that made *me* almost have a stroke."

"You mean the love-potion stuff?"

"Precisely."

"I knew you wouldn't toot your own horn, Sylv. So I

did it for you. Now you'll get all the recognition you ever wanted. Your mother and all your uptight relatives will be so proud of you, they'll probably burst their girdles."

"Earth to Luc. Who died and named you my road-show manager? I distinctly recall telling you that I never wanted to be in the spotlight for JBX . . . that all I ever wanted was behind-the-scenes peer recognition."

"Ooops."

"*Ooops?* You just turned me into the laughingstock of the country . . . a spectacle . . . a freak . . . and all you can say is *ooops.*"

"Don't you think you're overreacting a bit? Okay, so you didn't want to be the front man for the project. So, step back, and let Charles or some hired spokesperson take over. No big deal! The most important thing, Sylv, is that you and I are perfect proof that the love potion works."

"I've put a halt on the JBX project," she inserted brusquely.

"*What?*"

"You heard me. Your big announcement was for naught. There is no love potion project . . . for now."

Her news clearly floored him, and he blinked with confusion. "But why?"

"I learned a few things while ensconced in your little love hideaway," she said snidely. "Let's just say that the love potion needs a little work, in my opinion."

He waved a hand airily. "So, it's just a temporary delay. You had me scared there for a minute. You and I both know what a great thing that love potion is. It brought us together, didn't it?"

She glared at him.

But the fool just blathered on. "Look at us, honey. Two people who practically hated each other—*well, I didn't hate you but you hated me*—and with the help of a handful of jelly beans, we fell in love. That's important, sweetheart. And your invention did it all."

"You are incredible."

"I know. And by the way, you never actually said the words to me. Now might be a good time." He smiled enticingly at her and patted the couch next to him.

"You couldn't possibly be as thickheaded as you're pretending to be."

He stared at her quizzically, and she saw the moment that understanding dawned. "Spit it out, Sylv. What great sin have I committed now? I've been seeing that expression on people's faces since I was five years old. Even when I tried to do good, it came out wrong. 'Bad boy of the bayou.' What did I do this time?"

She almost felt sorry for him. Almost, but not quite. "There was no love potion."

"Huh?"

"You heard me. There was no love potion in the jelly beans you ate."

He gaped at her, wide-eyed with wonder. "How . . . why . . . but you said . . ."

"There was a mix-up in petri dishes. I thought you ate the ones with my enzymes in them, but apparently you ate the neutral set."

Then Luc did something she never expected. He began to laugh . . . and laugh . . . and laugh. He couldn't seem to stop. He slapped his knee. He swiped at his eyes. Every time he seemed to be over his bout of hysteria, he started up all over again.

"You think this is funny?"

"I think this is hilarious, and you should, too, Sylv. It means that I was in love with you all along, and I didn't need any damn love potion to jump-start my heart."

She gasped. "No, that's not what it means. It means that you played a game with me from the moment I told you that you'd swallowed those jelly beans. It was just one more form of teasing Sylvie Fontaine. How you must have been laughing behind my back!"

"Sylv, you can't possibly believe that," he said, jumping to his feet and pulling her up with him.

But she was deadly serious.

Luc felt everything that was important to him slipping away. Yanking a resisting Sylvie into his embrace forcibly, he hugged her fiercely, whispering against her neck, "Please, please, please . . ."

He wasn't sure what he was begging for. Understanding? A second chance? Forgiveness? What?

Then it occurred to him. All he wanted from Sylvie was love. Such a little thing, and yet so very much.

He took her face in both his hands and set her away from him slightly. Tears were streaming down her face, but he did not care now. There were more important things on his mind.

"Tell me," he demanded. "Tell me that you love me. Everything else can be worked out if we have that as a starting point. Oh, God, Sylv, just say the words."

Her lips worked, but nothing came out.

He dropped his hands from her face and stepped back . . . waiting.

Nothing.

This was just a misunderstanding . . . that she would actually think he'd pretended to be attracted to her . . . but saying the words now would be meaningless. And his intentions had been pure in making the announcement to the press about JBX. Hell, since when had it become a crime to make a mistake? Comprehension would come later for Sylvie, but there were greater things at stake first. Like love, and its foundation: trust.

If he hadn't known it before, he knew now just how

strong and deeply ingrained were the biases and pre-conceptions that people held about him.

"Sylvie, I love you," he said with all the earnestness he could muster. "Do you believe me?"

"I don't know what to believe about your feelings now. But not for one minute do I think you felt that way all those times in the beginning when you claimed to be under the spell of a love potion. And if you lied then, why not now?"

"For what purpose, Sylv?"

"Logic says—"

"Screw logic! What does your heart say?"

She flinched at his vehemence.

Luc raked the fingers of both hands through his hair, still unused to its shorter length, and stalked around the room. How to get through to the stubborn woman?

Suddenly, he stopped, noticing the two separate cages.

"What's wrong with Samson and Delilah? How come you separated them?"

Sylvie shrugged. "Delilah can't stand Samson anymore."

"Really? Just like that?"

She nodded, a sad expression in her eyes. "I guess the love potion wore off."

The silence between them was telling. If the love between Samson and Delilah faded so easily, why not theirs?

No, he refused to think like that.

"Sylv, what do you want from me?"

"N-nothing," she answered. If it weren't for the hesitancy in her voice, Luc would have reached over and shaken the bejesus out of her.

"Do you need more time?"

She shook her head. "I don't think time is going to heal this one, Luc."

Her words had the ring of finality to them.

"Do you want me to leave?" he inquired, not really expecting her to answer in the positive.

"I think that would be best," she said in a wavering whisper.

Luc could barely breathe past the lump in his throat. He was angry and frustrated and hurt. "I pity you, Sylv. I really do."

She tilted her head in question.

"I thought that each of us had grown in some way during those days we spent together . . . each as a result of the other. I know that I acknowledged some things about myself, realized I've spent a lifetime living down to other people's expectations. Well, no more. If people want to call me The Swamp Solicitor or 'the bad boy of the bayou,' well, let 'em. From now on, my self-identity comes from here," he said, pounding a fist over his heart. "You taught me that."

Sylvie put the fingertips of both hands to her mouth to stifle a sob, but he wasn't done with her yet.

"You, on the other hand, have been trying to live up to other people's expectations. And you're still doing it. Go ahead, Sylv, revert to your old crutch . . . the shyness and aloofness. Crawl back in your shell and look for a safe man. Judge me all you want, but it's got to be god-awful lonely up there on that pedestal all by yourself."

Luc turned on his heel and made his way toward the front door with a haze of tears in his eyes. His pride was the only thing carrying him forward.

Ironically, just before he left Sylvie's house, he had a crazy thought. Wouldn't it be nice if there really were a love potion? If only he could have Sylvie pop a pill and love him again!

He started up his Jeep, and if the jalopy hadn't been making its usual rumbling commotion, he might have heard the feminine voice behind him, calling out from Sylvie's front door, "Luc, come back!"

But it was too late.

Chapter Eighteen

It was a gift she couldn't refuse . . .

"I have a present for you," Tante Lulu said without preamble when Sylvie opened her front door.

It was a week later. Luc hadn't called her, she hadn't called him, and life was miserable. So, actually, Sylvie welcomed a little distraction. Only she'd been hoping it was Luc. They'd both been involved in an unspoken battle of wills over who would take the first step.

First steps were hell. She was learning that lesson too well as the days separating them grew.

Her life was going down the toilet and Luc had apparently given up on her, no thanks to Sylvie's stubborn pride, and here was his aunt about to give her a gift. "A pre-present?" she stammered.

"Yep," the old lady said. She was wearing bib over-alls today and a John Deere cap. There was a tiny insignia near the shoulder strap that read, "Redneck this!" surrounded by what looked like "the finger," but Sylvie didn't want to peer too close. Maybe it was a rake or rifle or cigarette or bottle of booze or something.

It was not surprising when Tante Lulu added with a jerk of her head toward the street, "Can you help me get your present out of my truck?"

A pickup truck. What else! "Can I assume you traded in the Harley?"

"Luc made me do it. The boy has no sense of humor anymore. I tell you, *chère*, he's lost his *joie de vivre*." She sliced Sylvie with a glower that clearly laid the blame on her.

But maybe that was a good sign . . . that Luc was no longer joyous. If he was as miserable as she was, perhaps he was ready to crack. Yep, he would probably be ready to take the first step any minute now.

Yeah, right.

Sylvie helped Tante Lulu carry a huge cardboard carton about the size of a refrigerator crate, only much lighter, into the house, with a little assistance from two passing neighbor boys. When it was sitting in Sylvie's den, Sylvie went for a butcher knife to cut open the box, and a puffing Tante Lulu glanced around the room, her gaze stopping on the two rat cages.

"Aren't you going to ask why I separated Samson and Delilah?" Sylvie inquired as she began working on the carton.

"Nope. I can see why. That mama's about ready to drop a litter of rats."

"Huh?" Sylvie straightened and glanced at the rat cage holding Delilah, who now that it was mentioned, did look a mite chubby. Then Sylvie glanced at Tante

Lulu. "I separated them when Delilah seemed to lose interest in Samson. I assumed it was because the love potion had worn off."

"Well, of course, she lost interest. I been catchin' babies down on the bayou for forty years and more. Mos' women start gettin' tetchy round their menfolks as the time approaches. Those randy goats are the one's who put them in this predicament, dontcha see? You should hear the language that comes out of the mouths of some of those females when the big pain hits." She rolled her eyes and made an "Aiyeee!" sound. "Don' worry none. Delilah will be hot to trot again, once the little ones are born."

Sylvie threw her head back and laughed gloriously . . . the first time she'd laughed in such a long time. How could she not have seen what was going on in front of her nose?

That thought brought her up short, and she tapped her forefinger against her chin pensively. Was it possible there were other things she'd failed to see, too? Suddenly, new hope sprang up in Sylvie . . . hope that the love potion really did work, and hope for her and Luc, too.

"You gonna open your present or not?" Tante Lulu grumbled. "I gotta get down to the bingo hall by seven. There's a thousand-dollar jackpot tonight. Wanna come?"

"Uh, I don't think so."

Sylvie worked quickly then, opening the carton, then discarding a ton of bubble paper. When she finally pulled her gift out, and set it in the middle of the room, Sylvie could only stare, slack-jawed with incredulity.

It was a four-foot-tall ceramic statue of St. Jude.

"I figure you could put it out in your rose garden," Tante Lulu suggested, smiling brightly.

Tante Lulu better not be still harboring ideas about
having cow manure delivered to enrich her mostly un-
successful rose-growing endeavors. It had taken Sylvie
all week to get rid of the chickens and clean up her
basement. To her surprise, there had also been a dozen
eggs.

Sylvie put a fist on one hip and tilted her head questioningly at Tante Lulu. "Are you trying to say that I'm
a hopeless case?"

"Ab-so-lute-ly!"

Sylvie had to smile at Tante Lulu's probably accurate
assessment of her. But she wasn't smiling for long. In
fact, when she opened a second package at the bottom
of the box, and saw that it contained an exquisite, hand-
embroidered wedding coverlet, she started to cry. Despite her first gift, Tante Lulu still had hope for her.

Charmaine arrived then with a suitcase full of beauty
supplies, immediately followed by Blanche and Claudia. None of them paid any attention to Sylvie's quickly
swiped tears; in fact, they acted as if weeping were expected of her. They all gave her lame excuses as to why
they'd come, but basically the silent message was that
they believed Sylvie needed to get her butt in gear and
straighten out her life. Tante Lulu nodded her approval
of the three women's endeavors and left for Bingo
Heaven.

Charmaine made a tsk-ing sound of dismay as she
viewed Tante Lulu's nonexistent backside in the cover-
alls as she departed. "God, I hope she finds herself pretty
soon."

To no one's surprise, the minute they were sitting
around her kitchen table with aluminum-foil wraps
sticking up from various portions of their heads, like
alien antennae, Remy and René arrived.

"Hubba-hubba," René said.

Remy just chuckled.

Claudia smiled up at Remy, undaunted by the green wax under her eyebrows. It was amazing how she never even blinked at the disfigured side of his face. But then, Sylvie rarely noticed now either.

Remy winked at Claudia.

She blushed. The pink went great with the puke-green.

"Who's the dude?" Remy asked with a laugh, glancing over at the corner, by the patio door.

"You don't recognize St. Jude?" Charmaine lifted a perfectly arched eyebrow.

Sylvie had moved the statue from the den to the kitchen. He did look a little different, Sylvie had to admit, with the roguish mustache Claudia had painted on him with eyeliner, the beret Blanche had plopped on his head, and the "Proud to be a Cajun" badge Charmaine had tacked on to his robe.

"Halloween coming early this year?" René inquired, and he wasn't referring to the statue. He was gaping at the three of them.

"I'm just giving them a few highlights," Charmaine said defensively of the foil hair spikes, "and Sylvie's gonna get a little pouf, too."

"No, no, no. I told you, Charmaine. No pouf," Sylvie protested, barely moving her lips. She didn't want to crack the hardened mask on her face.

Charmaine just patted her on the shoulder.

"I think a pouf would look good on you, Sylv," Blanche commented. "You need a change in your life, hon."

Not for the first time lately, Sylvie labeled her friend a traitor. Sylvie thought she'd had more than enough change lately, but she was unable to get out that many words. Besides, no one listened to her anyhow. They just kept talking about how miserable Luc was. Didn't they care how miserable *she* was?

"Yep, the best thing for a broken heart is a make-over," Charmaine was saying.

"Sylvie has a broken heart?" Remy and René asked hopefully.

"What are you two doing here?" Blanche inquired.

René tossed several flyers onto the table. "You're all invited."

It appeared that a *fais do do*—a Cajun dance—was being held to benefit the Southern Louisiana Shrimpers Association and two dozen families who'd lost their boats and their livelihood due to the recent pollution problems. It would include a talent show, dancing, and ethnic foods, all for a whopping one-hundred-dollar admission fee.

"What about the settlement money?" Sylvie questioned through thinned lips, still unable to speak normally because of her masked face.

"The five-million-dollar settlement is all well and good, but who knows when we'll actually receive it. Could be years. In the meantime, there are some families in dire need," René explained.

"We expect you all to be there," Remy pronounced. "If I can be bulldozed into helping, the least you all can do is show up."

Sylvie wanted to ask if Luc would attend, but her pride still stood in the way.

"You, especially." Remy stared pointedly at her.

"Me?" She put a palm over her heart.

"You," Remy emphasized. "You owe us after what you've done to our brother. He's actually turned"— Remy paused to shudder—"*respectable*." You'd think respectable was a dirty word by the way his upper lip curled with revulsion.

"Huh?" all the women said.

"Not only did he get a haircut, but he wears suits all the time. Doesn't drink. Works eight hours a day. Says he doesn't like booze anymore, except of course for beer, which doesn't count. And he even went to church with Tante Lulu last Sunday. Father Phillipe almost swallowed his tongue in the middle of his sermon when he recognized him," Remy elaborated.

"He's talkin' about tradin' in his Jeep for a BMW," René noted with horror.

"Sonofabitch! A coonass in a yuppiemobile!" Remy exclaimed, then immediately added, "Excuse me, ma'am"—a blanket apology to all the women.

"Don't you just melt when he says ma'am?" Claudia whispered to Sylvie.

"I was with him all day yesterday and he didn't swear, not even once," René remarked with a meaningful grimace.

"Bottom line, he's become boooring," Remy concluded.

The other women were laughing, but Sylvie started to weep. Big fat tears that no doubt made rivulets in her mud-caked face.

"What? What?" Remy appeared affronted that he might have caused her to fall apart. "You're crying 'cause Luc doesn't swear anymore?"

"No," she wailed, "I'm crying because Luc cut his hair." She felt her face crack then. What a sight she must be!

"Oh, well," Remy said, and everyone nodded, as if that was perfectly understandable.

After Remy and René left, Sylvie went to the bathroom to repair her face. It was a hopeless task. After washing off the mud mask, she just gave up.

As she passed St. Jude on her way back, she gave him

a pat on the head and offered up a silent prayer. "Please, St. Jude. If there ever was a more hopeless case, I can't imagine who it could be."

When she plopped down into her chair, Blanche, Claudia, and Charmaine beamed at her.

Uh-oh!

"We have an idea," they all said at once.

Uh-oh!

"It involves dancing," Blanche announced.

Uh-oh!

"And spandex," Charmaine added with a gleam in her eyes. "*Red* spandex, and poufy hair."

Uh-oh!

Blanche squeezed one of her hands reassuringly. "And Luc."

Thank you, St. Jude! Sylvie thought then, immediately followed by *I think*. And another *Uh-oh!*

The things a man will do for love! . . .

"This is the most half-baked idea you've ever talked us into," Luc grumbled to René. They were standing behind the stage at the community outdoor arena waiting their turn in the talent show. "There are five hundred people out there who are going to laugh their bloody heads off . . . at us!"

"I'll tell you one thing," Remy snarled at René, "I'm *not* dancing, or swinging my hips, or pretending to have sex with a metal pole, or nothin'. I'm standing still, pretending to sing, that's all."

Luc's eyes swept over Remy, and he decided things could have been worse.

"Don't . . . you . . . say . . . a . . . word," Remy gritted out to him.

Luc was annoyed with René for involving them in another of his shenanigans, but Remy was *really* pissed off. With good reason.

Luc was wearing his usual lawyer's suit, though his shirt was unbuttoned down practically to the navel, and there was a fake earring in one ear, while Remy was wearing tight jeans with cowboy boots and hat and a leather vest, sans shirt. Even Luc thought his brother looked sexy, and he was a guy . . . a heterosexual guy . . . though you wouldn't know it by the lack of women in his life.

René was wearing jeans, boots, and an accordion. That was all, except for the tattoo on his right shoulder that resembled an ink splotch but was probably a shrimp. Joining them in this madness were a few Cajun pals of René's: a fireman who no doubt looked spiffy to some people in his suspenders and plastic pants and boots, not to mention helmet; a second-team football player from the New Orleans Saints, who appeared to have no underwear on under his uniform; and Luc's old pal, Ambrose "Rosie" Mouton, in his cop outfit. Rosie seemed as uncomfortable as he did. Though he wasn't showing any skin, his boss might fire him over this misuse of official apparel.

Needless to say, they were going to be the Village People of Southern Louisiana. To the music of "Macho Man," they would be singing, "Ca-jun, Ca-jun man. I want to be a Ca-jun man."

If his heart wasn't broken and his brain in temporary meltdown over Sylvie, Luc never would have agreed to this insanity. He had put his pride in his pocket two weeks ago when he'd gone to Sylvie's home, but she'd pretty much told him to take a hike. He'd kept expecting her to change her mind, but no such luck. Each day that went by saw his dreams being chipped away bit by bit, till they were practically nonexistent now.

Everyone kept telling him not to give up hope, especially Tante Lulu, who was going overboard on the St. Jude stuff this week. He was almost afraid to look up at the sky for fear of seeing a Goodyear Blimp in the shape of St. Jude. Charmaine had even told him she'd heard a rumor that Tante Lulu had the ladies' auxiliary at Our Lady of the Bayou Church making a novena for him. Imagine that! A love novena.

It had been a foolish fantasy to begin with, he supposed. The Cajun bad boy and the Creole princess. An impossible mix.

But, God, it had been sweet while it lasted.

"It's all for a good cause," René was protesting for the zillionth time, calling Luc back to the present. He was still trying to justify the madness he'd conned them into.

"How come we couldn't make a hundred-dollar donation like everyone else?" the fireman griped. "And I'm not having sex with a pole, either, René, so just forget it."

"*Mon Dieu!* I never heard so much complaining in all my life. Those Cajun dockworkers from Morgan City are gonna be the Cajun-dales. You know, like the Chippendales. And all they'll be wearing are G-strings made of shrimp shells. *They* have no qualms about dancing with firemen's poles."

The jaws of a lawyer, cowboy, fireman, football player, and cop dropped open at that. You never knew for sure when René was kidding.

The only saving grace for Luc was knowing that Sylvie wouldn't see him like this. She'd never be caught dead at such a low-down, rowdy affair.

But, damn, he'd like to see her one more time.

* * *

The things a woman will do for love! . . .

Their Cajun version of the Village People was an over-whelming hit. The stage was spotlighted, but they could see out into the neon-lit darkness where people were standing and clapping and singing along and let-ting loose wild rebel yells.

All of them on stage got a little caught up in the magic, and, yes, they did swing their hips a bit. Hey, they were Cajuns, after all; there was music in their souls. Even the stoic Remy had the women drooling when he did an ever-so-subtle roll of the hips during one of their syncopated turns, like those old Motown groups . . . or like, well, the Village People. Rosie did this thing with his baton that was . . . well, there were no words for it. The crowd loved it, though. Every time the fireman snapped his suspenders, the young girls in the crowd practically fainted. When the football player shook his bootie at them, catcalls and wolf whistles filled the arena.

All Luc did was dance a little, and once he flashed the edge of his Valentine boxers, for which he'd developed a fondness. That seemed to satisfy the mob, though some women kept yelling at him to "Take it off! Take it all off!"

Then Luc saw Sylvie sitting in the front row, wide-eyed and slack-jawed with amazement. Good thing it was the end of their song. He did the only thing he could think of. He winked at her.

And bless her heart, she winked right back.

Was it a sign?

Luc would have jumped right off the stage to find out, but Remy and René grabbed him by the forearms and pulled him back. As they exited the stage area, the crowd was going wild.

"They want us to do an encore," René announced enthusiastically.

All the rest of them gave René a look that pretty well translated to "Get a Life!" and scooted off before he could talk them into something they might regret.

It was almost impossible for Luc to make his way through the tightly packed crowd to the front-row area where he'd seen Sylvie. Instead, he found himself drawn along with Remy and René toward a beer stand off to the side.

Along the way, they got lots of pats on the backs and more than a few propositions from the ladies. Some of them even brought a blush to his face.

Remy swore one woman pinched his butt. And he liked it.

The band was warming up for the next act, and through the fuzziness in Luc's brain—he was still feeling euphoric over Sylvie's wink—he began to register an increasingly worrisome fact. It sounded as if the band was about to play that old rock 'n' roll song "Love Potion Number Nine."

He almost dropped his beer.

He glanced at his brothers, who were suddenly grinning. He glanced at the stage, where four women had just come out wearing dark sunglasses and raincoats that covered them from neck to stiletto-heeled feet. Then he glanced at his aunt, whom he'd just noticed behind the bar wearing a sarong, a lei, and a black pageboy wig. God knows what kind of vehicle she had now . . . probably a boat. She waggled a St. Jude medal at him and smiled encouragingly.

But he couldn't think about that now. To the beat of the rock music, the women in raincoats strutted up to the four microphones planted along the front of the stage. With orchestrated panache, they flipped their sunglasses off and into the audience, then removed their raincoats, tossing them back and out of the way.

"Oh, my God!" he and Remy and René all said at once.

Sylvie, Blanche, Claudia, and Charmaine were wearing short-sleeved spandex dresses with rounded necklines that dipped practically to their butts in the back. They were so short they should have been outlawed. The colors were flame-red, pink, black, and white, with matching high-heeled shoes. About four miles of black silk stockings were displayed, ending in those sexysexy-sexy shoes . . . the kind of shoes that prompted a man to picture his woman wearing them, and nothing else.

Sylvie was the one in flame-red . . . which brought to mind something else she'd worn for him in flame-red. A nightie. Had she worn this red dress deliberately for him? Was it a message? Nah, he was dreaming again. Aside from the hooker dress, he noticed that her hair was a little . . . poufy. He recognized Charmaine's work. Most of all, he noticed that Sylvie looked scared as hell.

Why is she doing this?

Sylvie was a Creole chemist with no real ties to the Cajun community.

Sylvie was too high-class to wear such low-class clothes, especially in public, even for a good cause.

Sylvie was too mad to go anywhere near where he might be.

Sylvie was too shy to put herself on exhibition.

Why is she doing this?

With a crash of cymbals and roll of drums, the band ended their rendition of "Love Potion Number Nine," which the Happy Hookers had been singing while his mind had been wandering.

The stage darkened, except for a spotlight on Sylvie. Charmaine, Claudia, and Blanche stepped back a bit and took on the role of backup singers. Then Sylvie held onto the standing mike for dear life and began to sing that old torchy rock 'n' roll song "Do You Wanna Dance?"

She's singing to me, was the first thing Luc realized.

Dropping his beer to the ground, he began to make his way doggedly through the crowd and toward her. Her voice was quivery and her legs unsteady as she poured out her heart in a surprisingly clear and poignantly pleasant wail, "Oh, baby, do you wanna dance?" And the whole time she sang, she danced in place, her hips and shoulders swaying from side to side, her arms outstretched in a beckoning manner.

She's dancing for me, was the second thing he realized.

From the time they were kids, Luc had been teasing Sylvie about how someday she would dance with him. Well, she was sure as hell doing it now, except that she was dancing *for him*. With tears in her eyes and her heart in her wavering voice, she was making a monumental effort—*monumental, for a timid, publicity-shy person like Sylvie*—to prove something to him.

She loves me, was the third thing Luc realized, and it hit him square in the heart.

Now, she was exhorting her "baby" to squeeze her all night long, followed by the refrain "Oh, baby, do you wanna dance?"

He'd almost reached the stage after shoving aside two security guards, who were probably calling for backups. He saw the moment that Sylvie saw him. Her eyes went wide with pleading and her arms, which would appear beckoning in a sexual way to the audience, were clearly beckoning him to rescue her before she had one of her anxiety attacks in front of five hundred people.

He wanted to whack Charmaine and Claudia and Blanche on their heads. They'd probably talked Sylvie

into doing this, not realizing she wasn't up to this kind
of exposure.

But, God, he loved Sylvie for doing it.

With hands braced on the edge of the stage, he vaulted
himself up and rushed to Sylvie's side.

"Dance, dance, dance," the crowd shouted, misin-
terpreting his actions as those of a lover coming to join
Sylvie in her act . . . a rehearsed culmination to the
stage show.

He did just that, but only as a means to dance her off
the stage. Pulling her into his embrace, he whispered
against her ear, "Hold on, babe. Everything's gonna be
okay now."

She pulled away slightly, even as they danced slowly
toward the back of the stage while the three Dunce-
ettes shoobee-doo'd the lyrics. Gazing up at him, Sylvie smiled and said, "I did it, Luc. I actually got up on
a stage and sang. I guess that proves something, huh?"
Her voice was choked with pride and emotion and a
vulnerability that tugged at his heartstrings.

"You did great, darlin'. But why?"

She said something, but he couldn't hear over the
clapping of the excited crowd and the continued harmo-
nizing of the Dunce-ettes.

"What?" He leaned closer. In her killer high heels,
Sylvie was almost eye-level with him, and now that
he thought about it, their body parts were perfectly
aligned. That, of course, gave him ideas for later.

"I did it to prove to you that I wasn't pitiful."

"Huh?" he exclaimed, and whisked Sylvie through
the stage curtains and down the back steps.

The Dunce-ettes doo-whopped on without them,
"Do you do you do you . . . oh, baaaby!"

Luc pulled Sylvie close to his side and walked her toward the trees, away from the people who hung around

in clusters, even behind the stage. Once she was leaning back against the wide tree trunk, she wilted.

God, he wanted answers to so many things, but more than anything he wanted to take Sylvie into his arms and kiss her and kiss her and kiss her till no questions and no answers were necessary. Then, he'd like to kiss her some more.

"Why are you smiling?" Sylvie asked. Now she was calmed down somewhat. *God, I can't believe I actually got up on that stage and sang. And danced. Lordy, I don't think I'll ever be able to regress into shyness again.* Then she began to notice her surroundings. Had Luc really "rescued" her like that? *My very own Cajun Knight!*

"You're smiling, too, babe," he said in a husky voice that did wonderful, fluttery things to the pit of her stomach.

"I'm happy," she whispered.

"Me, too," he whispered back.

For now, that was enough. No explanations necessary.

"Do you want to tell me what you mean about proving you weren't pitiful?" Luc asked then.

"The last time I saw you, you told me I was pitiful, and—"

He gasped. "I said *that?*"

She nodded. "You did, and you were right. I wasn't willing to take a chance on you. It was easier to fall back on old preconceived ideas. I couldn't trust you on your word alone."

"And now?"

"Now, nothing seems to matter except . . ." Her voice trailed off, and she averted her face.

"Oh, God, Sylv, don't stop now," he pleaded, cupping her chin and tilting her face back.

"I love you," she said. Finally, finally, finally, she spoke the words, and it was as if a heavy load was lifted from her heart. She felt light as a feather and happier than she'd ever been in all her life.

Instead of telling her that he loved her, too, Luc slipped a fingertip under the shoulder of her dress and gave it a little ping. "Nice color, Sylv," he commented. "Any particular significance to your picking flame-red?"

She lifted her chin and refused to answer. If he was going to tease her, she refused to be a willing participant.

"I especially like the elasticity of this dress," he noted, putting his palm on her buttocks and rubbing up and down, causing the hem to be hiked dangerously high. She felt the shock of electricity from that seductive move of his fingers. "What are you wearing under it, anyhow?"

Aaah! Perfect setup! "Nothing."

She saw him gulp.

"Wanna see?" She winked at him.

He laughed. "Man, oh, man! Put a shy thing in a tart dress and who knows what will happen!"

Sylvie had had enough of games and teasing. "I'm sorry, Luc. I really am."

"Me, too." He leaned his mouth close to hers and spoke against her parted lips. "I love you, *chère*."

She whimpered at the ferocity of his kisses then. He couldn't seem to get enough of her. Sylvie wanted his kisses, but she wanted to hear the words, too. Cradling his face in her hands, she held him away from her. "I love you so much," she said.

"I know," he said.

She shoved him in the chest. He knew what she wanted to hear—*the louse!*—but continued to tease her. As always.

Finally, he gave in. "I have loved you for such a long

time, Sylv. I loved you when we were kids. I love you now. I will love you forever."

More beautiful words were never spoken.

They kissed and said the words a few hundred more times. Then Luc gazed at her through adoring eyes and asked something she hadn't expected. "Do you wanna dance?"

"Here?" she asked in surprise.

"No, not here," he responded. "Back at my apartment. I have a different kind of dancing in mind."

He looked at her and grinned.

She looked at him and grinned.

And they both said at the same time, "Nude dancing."

Epilogue

*L*ove, Cajun style . . . guar-an-teed! . . .

Two months later . . .

The Breaux plantation in Houma, Louisiana, rang with the sounds of rowdy Cajun music and soft Creole ballads. It was the wedding of Lucien Michael LeDeux and Sylvie Marie Fontaine.

Father Phillipe had performed the ceremony down at Our Lady of the Bayou Church, and the reception was being held outdoors at the home of Sylvie's mother, for appearance's sake—her mother's, not Sylvie's.

The catering tables groaned with myriad delicacies from both the Cajun and Creole cultures. At the bar, specialties of the day were oyster shooters and "pink" zinfandel . . . and beer, of course . . . lots of beer.

Remy was his brother's best man, and the ushers were René and Tee-John. Blanche was the maid of honor, with Claudia and Charmaine acting as bridesmaids, all in the Dunce-ettes' spandex dresses, for sentimental reasons, much to Inez Breaux-Fontaine's disapproval. Sylvie figured her mother was lucky she hadn't chosen flame-red for her bridal gown, instead of virginal-white. And besides, the bridesmaids' dresses had detachable net overgowns made up for the sake of respectability in the church.

Even Valcour LeDeux and his wife Jolie attended the festivities, though they were treated with marked coolness by his sons. The rift between them was still wide.

Tante Lulu was looking proud of herself in a pink suit and pumps and soft gray hair. Apparently, normal attire was to be her standard now that she'd gotten Luc married off. Maybe she had finally "found herself," even as she'd found a bride for Luc. On the other hand, there was a hint of problems to come when she called Remy over and inquired sweetly, "How's *your* hope chest, honey?"

Sylvie intended to return to work on her love-potion research at Terrebonne Pharmaceuticals after a short honeymoon at Luc's bayou cabin. In fact, each place setting at the reception had a little paper cup of jelly beans. There were lots of jokes about being under the influence.

Luc had more legal business than he could handle these days because of the publicity over Cypress Oil and the love potion. He was trying his best not to turn too respectable at the command of his new wife. In line with that, he had added a line to the brass plate on his law office door which now read, "Lucien LeDeux, Attorney-at-Law, The Swamp Solicitor."

Samson and Delilah were back together again, boinking away. Delilah had dropped four baby rats the month before. Their names were Eenie, Meanie, Miney, and Moe.

Reporters still continued to hound Luc and Sylvie,

refusing to believe there was no love potion. In fact, today's newspaper read: "Love Potion Wedding."

The day was winding down now, and the bridal couple was dancing again . . . this time to a tune that was becoming popular with many Louisiana radio stations, "Cajun Knight."

"Shall we leave soon, *chère?*" Luc drawled, nuzzling her neck. His bride was known to have a soft spot for his drawl. "I can't wait for you to try on my wedding gift." Luc had given her several sexy lingerie items with matching high heels, all in flame-red, of course.

"I'm ready when you are, Luc. Actually, I'm a little anxious for us to try out my gifts to you, as well." She'd given him licorice whips and a Luther Vandross CD.

Shortly after that, as the groom whisked the bride off to their honeymoon, someone overheard Luc let loose a wild, whooping rebel yell and the famous Cajun expression "*Laissez les bon temps rouler.*"

And his bride was said to have agreed, "Let the good times roll."

Reader Letter

You gotta love a Cajun man.

I know, I know, I said the same thing about Vikings. But, really, in many ways they are similar.

The Acadians (from which the shortened mispronunciation of Cajuns stems) are a proud people who always manage to land on their feet and thrive, despite being exiled out of one country after another . . . first France, then Canada. The Vikings were always looking for a new homeland, too, but in their case they blended in to the countries they conquered. Fortunately, the Cajuns have managed to maintain their unique culture in Southern Louisiana.

The Acadians were natives of Nova Scotia, originally of French descent. They left Canada rather than live under English rule. In 1755 they were disbanded by the British, with women and children being separated from their men and sent in all directions. One distinct group finally settled in Southern Louisiana, where they called themselves Cajuns. Longfellow's epic poem *Evangeline* tells their story so well.

If the Vikings were handsome devils with impressive height and long blond hair, you ought to see these Cajun men with their dark hair and dancing eyes. Ooh-la-la!

They have colorful first names like Valcour, Ambrose, and Remy, and surnames like Arcenaux, Doucet, Breaux, Fortier, and Guidry. Their lifestyle is based on good food, love of God and family, and a marvelous appreciation for *joie de vivre* or joy of life. Nowhere is their sense of humor more evident than in the titles they gave their beloved bayous: Bayou Go to Hell, Bayou Funny Louis, and Bayou *Mouchoir de l'Ourse* (handkerchief of a she-bear); or in the lyrics of their unique music; or in their most colorful language, which is a little bit Southern drawl, a dash of Cajun French, and a lot of unique, deliberate mispronunciations of words.

The Cajuns managed to flourish in the presumably unlivable swamplands of Louisiana, and not only survive but prosper. They built their homes on stilts and found ways to prepare dishes from the bayou's plentiful game and fish . . . some of which the more uppity Creoles wouldn't have touched till the Cajuns taught them how. There's a Cajun saying. "If it moves, we cook it." And cook it they do—crawfish, gumbo, blackened redfish, jambalaya. The spicier the better. No wonder they call Tabasco "Cajun Lightning."

The Cajuns love festivals and don't need an excuse to have one. One of the most colorful occurs at the Morgan City Shrimp and Petroleum Festival, where two big boats meet in a bow-to-bow kiss as the king and queen lean forward from their respective decks for a traditional champagne toast. But there are also frog derbies, crawfish boils, and, of course, their own outrageous interpretations of Mardi Gras.

I hope you come to love the Cajuns as much as I do. Enjoy reading this book, the first of my Cajun novels, and the seven books in the series that follow. And as they say in Southern Louisiana, and as my hero and heroine said at the end of their story: *"Laissez les bon temps rouler,"* or "Let the good times roll."

Sandra Hill
P.O. Box 604
State College, PA 16804
shill733@aol.com
www.sandrahill.net

Can't get enough of *USA Today* and
New York Times bestselling
author Sandra Hill?
Turn the page for glimpses of her amazing
books. From cowboys to Vikings, Navy
SEALs to Southern bad boys, every one
of Sandra's books has her unique blend of
passion, creativity, and unparalleled wit.

Welcome to the World of Sandra Hill!

The Viking Takes a Knight

For John of Hawks' Lair, the unexpected appearance of a beautiful woman at his door is always welcome. Yet the arrival of this alluring Viking woman, Ingrith Sigrundottir—with her enchanting smile and inviting curves—is different . . . for she comes accompanied by a herd of unruly orphans. And Ingrith needs more than the legendary knight's hospitality; she needs protection. For among her charges is a small boy with a claim to the throne—a dangerous distinction when murderous King Edgar is out hunting for Viking blood.

A man of passion, John will keep them safe—but in exchange, he wants something very dear indeed: Ingrith's heart, to be taken with the very first meeting of their lips . . .

Viking in Love

☯

*C*aedmon of Larkspur *was the most loathsome lout*
Breanne *had ever encountered. When she
arrived at his castle with her sisters, they were
greeted by an estate gone wild, while Caedmon
laid abed after a night of ale. But Breanne must
endure, as they are desperately in need of protection . . . and he is quite handsome.*

*After nine long months in the king's service, all
Caedmon wanted was peace, not five Viking prin-
cesses running about his keep. And the fiery red-
head who burst into his chamber was the worst of
them all. He should kick her out, but he has a far
better plan for Breanne of Stoneheim—one that
will leave her a Viking in lust.*

The Reluctant Viking

*T*he self-motivation tape was supposed to help Ruby Jordan solve her problems, not create new ones. Instead, she was lulled into an era of hard-bodied warriors and fair maidens. But the world ten centuries in the past didn't prove to be all mead and mirth. Even as Ruby tried to update medieval times, she had to deal with a Norseman whose view of women was stuck in the Dark Ages. And what was worse, brawny Thork had her husband's face, habits, and desire to avoid Ruby. Determined not to lose the same man twice, Ruby planned a bold seduction that would conquer the reluctant Viking—and make him an eager captive of her love.

The Outlaw Viking

As tall and striking as the Valkyries of legend, Dr. Rain Jordan was proud of her Norse ancestors despite their warlike ways. But she can't believe it when she finds herself on a nightmarish battlefield, forced to save the barbarian of her dreams.

He was a wild-eyed warrior whose deadly sword could slay a dozen Saxons with a single swing, yet Selik couldn't control the saucy wench from the future. If Selik wasn't careful, the stunning siren was sure to capture his heart and make a warrior of love out of **The Outlaw Viking**.

The Tarnished Lady

*B*anished from polite society, Lady Eadyth of Hawks' Lair spent her days hidden under a voluminous veil, tending her bees. But when her lands are threatened, Lady Eadyth sought a husband to offer her the protection of his name.

Notorious for loving—and leaving—the most beautiful damsels in the land, Eirik of Ravenshire was England's most virile bachelor. Yet when the mysterious lady offered him a vow of chaste matrimony in exchange for revenge against his most hated enemy, Eirik couldn't refuse. But the lusty knight's plans went awry when he succumbed to the sweet sting of the tarnished lady's love.

The Bewitched Viking

&

Even fierce Norse warriors have bad days. 'Twas enough to drive a sane Viking mad, the things Tykir Thorksson was forced to do—capturing a red-headed virago, putting up with the flock of sheep that follows her everywhere, chasing off her bumbling brothers. But what could a man expect from the sorceress who had put a kink in the King of Norway's most precious body part? If that wasn't bad enough, Tykir was beginning to realize he wasn't at all immune to the enchantment of brash red hair and freckles. Perhaps he could reverse the spell and hold her captive, not with his mighty sword, but with a Viking man's greatest magic: a wink and smile.

The Blue Viking

*F*or Rurik the Viking, life has not been worth living since he left Maire of the Moors. Oh, it's not that he misses her fiery red tresses or kissable lips. Nay, it's the embarrassing blue zigzag tattoo she put on his face after their one wild night of loving. For a fierce warrior who prides himself on his immense height, his expertise in bedsport, and his well-toned muscles, this blue streak is the last straw. In the end, he'll bring the witch to heel, or die trying. Mayhap he'll even beg her to wed . . . so long as she can promise he'll no longer be . . . **The Blue Viking**.

The Viking's Captive

(originally titled MY FAIR VIKING)

⊗

Tyra, Warrior Princess. She is too tall, too loud, too fierce to be a good catch. But her ailing father has decreed that her four younger sisters—delicate, mild-mannered, and beautiful—cannot be wed 'til Tyra consents to take a husband. And then a journey to save her father's life brings Tyra face to face with Adam the Healer. A god in human form, he's tall, muscled, perfectly proportioned. Too bad Adam refuses to fall in with her plans—so what's a lady to do but truss him up, toss him over her shoulder, and sail off into the sunset to live happily ever after.

A Tale of Two Vikings

✷

*T*oste and Vagn Ivarsson are identical Viking twins, about to face Valhalla together, following a tragic battle, or maybe something even more tragic: being separated for the first time in their thirty and one years. Alas, even the bravest Viking must eventually leave his best buddy behind and do battle with that most fearsome of all opponents—the love of his life. And what if that love was Helga the Homely, or Lady Esme, the world's oldest novice nun?

A Tale of Two Vikings will give you twice the tears, twice the sizzle, and twice the laughter . . . and make you wish for your very own Viking.

The Last Viking

He was six feet, four inches of pure, unadulterated male. He wore nothing but a leather tunic, and he was standing in Professor Meredith Foster's living room. The medieval historian told herself he was part of a practical joke, but with his wide gold belt, ancient language, and callused hands, the brawny stranger seemed so . . . authentic. And as he helped her fulfill her grandfather's dream of re-creating a Viking ship, he awakened her to dreams of her own. Until she wondered if the hand of fate had thrust her into the loving arms of . . . **The Last Viking**.

Truly, Madly Viking

$\oplus$

A *Viking named Joe? Jorund Ericsson is a tenth-century* Viking warrior who lands in a modern mental hospital. Maggie McBride is the lucky psychologist who gets to "treat" the gorgeous Norseman, whom she mistakenly calls Joe.

You've heard of *One Flew Over the Cuckoo's Nest*. But how about *A Viking Flew Over the Cuckoo's Nest*? The question is: Who's the cuckoo in this nest? And why is everyone laughing?

The Very Virile Viking

❧

*M*agnus Ericsson *is a simple man. He loves the* smell of fresh-turned dirt after springtime plowing. He loves the feel of a soft woman under him in the bed furs. He loves the heft of a good sword in his fighting arm.

But, Holy Thor, what he does not relish is the bothersome brood of children he's been saddled with. Or the mysterious happenstance that strands him in a strange new land—the kingdom of *Holly Wood*. Here is a place where the folks think he is an *act-whore* (whatever that is), and the woman of his dreams—a winemaker of all things—fails to accept that he is her soul mate . . . a man of exceptional talents, not to mention . . . **A Very Virile Viking.**

Wet & Wild

⊗

*W*hat do you get when you cross a Viking with a Navy SEAL? A warrior with the fierce instincts of the past and the rigorous training of America's most elite fighting corps? A totally buff hero-in-the-making who hasn't had a woman in roughly a thousand years? A dyed-in-the-wool romantic with a hopeless crush? Whatever you get, women everywhere can't wait to meet him, and his story is guaranteed to be . . . **Wet & Wild**.

Hot & Heavy

☘

*I*n and out, that's the goal as Lt. Ian MacLean prepares for his special ops mission. He leads a team of highly trained Navy SEALs, the toughest, buffest fighting men in the world and he has nothing to lose. Madrene comes from a time a thousand years before he was born, and she has no idea she's landed in the future. After tying him up, the beautiful shrew gives him a tongue-lashing that makes a drill sergeant sound like a kindergarten teacher. Then she lets him know she has her own special way of dealing with over-confident males, and things get . . . **Hot & Heavy**.

Frankly, My Dear . . .

⊛

*L*ost in the Bayou . . . *Selene had three great passions: men, food, and Gone with the Wind.* But the glamorous model always found herself starving—for both nourishment and affection. Weary of the petty world of high fashion, she headed to New Orleans for one last job before she began a new life. Little did she know that her new life would include a brand-new time—about 150 years ago! Selene can't get her fill of the food—or an alarmingly handsome man. Dark and brooding, James Baptiste was the only lover she gave a damn about. And with God as her witness, she vowed never to go without the man she loved again.

Sweeter Savage Love

&

*T*he stroke of surprisingly gentle hands, the flash
of fathomless blue eyes, the scorch of white-
hot kisses . . . Once again, Dr. Harriet Ginoza was
swept away into rapturous fantasy. The modern
psychologist knew the object of her desire was
all she should despise, yet time after time, she
lost herself in visions of a dangerously handsome rogue straight out of a historical romance.
Harriet never believed that her dream lover
would cause her any trouble, but then a twist of
fate cast her back to the Old South and she met
him in the flesh. To her disappointment, Etienne
Baptiste refused to fulfill any of her secret wishes.
If Harriet had any hope of making her amorous
dreams become passionate reality, she'd have to
seduce this charmer with a sweeter savage love
than she'd imagined possible . . . and savor every
minute of it.

The Love Potion

ame and fortune are surely only a swallow away
when Dr. Sylvie Fontaine discovers a chemical
formula guaranteed to attract the opposite sex.
Though her own love life is purely hypothetical,
the shy chemist's professional future is assured
. . . as soon as she can find a human guinea pig.
But bad boy Lucien LeDeux—best known as the
Swamp Lawyer—is more than she can handle
even before he accidentally swallowed a love
potion disguised in a jelly bean. When the dust
settles, Luc and Sylvie have the answers to some
burning questions—can a man die of testosterone overload? Can a straight-laced female lose
every single one of her inhibitions?—and they
learn that old-fashioned romance is still the best
catalyst for love.

Love Me Tender

O*nce upon a time, in a magic kingdom, there* lived a handsome prince. Prince Charming, he was called by one and all. And to this land came a gentle princess. You could say she was Cinderella . . . Wall Street Cinderella. Okay, if you're going to be a stickler for accuracy, in this fairy tale the kingdom is Manhattan. But there's magic in the Big Apple, isn't there? And maybe he can be Prince Not-So-Charming at times, and "gentle" isn't the first word that comes to mind when thinking of this princess. But they're looking for happily ever after just the same—and they're going to get it.

Desperado

❧

*M*istaken *for a notorious bandit and his infamously* scandalous mistress, L.A. lawyer Rafe Santiago and Major Helen Prescott found themselves on the wrong side of the law. In a time and place where rules had no meaning, Helen found Rafe's hard, bronzed body strangely comforting, and his piercing blue eyes left her all too willing to share his bedroll. His teasing remarks made her feel all woman, and she was ready to throw caution to the wind if she could spend every night in the arms of her very own . . . **Desperado**.

*G*ive in to your Impulses!

These unforgettable stories only take a second to buy and give you hours of reading pleasure!

Go to *www.AvonImpulse.com* and see what we have to offer.

Available wherever e-books are sold.

AVONIMPULSE

IMP 0811